TO THE GALACTIC RIM

TO THE
GALACTIC RIM

A. Bertram Chandler

TO THE GALACTIC RIM

The Road to the Rim, copyright © 1967 by A. Bertram Chandler.
To Prime the Pump, copyright ©1971 by A. Bertram Chandler.
The Hard Way Up, copyright © 1972 by A. Bertram Chandler.
The Broken Cycle, copyright ©1979 by A. Bertram Chandler.

A Baen Books Original

Baen Publishing Enterprises
P.O. Box 1403
Riverdale, NY 10471
www.baen.com

ISBN: 978-1-43913421-4

Cover art by Stephen Hickman

First Baen paperback printing, March 2011

Distributed by Simon & Schuster
1230 Avenue of the Americas
New York, NY 10020

Library of Congress Cataloging-in-Publication Data

Chandler, A. Bertram (Arthur Bertram), 1912-1984.
  [Selections. 2011]
  To the galactic rim / A. Bertram Chandler.
     p. cm.
  "A Baen Books original" --T.p. verso.
  ISBN 978-1-4391-3421-4 (trade pbk.)
  I. Title.
  PR6053.H325A6 2011
  823'.914--dc22
                                    2010052402
Printed in the United States of America

10 9 8 7 6 5 4 3 2 1

CONTENTS

THE
ROAD TO THE
RIM

LIEUTENANT JOHN GRIMES *of the Federation Survey Service: fresh out of the Academy—and as green as they come!*

"What do you think you're playing at?"

"Captain," said Wolverton, "I can no more than guess at what you intend to do—but I have decided not to help you do it."

"Give me the initiator, Wolverton. That's an order!"

"A *lawful* command, Captain? As lawful as those that armed this ship?"

"Hold him, Grimes!"

. . . They hung there, clinging to each other, but more in hate than in love. Wolverton's back was to the machine; he could not see, as could Grimes, that there was an indraught of air into the shimmering, spinning complexity. Grimes felt the beginnings of panic . . . all that mattered was that there was nothing to prevent him and Wolverton from being drawn into the machine. . . . Violently Grimes shoved away. To the action, there was a reaction . . .

When he had finished retching, Grimes forced himself to look again at the slimy, bloody obscenity that was a man turned inside out—heart still beating, intestines still writhing . . .

3

1

HIS UNIFORM was new, too new, all knife-edged creases, and the braid and buttons as yet un-dimmed by time. It sat awkwardly upon his chunky body—and even more awkwardly his big ears protruded from under the cap that was set too squarely upon his head. Beneath the shiny visor his eyes were gray (but not yet hard), and his face, for all its promise of strength, was as yet unlined, had yet to lose its immature softness. He stood at the foot of the ramp by which he had disembarked from the transport that had carried him from the Antarctic Base to Port Woomera, looking across the silver towers that were the ships, interplanetary and interstellar, gleaming in the desert. The westering sun was hot on his back, but he did not notice the discomfort. There were the ships, the *real* ships—not obsolescent puddle-jumpers like the decrepit cruiser in which he, with the other midshipmen of his class, had made the training cruise to the moons of Saturn. There were the ships, the star ships, that spun their web of commerce from Earth to the Centaurian planets, to the Cluster Worlds, to the Empire of Waverley, to the Shakespearian Sector and beyond.

(*But they're only merchantmen,* he thought, with a young man's snobbery.)

He wondered in which one of the vessels he would be taking passage. Merchantman or not, that big ship, the one that stood out from her neighbors like a city skyscraper among village church

5

steeples, looked a likely enough craft. He pulled the folder containing his orders from his inside breast pocket, opened it, read (not for the second time, even), the relevant page.

　　. . . *you are to report on board the Interstellar Transport Commission's* Delta Orionis . . .

He was not a spaceman yet, in spite of his uniform, but he knew the Commission's system of nomenclature. There was the *Alpha* class, and the *Beta* class, and there were the *Gamma* and *Delta* classes. He grinned wryly. His ship was one of the smaller ones. Well, at least he would not be traveling to Lindisfarne Base in an *Epsilon* class tramp.

Ensign John Grimes, Federation Survey Service, shrugged his broad shoulders and stepped into the ground car waiting to carry him and his baggage from the airport to the spaceport.

2

GRIMES LOOKED at the officer standing just inside *Delta Orionis'* airlock, and she looked at him. He felt the beginnings of a flush spreading over his face, a prickling of the roots of his close-cropped hair, and felt all the more embarrassed by this public display of his embarrassment. But spaceborn female officers, at this time, were almost as scarce as hens' teeth in the Survey Service—and such few as he had met all looked as though they shared a common equine ancestry. It was all wrong, thought Grimes. It was unfair that this girl (this attractive girl) should already be a veteran of interstellar voyages while he, for all his uniform and commission, should be embarking upon his first, his very first trip outside the bounds of the Solar System. He let his glance fall from her face (but not without reluctance), to the braid on her shoulderboards. Gold on a white facing. So it wasn't too bad. She was only some sort of paymaster— or, to use Merchant Service terminology, only some sort of purser.

She said, her clear, high voice almost serious, "Welcome aboard the *Delia O'Ryan,* Admiral."

"Ensign," corrected Grimes stiffly. "Ensign Grimes . . ."

" . . . of the Federation Survey Service," she finished for him. "But you are all potential admirals." There was the faintest of smiles flickering upon her full lips, a barely discernible crinkling at the corners of her eyes. *Her brown eyes,* thought Grimes. *Brown eyes, and what I can see of her hair under that cap seems to be auburn . . .*

She glanced at her wristwatch. She told him, her voice now crisp and businesslike, "We lift ship in precisely ten minutes' time, Ensign."

"Then I'd better get my gear along to my cabin, Miss . . . ?"

"I'll look after that, Mr. Grimes. Meanwhile, Captain Craven sends his compliments and invites you to the Control Room."

"Thank you." Grimes looked past and around the girl, trying to discover for himself the door that gave access to the ship's axial shaft. He was determined not to ask.

"It's labeled," she told him with a faint smile. "And the cage is waiting at this level. Just take it up as far as it goes, then walk the rest. Or do you want a pilot?"

"I can manage," he replied more coldly than he had intended, adding, "thank you." He could see the sign over the door now. It was plain enough. AXIAL SHAFT. So was the button that he had to press to open the door—but the girl pressed it for him. He thanked her again—and this time his coldness was fully intentional—and stepped into the cage. The door slid shut behind him. The uppermost of the studs on the elevator's control panel was marked CAPTAIN'S DECK. He pushed it, then stood there and watched the lights flashing on the panel as he was swiftly lifted to the nose of the ship.

When he was carried no further he got out, found himself on a circular walk surrounding the upper extremity of the axial shaft. On the outside of the shaft itself there was a ladder. After a second's hesitation he climbed it, emerged through a hatch into the control room.

It was like the control room of the cruiser in which he had made his training cruise—and yet subtly (or not so subtly), unlike it. Everything— but so had it been aboard the Survey Service vessel— was functional, but there was an absence of high polish, of polishing for polishing's sake. Instruments gleamed—but it was the dull gleam that comes from long and continual use, and matched the dull gleam of the buttons and rank marks on the uniforms of the officers already seated at their stations, the spacemen to whom, after all, a uniform was no more (and no less), than an obligatory working rig.

The big man with the four gold bars on each shoulder half

turned his head as Grimes came up through the hatch. "Glad to have you aboard, Ensign," he said perfunctorily. "Grab yourself a seat—there's a spare one alongside the Mate's. Sorry there's no time for introductions right now. We're due to get upstairs."

"Here!" grunted one of the officers.

Grimes made his way to the vacant acceleration chair, dropped into it, strapped himself in. While he was so doing he heard the Captain ask, "All secure, Mr. Kennedy?"

"No, sir."

"Then why the hell not?"

"I'm still waiting for the purser's report, sir."

"Are you?" Then, with a long-suffering sigh, "I suppose she's still tucking some passenger into her—or *his*—bunk . . . ."

"She could still be stowing some passenger's gear, sir," contributed Grimes. "Mine," he added.

"Indeed?" The Captain's voice was cold and elaborately uninterested.

Over the intercom came a female voice. "Purser to Control. All secure below."

"And bloody well time," grumbled the shipmaster. Then, to the officer at the transceiver, "Mr. Digby, kindly obtain clearance."

"Obtain clearance, sir," acknowledged that young man brightly. Then, into his microphone, "*Delta Orionis* to Port Control. Request clearance to lift ship. Over."

"Port Control to *Delta Orionis*. You may lift. Bon voyage. Over."

"Thank you, Port Control. Over and out."

Then the ship was throbbing to the rhythmic beat of her Inertial Drive, and Grimes felt that odd sense of buoyancy, of near weightlessness, that persisted until the vessel broke contact with the ground—and then the still gentle acceleration induced the reverse effect. He looked out through the nearest viewport. Already the ocher surface of the desert, streaked by the long, black shadows of ships and spaceport buildings, was far below them, with the vessels and the immobile constructions looking like toys, and one or two surface vehicles like scurrying insects. Far to the north, dull-ruddy against the blue of the sky, there was a sandstorm. *If that sky were darker,* thought Grimes, *this would look like Mars,* and the mental comparison reminded him that he, too, was a spaceman, that he, too, had been around (although only within the bounds of Sol's planetary system). Even so, he was Survey Service, and these others with him in Control were only merchant officers, fetchers and carriers, interstellar coach and truck drivers. (But he envied them their quiet competency.)

Still the ship lifted, and the spaceport below her dwindled, and the land horizon to the north and the now visible sea horizon to the south began to display the beginnings of curvature. Still she lifted, and overhead the sky was dark, and the first bright stars, Sirius and Canopus, Alpha and Beta Centauri, were sparkling there, beckoning, as they had beckoned for ages immemorial before the first clumsy rocket clambered heavenward up the ladder of its own fiery exhaust, before the first airplane spread its flimsy wings, before the first balloon was lifted by the hot, expanding gases from its airborne furnace . . . .

"Mr. Grimes," said the Captain suddenly, his voice neither friendly nor unfriendly.

"Sir?"

"We lift on I.D. until we're clear of the Van Allens."

"I know, sir," said Grimes—then wished that he could unsay the words. But it was too late. He was conscious of the shipmaster's hostile silence, of the amused contempt of the merchant officers. He shrank into his chair, tried to make himself as inconspicuous as possible. The ship's people talked among themselves in low voices, ignoring him. They allowed themselves a period of relaxation, producing and lighting cigarettes. Nobody offered the Ensign one.

Sulkily he fumbled for his pipe, filled it, lighted it. The Chief Officer coughed with quite unnecessary vigor. The Captain growled, "Put that out, please," and muttered something about stinking out the control room. He, himself, was puffing at a villainous black cigar.

The ship lifted, and below her the Earth was now a great sphere, three-quarters in darkness, the line of the terminator drawn across land masses, cloud formations and oceans. City lights twinkled in the gloom like star clusters, like nebulae. In a quiet voice an officer was calling readings from the radar altimeter.

To the throbbing of the Inertial Drive was added the humming, shrilling to a whine, of the directional gyroscopes as the ship turned about her short axis hunting the target star. The pseudo-gravity of centrifugal force was at an odd angle to that of acceleration—and the resultant was at an odder angle still. Grimes began to feel sick—and was actually thankful that the Captain had made him put his pipe out. Alarm bells sounded, and then somebody was saying over the intercom. "Prepare for acceleration. Prepare for acceleration. Listen for the countdown."

The countdown. Part of the long tradition of space travel, a hangover from the days of the first, unreliable rockets. Spaceships still used rockets—but only as auxiliaries, as a means of delivering thrust in a hurry, of building up acceleration in a short time.

At the word *Zero!* the Inertial Drive was cut and, simultaneously, the Reaction Drive flared into violent life. The giant hand of acceleration bore down heavily upon all in the ship—then, suddenly, at a curt order from the Captain, lifted.

Grimes became aware of a thin, high keening, the song of the ever-precessing gyroscopes of the Mannschenn Drive. He knew the theory of it—as what spaceman did not?—although the mathematics of it were beyond the comprehension of all but a handful of men and women. He knew what was happening, knew that the ship, now that speed had been built up, was, as one of his instructors had put it, going ahead in space and astern in time. He felt, as he had been told that he would feel, the uncanny sensation of *déjà vu,* and watched the outlines of the control room and of every person and instrument in the compartment shift and shimmer, the colors sagging down the spectrum.

Ahead, the stars were pulsating spirals of opalescence, astern, Earth and Moon were frighteningly distorted, uncanny compromises between the sphere and the tesseract. But this was no more than the merest subliminal glimpse; in the twinkling of an eye the Home Planet and her daughter were no more than dust motes whirling down the dark dimensions.

The Captain lit a fresh cigar. "Mr. Kennedy," he said, "you may set normal Deep Space watches." He turned to Grimes. His full beard almost hid his expression, that of one performing a social duty with no enthusiasm. "Will you join me in my day cabin, Ensign?"

"It will be my pleasure, sir," lied Grimes.

3

HANDLING HIS BIG BODY with easy grace in the Free Fall conditions, the Captain led the way from the control room. Grimes followed slowly and clumsily, but with a feeling of great thankfulness that after his training cruise he was no longer subject to spacesickness. There were drugs, of course, and passengers used them, but a spaceman was expected to be independent of pharmaceutical aids. Even so, the absence of any proper "up" or "down" bothered him more than he cared to admit.

The shipmaster slid open the door to his accommodation, motioned to Grimes to enter, murmuring sardonically, "Now you see how the poor live." The so-called poor, thought Grimes, didn't do at all badly. This Deep Space sitting room was considerably larger than the day cabin of the Survey Service cruiser's Captain had been. True, it was also shabbier—but it was far more comfortable. Its decorations would never have been approved aboard a warship, were obviously the private property of the Master. There were a full dozen holograms on the bulkhead, all of them widely differing but all of them covering the same subject matter. Not that the subject matter was covered.

"My harem," grunted the Captain. "That one there, the redhead, I met on Caribbea. Quite a stopover that was. The green-haired wench—and you can see that it's not a dye job, although I've often wondered why women can't be *thorough*— isn't human, of course.

13

But indubitably humanoid, and indubitably mammalian. Belongs to Brrrooonooorrrooo—one of the worlds of the Shaara Empire. The local Queen Mother offered to sell Lalia—that's her name—to me for a case of Scotch. And I was tempted . . ." He sighed. "But you Service Survey types aren't the only ones who have to live by Regulations."

Grimes said nothing, tried to hide his interest in the art gallery.

"But take a pew, Ensign. Spit on the mat and call the cat a bastard—this is Liberty Hall."

Grimes pulled himself to one of the comfortable chairs, strapped himself in. He said lamely, "I don't see any cat, sir."

"A figure of speech," growled the Captain, seating himself next to what looked like a drink cabinet. "Well, Mr. Grimes, your Commandant at the Academy, Commodore Bradshaw, is an old friend and shipmate of mine. He said that you were a very promising young officer"—like a balloon in a comic strip the unspoken words, "God knows why," hung between them—"and asked me to keep an eye on you. But I have already gained the impression that there is very little that a mere merchant skipper such as myself will be able to teach you."

Grimes looked at the bulky figure seated opposite him, at the radiation-darkened skin of the face above the black, silver-streaked beard, at the fiercely jutting nose, at the faded but bright and intelligent blue eyes, the eyes that were regarding him with more than a hint of amused contempt. He blushed miserably as he recalled his brash, "I know, sir," in this man's own control room. He said, with an effort, "This is my first Deep Space voyage, sir."

"I know." Surprisingly the Captain chuckled—and as though to celebrate this minor scoring over his guest opened the liquor cabinet. "Pity to have to suck this excellent Manzanila out of a bulb—but that's one of the hardships of Free Fall. Here!" He tossed a little pear-shaped container to Grimes, kept one for himself. "Your health, Ensign!"

"And yours, sir."

The wine was too dry for Grimes' taste, but he made a pretense of enjoying it. He was thankful that he was not asked to have a second drink. Meanwhile, his host had pulled a typewritten sheet from a drawer of his desk and was looking at it. "Let me see, now . . . You're in cabin 15, on D Deck. You'll be able to find your own way down, won't you?"

Grimes said that he would and unbuckled his lapstrap. It was obvious that the party was over.

"Good. Now, as an officer of the Survey Service you have the freedom of the control room and the engine rooms. . . ."

"Thank you, sir."

"Just don't abuse the privilege, that's all."

After that, thought Grimes, *I'm not likely to take advantage of it, let alone abuse it.* He let himself float up from his chair, said, "Thank you, sir." (For the drink, or for the admonition? What did it matter?) "I'll be getting down to my cabin, sir. I've some unpacking to do."

"As you please, Mr. Grimes."

The Captain, his social duty discharged, had obviously lost interest in his guest. Grimes let himself out of the cabin and made his way, not without difficulty, to the door in the axial shaft. He was surprised at the extent to which one not very large drink had interfered with the control of his body in Free Fall. Emerging from the elevator cage on D Deck he stumbled, literally, into the purser. "Let go of me," she ordered, "or I shall holler rape!"

That, he thought, *is all I need to make this trip a really happy one.*

She disengaged herself, moved back from him, her slim, sandaled feet, magnetically shod, maintaining contact with the steel decking, but gracefully, with a dancing motion. She laughed. "I take it that you've just come from a home truth session with B.B."

"B.B.?"

"The Bearded Bastard. But don't take it too much to heart. He's that way with *all* junior officers. The fact that you're Survey Service is only incidental."

"Thank you for telling me."

"His trouble," she went on. "His *real* trouble is that he's painfully shy."

He's not the only one, thought Grimes, looking at the girl.

She seemed even more attractive than on the occasion of their first meeting. She had changed into shorts-and-shirt shipboard uniform—and she was one of the rare women who could wear such a rig without looking lumpy and clumpy. There was no cap now to hide her hair—smooth, lustrous, with coppery glints, with a straight white part bisecting the crown of her finely shaped head.

She was well aware of his scrutiny. She said, "You must excuse me, Ensign. I have to look after the other customers. They aren't seasoned spacemen like you."

Suddenly bold, he said, "But before you go, what is your name?"

She smiled dazzlingly. "You'll find a list of all ship's personnel posted in your cabin. I'm included." Then she was gone, gliding rapidly around the curve of the alleyway.

He looked at the numbers over the cabin doors, outboard from the axial shaft, making a full circuit of that hollow pillar before he realized that this was only the inner ring, that he would have to follow one of the radial alleyways to reach his own accommodation. He finally found No. 15 and let himself in.

His first action was to inspect the framed notices on the bulkhead.

I.S.S. *Delta Orionis,* he read.

Captain J. Craven, O.G.S., S.S.R.

So the Old Man held a Reserve commission. And the Order of the Golden Star was awarded for something more than good attendance.

Mr. P. Kennedy, Chief Officer.

He ignored the other names on the list while he searched for one he wanted. Ah, here it was.

Miss Jane Pentecost, Purser.

He repeated the name to himself, thinking that, despite the old play on words, this Jane was not plain. (But Janes rarely are.) *Jane Pentecost . . .* Then, feeling that he should be showing some professional interest, he acquainted himself with the names of the other members of the ship's crew. He was intrigued by the manning scale, amazed that such a large vessel, relatively speaking, could be run by such a small number of people. But this was not a warship;

there were no weapons to be manned, there would never be the need to put a landing party ashore on the surface of a hostile planet. The Merchant Service could afford to automate, to employ machinery in lieu of ratings. The Survey Service could not.

Virtuously he studied the notices dealing with emergency procedures, ship's routine, recreational facilities and all the rest of it, examined with care the detailed plan of the ship. Attached to this was a card, signed by the Master, requesting passengers to refrain, as much as possible, from using the elevator in the axial shaft, going on to say that it was essential, for the good of their physical health, that they miss no opportunity for taking exercise. (In a naval vessel, thought Grimes, with a slight sneer, that would not be a request—it would be an order. And, in any case, there would be compulsory calisthenics for all hands.)

He studied the plan again and toyed with the idea of visiting the bar before dinner. He decided against it; he was still feeling the effects of the drink that the Captain had given him. So, to pass the time, he unpacked slowly and carefully, methodically stowing his effects in the drawers under the bunk. Then, but not without reluctance, he changed from his uniform into his one formal civilian suit. One of the officer-instructors at the Academy had advised this. "Always wear civvies when you're traveling as passenger. If you're in uniform, some old duck's sure to take you for one of the ship's officers and ask you all sorts of technical questions to which you don't know the answers."

While he was adjusting his frilled cravat in front of the mirror the sonorous notes of a gong boomed from the intercom.

$$\approx\approx 4\approx\approx$$

THE DINING SALOON was much more ornate than the gunroom of that training cruiser had been, and more ornate than her wardroom. The essentials were the same, of course, as they are in any ship—tables and chairs secured to the deck, each seat fitted with its strap so that the comforting pressure of buttocks on padding could give an illusion of gravity. Each table was covered with a gaily colored cloth—but beneath the fabric there was the inevitable stainless steel to which the stainless steel service would be held by its own magnetic fields. But what impressed Grimes was the care that had been taken, the ingenuity that had been exercised to make this compartment look like anything but part of a ship.

The great circular pillar of the axial shaft was camouflaged by trelliswork, and the trelliswork itself almost hidden by the luxuriance of some broad-level climbing plant that he could not identify. Smaller pillars were similarly covered, and there was a further efflorescence of living decoration all around the circular outer wall—the wall that must be the inner skin of the ship. And there were windows in this wall. No, Grimes decided, not windows, but holograms. The glowing, three dimensional pictures presented and maintained the illusion that this was a hall set in the middle of some great park. But on what world? Grimes could not say. Trees, bushes and flowers were unfamiliar, and the color of the sky subtly strange.

He looked around him at his fellow diners, at the dozen

passengers and the ship's officers, most of whom were already seated. The officers were in neat undress uniform. About half the male passengers were, like himself, formally attired; the others were sloppy in shorts and shirts. But this was the first night out and some laxity was allowable. The women, however, all seemed to have decided to outshine the glowing flowers that flamed outside the windows that were not windows.

There was the Captain, unmistakable with his beard and the shimmering rainbow of ribbons on the left breast of his blouse. There were the passengers at his table—the men inclined to portliness and pomposity, their women sleek and slim and expensive looking. Grimes was relieved to see that there was no vacant place— and yet, at the same time, rather hurt. He knew that he was only an Ensign, a one-ringer, and a very new Ensign at that—but, after all, the Survey Service was the Survey Service.

He realized that somebody was addressing him. It was a girl, a small, rather chubby blonde. She was in uniform—a white shirt with black shoulder-boards, each bearing a narrow white stripe, sharply creased slacks, and black, highly polished shoes. Grimes assumed, correctly, that she was a junior member of the purser's staff. "Mr. Grimes," she said, "will you follow me, please? You're at Miss Pentecost's table."

Willingly he followed the girl. She led him around the axial shaft to a table for four at which the purser with two passengers, a man and a woman, was already seated. Jane Pentecost was attired as was his guide, the severity of her gold-trimmed black and white in pleasing contrast to the pink and blue frills and flounces that clad the other woman, her slenderness in still more pleasing contrast to the other's untidy plumpness.

She smiled and said pleasantly, "Be seated, Admiral."

"Admiral?" asked the man at her left, unpleasantly incredulous. He had, obviously, been drinking. He was a rough looking customer, in spite of the attempt that he had made to dress for dinner. He was twice the Ensign's age, perhaps, although the heavily lined face under the scanty sandy hair made him look older. "Admiral?" He laughed, revealing irregular yellow teeth. "In what? The Space Scouts?"

Jane Pentecost firmly took control. She said, "Allow me to introduce Ensign Grimes, of the Survey Service . . ."

"Survey Service . . . Space Scouts . . . S.S. . . . What's the difference?"

"Plenty!" answered Grimes hotly.

The purser ignored the exchange. "Ensign, this is Mrs. Baxter. . . ."

"Pleased to meet you, I'm sure," simpered the woman.

"And Mr. Baxter."

Baxter extended his hand reluctantly and Grimes took it reluctantly. The amenities observed, he pulled himself into his seat and adjusted his lapstrap. He was facing Jane Pentecost. The man was on his right, the woman on his left. He glanced first at her, then at her husband, wondering how to start and to maintain a conversation. But this was the purser's table, and this was her responsibility.

She accepted it. "Now you're seeing how the poor live, Admiral," she remarked lightly.

Grimes, taking a tentative sip from his bulb of consommé, did not think that the self-styled poor did at all badly, and said as much. The girl grinned and told him that the first night out was too early to draw conclusions. "We're still on shoreside meat and vegetables," she told him, "and you'll not be getting your first taste of our instant table wine until tomorrow. Tonight we wallow in the unwonted luxury of a quite presentable Montrachet. When we start living on the produce of our own so-called farm, washing it down with our own reconstituted plonk, you'll see the difference."

The Ensign replied that, in his experience, it didn't matter if food came from tissue-culture vats or the green fields of Earth—what *was* important was the cook.

"Wide experience, Admiral?" she asked sweetly.

"Not very," he admitted. "But the gunroom cook in my last ship couldn't boil water without burning it."

Baxter, noisily enjoying his dinner, said that this preoccupation with food and drink was symptomatic of the decadence of Earth. As he spoke his knife grated unpleasantly on the steel spines that secured his charcoal broiled steak to the surface of his plate.

Grimes considered inquiring if the man thought that good table manners were also a symptom of decadence, then thought better of it. After all, this was not *his* table. Instead, he asked, "And where are you from, Mr. Baxter?"

"The Rim Worlds, Mr. Grimes. Where we're left to sink or swim—so we've no time for much else than keeping ourselves afloat." He sucked noisily from his bulb of wine. "Things might be a little easier for us if your precious Survey Service did something about keeping the trade routes open."

"That is our job," said Grimes stiffly. "And we do it."

"Like hell! There's not a pirate in the Galaxy but can run rings around you!"

"Practically every pirate has been hunted down and destroyed," Grimes told him coldly.

"Practically every pirate, the man says! A few small-time bunglers, he means!"

"Even the notorious Black Bart," persisted Grimes.

"Black Bart!" Baxter, spluttering through his full mouth, gestured with his laden fork at Grimes. "Black Bart! He wasn't much. Once he and that popsy of his split brass rags he was all washed up. I'm talkin' about the *real* pirates, the ones whose ships wear national colors instead o' the Jolly Roger, the ones that your precious Survey Service daren't say boo to. The ones who do the dirty work for the Federation."

"Such as?" asked Grimes frigidly.

"So now you're playin' the bleedin' innocent. Never heard o' the Duchy o' Waldegren, Mr. Ensign Grimes?"

"Of course. Autonomous, but they and the Federation have signed what's called a Pact of Perpetual Amity."

"Pretty words, ain't they? Suppose we analyze them. Suppose we analyze by analogy. D'yer know much about animals, Mr. Ensign Grimes?"

"Animals?" Grimes was puzzled. "Well, I suppose I do know something. I've taken the usual courses in xenobiology. . . ."

"Never mind that. You're a Terry. Let's confine ourselves to a selection of yer own Terran four-footed friends."

"What the hell are you driving at?" flared Grimes, losing his temper. He threw an apologetic glance in Jane Pentecost's direction, saw that she was more amused than shocked.

"Just think about a Pact of Perpetual Amity between an elephant and a tom cat," said Baxter. "A fat an' lazy elephant. A lean, scrawny, vicious tom cat. If the elephant wanted to he could convert that cat into a fur bedside rug just by steppin' on him. But he doesn't want to. He leaves the cat alone, just because the cat is useful to him. He does more than just leave him alone. He an' this feline pull out their pens from wherever they keep 'em an' sign their famous Pact.

"In case you haven't worked it out for yourself, the elephant's the Federation, and the tom cat's the Duchy of Waldegren."

"But why?" asked Grimes. *"Why?"*

"Don't they teach you puppies any interstellar politics? Or are those courses reserved for the top brass? Well, Mr. Grimes, I'll tell you. There's one animal that has the elephant *really* worried. Believe it or not, he's scared o' mice. An' there're quite a few mice inside the Federation, mice that make the elephant nervous by their rustlings an' scurryings an' their squeaky demands for full autonomy. That's where the cat comes in. By his free use of his teeth an' claws, by his very presence, he keeps the mice quiet."

"And just who are these famous mice, Mr. Baxter?" asked Grimes.

"Don't they teach you nothin' in your bleedin' Academy? Well, I'll tell you. In *our* neck o' the woods, the mice are the Rim Worlds, an' the tom cat, as I've already made clear, is the Duchy o' Waldegren. The Duchy gets away with murder—murder an' piracy. But accordin' to the Duchy, an accordin' to your big, stupid elephant of a Federation, it's not piracy. It's—now, lemme see, what fancy words have been used o' late? Contraband Control. Suppression of Espionage. Violation of the Three Million Mile Limit. Every time that there's an act of piracy there's some quote legal unquote excuse for it, an' it's upheld by the Federation's tame legal eagles, an' you Survey Service sissies just sit there on your big, fat backsides an' don't lift a pinkie against your dear, murderous pals, the Waldegrenese. If you did, they send you screaming back to Base, where some dear old daddy of an Admiral'd spank your little plump bottoms for you."

"Please, Mr. Baxter!" admonished Jane Pentecost.

"Sorry, Miss. I got sort of carried away. But my young brother was Third Reaction Drive Engineer of the old *Bunyip* when she went missing. Nothin' was ever proved—but the Waldegrenese Navy was holdin' fleet maneuvers in the sector she was passin' through when last heard from. Oh, they're cunnin' bastards. They'll never go for one o' these ships, or one of the Trans-Galactic Clippers; it'll always be some poor little tramp that nobody'll ever miss but the friends an' relatives o' the crew. And, I suppose, the underwriters—but Lloyds makes such a packet out o' the ships that don't get lost that they can well afford to shell out now an' again. Come to that, it must suit 'em. As long as there're a few 'overdues' an' 'missings' they can keep the premiums up."

"But I still can't see how piracy can possibly pay," protested Grimes.

"O' course it pays. Your friend Black Bart made it pay. An' if you're goin' to all the expense of building and maintaining a war fleet, it might just as well earn its keep. Even your famous Survey Service might show a profit if you were allowed to pounce on every fat merchantman who came within range o' your guns."

"But for the Federation to condone piracy, as you're trying to make out . . . That's utterly fantastic."

"If you lived on the Rim, you might think different," snarled Baxter.

And Jane Pentecost contributed, "Not piracy. Confrontation."

5

AS SOON AS the meal was finished the Baxters left rather hastily to make their way to the bar, leaving Grimes and Jane Pentecost to the leisurely enjoyment of their coffee. When the couple was out of earshot Grimes remarked, "So those are Rim Worlders. They're the first I've met."

"They're not, you know," the girl told him.

"But they are. Oh, there are one or two in the Survey Service, but I've never run across them. Now I don't particularly want to."

"But you did meet one Rim Worlder before you met the Baxters."

"The Captain?"

She laughed. "Don't let him hear you say that—not unless you want to take a space walk without a suit!"

"Then who?"

"Who could it be, Admiral? Whom have you actually met, to talk to, so far in this ship? Use your crust."

He stared at her incredulously. "Not you?"

"Who else?" She laughed again, but with a touch of bitterness. "We aren't all like our late manger companions, you know. Or should know. Even so, you'd count yourself lucky to have Jim Baxter by your side in any real jam. It boils down to this. Some of us have acquired veneer. Some of us haven't. Period."

"But how did you . . . ?" He groped for words that would not be offensive to conclude the sentence.

"How did I get into this galley? Easily enough. I started my spacefaring career as a not very competent Catering Officer in *Jumbuk,* one of the Sundowner Line's more ancient and decrepit tramps. I got sick in Elsinore. Could have been my own cooking that put me in the hospital. Anyhow, I was just about recovered when the Commission's *Epsilon Serpentis* blew in—and she landed *her* purser with a slightly broken leg. She'd learned the hard way that the Golden Rule—*stop whatever you're doing and secure everything when the acceleration warning sounds*—is meant to be observed. The Doctor was luckier. She broke his fall . . . ." Grimes was about to ask what the Doctor and the purser had been doing, then was thankful that he had not done so. He was acutely conscious of the crimson blush that burned the skin of his face.

"You must realize," said the girl dryly, "that merchant vessels with mixed crews are not monastic institutions. But where was I? Oh, yes. On Elsinore. Persuading the Master of the *Snaky Eppy* that I was a fit and proper person to take over his pursering. I managed to convince him that I was at least proper—I still can't see what my predecessor saw in that lecherous old goat of a quack, although the Second Mate had something. . . ." Grimes felt a sudden twinge of jealousy. Anyhow, he signed me on, as soon as I agreed to waive repatriation.

"It was a long voyage; as you know, the *Epsilon* class ships are little better than tramps themselves. It was a long voyage, but I enjoyed it— seeing all the worlds that I'd read about and heard about and always wanted to visit. The Sundowner Line doesn't venture far afield—just the four Rim Worlds, and now and again the Shakespearian Sector, and once in a blue moon one of the drearier planets of the Empire of Waverley. The Commission's tramps, of course, run *everywhere.*

"Anyhow, we finally berthed at Woomera. The Old Man must have put in a good report about me, because I was called before the Local Superintending Purser and offered a berth, as a junior, in one of the *Alpha* class liners. *Alpha Centauri,* if you must know. She was on the Sol-Sirius service. Nothing very glamorous in the way of ports of call, but she was a fine ship, beautifully kept, efficiently run. A couple of years there knocked most of the sharp corners off me.

After that—a spell as Assistant Purser of *Beta Geminorum*. Atlanta, Caribbea Carinthia and the Cluster Worlds. And then my first ship as Chief Purser. This one."

One of Jane's girls brought them fresh bulbs of coffee and ampoules of a sweet, potent liqueur. When she was gone Grimes asked, "Tell me, what are the Rim Worlds like?"

She waited until he had applied the flame of his lighter to the tip of her long, thin cigar, then answered, "Cold. Dark. Lonely. But . . . they have something. The feeling of being on a frontier. *The* frontier. The last frontier."

"The frontier of the dark . . ." murmured Grimes.

"Yes. The frontier of the dark. And the names of our planets. They have something too. A . . . poetry? Yes, that's the word. Lorn, Ultimo, Faraway and Thule . . . And there's that night sky of ours, especially at some times of the year. There's the Galaxy—a great, dim-glowing lenticulate nebula, and the rest is darkness. At other times of the year there's only the darkness, the blackness that's made even more intense by the sparse, faint stars that are the other Rim Suns, by the few, faint luminosities that are the distant island universes that we shall never reach . . . ."

She shivered almost imperceptibly. "And always there's that sense of being on the very edge of things, of hanging on by our finger-nails with the abyss of the eternal night gaping beneath us. The Rim Worlders aren't a spacefaring people; only a very few of us ever get the urge. It's analogous, perhaps, to your Maoris—I spent a leave once in New Zealand and got interested in the history of the country. The Maoris come of seafaring stock. Their ancestors made an epic voyage from their homeland paradise to those rather grim and dreary little islands hanging there, all by themselves, in the cold and stormy Southern Ocean, lashed by frigid gales sweeping up from the Antarctic. And something—the isolation? the climate?—killed the wanderlust that was an essential part of the makeup of their race. You'll find very few Maoris at sea—or in space—although there's no dearth of Polynesians from the home archipelagoes aboard the surface ships serving the ports of the Pacific. And there are quite a few, too, in the Commission's ships . . . ."

"We have our share in Survey Service," said Grimes. "But tell me, how do you man your vessels? This Sundowner Line of yours . . ."

"There are always the drifters, the no-hopers, the castoffs from the Interstellar Transport Commission, and Trans-Galactic Clippers, and Waverley Royal Mail and all the rest of them."

"And from the Survey Service?" The question lifted her out of her somber mood. "No," she replied with a smile. "Not yet."

"Not ever," said Grimes.

6

ONCE HIS INITIAL SHYNESS HAD WORN OFF—and with it much of his Academy-induced snobbery—Grimes began to enjoy the voyage. After all, Survey Service or no Survey Service, this was a ship and he was a spaceman. He managed to accept the fact that most of the ship's officers, even the most junior of them, were far more experienced spacemen than he was. Than he was *now,* he often reminded himself. At the back of his mind lurked the smug knowledge that, for all of them, a captaincy was the very limit of promotion, whereas he, one day, would be addressed in all seriousness as Jane Pentecost now addressed him in jest.

He was a frequent visitor to the control room but, remembering the Master's admonition, was careful not to get in the way. The watch officers accepted him almost as one of themselves and were willing to initiate him into the tricky procedure of obtaining a fix with the interstellar drive in operation—an art, he was told, rather than a science.

Having obtained the permission of the Chief Engineers he prowled through the vessel's machinery spaces, trying to supplement his theoretical knowledge of reaction, inertial and interstellar drives with something more practical. The first two, of course, were idle, and would be until the ship emerged from her warped Space-Time back into the normal continuum—but there was the Pile, the radio-active heart of the ship, and there was the auxiliary machinery that, in this tiny, man-made planet, did the work that on a natural world is performed by winds, rivers, sunlight and gravity.

There was the Mannschenn Drive Room—and, inside this holy of holies, no man need fear to admit that he was scared by the uncanny complexity of ever-precessing gyroscopes. He stared at the tumbling rotors, the gleaming wheels that seemed always on the verge of vanishing into nothingness, that rolled down the dark dimensions, dragging the ship and all aboard her with them. He stared, hypnotized, lost in a vague, disturbing dream in which Past and Present and Future were inextricably mingled—and the Chief Interstellar Drive Engineer took him firmly by the arm and led him from the compartment. "Look at the time-twister too long," he growled, "and you'll be meeting yourself coming back!"

There was the "farm"—the deck of yeast- and tissue-culture vats which was no more (and no less), than a highly efficient protein factory, and the deck where stood the great, transparent globes in which algae converted the ship's organic waste and sewage back into usable form (processed as nutriment for the yeasts and the tissue-cultures and as fertilizer for the hydroponic tanks, the biochemist was careful to explain), and the deck where luxuriant vegetation spilled over from the trays and almost barricaded the inspection walks, the source of vitamins and of flowers for the saloon tables and, at the same time, the ship's main air-conditioning unit. Grimes said to Jane Pentecost, who had accompanied him on this tour of inspection, "You know, I envy your Captain."

"From you, Admiral," she scoffed, "that *is* something. But why?"

"How can I put it? You people do the natural way what we do with chemicals and machinery. The Captain of a warship is Captain of a warship. Period. But your Captain Craven is absolute monarch of a little world."

"A warship," she told him, "is supposed to be able to go on functioning as such even with every compartment holed. A warship cannot afford to depend for the survival of her crew upon the survival of hosts of other air-breathing organisms."

"Straight from the book," he said. Then, puzzled, "But for a . . ." He hesitated.

"But for a woman, or for a purser, or for a mere merchant officer I know too much," she finished for him. "But I can read, you know. And when I was in the Sundowner Line, I, as well as all the other officers, was supposed to keep up with all the latest Survey Service publications."

"But why?" he asked.

"But why not? We'll have a Navy of our own, one day. Just stick around, Admiral."

"Secession?" he inquired, making it sound like a dirty word.

"Once again—why not?"

"It'd never work," he told her.

"The history of Earth is full of secessions that did work. So is the history of Interstellar Man. The Empire of Waverley, for example. The Duchy of Waldegren, for another—although that's one that should have come to grief. We should all of us be a great deal happier if it had."

"Federation policy . . ." he began.

"Policy, shmolicy! Don't let's be unkind to the Waldegrenese, because as long as they're in being they exercise a restraining influence upon the Empire of Waverley and the Rim Worlds . . ." Her pace slackened. Grimes noticed that they were passing through the alleyway in which she and her staff were accommodated. She went on, "But all this talking politics is thirsty work. Come in for a couple of drinks before lunch."

"Thank you. But, Jane"—she didn't seem to have noticed the use of her given name—"I don't think that either of us is qualified to criticize the handling of foreign and colonial affairs."

"Spoken like a nice, young, well-drug-up future admiral. Oh, I know, I know. You people are trained to be the musclemen of the Federation. Yours not to reason why, yours but to do and die, and all the rest of it. But I'm a Rim Worlder—and out on the Rim you learn to think for yourself." She slid her door open. "Come on in. This is Liberty Hall—you can spit on the mat and call the cat a bastard."

Her accommodation was a suite rather than a mere cabin. It was neither as large nor as well fitted as the Captain's, but it was better than the Chief Officer's quarters, in which Grimes had already been a guest. He looked with interest at the holograms on the bulkhead of the sitting room. They were—but in an altogether different way—as eye-catching as Captain Craven's had been. There was one that was almost physically chilling, that induced the feeling of utter cold and darkness and loneliness. It was the night sky of some planet—a range of dimly seen yet sharply serrated peaks bisecting a great, pallidly glowing, lenticulate nebula. "Home, sweet home," murmured the girl, seeing what he was looking at. "The Desolation Mountains on Faraway, with the Galactic Lens in the background."

"And you feel homesick for *that?*"

"Darn right I do. Oh, not all the time. I like warmth and comfort as well as the next woman. But . . ." She laughed. "Don't stand around gawking—you make the place look untidy. Pull yourself into a chair and belay the buttocks."

He did so, watching her as she busied herself at the liquor cabinet. Suddenly, in these conditions of privacy, he was acutely conscious of the womanliness of her. The rather tight and rather short shorts, as she bent away from him, left very little to the imagination. And her legs, although slender, were full where they should be full, with the muscles working smoothly under the golden skin. He felt the urge, which he sternly suppressed, to plant a kiss in the delectable hollow behind each knee. She turned suddenly. "Here! Catch!" He managed to grab the bulb that was hurtling toward his face, but a little of the wine spurted from the nipple and struck him in the right eye. When his vision cleared he saw that she was seated opposite him, was laughing (at or with him?). At, he suspected. A real demonstration of sympathy would have consisted of tears, not laughter. Her face grew momentarily severe. "Not the mess," she said reprovingly. "But the waste."

Grimes examined the bulb. "I didn't waste much. Only an eyeful."

She raised her drink in ritual greeting. "Here's mud in your eye," adding, "for a change."

"And in yours."

In the sudden silence that followed they sat looking at each other. There was a tension, some odd resultant of centrifugal and centripetal forces. They were on the brink of something, and both of them knew it, and there was the compulsion to go forward countered by the urge to go back.

She asked tartly, "Haven't you ever seen a woman's legs before?"

He shifted his regard to her face, to the eyes that, somehow, were brown no longer but held the depth and the darkness of the night through which the ship was plunging.

She said, "I think you'd better finish your drink and go."

He said, "Perhaps you're right."

"You better believe I'm right." She managed a smile. "I'm not an idler, like some people. I've work to do."

"See you at lunch, then. And thank you."

"Don't thank me. It was on the house, as the little dog said. Off with you, Admiral."

He unbuckled his lapstrap, got out of the chair and made his way to the door. When he was out of her room he did not go to his own cabin but to the bar, where he joined the Baxters. They, rather to his surprise, greeted him in a friendly manner. Rim Worlders, Grimes decided, had their good points.

It was after lunch when one of the purserettes told him that the Captain wished to see him. *What have I done now?* wondered Grimes—and answered his own question with the words, *Nothing. Unfortunately.*

Craven's manner, when he admitted Grimes into his dayroom, was severe. "Come in, Ensign. Be seated."

"Thank you, sir."

"You may smoke if you wish."

"Thank you, sir."

Grimes filled and lighted his pipe; the Captain ignited one of his pungent cigars, studied the eddying coils of smoke as though they were writing a vitally important message in some strange language.

"Er, Mr. Grimes, I believe that you have been seeing a great deal of my purser, Miss Pentecost."

"Not a great deal, sir. I'm at her table, of course."

"I am told that she has entertained you in her quarters."

"Just one bulb of sherry, sir. I had no idea that we were breaking ship's regulations."

"You were not. All the same, Mr. Grimes, I have to warn you."

"I assure you, sir, that nothing occurred between us."

Craven permitted himself a brief, cold smile. "A ship is not a Sunday school outing—especially a ship under my command. Some Masters, I know, do expect their officers to comport themselves like Sunday school pupils, with the Captain as the principal—but *I* expect *my* senior officers to behave like intelligent and responsible adults. Miss Pentecost is quite capable of looking after herself. It is you that I'm worried about."

"There's no need to be worried, sir."

The Captain laughed. "I'm not worried about your morals, Mr. Grimes. In fact, I have formed the opinion that a roll in the hay would do you far more good than harm. But Miss Pentecost is a dangerous woman. Before lifting ship, very shortly before lifting ship, I received a confidential report concerning her activities. She's an efficient purser, a highly efficient purser, in fact, but she's even more than that. Much more." Again he studied the smoke from his cigar. "Unfortunately there's no *real* proof, otherwise she'd not be sailing with us. Had I insisted upon her discharge I'd have been up against the Interstellar Clerical and Supply Officers' Guild."

"Surely not," murmured Grimes. Craven snorted. "You people are lucky. *You* haven't a mess of Guilds to deal with, each and every one of which is all too ready to rush to the defense of a Guild member, no matter what he or she is supposed to have done. As a Survey Service Captain you'll never have to face a suit for wrongful dismissal. You'll never be accused of victimization."

"But what has Miss Pentecost done, sir?" asked Grimes.

"Nothing—or too damn much. You know where she comes from, don't you? The Rim Worlds. The planets of the misfits, the rebels, the nonconformists. There's been talk of secession of late—but even those irresponsible anarchists know full well that secession will never succeed unless they build up their own space power. There's the Duchy of Waldegren, which would pounce as soon as the Federation withdrew its protection. And even the Empire of Waverley might be tempted to extend its boundaries. So . . ."

"They have a merchant fleet of sorts, these Rim Worlders. The Sundowner Line. I've heard rumors that it's about to be nationalized. But they have no fighting navy."

"But what's all this to do with Miss Pentecost, sir?"

"If what's more than just hinted at in that confidential report is true—plenty. She's a recruiting sergeant, no less. Any officer with whom she's shipmates who's disgruntled, on the verge of throwing his hand in—or on the verge of being emptied out—she'll turn on the womanly sympathy for, and tell him that there'll always be a job waiting out on the Rim, that the Sundowner Line is shortly going to expand, so there'll be quick promotion and all the rest of it."

"And what's that to do with *me*, Captain? "

"Are all Survey Service ensigns as innocent as you, Mr. Grimes? Merchant officers the Rim Worlds want, and badly. Naval officers they'll want more badly still once the balloon goes up."

Grimes permitted himself a superior smile. "It's extremely unlikely, sir, that I shall ever want to leave the Survey Service."

"Unlikely perhaps—but not impossible. So bear in mind what I've told you. I think that you'll be able to look after yourself now that you know the score."

"I think so too," Grimes told him firmly. He thought, *The old bastard's been reading too many spy stories.*

7

THEY WERE DANCING.

Tables and chairs had been cleared from the ship's saloon, and from the big, ornate playmaster throbbed the music of an orchestra so famous that even Grimes had heard of it—The Singing Drums.

They were dancing.

Some couples shuffled a sedate measure, never losing the contact between their magnetically shod feet and the polished deck. Others— daring or foolhardy—cavorted in Nul-G, gamboled fantastically but rarely gracefully in Free Fall.

They were dancing.

Ensign Grimes was trying to dance.

It was not the fault of his partner that he was making such a sorry mess of it. She, Jane Pentecost, proved the truth of the oft-made statement that spacemen and spacewomen are expert at this form of exercise. He, John Grimes, was the exception that proves the rule. He was sweating, and his feet felt at least six times their normal size. Only the fact that he was holding Jane, and closely, saved him from absolute misery.

There was a pause in the music. As it resumed Jane said, "Let's sit this one out, Admiral."

"If you wish to," he replied, trying not to sound too grateful.

"That's right. I wish to. I don't mind losing a little toenail varnish, but I think we'll call it a day while I still have a full set of toenails."

"I'm sorry," he said.

"So am I." But the flicker of a smile robbed the words of their sting.

She led the way to the bar. It was deserted save for the bored and sulky girl behind the gleaming counter. "All right, Sue," Jane told her. "You can join the revels. The Admiral and I will mind the shop."

"*Thank* you, Miss Pentecost." Sue let herself out from her little cage, vanished gracefully and rapidly in the direction of the saloon. Jane took her place.

"I *like* being a barmaid," she told the ensign, taking two frosted bulbs out of the cooler.

"I'll sign for these," offered Grimes.

"You will not. This comes under the heading of entertaining influential customers."

"But I'm not. Influential, I mean."

"But you will be." She went on dreamily. "I can see it. I can just see it. The poor old *Delia O'Ryan,* even more decrepit that she is now, and her poor old purser, about to undergo a fate worse than death at the hands of bloody pirates from the next Galaxy but three . . . . But all is not lost. There, light years distant, is big, fat, Grand Admiral Grimes aboard his flagship, busting a gut, to say nothing of his Mannschenn Drive unit, to rush to the rescue of his erstwhile girlfriend. 'Dammitall,' I can hear him muttering into his beard. 'Dammitall. That girl used to give me free drinks when I was a snotty nosed ensign. I will repay. Full speed ahead, Gridley, and damn the torpedoes!'"

Grimes laughed—then asked sharply, "Admiral in which service?"

"What do you mean, John?" She eyed him warily.

"*You* know what I mean."

"So . . ." she murmured. "So . . . I know that you had another home truth session with the Bearded Bastard. I can guess what it was about."

"And is it true?" demanded Grimes.

"Am I Olga Popovsky, the Beautiful Spy? Is that what you mean?"

"More or less."

"Come off it, John. How the hell can I be a secret agent for a non-existent government?"

"You can be a secret agent for a subversive organization."

"What *is* this? Is it a hangover from some half-baked and half-understood course in counterespionage?"

"There was a course of sorts," he admitted. "I didn't take much interest in it. At the time."

"And now you wish that you had. Poor John."

"But it wasn't espionage that the Old Man had against you. He had some sort of story about your acting as a sort of recruiting sergeant, luring officers away from the Commission's ships to that crumby little rabble of star tramps calling itself the Sundowner Line . . . ."

She didn't seem to be listening to him, but was giving her attention instead to the music that drifted from the saloon. It was one of the old, Twentieth Century melodies that were enjoying a revival. She began to sing in time to it.

> *"Goodbye, I'll run*
> *To seek another sun*
> *Where I May find*
> *There are hearts more kind*
> *Than the ones left behind . . ."*

She smiled somberly and asked, "Does that answer your question?"

"Don't talk in riddles," he said roughly.

"Riddles? Perhaps—but not very hard ones. That, John, is a sort of song of farewell from a very old comic opera. As I recall it, the guy singing it was going to shoot through and join the French Foreign Legion. (But there's no French Foreign Legion anymore. . . .) We, out on the Rim, have tacked our own words on to it. It's become almost a national anthem to the Rim Runners, as the people who man our ships—such as they are—are already calling themselves.

"There's no French Foreign Legion anymore—but the misfits

and the failures have to have somewhere to go. I haven't *lured* anybody away from this service—but now and again I've shipped with officers who've been on the point of getting out, or being emptied out, and when they've cried into my beer I've given them advice. Of course, I've a certain natural bias in favor of my own home world. If I were Sirian born I'd be singing the praises of the Dog Star Line."

"Even so," he persisted, "your conduct seems to have been somewhat suspect."

"Has it? And how? To begin with, *you* are not an officer in this employ. And if you were, I should challenge you to find anything in the Commission's regulations forbidding me to act as I have been doing."

"Captain Craven warned me," said Grimes.

"Did he, now? That's his privilege. I suppose that he thinks that it's also his duty. I suppose he has the idea that I offered you admiral's rank in the Rim Worlds Navy as soon as we secede. *If* we had our own Navy—which we don't—we might just take you in as Ensign, Acting, Probationary."

"Thank you."

She put her elbows on the bar counter, propping her face between her hands, somehow conveying the illusion of gravitational pull, looking up at him. "I'll be frank with you, John. I admit that we do take the no-hopers, the drunks and the drifters into our merchant fleet. I know far better than you what a helluva difference there is between those rustbuckets and the well-found, well-run ships of the Commission and, come to that, Trans-Galactic Clippers and Waverley Royal Mail. But when we do start some kind of a Navy we shall want better material. Much better. We shall want highly competent officers who yet, somehow, will have the Rim World outlook. The first batch, of course, will have to be outsiders, to tide us over until our own training program is well under way."

"And I don't qualify?" he asked stiffly.

"Frankly, no. I've been watching you. You're too much of a stickler for rules and regulations, especially the more stupid ones. Look at the way you're dressed now, for example. Evening wear, civilian, junior officers, for the use of. No individuality. *You* might as well be in uniform. Better, in fact. There'd be some touch of brightness."

"Go on."

"And the way you comport yourself with women. Stiff. Starchy. Correct. And you're all too conscious of the fact that I, even though I'm a mere merchant officer, and a clerical branch at that, put up more gold braid than you do. I noticed that especially when we were dancing. I was having to lead all the time."

He said defensively, "I'm not a very good dancer."

"You can say that again." She smiled briefly. "So there you have it, John. You can tell the Bearded Bastard, when you see him again, that you're quite safe from my wiles. I've no doubt that you'll go far in your own Service—but you just aren't Rim Worlds material."

"I shouldn't have felt all that flattered if you'd said that I was," he told her bluntly—but he knew that he was lying.

8

"YES?" JANE WAS SAYING. "Yes, Mr. Letourneau?"

Grimes realized that she was not looking at him, that she was looking past him and addressing a newcomer. He turned around to see who it was. He found—somehow the name hadn't registered—that it was the Psionic Radio Officer, a tall, pale, untidily put together young man in a slovenly uniform. He looked scared—but that was his habitual expression, Grimes remembered. They were an odd breed, these trained telepaths with their Rhine Institute diplomas, and they were not popular, but they were the only means whereby ships and shore stations could communicate instantaneously over the long light years. In the Survey Service they were referred to, slightingly, as Commissioned Teacup Readers. In the Survey Service and in the Merchant Service they were referred to as Snoopers. But they were a very necessary evil.

"Yes, Mr. Letourneau?"

"Where's the Old Man? He's not in his quarters."

"The Master"—Jane emphasized the title—"is in the saloon." Then, a little maliciously, "Couldn't you have used your crystal ball?"

Letourneau flushed. "You know very well, Miss Pentecost, that we have to take an oath that we will always respect the mental privacy of our shipmates . . . . But I must find him. Quickly."

"Help yourself. He's treading the light fantastic in there." When he was gone she said, "Typical. Just typical. If it were a real emergency he could get B.B. on the intercom. But no. Not him. He has to parade his distrust of anything electronic and, at the same time, make it quite clear that he's not breaking his precious oath . . . . Tell me, how do you people handle your spaceborne espers?"

He grinned. "We've still one big stick that you people haven't. A court martial followed by a firing party. Not that I've ever seen it used."

"Hardly, considering that you've only been in Space a dog watch." Her face froze suddenly. "Yes, Sue?"

It was the girl whom Jane had relieved in the bar. "Miss Pentecost, will you report to the Captain in Control, please. At once."

"What have I done now?"

"It's some sort of emergency, Miss Pentecost. The Chief Officer's up there with him, and he's sent for the Doctor and the two Chief Engineers."

"Then I must away, John. Look after the bar again, Sue. Don't let the Admiral have too many free drinks."

She moved fast and gracefully, was gone before Grimes could think of any suitable repartee. He said to the girl, "What *is* happening, Sue?"

"I don't know, Ad—" She flushed. "Sorry, Ensign. And, in any case, I'm not supposed to talk to the passengers about it."

"But I'm not a real passenger," he said—and asked himself, *Am I a* real *anything?*

"No, I suppose you're not, Mr. Grimes. But you're not on duty."

"An officer of the Survey Service is *always* on duty," he told her, with some degree of truth. "Whatever happens on the spacelanes is our concern." It sounded good.

"Yes," she agreed hesitantly. "That's what my fiancé—he's a Lieutenant J.G.—is always telling me."

"So what's all the flap about?"

"Promise not to tell anybody?"

"Of course."

"Mr. Letourneau came wandering into the Saloon. He just stood there staring about, the way he does, then he spotted the Captain. He was actually dancing with me at the time. . . ." She smiled reminiscently, and added, "He's a very good dancer."

"He would be. But go on."

"He came charging across the dance floor—Mr. Letourneau, I mean. He didn't care whose toes he trod on or who he tripped over. I couldn't help overhearing when he started babbling away to Captain Craven. It's a distress call. From one of our ships—*Epsilon Sextans.*'" Her voice dropped to a whisper. "And it's piracy."

"Piracy? Impossible."

"But, Mr. Grimes, it's what he said."

"Psionic Radio Officers have been known to go around the bend before now," Grimes told her, "and to send false alarm calls. And to receive non-existent ones."

"But the *Sexy Eppy*—sorry, *Epsilon Sextans*—has a cargo that'd be worth pirating. Or so I heard. The first big shipment of Antigeriatridine to Waverly. . . ."

Antigeriatridine, the so-called Immortality Serum. Manufactured in limited, but increasing quantities only on Marina (often called by its colonists Submarina), a cold, unpleasantly watery world in orbit about Alpha Crucis. The fishlike creatures from which the drug was obtained bred and flourished only in the seas of their own world.

But piracy . . . .

But the old legends were full of stories of men who had sold their souls for eternal youth.

The telephone behind the bar buzzed sharply. Sue answered it. She said, "It's for you, Mr. Grimes."

Grimes took the instrument. "That you, Ensign?" It was Captain Craven's voice. "Thought I'd find you there. Come up to Control, will you?" It was an order rather than a request.

All the ship's executive officers were in the Control Room, and the Doctor, the purser and the two Chief Engineers. As Grimes emerged from the hatch he heard Kennedy, the Mate, say, "Here's the Ensign now."

"Good. Then dog down, Mr. Kennedy, so we get some privacy."
Craven turned to Grimes. "'You're on the Active List of the Survey
Service, Mister, so I suppose you're entitled to know what's going
on. The situation is this. *Epsilon Sextans,* Marina to Waverley with a
shipment of Antigeriatridine, has been pirated." Grimes managed,
with an effort, to refrain from saying "I know." Craven went on.
"Her esper is among the survivors. He says that the pirates were two
frigates of the Waldegren Navy. Anyhow, the Interstellar Drive
Engineers aboard *Epsilon Sextans* managed to put their box of tricks
on random precession, and they got away. But not in one piece. . . ."

"Not in one piece?" echoed Grimes stupidly.

"What the hell do you expect when an unarmed merchantman
is fired upon, without warning, by two warships? The esper says that
their Control has had it, and all the accommodation spaces. By some
miracle the Psionic Radio Officer's shack wasn't holed, and neither
was the Mannschenn Drive Room."

"But even one missile . . ." muttered Grimes.

"If you want to capture a ship and her cargo more or less intact,"
snapped Craven, "you don't use missiles. You use laser. It's an ideal
weapon if you aren't fussy about how many people you kill."

"Knowing the Waldegrenese as *we* do," said Jane Pentecost
bitterly, "there wouldn't have been any survivors anyhow."

"Be quiet!" roared Craven. Grimes was puzzled by his outburst.
It was out of character. True, he could hardly expect a shipmaster
to react to the news of a vicious piracy with equanimity—but this
shipmaster was an officer of the Reserve, had seen service in warships
and had been highly decorated for outstanding bravery in battle.

Craven had control of himself again. "The situation is this.
There are people still living aboard *Epsilon Sextans.* Even though all
her navigators have been killed I think that I shall be able to find her
in time. Furthermore, she has a very valuable cargo and, in any case,
cannot be written off as a total loss. There is little damage that cannot
be repaired by welded patches. I have already sent a message to
Head Office requesting a free hand. I have salvage in mind. I see no
reason why the ship and her cargo should not be taken on to
Waverley."

"A prize crew, sir?"

"If you care to put it that way. This will mean cutting down the number of officers aboard my own vessel—but I am sure, Mr. Grimes, that you will be willing to gain some practical watch-keeping experience. All that's required is your autograph on the ship's Articles of Agreement."

"Thank you, sir."

"Don't thank me. I may be thanking you before the job's over and done." He turned to his Chief Officer. "Mr. Kennedy, keep in touch with Mr. Letourneau and let me know if anything further comes through either from *Epsilon Sextans* or from Head Office. The rest of you—keep this to yourselves. No sense in alarming the passengers. I'm sure that the Doctor and Miss Pentecost between them can concoct some soothing story to account for this officers' conference."

"Captain Craven," said Jane Pentecost.

"Well?"

"The other man at my table, Mr. Baxter. I knew him out on the Rim. He holds Chief Reaction Drive Engineer's papers."

"Don't tell him anything yet. But I'll keep him in mind. Now, Mr. Grimes, will you join me in my day cabin?"

9

THE HOLOGRAMS were all gone from the bulkheads of Captain Craven's cabin. To replace them there was just one picture—of a woman, not young, but with the facial bone structure that defies age and time. She was in uniform, and on her shoulderboards were the two and a half stripes of a Senior Purser. The shipmaster noticed Grimes' interest and said briefly and bitterly. "She was too senior for an *Epsilon* class ship—but she cut her leave short, just to oblige, when the regular purser went sick. She should have been back on Earth at the same time as me, though. Then we were going to get married. . . ."

Grimes said nothing. He thought, *Too senior for an* Epsilon *class ship? Epsilon Sextans, for example?* What could he say?

"And that," said Craven savagely, *"was* that."

"I'm sorry, sir," blurted Grimes, conscious of the inadequacy of his words. Then, foolishly, "But there are survivors, sir."

"Don't you think that I haven't got Letourneau and his opposite number checking? And have *you* ever seen the aftermath of a Deep Space battle, Mister? Have you ever boarded a ship that's been slashed and stabbed to death with laser beams?" He seemed to require no answer; he pulled himself into the chair by his desk, strapped himself in and motioned to Grimes to be seated. Then he pulled out from a drawer a large sheet of paper, which he unfolded. It was a cargo plan. "Current voyage," he grunted. "And we're carrying more to Lindisfarne than one brand-new ensign."

45

"Such as, sir?" ventured Grimes.

"Naval stores. I don't mind admitting that I'm more than a little rusty insofar as Survey Service procedure is concerned, even though I still hold my Reserve Commission. You're more familiar with fancy abbreviations than I am. Twenty cases RERAT, for example . . . ."

"Reserve rations, sir. Canned and dehydrated."

"Good. And ATREG?"

"Atmospheric regeneration units, complete."

"So *if Epsilon Sextans'* 'farm' has been killed we shall be able to manage?"

"Yes, sir."

"Do you think you'd be able to install an ATREG unit?"

"Of course, sir. They're very simple, as you know. Just synthetic chlorophyll and a UV source . . . . In any case, there are full instructions inside every container."

"And this? A double M, Mark XV?"

"Anti-Missile Missile."

"And ALGE?"

"Anti-Laser Gas Emitter."

"The things they do think of. I feel more at home with these AVMs—although I see that they've got as far as Mark XVII now."

"Anti-Vessel Missiles," said Grimes. A slight enthusiasm crept into his voice. "The XVII's a real honey."

"What does it do?"

"I'm sorry, sir. Even though you are a Reserve Officer, I can't tell you."

"But they're effective?"

"Yes. Very."

"And I think you're Gunnery Branch, Mr. Grimes, aren't you?"

"I am sir." He added hastily, "But I'm still quite capable of carrying out a watch officer's duties aboard this vessel should the need arise."

"The main thing is, you're familiar with naval stores and equipment. When we find and board *Epsilon Sextans* I shall be transshipping certain items of cargo . . . "

"RERAT and ATREG, sir?"

"Yes. And the others."

"But, sir, I can't allow it. Not unless I have authority from the Flag Officer commanding Lindisfarne Base. As soon as your Mr. Letourneau can be spared I'll get him to try and raise the station there."

"I'm afraid that's out of the question, Mr. Grimes. In view of the rather peculiar political situation, I think that the answer would be No. Even if it were 'Yes', you know as well as I how sluggishly the tide flows through official channels. Furthermore, just in case it has escaped your notice, *I* am the Master."

"And I, sir, represent the Survey Service. As the only commissioned officer aboard this vessel *I* am responsible for Survey Service cargo."

"As a Reserve Officer, Mr. Grimes, I rank you."

"Only when you have been recalled to Active Service. Sir."

Craven said, "I was rather afraid that you'd take this attitude. That's why I decided to get this interview over and done with, just so we all know where we stand." He put away the cargo plan, swiveled his chair so that he could reach out to his liquor cabinet. He pulled out two bulbs, tossed one to Grimes. "No toasts. If we drank to Law and Order we should mean different things. So just drink. And listen.

"To begin with, *Epsilon Sextans* doesn't know where she is. But Letourneau is one of the rare telepaths with the direction finding talent, and as soon as he's able to get lined up we shall alter course to home on the wreck. That's what he's trying to do now.

"When we find her, we shall synchronize and board, of course. The first thing will be medical aid to the survivors. Then we patch the ship up. And then we arm her. And then, with a prize crew under myself, we put ourselves on the trajectory for Waverley—hoping that those Waldegrenese frigates come back for another nibble."

"They'd never dare, sir."

"Wouldn't they? The original piracy they'll try to laugh off by saying that it was by *real* pirates— no, that's not quite right, but you know what I mean—wearing Waldegren colors. The second piracy— they'll make sure that there are no survivors."

"But I still can't see how they can hope to get away with it. It's always been an accepted fact that the main weapon against piracy has been psionic radio."

"And so it was—until some genius developed a jamming technique. *Epsilon Sextans* wasn't able to get any messages out until her crazy random precession pulled her well clear."

"And you hope, sir, that they *do* attack you?"

"I do, Mr. Grimes. I had hoped, that I should have a good gunnery officer under me, but"—he shrugged his massive shoulders—"I think that I shall be able to manage."

"And you hope that you'll have your weapons," persisted Grimes.

"I see no reason why I should not, Ensign."

"There is one very good reason, sir. That is that I, a commissioned officer of the Survey Service, am aboard your vessel. I insist that you leave the tracking down and destruction of the pirates to the proper authorities. I insist, too, that no Survey Service stores be discharged from this ship without my written authority."

For the first time the hint of a smile relieved the somberness of Craven's face. "And to think that I believed that Jane Pentecost could recruit *you*," he murmured. Then, in a louder voice, "And what if I just go ahead without your written authority, Ensign?"

Grimes had the answer ready. "Then, sir, I shall be obliged to order your officers not to obey your unlawful commands. If necessary, I shall call upon the male passengers to assist me in any action that is necessary."

Craven's bushy eyebrows went up and stayed up. "Mr. Grimes," he said in a gritty voice, "it is indeed lucky for you that I have first-hand experience of the typical Survey Service mentality. Some Masters I know would, in these circumstances, send you out on a spacewalk without a suit. But, before I take drastic action, I'll give you one more chance to cooperate." His tone softened. "You noticed the portrait I've put up instead of all the temporary popsies. Every man, no matter how much he plays around, has one woman who is *the* woman. Gillian was *the* woman as far as I was concerned—as far as I *am* concerned. I've a chance to bring her murderers under my guns—and, by God, I'm taking that chance, no matter what it means either to my career or to the somewhat odd foreign policy of the Federation. I used to be annoyed by Jane Pentecost's outbursts on that subject—but now I see that she's right. And she's right, too, when it comes to the Survey Service's reluctance to take action against Waldegren.

"So I, Mr. Grimes, am taking action."

"Sir, I forbid you . . ."

"*You* forbid *me*? Ensign, you forget yourself. Perhaps this will help you remember."

This was a Minetti automatic that had appeared suddenly in the Captain's hand. In his hairy fist the little, glittering weapon looked no more than a toy—but Grimes knew his firearms, knew that at the slightest pressure of Craven's finger the needle-like projectiles would stitch him from crown to crotch.

"I'm sorry about this, Mr. Grimes." As he spoke, Craven pressed a button set in his desk with his free hand. "I'm sorry about this. But I realize that I was expecting rather too much of you. After all, you have your career to consider . . . . Time was," he went on, "when a naval officer could put his telescope to his blind eye as an excuse for ignoring orders—and get away with it. But the politicians had less power in those days. We've come a long way—and a wrong way—since Nelson."

Grimes heard the door behind him slide open. He didn't bother to look around, not even when hard hands were laid on his shoulders.

"Mr. Kennedy," said Craven, "things turned out as I feared that they would. Will you and Mr. Ludovic take the Ensign along to the Detention Cell?"

"I'll see you on trial for piracy, Captain!" flared Grimes.

"An interesting legal point, Ensign—especially since you are being entered in my Official Log as a mutineer."

10

THE DETENTION CELL was not uncomfortable, but it was depressing. It was a padded cell— passengers in spacecraft have been known to exhibit the more violent symptoms of mania—which detracted from its already inconsiderable cheerfulness if not from its comfort. However, Grimes was not mad—not in the medical sense, that is—and so was considered able to attend to his own bodily needs. The little toilet was open to him, and at regular intervals a bell would sound and a container of food would appear in a hatch recessed into the bulkhead of the living cabin. There was reading matter too—such as it was. The Ensign suspected that Jane Pentecost was the donor. It consisted of pamphlets published by some organization calling itself The Rim Worlds Secessionist Party. The almost hysterical calls to arms were bad enough—but the ones consisting mainly of columns of statistics were worse. Economics had never been Grimes' strong point.

He slept, he fed at the appointed times, he made a lengthy ritual of keeping himself clean, he tried to read—and, all the time, with only sounds and sensations as clues, he endeavored to maintain a running plot of the ship's maneuvers.

Quite early there had been the shutting down of the Mannschenn Drive, and the consequent fleeting sensation of temporal disorientation. This had been followed by the acceleration warning—the cell had an intercom speaker recessed in the

50

padding—and Grimes, although it seemed rather pointless in his sponge rubber environment, had strapped himself into his couch. He heard the directional gyroscopes start up, felt the effects of centrifugal force as the ship came around to her new heading. Then there was the pseudo-gravity of acceleration, accompanied by the muffled thunder of the reaction drive. It was obvious, thought the Ensign, that Captain Craven was expending his reaction mass in a manner that, in other circumstances, would have been considered reckless.

Suddenly—silence and Free Fall, and almost immediately the off-key keening of the Mannschenn Drive. Its note was higher, much higher, than Grimes remembered it, and the queasy feeling of temporal disorientation lasted much longer than it had on previous occasions. And that, for a long time, was all. Meals came, and were eaten. Every morning—according to his watch—the prisoner showered and applied depilatory cream to his face. He tried to exercise—but to exercise in a padded cell, with no apparatus, in Free Fall, is hard. He tried to read—but the literature available was hardly more interesting to him than a telephone directory would have been. And, even though he never had been gregarious, the lack of anybody to talk to was wearing him down.

It was a welcome break from the monotony when he realized that, once again, the ship was maneuvering. This time there was no use of the directional gyroscopes; there were no rocket blasts, but there was a variation of the whine of the Drive as it hunted, hunted, as the temporal precession rate was adjusted by tens of seconds, by seconds, by microseconds.

And then it locked.

The ship shuddered slightly—once, twice.

Grimes envisaged the firing of the two mooring rockets, one from the bow and one from the stern, each with the powerful electromagnet in its nose, each trailing its fathoms of fine but enormously strong cable. Merchant vessels, he knew, carried this equipment, but unlike naval ships rarely used it. But Craven, as a Reservist, would have seen and taken part in enough drills.

The ship shuddered again—heavily.

So the rendezvous had been made. So *Delta Orionis* and *Epsilon Sextans,* their Drives synchronized, bound together by the rescue ship's cables, were now falling as one unit through the dark immensities.

So the rendezvous had been made—and already the survivors of the wreck were being brought aboard the *Delia O'Ryan,* were being helped out of their stinking spacesuits, were blurting out their story to Craven and his officers. Grimes could visualize it all, almost as clearly as though he were actually watching it. He could visualize, too, the engineers swarming over the wreck, the flare of their burning and welding torches, the cannibalizing of nonessential plating from the ship's structure for hull patches. It was all laid down in the Survey Service's Damage Control Manual—and Captain Craven, at least, would know that book as thoroughly as did Grimes.

And what of the cargo, the Survey Service stores, *Grimes'* stores? A trembling in the ship's structure, a barely felt vibration, told him that gantries and conveyor belts were being brought into operation. There would be no great handling problems. Lindisfarne *was Delta Orionis'* first port of call, and the Survey Service consignment would be top stowage. But there was nothing that Grimes could do about it—not a thing. In fact, he was beginning to doubt the legality of the stand he had made against the Master. And he was the small frog in this small puddle, while Captain Craven had made it quite clear that he was the big frog. Grimes wished that he was better versed in astronautical law—although a professional lawyer's knowledge would be of no use to him in his present situation.

So, with some hazy idea that he might need all his strength, both mental and physical, for what was to befall him (but *what?*), in the near future, he strapped himself into his bunk and did his best to forget his worries in sleep. He was well enough acquainted with the psychiatrists' jargon to know that this was no more than a return to the womb but, before dropping off into a shallow slumber, shrugged, *So what?*

He jerked into sudden wakefulness.

Jane Pentecost was there by his bunk, looking down at him.

"Come in," he said. "Don't bother to knock. Now you see how the poor live. This is Liberty Hall; you can spit on the mat and call the cat a bastard."

She said, "That's not very funny."

"I know it's not. Even the first time that I heard it aboard this blasted ship I was able to refrain from rolling in the aisles."

She said, "There's no need to be so bitchy, John."

"Isn't there? Wouldn't you be bitchy if you'd been thrown into this padded cell?"

"I suppose I would be. But you asked for it, didn't you?"

"If doing my duty—or trying to do my duty—is asking for it, I suppose that I did. Well—and has our pirate Captain cast off yet, armed to the teeth with the weapons he's stolen?"

"No. The weapons are still being mounted. But let's not argue legalities, John. There's not enough time. I . . . I just wanted to say goodbye."

"Goodbye?" he echoed.

"Yes. Somebody has to do the cooking aboard *Epsilon Sextans*—and I volunteered."

"You?"

"And why the hell not?" she flared. "Captain Craven has been pushed over to *our* side of the fence, and it'd be a pretty poor show if we Rim Worlders weren't prepared to stand by him. Baxter's gone across to take over as Reaction Drive Engineer; the only survivor in that department was the Fourth, and he's only a dog watch in Space."

"And who else?"

"Nobody. The *Sexy Eppy's* Chief, Second and Third Interstellar Drive Engineers survived, and they're willing—anxious, in fact, now that their ship's being armed—to stay on. And the Psionic Radio Officer came through, and is staying on. All of our executive officers volunteered, of course, but the Old Man turned them down. He said that, after all, he could not hazard the safety of this ship by stripping her of her trained personnel. Especially since we carry passengers."

"That's his worry," said Grimes without much sympathy. "But how does he hope to fight his ship if those frigates pounce again?"

"He thinks he'll be able to manage—with remote controls for every weapon brought to his main control panel."

"Possible," admitted Grimes, his professional interest stirred. "But not very efficient. In a naval action the Captain has his hands full just handling the ship alone, without trying to control her weaponry."

"And you'd know, of course."

"Yes."

"Yes, you've read the books. And Captain Craven commanded a light cruiser during that trouble with the Dring, so he knows nothing."

"He still hasn't got four hands and two heads."

"Oh, let's stop talking rubbish," she cried. "I probably shan't see you again, John and . . . and . . . oh, hell, I want to say goodbye properly, and I don't want you to think too badly about either the Old Man or . . . or myself."

"So what are we supposed to do about it?"

"Damn you, Grimes, you snotty-nosed, stuck-up spacepuppy! Look after yourself!"

Suddenly she bent down to kiss him. It was intended to be no more than a light brushing of lips, but Grimes was suddenly aware, with his entire body, of the closeness of her, of the warmth and the scent of her, and almost without volition his arms went about her, drawing her closer still to him. She tried to break away, but it was only a halfhearted effort. He heard her murmur, in an odd, sardonic whisper, "wotthehell, wotthehell," and then, "toujours gai." It made no sense at the time but, years later, when he made the acquaintance of the Twentieth Century poets, he was to remember and to understand. What was important now was that her own arms were about him.

Somehow the buttons of her uniform shirt had come undone, and her nipples were taut against Grimes' bare chest. Somehow her shorts had been peeled away from her hips—unzipped by whom? and how?—and somehow Grimes' own garments were no longer the last barrier between them.

He was familiar enough with female nudity; he was one of the great majority who frequented the naked beaches in preference to those upon which bathing costumes were compulsory. He knew what a naked woman looked like—but this was different. It was not the first time that he had kissed a woman—but it was the first time that he had kissed, and been kissed by, an unclothed one. It was the first time that he had been alone with one.

What was happening he had read about often enough—and, like most young men, he had seen his share of pornographic films. But this was different. This was happening to *him*.

And for the first time.

When it was over, when, still clasped in each others' arms they drifted in the center of the little cabin, impelled there by some odd resultant of forces, their discarded clothing drifting with them, veiling their perspiration-moist bodies, Grimes was reluctant to let her go.

Gently, Jane tried to disengage herself.

She whispered, "That was a warmer goodbye that I intended. But I'm not sorry. No. I'm not sorry . . . ."

Then, barely audibly, "It was the first time for you, wasn't it?"

"Yes."

"Then I'm all the more glad it happened. But this *is* goodbye."

"*No.*"

"Don't be a fool, John. You can't keep me here."

"But I can come with you."

She pushed him from her. Somehow he landed back on the bed. Before he could bounce he automatically snapped one of the confining straps about his middle. Somehow—she was still wearing her sandals but nothing else—she finished up standing on the deck, held there by the contact between the magnetic soles and the ferrous fibers in the padding. She put out a long, graceful arm and caught her shirt. She said harshly, "*I'm* getting dressed and out of here. *You* stay put. Damn you, Grimes, for thinking that I was trying to lure you aboard the *Sexy Eppy* with the body beautiful. I told you before that I am not, repeat not, Olga Popovsky, the Beautiful Spy. And I'm not a prostitute. There's one thing I wouldn't *sell* if I were offered the services of the finest Gunnery Officer (which you aren't), in the whole bloody Galaxy in payment!"

"You're beautiful when you flare up like that," said Grimes sincerely. "But you're *always* beautiful." Then, in a louder voice, "Jane, I love you."

"Puppy love," she sneered. "And I'm old enough to be your . . ." A faint smile softened her mouth. "Your maiden aunt."

"Let me finish. All right, it's only puppy love—*you* say. But it's still love. But"—he was extemporizing—convincingly, he hoped—"but my real reason for wanting to come with you is this. I can appreciate now what Captain Craven lost when *Epsilon Sextans* was pirated. I can see—I can *feel*—why he's willing to risk his life and his career to get his revenge. And I think that it's worth it. And I want to help him."

She stood there, her shirt half on, eying him suspiciously. "You mean that? You really mean that?"

"Yes."

"Then you're a liar, Grimes."

"No," he said slowly. "No. Not altogether. I want to help the Old Man—and I want to help *you*. This piracy has convinced me that you Rim Worlders *are* getting the dirty end of the stick. I may not be the finest Gunnery Officer in the whole Galaxy—but I'm better acquainted with the new stuff than Captain Craven is."

Her grin was openly derisive. "First it's fellow-feeling for another spaceman, then it's international politics. What next?"

"Where we started. I *do* love you, Jane. And if there's going to be any shooting, I want to be on hand to do the shooting back on your behalf. I'll admit that . . . that what's happened has influenced my decision. But you didn't buy me, or bribe me. Don't think that. Don't ever think that." There was a note of pleading in his voice. "Be realistic, Jane. With another officer along, especially an officer with recent gunnery training, you stand a damn sight better chance than you would otherwise."

"I . . . I suppose so. But I still don't like it."

"You don't have to. But why look a gift horse in the mouth?"

"All right. You win. Get your clothes on and come and see the Old Man."

11

JANE PENTECOST led Grimes to the airlock. The ship seemed oddly deserted, and he remarked on this. The girl explained that the passengers had been requested to remain in their accommodations, and that most of *Delta Orionis'* personnel were employed in work aboard *Epsilon Sextans.*

" So I haven't been the only one to be kept under lock and key," commented Grimes sardonically.

"You're the only one," retorted the girl, "who's been compensated for his imprisonment."

There was no answer to that, so the Ensign remained silent. Saying nothing, he inspected with interest the temporary tunnel that had been rigged between the airlocks of the two ships. *So Epsilon Sextans'* pressure hull had been made good, her atmosphere restored. That meant that the work of installing the armament had been completed. He hoped that he would not have to insist upon modifications.

The wreck—although she was a wreck no longer—bore her scars. The worst damage had been repaired, but holes and slashes that did not impair her structural strength were untouched, and spatters of once molten metal still made crazy patterns on beams and frames, stanchions and bulkheads. And there were the scars made by Craven's engineers—the raw, bright cicatrices of new welding.

Forward they made their way, deck after deck. The elevator in the axial shaft was not yet working, so Grimes had time and opportunity to appreciate the extent of the damage. They passed through the wreckage of the "farm"—the burst algae tanks, the ruptured vats in which yeast and tissue cultures were black and dead, frostbitten and dehydrated. They brushed through alleyways choked with the brittle fronds of creeping plants killed by the ultimate winter.

And then they were passing through the accommodation levels. Bulkheads had been slashed through, destroying the privacy of the cabins that they had once enclosed. Destroying the privacy—and the occupants. There were no longer any bodies; for this Grimes was deeply thankful. (He learned later that Craven's first action had been to order and conduct a funeral service.) There were no bodies—but there were still stains. Men and women die quickly in hard vacuum— quickly and messily.

Captain Craven was alone in the Control Room. He was working, rather slowly and clumsily, wiring up an obviously makeshift panel that was additional to the original one installed before the Master's acceleration chair. It was obvious what it was—the remote controls for the newly fitted weaponry. Grimes said quickly, "There's no need for that, sir."

Craven started, let go of his screwdriver, made a fumbling grab for it as it drifted away from him. He stared at Grimes, then growled, "So it's *you*, is it?" Then, to Jane, "What the hell do you mean by letting this puppy out of his kennel?"

"Captain Craven," she told him quietly, "Mr. Grimes wants to come with us."

"*What?* I warn you, Miss Pentecost, I'm in no mood for silly jokes."

"This is not a silly joke, Captain," said Grimes. "I've had time to think things over. I feel, I really feel that you have a far better chance if there's a qualified officer along to handle the gunnery."

Craven looked at them, from the girl to Grimes, then back again. He said, "Ensign, didn't I warn you?"

"It's not that way at all, sir," Grimes told him, flushing. "In fact, Miss Pentecost has been trying hard to dissuade me."

"*Oh*?"

"It's true," said Jane. "But he told me that we couldn't afford to look a gift horse in the mouth."

"I don't know what's been happening," rasped Craven. "I don't want to know what's been happening between the pair of you. This change of mind, this change of heart is rather . . . sudden. No matter. One volunteer, they say, is worth ten pressed men." He glared coldly at the Ensign. "And you volunteer?"

"Yes, Captain."

"I believe you. I have no choice in the matter. But you realize the consequences?"

"I do."

"Well, I *may* be able to do something to clear your yardarm. I've still to make my last entries in the Official Log of *Delta Orionis*, before I hand over to Captain Kennedy. And when it comes to such documentation, nobody cares to accuse a shipmaster of being a liar. Not out loud." He paused, thinking. "How does this sound, Miss Pentecost? Date, Time, Position, etc., etc. Mr. John Grimes, passenger, holding the rank of Ensign in the Federation Survey Service, removed by force from this vessel to *Epsilon Sextans*, there to supervise the installation and mounting of the armament, Survey Service property, discharged on my orders from No. 1 hold, also to advise upon the use of same in the subsequent event of an action's being fought. Signed, etc., etc. And witnessed."

"Rather long-winded, sir. But it seems to cover the ground."

"I intend to do more than advise!" flared Grimes.

"Pipe down. Or, if you must say it, make sure that there aren't any witnesses around when you say it. Now, when it comes to the original supervision, you see what I'm trying to do. Will it work?"

"After a fashion, sir. But it will work much better if the fire control panel is entirely separate from maneuvering control."

"You don't think that I could handle both at once?"

"You *could*. But not with optimum efficiency. No humanoid could. This setup of yours might just work if we were Shaara, or any of the other multi-limbed arthropods. But even the Shaara, in their warships, don't expect the Queen-Captain to handle her ship *and* her guns simultaneously."

"You're the expert. I just want to be sure that you're prepared to, quote, advise, unquote, with your little pink paws on the actual keyboard of your battle organ."

"That's just the way that I propose to advise."

"Good. Fix it up to suit yourself, then. I should be able to let you have a mechanic shortly to give you a hand."

"Before we go any further, sir, I'd like to make an inspection of the weapons themselves. Just in case . . ."

"Just in case I've made some fantastic bollix, eh?" Craven was almost cheerful. "Very good. But try to make it snappy. It's time we were on our way."

"Yes," said Jane, and it seemed that the Captain's discarded somberness was hanging about her like a cloud. "It's time."

12

AT ONE TIME, before differentiation between the mercantile and the fighting vessel became pronounced, merchant vessels were built to carry a quite considerable armament. Today, the mounting of weapons on a merchantman presents its problems. After his tour of inspection Grimes was obliged to admit that Captain Craven had made cunning use of whatever spaces were available— but Craven, of course, was a very experienced officer, with long years of service in all classes of spacecraft. Too—and, perhaps, luckily—there had been no cannon among the Survey Service ordnance that had been requisitioned, so recoil had not been among the problems.

When he was finished, Grimes returned to the Control Room. Craven was still there, and with him was Jane Pentecost. They had, obviously, been discussing something. They could, perhaps, have been quarreling; the girl's face was flushed and her expression sullen.

"Yes?" snapped the Captain.

"You've done a good job, sir. She's no cruiser, but she should be able to defend herself."

"Thank you. Then we'll be on our way."

"Not so fast, sir. I'd like to wire up my control panel properly before we shove off."

Craven laughed. "You'll have time, Mr. Grimes. I still have a few last duties to discharge aboard *Delta Orionis*. But be as quick as you can."

He left the compartment, followed by Jane Pentecost. She said, over her shoulder, "I'll send Mr. Baxter to help you, John."

The Rim Worlder must have been somewhere handy; in a matter of seconds he was by Grimes' side, an already open tool satchel at his belt. As he worked, assisting deftly and then taking over as soon as he was sure of what was required, he talked. He said, "Mum wanted to come along, but I soon put the damper on that. But I was bloody amazed to find *you* here."

"Were you?" asked Grimes coldly.

"You bet I was. Never thought you were cut out to be a bloody pirate." He cursed briefly as a spatter of hot metal from his sizzling soldering iron stung his hand. "A cold weld'd be better, but it'd take too much time. But where was I? Oh, yes. The shock to me system when I saw you comin' aboard this wagon."

"I have my quite valid reasons," Grimes told him stiffly.

"You're tellin' me. Just as my missus had quite valid reasons for wantin' to come with me. But she ain't a gunnery expert." He added piously, "Thank Gawd."

"And I am one," said the Ensign, trying to change the drift of the conversation before he lost his temper. "Yes. that's right. Just stick to the color code. The blue wiring's the ALGE . . ."

"I know," Baxter told him. "Tell me, is it any good?"

"*Yes.* Of course, if an enemy held us in her beams for any prolonged period we should all be cooked, but as far as it goes it's effective enough."

"Hope you're right." He made the last connections, then replaced the panel on the open shallow box. "Here's yer magic cabinet, Professor. All we have ter see now is what rabbits yer can pull outer the hat."

"Plenty, I hope," said Captain Craven, who had returned to Control. "And are you ready now, Mr. Grimes?"

"Yes, sir."

"Good. Then we'll make it stations. If you will take the copilot's chair, while Mr. Baxter goes along to look after his rockets."

"Will do, Skipper," said the engineer, packing away his tools as he pulled himself toward the exit hatch.

The ship's intercom came to life, in Jane Pentecost's voice. "Connection between vessels severed. Airlock door closed."

"We're still connected," grumbled Craven. "*Delia O'Ryan* still has her magnetic grapnels out." He spoke into the transceiver microphone: "*Epsilon Sextans* to *Delta Orionis*. Cast off, please. Over."

"*Delta Orionis* to *Epsilon Sextans*. Casting off." Through a viewport Grimes could see one of the bright mooring wires snaking back into its recess. "All clear, Captain."

"Thank you, *Captain* Kennedy." And in a softer voice, "And I hope you keep that handle to your name, Bill."

"Thank you, sir. And all the best, Captain, from all of us, to all of you. And good hunting."

"Thanks. And look after the old *Delia*, Captain. And yourself. Over—and out."

"*Delta Orionis* to *Epsilon Sextans*. Over and out."

(There was something very final, thought Grimes, about those outs.)

He was aware that the ships were drifting slowly apart. Now he could see all *of Delta Orionis* from his viewport. He could not help recalling the day on which he had first seen her, at the Woomera spaceport. So much had happened since that day. (And so much was still to happen—he hoped.) He heard Craven say into the intercom, "Stand by for temporal precession. We're desynchronizing." Then, there was the giddiness, and the off-beat whine of the Mannschenn Drive that pierced his eardrums painfully, and beyond the viewports the great, shining shape of the other ship shimmered eerily and was suddenly warped into the likeness of a monstrous Klein flash—then vanished. Where she had been (where she still was, in space but not in time) shone the distant stars, the stars that in this distorted continuum were pulsing spirals of iridescence.

"Mannschenn Drive. *Cut!*"

The thin, high keening died abruptly. Outside, the stars were glittering points of light, piercingly bright against the blackness.

"Mr. Grimes!" Craven's voice was sharp. "I hope that you take more interest in gunnery than you do in ship handling. In case it has escaped your notice, I would remind you that you are second in command of this vessel, and in full charge in the event of my demise."

"Sorry, sir," stammered Grimes. Then, suddenly bold, "But I'm not your second in command, sir. I've signed no Articles."

Surprisingly, Craven laughed. "A spacelawyer, yet! Well, Mr. Grimes, as soon as we get this vessel on course we'll attend to the legal formalities. Meanwhile, may I request your close attention to what I am doing?"

"You may, sir."

Thereafter he watched and listened carefully. He admired the skill with which Craven turned the ship on her directional gyroscopes until the red-glowing target star was centered exactly in the cartwheel sight. He noted that the Captain used his reaction drive at a longer period and at a higher rate of acceleration than usual, and said as much. He was told, the words falling slowly and heavily in the pseudo-gravity, "They . . . will . . . expect . . . us . . . to . . . be . . . in . . . a . . . hurry. We must . . . not . . . disappoint . . . them."

Speed built up, fast—but it was a velocity that, in the context of the interstellar distances to be traversed, was no more than a snail's crawl. Then—and the sudden silence was like a physical blow—the thunder of the rockets ceased. The screaming roar had died, but the ship was not quiet. The whine of the Mannschenn Drive pervaded her every compartment, vibrated through every member of her structure. She was falling, falling through space and time, plunging through the warped continuum to her rendezvous with Death. . . .

And whose death? wondered Grimes.

He said, "I should have asked before, sir. But how are . . . how are *they* going to find us?"

"I don't know," said Craven. "I don't know. But they've found other ships when they've wanted to. They've never used the old pirate's technique of lying in wait at breaking-out points. A Mass Proximity Indicator? Could be. It's theoretically possible. It could be for a ship under Mannschenn Drive what radar is for a ship in normal space-time. Or some means of homing on a temporal precession field? That's more like it, I think, as this vessel was able to escape when she went random.

"But if they want us—and they will—they'll find us. And then"—he looked at Grimes, his blue gaze intense—"and then it's up to you, Ensign."

"To all of us," said Grimes.

13

SHE WAS UNDERMANNED, this *Epsilon Sextans,* but she functioned quite efficiently. Craven kept a Control Room watch himself, and the other two watchkeepers were Grimes and Jane Pentecost. Four on and eight off were their hours of duty— but there was plenty of work to be done in the off duty periods. The Captain, of course, was in over-all charge, and was trying to bring his command to the pitch of efficiency necessary for a fighting ship. Jane Pentecost was responsible for meals—although these, involving little more than the opening of cans, did not take up too much of her time. She had also taken over biochemist's duties, but called now and again upon Grimes to help her with the ATREG unit. Its operation was simple enough, but it was inclined to be temperamental and, now and again, allowed the carbon dioxide concentration to reach a dangerous level. Grimes' main concern was his armament. He could not indulge in a practice shot—the expulsion of mass by a ship running under interstellar drive is suicidal; even the employment of laser weapons is dangerous. But there were tests that he could make; there was, in the ship's stores, a spare chart tank that he was able to convert to a battle simulator.

Craven helped him, and set up targets in the tank, glowing points of light that were destroyed by the other sparks that represented Grimes' missiles. After one such drill he said, "You seem to know your stuff, Ensign. Now, what's your grasp of the tactical side of it?"

Grimes considered his words before speaking. "Well, sir, we *could* use laser with the Drive in operation—but we haven't got laser. The pirates have. They can synchronize and just carve us up at leisure. This time, I think they'll go for the interstellar drive engine room first, so that we can't get away by the use of random precession."

"Yes. That's what they'll do. That's why I have that compartment literally sealed in a cocoon of insulation. Oh, I know it's not effective, but it will give us a second or so of grace. No more."

"We can't use our reflective vapor," went on Grimes. "That'd be almost as bad, from our viewpoint, as loosing off a salvo of missiles. But, sir, when this ship was first attacked there must have been a considerable loss of mass when the atmosphere was expelled through the rents in the shell plating . . . the Drive was running. How was it that the ship wasn't flung into some other space-time?"

"Come, come, Mr. Grimes. You should know the answer to that one. She was held by the powerful temporal precession fields of the drive units of the two pirates. And then, of course, when the engineers managed to set up their random precession there was no mass left to be expelled."

"H'm. I see. Or I think I see. Then, in that case, why shouldn't I use my ALGE as soon as we're attacked?"

"No. Better not. Something might just go wrong—and I don't want to become one of my own ancestors."

"Then . . . ?"

"You tell me, Mr. Grimes."

"Cut our Drive . . . ? Break out into the normal continuum? Yes . . . it could work." He was becoming enthusiastic. "And then we shall be waiting for them, with our missile batteries, when *they* break out."

"We'll make an admiral of you yet, young Grimes."

With watchkeeping and with off-watch duties time was fully occupied. And yet there was something missing. There was, Grimes said to himself, one hell of a lot missing. Jane Pentecost had her own watch to keep, and her own jobs to do when she was not in the

control room—but she and Grimes had some free time to share. But
they did not share it.

He broached the subject when he was running a test on the
artificial chlorophyll in the ATREG. "Jane, I was hoping I'd see more
of you."

"You're seeing plenty of me."

"But not enough."

"Don't be tiresome," she snapped. Then, in a slightly softer
voice, "Don't . . ."

" . . . spoil everything?" he finished for her sardonically.

"You know what I mean," she told him coldly.

"Do I?" He groped for words. "Jane . . . Damn it all, I hoped . . .
After what happened aboard the *Delia O'Ryan* . . ."

"That," she said, "was different." Her face flushed. "I tell you
this, Grimes, if I'd known that you were coming along with us it
never would have happened."

"No?"

"*NO!*"

"Even so . . . I don't see any reason why we shouldn't . . ."

"Why we shouldn't what? Oh, all right, all right. I know what
you mean. But it's out of the question. I'll tell you why, in words of
one syllable. In a ship such as *Delta Orionis* discreet fun and games
were permissible, even desirable. No shortage of women—both crew
and passengers. Here, I'm the only female. Your friend Mr. Baxter
has been sniffing after me. And Mr. Wolverton, the Interstellar
Chief. *And* his Second. And even, bereaved though he is, the
Bearded Bastard. *He* might get away with it—the privileges of rank
and all that. But nobody else would—most certainly not yourself.
How long would it remain a secret if we went to bed together?"

"I suppose you're right, but . . ."

"But what? Oh John, John, you *are* a stubborn cow."

"*Cow*?"

"Sorry. Just Rimworldsese. Applicable to both sexes."

"Talking of sex . . ."

"Oh, shut *up*!"

"I'll not." She looked desirable standing there. A small smudge of grease on her flushed cheek was like a beauty spot. "I'll not," he said again. She was close to him, and he was acutely conscious that beneath the thin uniform shirt and the short shorts there was only Jane. He had only to reach out. He did so. At first she did not resist—and then exploded into a frenzy of activity. Before he could let go of her a hard, rough hand closed on his shirt collar and yanked him backwards.

"Keep yer dirty paws off her!" snarled a voice. It was Baxter's. "Keep yer dirty paws off her! If we didn't want yer ter let off the fireworks I'd do yer, here an' now."

"And keep *your* dirty paws off me!" yelped Grimes. It was meant to be an authentic quarterdeck bark, but it didn't come out that way.

"Let him go, Mr. Baxter," said Jane, adding, "please."

"Oh, orl right. If yer says so. But I still think we should run him up ter the Old Man."

"No. Better not." She addressed Grimes, "Thank you for your help on the ATREG, Mr. Grimes. And thank *you*, Mr. Baxter, for your help. It's time that I started looking after the next meal."

She left, not hastily, but not taking her time about it either. When she was gone Baxter released Grimes. Clumsily the Ensign turned himself around, with a wild flailing motion. Unarmed combat had never been his specialty, especially unarmed combat in Free Fall conditions. But he knew that he had to fight, and the rage and the humiliation boiling up in him made it certain that he would do some damage.

But Baxter was laughing, showing all his ugly, yellow teeth. "Come orf it, Admiral! An' if we must have a set-to—not in here. Just smash the UV projector—an' bang goes our air conditioning! Simmer down, mate. Simmer down!"

Grimes simmered down, slowly. "But I thought you were out for my blood, Mr. Baxter."

"Have ter put on a show for the Sheilas now an' again. Shouldn't mind puttin' on another kind o' show *with* her. But not in public—like you was goin' to. It just won't do—not until the shootin' is over, anyhow. An' even then. . . . So, Admiral, it's paws off as far as you're concerned. An' as far as I'm concerned—*an'* the Chief Time Twister an' his sidekick. But, if yer can spare the time, I propose we continue the conversation in my palatial dogbox."

Grimes should have felt uneasy as he followed the engineer to his accommodation but, oddly enough, he did not. The rough friendliness just could not be the prelude to a beating up. And it wasn't.

"Come in," said Baxter, pulling his sliding door to one side. "Now yer see how the poor live. This is . . ."

"No," protested Grimes. "No."

"Why? I was only goin' to say that this is me 'umble 'umpy. An' I'd like yer to meet a coupla friends o' mine—and there's more where they came from."

The "friends" were two drinking bulbs. Each bore proudly no less than four stars on its label. The brandy was smooth, smooth and potent. Grimes sipped appreciatively. "I didn't know that we had any of *this* aboard *Delia O'Ryan.*"

"An' nor did we. You'll not find this tipple in the bar stores of any merchantman, nor aboard any of yer precious Survey Service wagons. Space stock for the Emperor's yacht, this is. So here's ter the Waverley taxpayers!"

"But where did you get this from, Mr. Baxter?"

"Where d'yer think? I've had a good fossick around the holds o' this old bitch, an' there's quite a few things too good to let fall inter the hands o' those bloody Waldegrenese."

"But that's pillage."

"It's common sense. Mind yer, I doubt if Captain Craven would approve, so yer'd better chew some dry tea—that's in the cargo too—before yer see the Old Man again. All the bleedin' same—it's no worse than him borrowing your Survey Service stores an' weapons from *his* cargo."

"I suppose it's not," admitted Grimes. All the same, he still felt guilty when he was offered a second bulb of the luxurious spirit. But he did not refuse it.

14

HE WAS A GOOD FOSSICKER, was Baxter.

Two days later, as measured by the ship's chronometer, he was waiting for Grimes as he came off watch. "Ensign," he announced without preamble, "I've found somethin' in the cargo."

"Something new, you mean?" asked Grimes coldly. He still did not approve of pillage, although he had shared the spoils.

"Somethin' that shouldn't be there. Somethin' that's up *your* alley, I think."

"There's no reason why equipment for the Waverley Navy shouldn't be among the cargo."

"True enough. But it wouldn't be in a case with *Beluga Caviar* stenciled all over it. I thought I'd found somethin' to go with the vodka I half pinched, but it won't."

"Then what is it?"

"Come and see."

"All right." Briefly Grimes wondered if he should tell Craven, who had relieved the watch, then decided against it. The Old Man would probably insist on making an investigation in person, in which case Grimes would have to pass another boring hour or so in the Control Room.

The two men made their way aft until they came to the forward bulkhead of the cargo spaces. Normally these would have been pressurized, but, when *Epsilon Sextans'* atmosphere had been

71

replenished from *Delta Orionis'* emergency cylinders, it had seemed pointless to waste precious oxygen. So access was through an airlock that had a locker outside, in which suits, ready for immediate use, were stowed.

Grimes and Baxter suited up, helping each other as required. Then the engineer put out his gloved hand to the airlock controls. Grimes stopped him, bent forward to touch helmets. He said, "Hang on. If we open the door it'll register on the panel in Control."

"Like hell it will!" came the reply. "Most of the wiring was slashed through during the piracy. I fixed the hold lights—but damn all else." Grimes, through the transparency of the visors, saw the other's grin. "For obvious reasons."

Grimes shrugged, released Baxter. Everything was so irregular that one more, relatively minor, irregularity hardly mattered. He squeezed with the engineer into the small airlock, waited until the atmosphere it held had been pumped back into the body of the ship, then himself pushed the button that actuated the mechanism of the inner valve.

This was not the first time that he had been in the cargo spaces. Some of the weapons "borrowed" from *Delta Orionis'* cargo had been mounted in the holds. When he had made his inspections it had never occurred to him that the opening and closing of the airlock door had not registered in Control.

He stood back and let Baxter lead the way. The engineer pulled himself to one of the bins in which he had been foraging. The door to it was still open, and crates and cartons disturbed by the pillager floated untidily around the opening.

"You'll have to get all this restowed," said Grimes sharply. "If we have to accelerate there'll be damage." But he might as well have been speaking to himself. The suit radios had not been switched on and, in any case, there was no air to carry sound waves, however faintly.

Baxter had scrambled into the open bin. Grimes followed him, saw him standing by the case, its top prised open, that carried the lettering, BELUGA CAVIAR. PRODUCE OF THE RUSSIAN SOCIAL DEMOCRATIC REPUBLIC. Baxter beckoned. Grimes edged his way past the drifting packages to join him.

There was something in the case—but it was not jars or cans of salted sturgeon's eggs. It looked at first like a glittering, complex piece of mobile statuary, although it was motionless. It was a metal mismating of gyroscope and Moebius Strip. It did not look wrong— nothing functional ever does—but it did look *odd*.

Grimes was standing hard against Baxter now. Their helmets were touching. He asked, "What . . . what is it?"

"I was hopin' you'd be able ter tell me, Admiral." Then, as Grimes extended a cautious hand into the case, "Careful! Don't touch nothin'!"

"Why not?"

" 'Cause this bloody lot was booby-trapped, that's why. See that busted spring? An' see that cylinder in the corner? That's a thermite bomb, or somethin' worse. Shoulda gone orf when I pried the lid up—but luckily I buggered the firin' mechanism with me bar when I stuck it inter just the right crack. But I think the bastard's deloused now."

"It looks as though it—whatever it is—is hooked up to one of the electrical circuits."

"Yair. An' it's not the lightin' circuit. Must be the airlock indicators."

"Must be." As a weapons expert, Grimes could see the thermite bomb—if that was what it was— had been rendered ineffective. It hadn't been an elaborate trap, merely a device that would destroy the—the *thing* if the case housing it were tampered with. Baxter had been lucky—and, presumably, those who had planted the—what the hell was it?—unlucky.

With a cautious finger he nudged the rotor.

It turned—and he was reminded of those other rotors, the ever-precessing gyroscopes of the Mannschenn Drive.

He remembered, then. He remembered a series of lectures at the Academy on future weapons and navigational devices. Having decided upon his specialty he had been really interested only in the weapons. But there had been talk of a man called Carlotti, who was trying to develop a device that would induce temporal precession in radio signals, so that instantaneous communications would be possible throughout the Galaxy without ships and shore stations having to rely upon the temperamental and unreliable telepaths. And beacons, employing the same principle, could be used for navigation by ships under interstellar drive. . . .

So this could be one of Signor Carlotti's gadgets. Perhaps the Empire of Waverley had offered him a higher price than had the Federation. But why the BELUGA CAVIAR? To deter and confuse industrial spies? But *Epsilon Sextans* possessed excellent strong rooms for the carriage of special cargo.

And why was the thing wired up?

Suddenly it was obvious. Somehow, the Duchy of Waldegren possessed Carlotti equipment. This . . . this beacon had been transmitting, unknown to anybody aboard the ship, during the voyage. The frigates had homed upon her. When, inadvertently, its power supply had been shut off the victim, using random precession, had been able to make her escape.

So, if the pirates were to make a second attack it would have to be reactivated.

"We'd better throw this lot on to the Old Man's plate," said Grimes.

Captain Craven listened intently as Grimes and Baxter told their story. They feared that he was going to lose his temper when told of the engineer's cargo pillaging, but he only remarked, in a dry voice, "I guess that the consignees can afford to compensate us for our time and trouble. Even so, Mr. Baxter, I insist that this practice must cease forthwith." And then, when Grimes described the device, he said, "Yes, I have heard of Carlotti's work. But I didn't think that he'd got as far as a working model. But the thing could have been developed by Waldegrenese scientists from the data in his published papers."

"So you agree, sir, that it is some kind of beacon upon which the pirates can home?"

"What else can it be? Now, gentlemen, we find ourselves upon the horns of a dilemma. If we don't reactivate the bloody thing, the chances are that we shall deliver the ship and cargo intact, at no great risk to ourselves, and to the joy of the underwriters. If we *do* reactivate it—then the chances are that we shall have to fight our way through. And there's no guarantee that we shall be on the winning side."

"I was shanghaied away here as a gunnery officer," said Grimes.

"Shanghaied—or press-ganged?" queried Craven.

"The technique was more that of the shanghai," Grimes told him.

"Indeed?" Craven's voice was cold. "But no matter. You're here, and you're one of my senior officers. What course of action do *you* recommend?"

Grimes replied slowly and carefully. "Legally speaking, what we're involved in isn't a war. But it *is* a war, of sorts. And a just war. And, in any case, the Master of a merchant vessel has the legal right to resist illegal seizure or destruction by force of arms. Of course, we have to consider the illegal circumstances attending the arming of this ship . . . ."

"Let's not get bogged down in legalities and illegalities," said Craven, with a touch of impatience. "The lawyers can sort it all out eventually. Do we reactivate?"

"Yes," said Grimes.

"And you, Mr. Baxter. What do you say?"

"We Rim Worlders just don't like Waldegren. I'll not pass up a chance ter kick the bastards in the teeth. Reactivate, Skipper."

"Good. And how long will it take you to make good the circuit the beacon's spliced in to?"

"Twenty minutes. No more. But d'yer think we oughter put the whole thing to the vote first?"

"No. Everybody here was under the impression that we should be fighting. With one possible exception, they're all volunteers."

"But I did volunteer, sir," objected Grimes.

"Make your mind up, Ensign. You were telling me just now that you'd been shanghaied. All right. Everybody is a volunteer. So we just rebait the trap without any more yapping about it. Let me know as soon as you're ready, Mr. Baxter. Will you require assistance?"

"I'll manage, Skipper."

When he was gone Craven turned to Grimes. "You realize, Ensign, that this puts me in rather a jam. Let me put it this way. Am I justified in risking the lives of all my officers to carry out a private act of vengeance?"

"I think that you can take Mr. Baxter and myself as being representative, sir. As for the others—Miss Pentecost's a Rim Worlder, and her views will coincide with Baxter's. And the original crew members—they're just as entitled to vengeance as you are. I know that if I'd been an officer of this ship at the time of the original piracy I'd welcome the chance of hitting back."

"*You* would. Yes. Even if, as now, an alternative suddenly presented itself. But . . ."

"I honestly don't see what you're worrying about, sir."

"You wouldn't. It's a matter of training. But, for all my Reserve commission, I'm a merchant officer. Oh, I know that any military commander is as responsible for the lives of his men as I am—but he also knows that those lives, like his own, are expendable."

"It's a pity that Baxter found the beacon," said Grimes.

"It is—and it isn't. If he hadn't found it, I shouldn't be soliloquizing like a spacefaring Hamlet. And we should have brought the ship in intact and, like as not, all been awarded Lloyd's Medals. On the other hand—if he hadn't found it we—or I?—should have lost our chance of getting back at the pirates."

"You aren't Hamlet, sir." Grimes spoke with the assurance of the very young, but in later years he was to remember his words, and to feel neither shame nor embarrassment, but only a twinge of envy and regret. "You aren't Hamlet. You're Captain Craven, Master under God. Please, sir, for once in your life do something you want to do, and argue it out later with the Almightly if you must."

"And with my owners?" Grimes couldn't be sure, but he thought he saw something like a smile beneath Craven's full beard. "And with my owners?"

"Master Astronauts' certificates aren't all that common, sir. If worst comes to worst, there's always the Rim Worlds. The Sundowner Line, isn't it?"

"I'd already thought of that." There was no doubt about it.

Craven was smiling. "After all that you've been saying to me, I'm surprised *that you* don't join forces with our Miss Pentecost."

"Go out to the Rim, sir? Hardly."

"Don't be so sure, young Grimes. Anyhow, you'd better get Miss Pentecost up here now so that we can see how friend Baxter is getting on. There's always the risk that he'll find a few more things among the cargo that aren't nailed down."

15

GRIMES CALLED Jane Pentecost on the intercom; after a minute or so she made her appearance in Control. Craven told her what Baxter had discovered and what he, Craven, intended doing about it. She nodded in emphatic agreement. "Yes," she said. "The thing's here to be used—and to be used the way that *we* want to use it. But I don't think that we should make it public."

"Why not, Miss Pentecost?"

"I could be wrong, Captain, but in my opinion there are quite a few people in this ship who'd welcome the chance of wriggling out of being the cheese in the mousetrap. When there's no alternative they're brave enough. When there's a face-saving alternative . . ."

Baxter's voice came from the intercom speaker. "Chief Reaction Drive Engineer to Control. Repairs completed. Please check your panel."

Yes, the circuit had been restored. The buzzer sounded, and on the board a glowing red light showed that the outer door to the cargo hold airlock was open. How much of the failure of the indicators was due to battle damage and how much to Baxter's sabotage would never be known. Craven's heavy eyebrows lifted ironically as he looked at Grimes, and Grimes shrugged in reply.

Then, the watch handed over to the girl, the two men made their way aft from the Control Room. Outside the airlock they found Baxter, already suited up save for his helmet. There had been only two suits in the locker, and the engineer had brought another one along for the Captain from somewhere.

The little compartment would take only two men at a time. Craven and Grimes went through first, then were joined by Baxter. There was no longer any need for secrecy, so the suit radios were switched on. The only person likely to be listening in was Jane Pentecost in Control.

Grimes heard Craven muttering angrily as they passed packages that obviously had been opened and pillaged, but the Captain did no more than mutter. He possessed the sense of proportion so essential to his rank—and a few bulbs of looted liquor were, after all, relatively unimportant.

They came to the bin in which the case allegedly containing caviar had been stowed, in which some secret agent of Waldegren had tapped the circuit supplying power to the beacon. Inside the box the gleaming machine was still motionless. Craven said, "I thought you told me the current was on."

"It is, Skipper." Baxter's voice was pained. "But I switched it off before I fixed the wiring." He extended a gloved finger, pressed a little toggle switch.

And nothing happened.

"Just a nudge." whispered the engineer.

The oddly convoluted rotor turned easily enough, and as it rotated it seemed almost to vanish in a mist of its own generating— a mist that was no more than an optical illusion.

It rotated, slowed—and stopped.

Baxter cast aspersions upon the legitimacy of its parenthood. Then, still grumbling, he produced a volt-meter. Any doubt that power was being delivered to the machine was soon dispelled. Power was being delivered—but it was not being used.

"Well, Mr. Baxter?" demanded Craven.

"I'm a fair mechanic, Skipper—but I'm no physicist."

"Mr. Grimes?"

"I specialized in gunnery, sir."

Craven snorted, the sound unpleasantly loud in the helmet phones. He said sarcastically, "I'm only the Captain, but I have some smatterings of Mannschenn Drive maintenance and operation. This thing isn't a Mannschenn Drive unit—but it's first cousin to one. As I recall it, some of the earlier models couldn't be started without the employment of a small, temporal precession field initiator. Furthermore, these initiators, although there is no longer any need for them, are still carried as engine room spares in the Commission's ships."

"And that gadget'll start *this* little time-twister, Skipper?" asked the engineer.

"It might, Mr. Baxter. It might. So, Mr. Grimes, will you go along to the Mannschenn Drive room and ask Mr. Wolverton for his initiator? No need to tell him what it's for."

WOLVERTON was in the Mannschenn Drive room, staring moodily at the gleaming complexity of precessing rotors. Grimes hastily averted his eyes from the machine. It frightened him, and he didn't mind admitting it. And there was something about the engineer that frightened him, too. The tall, cadaverous man, with the thin strands of black hair drawn over his gleaming skull, looked more like a seer than a ship's officer, looked like a fortune-teller peering into the depths of an uncannily mobile crystal ball. He was mumbling, his voice a low, guttural muttering against the thin, high keening of his tumbling gyroscopes. The Ensign at last was able to make out the words.

"Divergent tracks.... To be, or not to be, that is the question—"

Grimes thought, *This ship should be renamed the* State of Denmark. *There's something rotten here* .... He said sharply, "Mr. Wolverton!"

Slowly the Chief Interstellar Drive Engineer turned his head, stared at Grimes unseeingly at first. His eyes came into focus. He whispered, "It's you."

"Who else, Chief? Captain's compliments, and he'd like to borrow your temporal precession field initiator."

"He would, would he? And why?"

"An—an experiment." said Grimes, with partial truth. The fewer people who knew the whole truth the better.

"An experiment?"

"Yes. If you wouldn't mind letting me have it now, Chief. . . ."

"But it's engine room stores. It's the Commission's stores. It's a *very* delicate instrument. It is against the Commission's regulations to issue it to unqualified personnel."

"But Mr. Baxter is helping with the . . . experiment."

"Mr. Baxter! That letter-off of cheap fireworks. That . . . *Rim Runner!* No. No. Mr. Baxter is not qualified personnel."

"Then perhaps you could lend us one of your juniors."

"No. No, I would not trust them. Why do you think that I am here, Mr. Grimes? Why do you think that I have been tied to my gyroscopes? Literally tied, almost. If I had not been here, keeping my own watch, when the pirates struck, this ship would have been utterly destroyed. I *know* the Drive, Mr. Grimes." He seized the Ensign's arm, turned him so that he was facing the gleaming, spinning rotors, endlessly precessing, endlessly tumbling down the dark dimensions, shimmering on the very verge of invisibility. Grimes wanted to close his eyes, but could not. "I *know* the Drive, Mr. Grimes. It talks to me. It shows me things. It warned me, that time, that Death was waiting for this ship and all in her. And now it warns me again. But there is a . . . a divergence. . . ."

"Mr. Wolverton, please! There is not much time."

"But what is Time, Mr. Grimes? What *is* Time? What do you know of the forking World Lines, the Worlds of If? I've lived with this machine, Mr. Grimes. It's part of me—or am I part of *it*? Let me show you . . . ." His grip on the Ensign's arm was painful. "Let me show you. Look. Look into the machine. What do you see?"

Grimes saw only shadowy, shimmering wheels and a formless darkness.

"I see you, Mr. Grimes," almost sang the engineer. "I see you—but not as you *will* be. But as you might be. I see you on the bridge of your flagship, your uniform gold-encrusted and medal-bedecked, with commodores and captains saluting you and calling you 'sir' . . . but I see you, too, in the control room of a shabby little ship, a single ship, in shabby clothes, and the badge on your cap is one that I have never seen, is one that does not yet exist. . . ."

"Mr. Wolverton! That initiator. *Please!*"

"But there is no hurry, Mr. Grimes. There is no hurry. There is time enough for everything—for everything that is, that has been, that will be and that might be. There is time to decide, Mr. Grimes. There is time to decide whether or not we make our second rendezvous with Death. The initiator is part of it all, Mr. Grimes, is it not? The initiator is the signpost that stands at the forking of the track. You weren't here, Mr. Grimes, when the pirates struck. You did not hear the screams, you did not smell the stench of burning flesh. You're young and foolhardy; all that you want is the chance to play with your toys. And all that I want, now that I know that alternatives exist, is the chance to bring this ship to her destination with no further loss of life."

"Mr. Wolverton . . ."

"Mr. Grimes!" It was Captain Craven's voice, and he was in a vile temper. "What the hell do you think you're playing at?"

"Captain," said Wolverton. "I can no more than guess at what you intend to do—but I have decided not to help you to do it."

"Then give us the initiator. We'll work it ourselves."

"No, Captain."

"Give me the initiator, Mr. Wolverton. That's an order."

"A *lawful* command, Captain? As lawful as those commands of yours that armed this ship?"

"Hold him, Grimes!" (*And who's supposed to be holding whom?* wondered the Ensign. Wolverton's grip was still tight and painful on his arm.) "Hold him, while I look in the storeroom!"

"Captain! Get away from the door! You've no right . . ."

Wolverton relinquished his hold on Grimes who, twisting with an agility that surprised himself, contrived to get both arms about the engineer's waist. In the scuffle the contact between their magnetic shoe soles and the deck was broken. They hung there, helpless, with no solidity within reach of their flailing limbs to give them purchase. They hung there, clinging to each other, but more in hate than in love. Wolverton's back was to the machine; he could not see, as could Grimes, that there was an indraught of air into the spinning, shimmering complexity. Grimes felt the beginnings of panic, more than the mere beginnings. There were no guardrails; he had read somewhere why this was so, but the abstruse physics involved did not matter—all that mattered was that there was nothing to prevent him and Wolverton from being drawn into the dimension-twisting field of the thing.

He freed, somehow, his right hand, and with an effort that sprained his shoulder brought it around in a sweeping, clumsy and brutal blow to the engineer's face. Wolverton screamed and his grip relaxed. Violently, Grimes shoved away. To the action there was reaction.

Craven emerged from the storeroom, carrying something that looked like a child's toy gyroscope in a transparent box. He looked around for Grimes and Wolverton at deck level and then, his face puzzled, looked up. He did not, as Grimes had been doing for some seconds, vomit—but his face, behind the beard, went chalk-white. He put out his free hand and, not ungently, pulled Grimes to the deck.

He said, his voice little more than a whisper, "There's nothing we can do. Nothing—except to get a pistol and finish him off. . . ."

Grimes forced himself to look again at the slimy, bloody obscenity that was a man turned, literally, inside-out—heart (if it was the heart) still beating, intestines still writhing.

16

IT WAS GRIMES who went for a pistol, fetching a Minetti from the weapons rack that he, himself, had fitted up in the Control Room. He told Jane Pentecost what he wanted it for. He made no secret of either his horror or his self blame.

She said, "But this is a war, even if it's an undeclared one. And in a war you must expect casualties."

"Yes, yes. I know. But *I* pushed him into the field."

"It was an accident. It could easily have been you instead of him. And I'm glad that it wasn't."

"But you haven't seen . . ."

"And I don't want to." Her voice hardened. "Meanwhile, get the hell out of here and back to the Mannschenn Drive room. If you're so sorry for the poor bastard, do something about putting him out of his misery."

"But . . ."

"Don't be such a bloody coward, Grimes."

The words hurt—mainly because there was so much truth in them. Grimes was dreading having to see again the twisted obscenity that had once been a man, was dreading having to breathe again the atmosphere of that compartment, heavy with the reek of hot oil, blood and fecal matter. But, with the exception of Craven, he was the only person in the ship trained in the arts of war. He recalled the words of a surgeon-commander who had lectured the midshipmen of his course on the handling of battle casualties—and recalled, too, how afterward the young gentlemen had sneered at the bloodthirstiness of one who was supposed to be a professional healer. *"When one of your shipmates has really had it, even if he's your best friend, don't hesitate a moment about finishing him off. You'll be doing him a kindness. Finish him off—and get him out of sight. Shockingly wounded men are bad for morale."*

"What are you waiting for?" demanded Jane Pentecost. "Do you want *me* to do it?"

Grimes said nothing, just hurried out of the Control Room.

Craven was still in the Mannschenn Drive room when Grimes got back there. With him were two of the interstellar drive engineers—the Second and the Third. Their faces were deathly white, and the Second's prominent Adam's apple was working spasmodically, but about them there was an air of grim resolution. The Third—how could he bear to touch that slimy, reeking mess?—had hold of its shoulders (white, fantastically contorted bone gleaming pallidly among red convolutions of flesh), while the Second, a heavy spanner in his hand, was trying to decide where to strike.

The Captain saw Grimes. "Give me that!" he snapped, and snatched the pistol from the Ensign's hand. Then, to the engineers, "Stand back!"

The little weapon rattled sharply and viciously. To the other smells was added the acridity of burned propellant. What had been Wolverton was driven to the deck by the impact of the tiny projectiles, and adhered there. There was surprisingly little blood, but the body had stopped twitching.

Craven handed the empty pistol back to the Ensign. He ordered, "You stay here, Mr. Grimes, and organize the disposal of the body." He went to the locker where he had put the initiator, took out the little instrument and, carrying it carefully, left the Mannschenn Drive room. Neither of the engineers, still staring with horrified fascination at their dead Chief, noticed.

"How . . . how did it happen?" asked the Second, after a long silence.

"He fell into the field," said Grimes.

"But how? How? He was always getting on us about being

careless, and telling us what was liable to happen to us, and now it's happened to him—"

"That's the way of it," contributed the Third, with a certain glum satisfaction. "Don't do as I do, do as I say."

"Have you a box?" asked Grimes.

"A box?" echoed the Second.

"Yes. A box." Now that he was doing something, doing something useful, Grimes was beginning to feel a little better. "We can't have a funeral while we're running under interstellar drive. We have to . . . to put him somewhere." *Out of sight,* he mentally added.

"That chest of spares?" muttered the Second.

"Just the right size," agreed the Third.

"Then get it," ordered Grimes.

The chest, once the spares and their packing had been removed and stowed elsewhere, was just the right size. Its dimensions were almost those of a coffin. It was made of steel, its bottom magnetized, and remained where placed on the deck while the three men, fighting down their recurring nausea, handled the body into it. All of them sighed audibly in relief when, at last, the close-fitting lid covered the remains. Finally, the Third ran a welding torch around the joint. As he was doing so the lights flickered.

Was it because of the torch? wondered Grimes. Or was it because the beacon in the hold had been reactivated?

Somehow he could not feel any real interest.

Cleaned up after a fashion, but still feeling physically ill, he was back in the Control Room. Craven was there, and Baxter was with him. Jane Pentecost had been relieved so that she could attend to her duties in the galley. "Not that *I* feel like a meal," the Captain had said. "And I doubt very much that Mr. Grimes does either."

"Takes a lot ter put *me* off me tucker," the engineer declared cheerfully as he worked on the airlock door telltale panel.

"You didn't see Mr. Wolverton, Mr. Baxter," said Craven grimly.

"No, Skipper. An' I'm not sorry I didn't." He paused in his work to rummage in his tool bag. He produced bulbs of brandy. "But I thought you an' the Ensign might need some o' this."

Craven started to say something about cargo pillage, then changed his mind. He accepted the liquor without further quibbling. The three men sipped in silence.

Baxter carelessly tossed his squeezed empty bulb aside, continued with what he had been doing. The Captain said to Grimes, "Yes. We got the thing started again. And we've improved upon it."

"Improved upon it, sir? How?"

"It's no longer only a beacon. It's also an alarm. As soon as it picks up the radiation from the similar pieces of apparatus aboard the enemy frigates, the buzzer that Mr. Baxter is fitting up will sound, the red light will flash. We shall have ample warning. . . ."

"She'll be right, Skipper," said the engineer.

"Thank you, Mr. Baxter. And now; if you don't mind, I'd like a few words in private with Mr. Grimes."

"Don't be too hard on him, Skipper."

Baxter winked cheerfully at Grimes and left the control room.

"Mr. Grimes," Craven's voice was grave. "Mr. Grimes, today, early in your career, you have learned a lesson that some of us never have to learn. You have killed a man—yes, yes, I know that it was not intentional—and you have been privileged to see the end result of your actions.

"There are many of us who are, who have been, killers. There are many of us who have pushed buttons but who have never seen what happens at the other end of the trajectory. Perhaps people slaughtered by explosion or laser beam do not look quite so horrible as Wolverton—but, I assure you, they often look horrible enough, and often die as slowly and as agonizingly. You know, now, what violent death looks like, Mr. Grimes. So tell me, are you still willing to push your buttons, to play pretty tunes on your battle organ?"

"And what did the bodies in this ship look like, Captain?" asked Grimes. Then, remembering that one of the bodies had belonged to the woman whom Craven had loved, he bitterly regretted having asked the question.

"Not pretty," whispered Captain Craven. "Not at all pretty."

"I'll push your buttons for you," Grimes told him.

And for Jane Pentecost, he thought. *And for the others. And for myself? The worst of it all is that I haven't got the excuse of saying that it's what I'm paid for. . . .*

17

DOWN THE DARK dimensions fell *Epsilon Sextans,* falling free through the warped continuum. But aboard the ship time still possessed meaning, the master chronometer still ticked away the seconds, minutes and hours; the little man-made world was still faithful to that puissant god of scientific intelligences everywhere in the universe—the Clock. Watch succeeded watch in Control Room and engine room. Meals were prepared and served on time. There was even, toward the end, a revival of off-duty social activities: a chess set was discovered and brought into use, playing cards were produced and a bridge school formed.

But there was one social activity that, to Grimes' disappointment was not resumed—the oldest social activity of them all. More than once he pleaded with Jane—and every time she laughed away his pleas. He insisted—and that made matters worse. He was (as he said), the donkey who had been allowed one nibble of the carrot and who could not understand why the carrot had been snatched away. He was (she said), a donkey. Period.

He should have guessed what was happening, but he did not. He was young, and inexperienced in the ways of women—of men *and* women. He just could not imagine that Jane would spare more than a casual glance for any of the engineers or for the flabby, pasty youth who was the psionic radio officer—and in this he was right.

Epsilon Sextans was, for a ship of her class, very well equipped.

In addition to the usual intercom system she was fitted with closed circuit television. In the event of emergency the Captain or watch officer, by the flip of a switch, could see what was happening in any compartment of the vessel. Over the control panel, in big, red letters, were the words: EMERGENCY USE ONLY. Grimes did not know what was the penalty for improper use of the apparatus in the Merchant Navy—but he did know that in the Survey Service officers had been cashiered and given an ignominious discharge for this offense. The more cramped and crowded the conditions in which men—and women—work and live, the more precious is privacy.

It was Grimes' watch.

When he had taken over, all the indications were that it would be as boring as all the previous watches. All that was required of the watchkeeper was that he stay awake. Grimes stayed awake. He had brought a book with him into Control, hiding it inside his uniform shirt, and it held his attention for a while. Then, following the example of generations of watch officers, he set up a game of three dimensional tic-tac-toe in the chart tank and played, right hand against left. The left hand was doing remarkably well when a buzzer sounded. The Ensign immediately cleared the tank and looked at the airlock indicator panel. But there were no lights on the board, and he realized that it was the intercom telephone.

"Control," he said into his microphone.

"P.R.O. here. I . . . I'm not happy, Mr. Grimes. . . ."

"Who is?" quipped Grimes.

"I . . . I feel . . . smothered."

"Something wrong with the ventilation in your shack?"

"No. NO. It's like . . . it's like a heavy blanket soaked in ice-cold water. . . . You can't move . . . you can't shout . . . you can't *hear*. . . . *It's like it was before.* . . ."

"*Before what?*" snapped Grimes—and then as the other buzzer sounded, as the additional red light flashed on the telltale panel, he realized the stupidity of his question.

At once he pressed the alarm button. This was it, at last. Action Stations! Throughout the ship the bells were shrilling, the klaxons squawking. Hastily Grimes vacated the pilot's chair, slipped into the one from which he could control his weapons—and from which he could reach out to other controls. But where was the Old Man? Where was Captain Craven? This was the moment that he had longed for, this was the consummation toward which all his illegalities had been directed. Damn it all, *where was he?*

Perhaps he was floating stunned in his quarters—starting up hurriedly from sleep he could have struck his head upon some projection, knocked himself out. If this were the case he, Grimes, would have to call Jane from her own battle station in Sick Bay to render first aid. But there was no time to lose.

The Ensign reached out, flipped the switches that would give him the picture of the interior of the Captain's accommodation. The screen brightened, came alive. Grimes stared at the luminous presentation in sick horror. Luminous it was—with that peculiar luminosity of naked female flesh. Jane was dressing herself with almost ludicrous haste. Of the Captain there was no sign—*on the screen.*

Craven snarled, with cold ferocity, "You damned, sneaking, prurient puppy!" Then, in a louder voice, "Switch that damn thing off! I'll deal with you when this is over."

"But, sir . . ."

"Switch it off, I say!"

Cheeks burning, Grimes obeyed. Then he sat staring at his armament controls, fighting down his nausea, his physical sickness. Somehow, he found time to think bitterly, *So I was the knight, all set and ready to slay dragons for his lady. And all the time, she . . .* He did not finish the thought.

He heard a voice calling over the intercom, one of the engineers. "Captain, they're trying to lock on! Same as last time. Random precession, sir?"

"No. Cut the Drive!"

"Cut the Drive?" Incredulously. "You heard me. *Cut!*" Then, to Grimes, "And what the hell are *you* waiting for?"

The Ensign knew what he had to do; he had rehearsed it often enough. He did it. From the nozzles that pierced the outer shell spouted the cloud of reflective vapor, just in time, just as the enemy's lasers lashed out at their target. It seemed that the ship's internal temperature rose suddenly and sharply—although that could have been illusion, fostered by the sight of the fiery fog glimpsed through the viewports before the armored shutters slammed home.

There were targets now on Grimes' fire control screen, two of them, but he could not loose a missile until the tumbling rotors of the Drive had ceased to spin, to precess. The use of the anti-laser vapor screen had been risky enough. Abruptly the screens went blank—which signified that the temporal precession rates of hunted and hunters were no longer in synchronization, that the fields of the pirates had failed to lock on. In normal spacetime there would be no need to synchronize—and then the hunters would discover that their quarry had claws and teeth.

Aboard *Epsilon Sextans* the keening note of the Drive died to a whisper, a barely audible murmur, fading to silence. There was the inevitable second or so of utter disorientation when, as soon as it was safe, the engineers braked the gyroscopes.

Craven acted without hesitation, giving his ship headway and acceleration with Inertial Drive. He was not running—although this was the impression that he wished to convey. He was inviting rather than evading combat—but if the Waldegren captains chose to assume that *Epsilon Sextans* was, as she had been, an unarmed merchantman (after all, the anti-laser screen could have been jury rigged from normal ship's stores and equipment), taking evasive action, that was *their* error of judgment.

Grimes watched his screens intently. Suddenly the two blips reappeared, astern, all of a hundred kilos distant, but closing. This he reported.

"Stand by for acceleration!" ordered Craven. "Reaction Drive—stand by!"

It was all part of the pattern—a last, frantic squandering of reaction mass that could do no more than delay the inevitable. It would look good from the enemy control rooms.

"Reaction Drive ready!" reported Baxter over the intercom.

"Thank you. Captain to all hands, there will be no countdown. *Fire!*"

From the corner of his eye Grimes saw Craven's hand slam

down on the key. Acceleration slammed him brutally back into his chair. There was a roar that was more like an explosion than a normal rocket firing, a shock that jarred and rattled every fitting in the Control Room.

Craven remarked quietly. "That must have looked convincing enough—but I hope that Baxter didn't really blow a chamber."

There was only the Inertial Drive now, and the two blips that, very briefly, had fallen astern, were now creeping up again, closing the range. "Anti-laser," ordered Craven briefly.

"But, sir, it'll just be wasting it. They'll not be using laser outside twenty kilometers."

"They'll not be expecting a gunnery specialist aboard this wagon, either."

Once again the nozzles spouted, pouring out a cloud that fell rapidly astern of the running ship, dissipating uselessly.

Craven looked at his own screens, frowned, muttered, "They're taking their sweet time about it . . . probably low on reaction mass themselves." He turned to Grimes. "I think a slight breakdown of the I.D.'s in order."

"As you say, sir." The Ensign could not forget having been called a damned, sneaking, prurient puppy. Let Craven make his own decisions.

"Stand by for Free Fall," ordered the Captain quietly. The steady throbbing of the Inertial Drive faltered, faltered and ceased. There were two long minutes of weightlessness, and then, for five minutes, the Drive came back into operation. *A breakdown,* the enemy must be thinking. *A breakdown, and the engineers sweating and striving to get the ship under way again.* A breakdown—it would not be surprising after the mauling she had endured at the first encounter.

She hung there, and although her actual speed could be measured in kilometers a second she was, insofar as her accelerating pursuers were concerned, relatively motionless. Grimes wondered why the warships did not use their radio, did not demand surrender—*Epsilon Sextans'* transceiver was switched on, but no sound issued from the speaker but the hiss and crackle of interstellar static. He voiced his puzzlement to Craven.

Craven laughed grimly. "They know who *we* are—or they think that they know. And they know that we know who *they* are. After what happened before, why should we expect mercy? All that we can do now—they think—is to get the Mannschenn Drive going again. But with that comic beacon of theirs working away merrily they'll be able to home on us, no matter how random our precession." He laughed again. "They haven't a care in the world, bless their little black hearts."

Grimes watched his screens. Forty kilometers—thirty—"Sir, the ALGE?" he asked.

"Yes. It's your party now."

For the third time reflective vapor gushed from the nozzles, surrounding the ship with a dense cloud. Craven, who had been watching the dials of the external temperature thermometers, remarked quietly, "They've opened fire. The shell plating's heating up. Fast."

And in the Control Room it felt hot—and hotter, Grimes pressed the button that unmasked his batteries. The gas screen, as well as affording protection from laser, hid the ship from visual observation. The enemy would not be expecting defense by force of arms.

He loosed his first salvo, felt the ship tremble as the missiles ejected themselves from their launching racks. There they were on the screens—six tiny sparks, six moronic mechanical intelligences programmed to home upon and destroy, capable of countering evasive action so long as their propellant held out. There they were on the screens—six of them, then four, then one. This last missile almost reached its target—then it, too, blinked out. The Waldegren frigates were now using their laser for defense, not attack.

"I don't think," remarked Craven quietly, "that they'll use missiles. Not yet, anyhow. They want our cargo intact." He chuckled softly. "But we've got them worried."

Grimes didn't bother to reply. The telltale lights on his panel told him that the six AVM launchers were reloaded. The AMMs—the anti-missile missiles—had not yet been fired. Dare he risk their use against big targets? He carried in his magazines stock sufficient

for three full salvos only— and with no laser for anti-missile work
dare he deplete his supply of this ammunition?

He had heard the AMMs described as "vicious little brutes."
They were to the Anti-Vessel Missiles as terriers are to mastiffs.
Their warheads were small, but this was compensated for by their
greater endurance. They were, perhaps, a little more "intelligent"
than the larger rockets—and Grimes, vaguely foreseeing this present
contingency, had made certain modifications to their "brains."

He pushed the button that actuated his modifications, that
overrode the original programming. He depressed the firing stud.
He felt the vibration as the war-rockets streaked away from the ship,
and on his screens watched the tiny points of light closing the range
between themselves and the two big blips that were the targets. They
were fast, and they were erratic. One was picked off by laser within
the first ten seconds, but the others carried on, spurting and
swerving, but always boring toward their objectives. Grimes could
imagine the enemy gunnery officers flailing their lasers like men,
armed only with sticks, defending themselves against a horde of
small, savage animals. There was, of course, one sure defense—to
start up the Mannschenn Drive and to slip back into the warped
continuum where the missiles could not follow. But, in all probability,
the Waldegren captains had yet to accept the fact, emotionally, that
this helpless merchantman had somehow acquired the wherewithal
to strike back.

Two of the AMMs were gone now, picked off by the enemy
laser. Three were still closing on the target on *Epsilon Sextans'* port
quarter, and only one on the target abaft the starboard beam.
Grimes loosed his second flight of AMMs, followed it with a full
salvo of AVMs. Then, knowing that the protective vapor screen
must have been thinned and shredded by his rocketry, he sent out
a replenishing gush of reflective gas.

He heard Craven cry out in exultation. The three AMMs of
the first flight had hit their target, the three sparks had fused with
the blip that represented the raider to port. The three sparks that
were the second flight were almost there, and overtaking them
were the larger and brighter sparks of the second AVM salvo.

The Anti-Missile Missiles would cause only minor damage to a ship—but, in all probability, they would throw fire control out of kilter, might even destroy laser projectors. In theory, one AVM would suffice to destroy a frigate; a hit by three at once would make destruction a certainty.

And so it was.

Seen only on the radar screen, as a picture lacking in detail painted on a fluorescent surface by an electron brush, it was anticlimactic. The blips, the large one, the three small ones and the three not so small, merged. And then there was an oddly shaped blob of luminescence that slowly broke up into a cluster of glowing fragments, a gradually expanding cluster, a leisurely burgeoning flower of pale fire.

Said Craven viciously, "The other bastard's got cold feet. . . ."

And so it was. Where she had been on the screen was only darkness, a darkness in which the sparks that were missiles and anti-missiles milled about aimlessly. They would not turn upon each other—that would have been contrary to their programming. They would not, in theory, use their remaining fuel to home upon the only worthwhile target remaining—*Epsilon Sextans* herself. But, as Craven knew and as Grimes knew, theory and practice do not always coincide. Ships have been destroyed by their own missiles.

With reluctance Grimes pushed the DESTRUCT button. He said to the Captain, gesturing toward the wreckage depicted on the screen, "Pick up survivors, sir? If there are any."

"If there are any," snarled Craven, "that's their bad luck. No—we give chase to the other swine!"

18

GIVE CHASE...

It was easier said than done. The surviving frigate had restarted her Mannschenn Drive, had slipped back into the warped continuum where, unless synchronization of precession rates was achieved and held, contact between vessels would be impossible. The Carlotti Beacon in *Epsilon Sextans'* hold was worse than useless; it had been designed to be homed upon, not to be a direction-finding instrument. (In any case, it could function as such only if the beacon aboard the Waldegren ship were working.) Neither Craven nor Grimes knew enough about the device to effect the necessary modifications. The interstellar drive engineers thought that they could do it, but their estimates as to the time required ranged from days to weeks. Obviously, as long as it was operating it would be of value to the enemy only.

So it was switched off.

There was only one method available to Craven to carry out the pursuit—psionic tracking. He sent for his Psionic Radio Officer, explained the situation. The telepath was a young man, pasty faced, unhealthy looking, but not unintelligent. He said at once, "Do you think, Captain, that the other officers and myself are willing to carry on the fight? After all, we've made our point. Wouldn't it be wisest to carry on, now, for Waverley?"

"Speaking for meself," put in Baxter, who had accompanied Jane Pentecost to Control, "an' fer any other Rim Worlders present,

97

I say that now the bastards are on the run it's the best time ter smack 'em again. An' hard. An' the tame time-twisters think the same as we do. I've already had words with 'em." He glared at the telepath. "Our snoopin' little friend here should know very well what the general consensus of opinion is."

"We do not pry," said the communications officer stiffly. "But I am willing to abide by the will of the majority."

"And don't the orders of the Master come into it?" asked Craven, more in amusement than anger.

"Lawful commands, sir?" asked Grimes who, until now, had been silent.

"Shut up!" snapped Jane Pentecost.

"Unluckily, sir," the young man went on, "I do not possess the direction-finding talent. It is, as you know, quite rare."

"Then what *can* you do?" demanded Craven.

"Sir, let me finish, please. The psionic damping device—I don't know what it was, but I suspect that it was the brain of some animal with which I am unfamiliar—was in the ship that was destroyed. The other vessel carries only a normal operator, with normal equipment—himself and some sort of organic amplifier. He is still within range, and I can maintain a listening watch—"

"And suppose *he* listens to you?" asked the Captain. "Even if you transmit nothing—as you will not do, unless ordered by myself—there could be stray thoughts. And that, I suppose, applies to all of us."

The telepath smiled smugly. "Direction-finding is not the only talent. I'm something of a damper myself—although not in the same class as the one that was blown up. I give you my word, sir, that this vessel is psionically silent." He raised his hand as Craven was about to say something. "Now, sir, I shall be able to find out where the other ship is heading. I know already that her Mannschenn Drive unit is not working at full capacity; it sustained damage of some kind during the action. I'm not a navigator, sir, but it seems to me that we could be waiting for her when she reemerges into the normal continuum."

"You're not a navigator," agreed Craven, "and you're neither a tactician nor a strategist. We should look rather silly, shouldn't we, hanging in full view over a heavily fortified naval base, a sitting duck. Even so . . ." His big right hand stroked his beard. "Meanwhile, I'll assume that our little friends are headed in the general direction of Waldegren, and set course accordingly. If Mr. Grimes will be so good as to hunt up the target star in the Directory . . ."

Grimes did as he was told. He had made his protest, such as it was, and, he had to admit, he was in favor of continuing the battle. It was a matter of simple justice. Why should one shipload of murderers be destroyed, and the other shipload escape unscathed? He was still more than a little dubious of the legality of it all, but he did not let it worry him.

He helped Craven to line the ship up on the target star, a yellow, fifth magnitude spark. He manned the intercom while the Captain poured on the acceleration and then, with the ship again falling free, cut in the Mannschenn Drive. When the vessel was on course he expected that the Old Man would give the usual order— "Normal Deep Space routine, Mr. Grimes,"—but this was not forthcoming.

"Now," said Craven ominously.

"Now *what*, sir?"

"You have a short memory, Ensign. A conveniently short memory, if I may say so. Mind you, I was favorably impressed by the way you handled your armament, but that has no bearing upon what happened before."

Grimes blushed miserably. He knew what the Captain was driving at. But, playing for time, he asked, "What do you mean, sir?"

Craven exploded. "What do I mean? You have the crust to sit there and ask me that! Your snooping, sir. Your violation of privacy. Even worse, your violation of the Master's privacy! I shall not tell Miss Pentecost; it would be unkind to embarrass her. But . . ."

Grimes refrained from saying that he had seen Miss Pentecost wearing even less than when, inadvertently, he had spied upon her. He muttered, "I can explain, sir."

"You'd better. Out with it."

"Well, sir, it was like this. I knew that we'd stumbled on the enemy—or that the enemy had stumbled upon us. I'd sounded Action Stations. And when you were a long time coming up to Control I thought that you must have hurt yourself, somehow . . . there have been such cases, as you know. So I thought I'd better check—"

"You thought . . . *you* thought. I'll not say that you aren't paid to think—because that's just what an officer *is* paid for. But you didn't think hard enough, or along the right lines." Grimes could see that Craven had accepted his explanation and that all would be well. The Captain's full beard could not hide the beginnings of a smile. "Did you ever hear of Sir Francis Drake, Ensign?"

"No, sir."

"He was an admiral—one of Queen Elizabeth's admirals. The first Elizabeth, of course. When the Spanish Armada was sighted he did not rush down to his flagship yelling 'Action Stations!' He knew that there was time to spare, and so he quietly finished what he was doing before setting sail."

"And what was he doing, sir?" asked Grimes innocently.

Craven glared at him, then snapped, "Playing bowls."

Then, suddenly, the tension was broken and both men collapsed in helpless laughter. In part it was reaction to the strain of battle—but in greater part it was that freemasonry that exists only between members of the same sex, the acknowledgment of shared secrets and shared experiences.

Grimes knew that Jane Pentecost was not for him—and wished Craven joy of her and she of the Captain. Perhaps they had achieved a permanent relationship, perhaps not—but, either way, his best wishes were with them.

Craven unbuckled his seat strap.

"Deep Space routine, Mr. Grimes. It is your watch, I believe."

"Deep Space routine it is, sir."

Yes, it was still his watch (although so much had happened). It was still his watch, although there were barely fifteen minutes to go before relief. He was tired, more tired than he had ever been in his life before. He was tired, but not unhappy. He knew that the fact that he had killed men should be weighing heavily upon his conscience—but it did not. They, themselves, had been killers—and they had had a far better chance than any of their own victims had enjoyed.

He would shed no tears for them.

19

CRAVEN CAME BACK to the Control Room at the change of watch, when Grimes was handing over to Jane Pentecost. He waited until the routine had been completed, then said, "We know where our friends are headed. They were, like us, running for Waldegren—but they're having to change course." He laughed harshly. "There must be all hell let loose on their home planet."

"Why? What's happened?" asked Grimes.

"I'll tell you later. But, first of all, we have an alteration of course ourselves. Look up Dartura in the Directory, will you, while I get the Drive shut down."

Epsilon Sextans was falling free through normal spacetime before Grimes had found the necessary information. And then there was the hunt for and the final identification of the target star, followed by the lining up by the use of the directional gyroscopes. There was the brief burst of acceleration and then, finally, the interstellar drive was cut in once more.

The Captain made a business of selecting and lighting a cigar. When the pungent combustion was well under way he said, "Our young Mr. Summers is a good snooper. Not as good as some people I know, perhaps." Grimes flushed and Jane Pentecost looked puzzled. "He's a super-sensitive. He let me have a full transcript of all the signals, out and in. It took us a little time to get them sorted out—but not too long, considering. *Adler*—that's the name of the surviving frigate—*was* running for home. Her Captain sent a rather heavily edited report of the action to his Admiral. It seems that *Adler* and the unfortunate *Albatross* were set upon and beaten up by a heavily armed Survey Service cruiser masquerading as an innocent merchantman. The Admiral, oddly enough, doesn't want a squadron of Survey Service battlewagons laying nuclear eggs on his base. So *Adler* has been told to run away and lose herself until the flap's over. . . ."

"And did they send all that *en clair?*" demanded Grimes. "They must be mad!"

"No, they aren't mad. The signal's weren't *en clair.*"

"But . . ."

"Reliable merchant captains," said Craven, "are often entrusted with highly confidential naval documents. There were some such in my safe aboard *Delta Orionis,* consigned to the Commanding Officer of Lindisfarne Base. The officer who delivered them to me is an old friend and shipmate of mine, and he told me that among them was the complete psionic code used by the Waldegren Navy. Well, when I had decided to take over this ship, I'd have been a bloody fool not to have Photostatted the whole damned issue.

"So that's the way of it. Herr Kapitan von Leidnitz thinks he can say what he likes to his superiors without anybody else knowing what he's saying. And all the while . . ." Craven grinned wolfishly. "It seems that there's a minor base, of sorts, on Dartura. Little more than repair yards, although I suppose that there'll be a few batteries for their protection. I can imagine the sort of personnel they have running the show—passed-over commanders and the like, not overly bright. By the time that we get there we shall have concocted a convincing story—convincing enough to let us hang off in orbit until *Adler* appears on the scene. After all, we have their precious code. Why should they suspect us?"

"Why shouldn't *we* be *Adler?*" asked Grimes.

"What do you mean, Ensign?"

"The Waldegren Navy's frigates are almost identical, in silhouette, with the Commission's *Epsilon* class freighters. We could disguise this ship a little by masking the dissimilarities by a rough patching of plating. After all, *Adler* was in action and sustained some damage—"

"Complicated," mused the Captain. "Too complicated. And two *Adlers*—each, presumably, in encoded psionic communication with both Waldegren and Dartura. . . . You've a fine, devious mind, young Grimes—but I'm afraid you've out-foxed yourself on that one."

"Let me talk, sir. Let me think out loud. To begin with—a ship running on Mannschenn Drive *can* put herself into orbit about a planet, but it's not, repeat not, recommended."

"Damn right it's not."

"But we have the heels *of Adler?* Yes? Then we could afford a slight delay to carry out the modifications—the disguise—that I've suggested. After all, forty odd light years is quite a long way."

"But what do we gain, Mr. Grimes?"

"The element of confusion, sir. Let me work it out. We disguise ourselves as well as we can. We find out, from intercepted and decoded signals, *Adler's* ETA—*and* the coordinates of her break-through into the normal continuum. We contrive matters to be more or less in the same place at exactly the same time. And when the shore batteries and the guardships see no less than two *Adlers* slugging it out, each of them yelling for help in the secret code, they won't know which of us to open fire on."

"Grimes," said Craven slowly, "I didn't know you had it in you. All I can say is that I'm glad that you're on *our* side."

"Am I?" asked Grimes wonderingly, suddenly deflated. He looked at the Captain who, after all, was little better than a pirate, whose accomplice he had become. He looked at the girl, but for whom he would not be here. "Am I? Damn it all, whose side *am* I on?"

"You'd better go below," Craven told him gently. "Go below and get some sleep. You need it. You've earned it."

"Jeremy," said Jane Pentecost to Craven, "would you mind looking after the shop for half an hour or so? I'll go with John."

"As you please, my dear. As you please."

It was the assurance in the Captain's voice that hurt. *It won't make any difference to us, it* implied. *It can't make any difference. Sure, Jane, go ahead. Throw the nice little doggie a bone. . . . we can spare it.*

"No thank you," said Grimes coldly, and left the Control Room. But he couldn't hate these people.

20

AFTER A LONG SLEEP Grimes felt better. After a meal he felt better still. It was a good meal, even though the solid portion of it came from tins. Craven's standards were slipping, thought the Ensign. He was reasonably sure that such items as caviar, escargots, pâé de foie gras, Virginia ham, Brie, and remarkably alcoholic cherries were not included in the Commission's inventory of emergency stores. And neither would be the quite reasonable Montrachet, although it had lost a little by being decanted from its original bottles into standard squeeze bulbs. But if the Captain had decided that the laborer was worthy of his hire, with the consignees of the cargo making their contribution toward that hire, that was his privilege . . .? Responsibility?—call it what you will.

Jane Pentecost watched him eat. As he was finishing his coffee she said, "Now that our young lion has fed, he is required in the Control Room."

He looked at her both gratefully and warily. "What have I done now?"

"Nothing, my dear. It is to discuss what you—we—will do. Next."

He followed her to Control. Craven was there, of course, and so were Baxter and Summers. The Captain was enjoying one of his rank cigars, and a limp, roll-your-own cigarette dangled from the engineer's lower lip. The telepath coughed pointedly every time that acrid smoke expelled by either man drifted his way. Neither paid any attention to him, and neither did Grimes when he filled and lighted his own pipe.

Craven said, "I've been giving that scheme of yours some thought. It's a good one."

"Thank you, sir."

"Don't thank me. I should thank you. Mr. Summers, here, has been maintaining a careful listening watch. *Adler's* ETA is such that we can afford to shut down the Drive to make the modifications that you suggest. To begin with, we'll fake patching plates with plastic sheets—we can't afford to cannibalize any more of the ship's structure—so as to obscure our name and identification letters. We'll use more plastic to simulate missile launchers and laser projectors—luckily there's plenty of it in the cargo."

"We found more than plastic while we were lookin' for it," said the engineer, licking his lips.

"That will do, Mr. Baxter. Never, in normal circumstances, should I have condoned . . ."

"These circumstances ain't normal, Skipper, an' we all bloody well know it."

"That will do, I say." Craven inhaled deeply, then filled the air of the Control Room with a cloud of smoke that, thought Grimes, would have reflected laser even at close range. Summers almost choked, and Jane snapped, "Jeremy!"

"This, my dear, happens to be *my* Control Room." He turned again to the Ensign. "It will not be necessary, Mr. Grimes, to relocate the real weapons. They functioned quite efficiently where they are and, no doubt, will do so again. And now, as soon as I have shut down the Drive, I shall hand the watch over to you. You are well rested and refreshed."

"Come on," said Jane to Baxter. "Let's get suited up and get that sheeting out of the airlock."

"Couldn't Miss Pentecost hold the fort, sir?" asked Grimes. He added, "I've been through the camouflage course at the Academy."

"And so have I, Mr. Grimes. Furthermore, Miss Pentecost has had experience in working outside, but I don't think that you have."

"No, sir. But . . . "

"That will be all, Mr. Grimes."

At Craven's orders the Drive was shut down, and outside the viewports the sparse stars became stars again, were no longer pulsing spirals of multi-colored light. Then, alone in Control, Grimes actuated his scanners so that he could watch the progress of the work outside the hull, and switched on the transceiver that worked on the spacesuit frequency.

This time he ran no risk of being accused of being a Peeping Tom.

He had to admire the competence with which his shipmates worked. The plastic sheeting had no mass to speak of, but it was awkward stuff to handle. Torches glowed redly as it was cut, and radiated invisibly in the infrared as it was shaped and welded. The workers, in their bulky, clumsy suits, moved with a grace that was in startling contrast to their attire—a Deep Space ballet, thought Grimes, pleasurably surprised at his own way with words. From the speaker of the transceiver came Craven's curt orders, the brief replies of the others.

"*This way a little . . . that's it.*"

"*She'll do, Skipper.*"

"*No she won't. Look at the bend on it!*"

Then Jane's laughing voice. "*Our secret weapon, Jeremy. A laser that fires around corners!*"

"*That will do, Miss Pentecost. Straighten it, will you?*"

"*Ay, ay, sir. Captain, sir.*"

The two interstellar drive engineers were working in silence, but with efficiency. Aboard the ship were only Grimes and Summers, the telepath.

Grimes felt out of it, but somebody had to mind the shop, he supposed. But the likelihood of any customers was remote.

Then he stiffened in his chair. One of the spacesuited figures was falling away from the vessel, drifting out and away, a tiny, glittering satellite reflecting the harsh glare of the working floods, a little, luminous butterfly pinned to the black velvet of the Ultimate Night. Who was it? He didn't know for certain, but thought that it was Jane. The ship's interplanetary drives—reaction and inertial— were on remote control, but reaction drive was out; before employing it he would have to swing to the desired heading by use of the directional gyroscopes. But the inertial drive was versatile.

He spoke into the microphone of the transceiver. "Secure yourselves. I am proceeding to rescue."

At once Craven's voice snapped back, "Hold it, Grimes. Hold it! There's no danger."

"But, sir . . ."

"Hold it!"

Grimes could see the distant figure now from a viewport, but it did not seem to be receding any longer. Hastily he checked with the radar. Range and bearing were not changing. Then, with relative bearing unaltered, the range was closing. He heard Jane call out, "Got it! I'm on the way back!"

Craven replied, "Make it snappy—otherwise young Grimes'll be chasing you all over the Universe!"

Grimes could see, now, the luminous flicker of a suit reaction unit from the lonely figure.

Later, he and the others examined the photographs that Jane had taken.

Epsilon Sextans looked as she was supposed to look—like a badly battle-scarred frigate of the Waldegren Navy.

21

IN TERMS OF SPACE and of time there was not much longer to go.

The two ships—one knowing and one unknowing—raced toward their rendezvous. Had they been plunging through the normal continuum there would have been, toward the finish, hardly the thickness of a coat of paint between them, the adjustment of a microsecond in temporal precession rates would have brought inevitable collision. Craven knew this from the results of his own observations and from the encoded position reports, sent at six hourly intervals, by *Adler.* Worried, he allowed himself to fall astern, a mere half kilometer. It would be enough—and, too, it would mean that the frigate would mask him from the fire of planet-based batteries.

Summers maintained his listening watch. Apart from the position reports he had little of interest to tell the Captain. *Adler,* once or twice, had tried to get in contact with the Main Base on Waldegren—but, other than from a curt directive to proceed as ordered there were no signals from the planet to the ship. Dartura Base was more talkative. That was understandable. There was no colony on the planet and the Base personnel must be bored, must be pining for the sight of fresh faces, the sound of fresh voices. They would have their excitement soon enough, promised Craven grimly.

Through the warped continuum fell the two ships, and ahead

the pulsating spiral that was the Dartura sun loomed ever brighter, ever larger. There were light years yet to go, but the Drive-induced distortions made it seem that tentacles of incandescent gas were already reaching out to clutch them, to drag them into the atomic furnace at the heart of the star.

In both Control Rooms watch succeeded watch—but the thoughts and the anticipations of the watchkeepers were not the same. Aboard *Adler* there was the longing for rest, for relaxation—although *Adler's* Captain must have been busy with the composition of a report that would clear him (if possible) of blame for his defeat. Aboard *Epsilon Sextans* there was the anticipation of revenge—insofar as Craven, Baxter, Jane Pentecost and the survivors of the ship's original personnel were concerned. Grimes? As the hour of reckoning approached he was more and more dubious. He did not know what to think, what to feel. There was the strong personal loyalty to Craven—and, even now, to Jane Pentecost. There was the friendship and mutual respect that had come into being between himself and Baxter. There was the knowledge that *Adler's* crew were no better than pirates, were murderers beyond rehabilitation. There was the pride he felt in his own skill as a gunnery officer. (But, as such, was he, himself, any better than a pirate, a murderer? The exercise of his craft aboard a warship would be legal—but here, aboard a merchantman, and a disguised merchantman at that, the legality was doubtful. What had his motives been when he volunteered—and as a commissioned officer of the Survey Service he had had no right to do so—and what were his motives now?)

He, Grimes, was not happy. He had far too much time to ponder the implications. He was an accessory before, during and after the fact. He had started off correctly enough, when he had tried to prevent Craven from requisitioning the Survey Service cargo aboard *Delta Orionis,* but after that . . . after he and Jane . . . (that, he admitted, was a memory that he wanted to keep, always, just as that other memory, of the bright picture of naked female flesh on the screen, he wished he could lose forever.)

He had started off correctly enough—and then, not only had he helped install the purloined armament but had used it. (*And used it well,* he told himself with a brief resurgence of pride.) Furthermore, the disguise *of Epsilon Sextans* had been his idea.

Oh, he was in it, all right. He was in up to his neck. What the final outcome of it all would be he did not care to contemplate.

But it would soon be over. He had no fears as to the outcome of the battle. The element of surprise would be worth at least a dozen missile launchers. *Adler* would never have the chance to use her laser.

Adler, reported Summers, had shut down her Mannschenn Drive and emerged briefly into normal spacetime to make her final course adjustment. She was now headed not for the Dartura Sun but for the planet itself—or where the planet would be at the time of her final—and fatal— reemergence into the continuum. The last ETA was sent, together with the coordinates of her planetfall. *Epsilon Sextans* made her own course adjustment—simultaneity in time and a half kilometer's divergence in space being Craven's objective. It was finicky work, even with the use of the ship's computer, but the Captain seemed satisfied.

The race—the race that would culminate in a dead heat—continued. Aboard the frigate there was, reported Summers, a lessening of tension, the loosening up that comes when a voyage is almost over. Aboard the merchantman the tension increased. The interstellar drive engineers, Grimes knew, were no happier about it all than he was—but they could no more back out than he could. Craven was calm and confident, and Baxter was beginning to gloat. Jane Pentecost assumed the air of dedication that in women can be so infuriating. Grimes glumly checked and rechecked his weaponry. It passed the time.

Dartura itself was visible now—not as tiny disk of light but as a glowing annulus about its distorted primary. The thin ring of luminescence broadened, broadened. The time to go dwindled to a week, to days, to a day, and then to hours . . .

To minutes . . .

To seconds. . . .

Craven and Grimes were in the Control Room; the others were

at their various stations. From the intercom came the telepath's voice, "He's cutting the Drive—"

"Cut the Drive!" ordered the Captain.

In the Mannschenn Drive room the spinning, precessing gyroscopes slowed, slowed, ceased their endless tumbling, assumed the solidity that they exhibited only when at rest. For perhaps two seconds there was temporal confusion in the minds of all on board as the precession field died, and past, present and future inextricably mingled. Then there was a sun glaring through the viewports, bright in spite of the polarization—a sun, and, directly ahead, a great, green-orange planet. There was a ship. . . .

There were ships—ahead of them, astern, on all sides.

There were ships—and, booming from the intership transceiver, the transceiver that was neither tuned nor switched on (but navies could afford induction transmitters with their fantastic power consumption), came the authorative voice: "*Inflexible* to *Adler*! Heave to for search and seizure ! Do not attempt to escape—our massed fields will hold you!"

The effect was rather spoiled when the same voice added, in bewilderment, "Must be seeing double . . . there's two of the bastards." The bewilderment did not last long. "*Inflexible* to *Adler* and to unidentified vessel. Heave to for search and seizure!"

"Hold your fire, Mr. Grimes," ordered Craven, quietly and bitterly. "It's the Survey Service."

"I know," replied Grimes—and pressed the button.

22

HE NEVER KNEW just why he had done so.

Talking it over afterward, thinking about it, he was able to evolve a theory that fitted the facts. During the brief period immediately after the shutting down of the Drive, during the short session of temporal disorientation, there had been prescience, of a sort. He had known that *Adler,* come what may, would attempt one last act of defiance and revenge, just as *Adler's* Captain or Gunnery Officer must have known, in that last split second, that Nemesis was treading close upon his heels.

He pushed the button—and from the nozzles in the shell plating poured the reflective vapor, the protective screen that glowed ruddily as *Adler's* lasers slashed out at it.

From the speaker of the dead transceiver, the transceiver that should have been dead, roared the voice of the Survey Service Admiral. *"Adler!* Cease fire! Cease fire, damn you!" There was a pause, then: "You've asked for it!"

She had asked for it—and now she got it. Suddenly the blip on Grimes' screen that represented the Waldegren frigate became two smaller blips, and then four. The rolling fog outside *Epsilon Sextans'* viewports lost its luminosity, faded suddenly to drab grayness. The voice from the transceiver said coldly, "And *now you,* whoever you are, had better identify yourself. And fast."

Craven switched on the communications equipment. He spoke

113

quietly into the microphone. "Interstellar Transport Commission's *Epsilon Sextans.* Bound Waverly, with general cargo . . ."

"Bound Waverley? Then what the hell are you doing here? And what's that armament you're mounting?"

"Plastic," replied the Captain. "Plastic dummies."

"And I suppose your ALGE is plastic, too. Come off it, Jerry. We've already boarded your old ship, and although your ex-Mate was most reluctant to talk we got a story of sorts from him."

"I thought I recognized your voice, Bill. May I congratulate you upon your belated efforts to stamp out piracy?"

"And may I deplore your determination to take the law into your own hands? Stand by for the boarding party."

Grimes looked at Craven, who was slumped in his seat. The Master's full beard effectively masked his expression. "Sir," asked the Ensign. "What can they do? What will they do?"

"You're the space lawyer, Grimes. You're the expert on Survey Service rules and regulations. What will it be, do you think? A medal—or a firing squad? Praise or blame?"

"You know the Admiral, sir?"

"Yes. I know the Admiral. We're old shipmates."

"Then you should be safe."

"Safe? I suppose so. Safe from the firing squad—but not safe from my employers. I'm a merchant captain, Grimes, and merchant captains aren't supposed to range the spacelanes looking for trouble. I don't think they'll dare fire me—but I know that I can never expect command of anything better than *Delta* class ships, on the drearier runs." Grimes saw that Craven was smiling. "But there're still the Rim Worlds. There's still the Sundowner Line, and the chance of high rank in the Rim Worlds Navy when and if there is such a service."

"You have . . . inducements, sir?"

"Yes. There are . . . inducements. Now."

"I thought, once," said Grimes, "that I could say the same. But not now. Not any longer. Even so . . . I'm Survey Service, sir, and I should be proud of my service. But in this ship, this merchant vessel, with her makeshift armament, we fought against heavy odds, and won. And, just now, we saved ourselves. It wasn't the Survey Service that saved us."

"Don't be disloyal," admonished Craven.

"I'm not being disloyal, sir. But . . . or, shall we say, I'm being loyal. You're the first captain under whom I served under fire. If you're going out to the Rim Worlds I'd like to come with you."

"Your commission, Grimes. You know that you must put in ten years' service before resignation is possible."

"But I'm dead."

"Dead!"

"Yes. Don't you remember? I was snooping around in the Mannschenn Drive room and I got caught in the temporal precession field. My body still awaits burial; it's in a sealed metal box in the deep freeze. It can never be identified."

Craven laughed. "I'll say this for you. You're ingenious. But how do we account for the absence of the late Mr. Wolverton? And your presence aboard this ship?"

"I can hide, sir, and . . ."

"And while you're hiding you'll concoct some story that will explain everything. Oh Grimes, Grimes—you're an officer I wish I could always have with me. But I'll not stand in the way of your career. All I can do, all I will do, is smooth things over on your behalf with the Admiral. I should be able to manage that."

Jane Pentecost emerged from the hatch in the Control Room deck. Addressing Craven she said formally, "Admiral Williams, sir." She moved to one side to make way for the flag officer.

"Jerry, you bloody pirate!" boomed Williams, a squat, rugged man the left breast of whose shirt was ablaze with ribbons. He advanced with outstretched hand.

"Glad to have you aboard, Bill. This is Liberty Hall—you can spit on the mat and call the cat a bastard!"

"Not again!" groaned Grimes.

"And who is this young man?" asked the Admiral.

"I owe you—or your Service—an apology, Bill. This is Ensign Grimes, who was a passenger aboard *Delta Orionis*. I'm afraid that I . . . er . . . press-ganged him into my service. But he has been most . . . cooperative? Uncooperative? Which way do you want it?"

"As we are at war with Waldegren—I'd say cooperative with reservations. Was it he, by the way, who used the ALGE? Just as well for you all that he did."

"At war with Waldegren?" demanded Jane Pentecost. "So you people have pulled your fingers out at last."

The Admiral raised his eyebrows.

"One of my Rim Worlders," explained Craven. "But I shall be a Rim Worlder myself shortly."

"You're wise, Jerry. I've got the buzz that the Commission is taking a very dim view of your piracy or privateering or whatever it was, and my own lords and masters are far from pleased with you. You'd better get the hell out before the lawyers have decided just what crimes you are guilty of."

"As bad as that?"

"As bad as that."

"And young Grimes, here?"

"We'll take him back. Six months' strict discipline aboard my flagship will undo all the damage that you and your ideas have done to him. And now, Jerry, I'd like your full report."

"In my cabin, Bill. Talking is thirsty work."

"Then lead on. It's your ship."

"And it's your watch, Mr. Grimes. She'll come to no harm on this trajectory while we get things sorted out."

Grimes sat with Jane Pentecost in the Control Room. Through the ports, had he so desired, he could have watched the rescue teams extricating the survivors from the wreckage of *Adler;* he could have stared out at the looming bulk of Dartura on the beam. But he did not do so, and neither did he look at his instruments.

He looked at Jane. There was so much about her that he wanted to remember—and, after all, so very little that he was determined to forget.

The intercom buzzed. "Mr. Grimes, will you pack whatever gear you have and prepare to transfer with Admiral Williams to the flagship? Hand the watch over to Miss Pentecost."

"But you'll be shorthanded, sir."

"The Admiral is lending me a couple of officers for the rest of the voyage."

"Very good, sir."

Grimes made no move. He looked at Jane—a somehow older, a tireder, a more human Jane than the girl he had first met. He said, "I'd have liked to have come out to the Rim with you. . . ."

She said, "It's impossible, John."

"I know. But . . ."

"You'd better get packed."

He unbuckled his seat belt, went to where she was sitting. He kissed her. She responded, but it was only the merest flicker of a response.

He said, "Goodbye."

She said, "Not goodbye. We'll see you out on the Rim, sometime."

With a bitterness that he was always to regret he replied, "Not bloody likely."

TO
PRIME THE
PUMP

THE GIRL LAY SPREAD-EAGLED ON THE ALTAR . . .

"The white goat!" they shouted . . . "The goat without horns . . ."

Two men set the animal down on the girl's naked body, its back to her breasts and belly, its head between her legs. The drums throbbed softly, insistently. The priest's knife swept down; the animal's cries ceased in mid-bleat, although its now released limbs kicked spasmodically. The girl, free herself from restraining hands, held the dying body to her.

ॐ Chapter 1 ॐ

GRIMES—Lieutenant John Grimes, Federation Survey Service, to give him his full name and title—had the watch. Slowly, careful not to break the contact of the magnetized soles of his shoes with the deck, he shuffled backwards and forwards in the narrow confines of the control room. Captain Daintree, commanding officer of the cruiser *Aries,* was a martinet, and one of the many things that he would not tolerate was a watchkeeper spending his spell of duty lounging in an acceleration chair, not even in (as now) Free Fall conditions. Not that Grimes really minded. He was a young and vigorous man and still not used to the enforced inactivity that is an inescapable part of spacefaring. This regulation pacing was exercise of a sort, was better than nothing.

He was a stocky young man, this Grimes, and the stiff material of his uniform shirt did little to hide the muscular development of his body. His face was too craggy for conventional handsomeness, but women, he already had learned, considered him good-looking enough. On the rare occasions that he thought about it he admitted that he was not dissatisfied with his overall appearance, even his protuberant ears had their uses, having more than once served as convenient handles by which his face could be pulled down to a waiting and expectant female face below. To complete the inventory, his close-cropped hair was darkly brown and his eyes, startlingly pale in his space-tanned face, were gray, at times a very bleak gray.

So this was Lieutenant John Grimes, presently officer-of-the-watch of the Survey Service cruiser *Aries,* slowly shuffling back and forth between the consoles, the banked instruments, alert for any information that might suddenly be displayed on dials or screens. He was not expecting any; the ship was in deep space, failing free through the warped continuum induced by her Mannschenn Drive through regions well clear of the heavily frequented trade routes. There was only one human colony, Grimes knew, in this sector of the Galaxy, the world that had been named, not very originally but aptly, *El Dorado;* and two ships a standard year served the needs of that fabulous planet.

El Dorado . . .

Idly—but a watch officer has to think about something— Grimes wondered what it was really like there. There were stories, of course, but they were no more than rumors, exaggerated rumors, like as not. The El Doradans did not encourage visitors, and the two ships that handled their small trade—precious ores outwards, luxury goods inwards—were owned and manned by themselves, not that the vessels, space-borne miracles of automation, required more than two men, captain and engineer, apiece.

Grimes looked out through the viewports, roughly to where El Dorado should be. He did not see it, of course, nor did he expect to do so. He saw only warped Space, suns near and far that had been twisted to the semblance of pulsating, multicolored spirals, blackness between the suns that had been contorted into its own vast convolutions, sensed (but with what sense?) rather than seen. It was, as always, a fascinating spectacle; it was, as always, a frightening one. It was not good to look at it for too long.

Grimes turned his attention to the orderly universe in miniature displayed in the chart tank.

"Mr. Grimes!"

"Sir!" The Lieutenant started. He hadn't heard the old bastard come into the control room. He looked up to the tall, spare figure of Captain Daintree, to the cold blue eyes under the mane of white hair. "Sir?"

"Warn the engine room that we shall be requiring Inertial Drive shortly. And then, I believe that you're qualified in navigation, you may work out the trajectory for El Dorado."

∾ Chapter 2 ∾

LIEUTENANT COMMANDER COOPER, the Navigating Officer of *Aries,* was in a bad mood, a sulky expression on his plump, swarthy face, his reedy voice petulant. "Damn it all," he was saying. "Damn it all, what am *I* supposed to be here for? An emergency alteration of trajectory comes up and am I called for? Oh, no, that'd be far too simple. So young Grimes has to fumble his way through the sums that *I* should be doing, and the first that *I* know is when somebody condescends to sound the acceleration alarm . . ."

"Was there anything wrong with my trajectory, *sir?*" asked Grimes coldly.

"No, Mr. Grimes. Nothing at all wrong, although *I* was brought up to adhere to the principle that interstellar dust clouds should be avoided . . ."

"With the Mannschenn Drive in operation there's no risk."

"Isn't there? A little knowledge is a dangerous thing, Mr. Grimes. Inside some of these dark nebulae the Continuum is dangerously warped."

"But CCD736 can hardly be classed as a nebula . . ."

"Even so, the first principle of all navigation should be caution, and it's high time that you learned that."

Doctor Passifern, the Senior Medical Officer, broke in. "Come off it, Pilot. Young Grimes *is* learning, and this idea of the Old Man's that every officer in the ship should be able to take over from the specialists is a very sound one . . ."

"Ha! It might be an idea if some of us were encouraged to take over *your* job, Doc!"

A flush darkened Passifern's already ruddy face. He growled, "That's not the same and you know it."

"Isn't it? Oh, I know that ever since the dawn of history you pill peddlers have made a sacred mystery of your technology . . ."

Grimes got to his feet, said, "What about some more coffee?" He collected the three mugs from the table, walked to the espresso machine that stood in a corner of the comfortable wardroom. He found it rather embarrassing when his seniors quarreled—the long-standing feud between the Navigator and the Doctor was more than good-natured bickering—and thought that a pause for refreshment would bring the opportunity for a change of subject. As he filled the mugs he remarked brightly, "At least this acceleration allows us to enjoy our drinks. I hate having to sip out of a bulb."

"Do you?" asked Cooper nastily. "I'd have thought that one of your tender years would enjoy a regression to the well-remembered and well-beloved feeding bottle."

Grimes ignored this. He set the mugs down on the low table, then dropped ungracefully into his easy chair. He said to Passifern, "But what *is* the hurry, Doc? I know that I'm only the small boy around here and that I'm not supposed to be told anything, but would you be breaking any vows of secrecy if you told us the nature of the emergency on El Dorado?"

"I don't know myself, Grimes. All I know is that there shouldn't be one. Those filthy rich El Doradans have the finest practitioners and specialists in the known Universe in residence; and they, by this time, must be almost as filthy rich as their patients! All *I* know is that *they* knew that we were in the vicinity of their planet, and requested a second opinion on something or other . . ."

"And our Lord and Master," contributed Cooper, "decided that it was a good excuse to give the Inertial Drive a gallop. He doesn't like Free Fall." He obliged with a surprisingly good imitation of Captain Daintree's deep voice: "Too much Free Fall makes officers soft."

"He could be right," said Passifern.

Cooper ignored this. "What puzzles me," he said, "is why these outstanding practitioners and specialists should call in a humble ship's quack . . ."

"As a major vessel of the Survey Service," Passifern told him coldly, "we carry a highly qualified and expert team of physicians, surgeons and technicians. And our hospital and research facilities would be the envy of many a planet. Furthermore, *we* have the benefit of experience denied to any planet-bound doctor . . ."

"And wouldn't *you* just love to be planetbound on a world like El Dorado?" asked Cooper.

Before the Doctor could make an angry reply, Grimes turned to the Navigator. "And what *is* El Dorado like, sir? I was going to look it up, but the Old Man's taken the Pilot Book covering it out of the control room."

"Doing his homework," said Cooper. "Luckily it's not everybody who has to rush to the books when the necessity for an unscheduled landing crops up. We specialists, unlike the jacks-of-all-trades, tend to be reasonably expert in our own fields." He took a noisy gulp of coffee. "All right. El Dorado. An essentially Earth-type planet in orbit about a Sol-type primary. A very ordinary sort of world, you might say. But it's not. And it wasn't."

It was Passifern who broke the silence. "What's so different about it?"

"Don't you know, Doc? You were hankering for its fleshpots only a minute ago. I suppose you have some sort of idea of what it's like now, but not how it got that way. Well, to begin with, it was an extraordinary world. It was one of those planets upon which life—life-as-we-know-it or any other kind of life—had never taken hold. There it was, for millions upon millions of years, just a sterile ball of rock and mud and water.

"And then it was purchased from the Federation by the so-called El Dorado Corporation.

"Even you, young Grimes, must know something of history. Even you must know how, on world after world, the trend has been towards socialism. Some societies have gone the whole hog, preaching and practicing the Gospel According to St. Marx. Some have contented themselves with State control of the means of production and supply, with ruinous taxation of the very well-to-do thrown in. There have been levelling up processes and levelling down processes, and these have hurt the aristocracies of birth and breeding as much as they have hurt the aristocracies of Big Business and industry.

"And so the Corporation was formed. Somehow its members managed to get most of their wealth out of their home worlds, and much of it was used for the terraforming of El Dorado. Terraforming? Landscape gardening would be a better phrase. Yes, that world's no more, and no less, than a huge, beautiful park, with KEEP OFF THE GRASS signs posted insofar as the common herd is concerned."

"What about servants? Technicians?" asked Grimes.

"The answer to that problem, my boy, was automation, automation and still more automation. Automation to an extent that would not have been practical on a world where the economics of it had to be considered. And on the rare occasions that the machines do need attention there are a few El Doradans to whom mechanics, electronics and the like are amusing and quite fascinating hobbies. And there will be others, of course, who enjoy playing around at gardening, or even farming."

"A world, in fact, that's just a rich man's toy," said Grimes.

"And don't forget the rich bitches," Cooper told him.

"I don't think I'd like it," went on Grimes.

"And I don't think that the El Doradans would like you," Cooper remarked. "Or any of us. As far as they're concerned, we're just snotty-nosed ragamuffins from the wrong side of the tracks."

"Still," said Passifern smugly, "they requested *my* services."

"God knows why," sneered Cooper.

There was silence while the Doctor tried to think of a scathing rejoinder. It was broken by Grimes. "Ah, here's Mr. Bose. Perhaps he can tell us."

"Our commissioned teacup reader," grunted the Navigator sardonically. "Singing and dancing."

Mr. Bose, the cruiser's Psionic Radio Officer, did not look the sort of man who would ever be heard or seen indulging in such activities. He was short and fat, and the expression of his shiny, chocolate-colored face was one of unrelieved gloom. On the occasions when a shipmate would tell him, for the love of all the odd gods of the Galaxy, to cheer up, he would reply portentously, "But I *know* too much." What he knew of what went on in the minds of his shipmates he would never divulge; insofar as they were concerned, he always observed and respected the oath of secrecy taken by all graduates of the Rhine Institute. Now and again, however, he seemed to consider outsiders fair game and would pass on to his fellow officers what he had learned by telepathic eavesdropping.

"What cooks on El Dorado, Bosey Boy?" demanded Cooper.

"What cooks, Commander, sir? The flesh of animals. They are a godless people and partake of unclean foods."

"The same as we do, in this ship. But you know what I mean."

Surprisingly, the telepath laughed, a high-pitched giggle. "Yes, I know what you mean, Commander, sir."

"Of course you do, you damned snooper. But what cooks?"

"I . . . I cannot understand. I have tried to . . . to tune in on the thoughts of all the people. From their Psionic Radio officers I have learned nothing, nothing at all. They are experts, highly trained, with their minds impenetrably screened. But the dreams, the secret thoughts of the ordinary people are vague, confused. There is unease and there is fear, but it is not the fear of an immediate danger. But it is a very real fear . . ."

"Probably just an increasing incidence of tinea," laughed Cooper. "Right up your alley, Doc."

Passifern was not amused.

∼ Chapter 3 ∼

ARIES **WAS IN ORBIT** about El Dorado. It was very quiet in the control room where Captain Daintree and his officers looked out, through the wide viewports, to the green, blue and golden, cloud-girdled planet that the ship was circling. The absence of the familiar, shipboard noises—the thin, high keening of the Mannschenn Drive, the odd, irregular throbbing of the inertial drive—engendered a feeling of tension, a taut expectancy. And this was more than just a routine planetfall. El Dorado was a new world to all of *Aries'* people. True, they had landed on new worlds before, worlds upon which they had been the first humans to set foot; but this fabled planet was—different. Grimes thought of the Moslem paradise with its timeless *houris* and grinned wryly. Such beauties would never confer their favours on—how had Cooper put it?—on a snotty-nosed ragamuffin from the wrong side of the tracks.

"And what do you find so amusing, Mr. Grimes?" asked Daintree coldly. "Perhaps you will share the joke with us."

"I . . . I was thinking, sir." Grimes felt his prominent ears redden.

"You aren't paid to think," came the age-old, automatic reply, the illogical rejoinder that has persisted through millennia. Grimes was tempted to point out that officers *are* paid to think, but thought better of it.

Commander Griffin, the Executive Officer, broke the silence. "The pinnace is all cleared away, sir, for the advance party."

"The *pinnace*, Commander? By whose orders?"

"I . . . I thought, sir . . ."

Another one! Grimes chuckled inwardly, permitted himself a slight grin as he looked at the embarrassed Griffin. Griffin looked back at him in a way that boded ill for the Lieutenant.

Daintree said, "I admit, Commander, that you are permitted to think. Even so, you should think to more purpose. How long is it since the rocket re-entry boat was exercised? Did you not consider that this would be an ideal opportunity to give the craft a test and training flight?"

"Why, yes, sir. It would be an ideal opportunity."

"Then have it cleared away, Commander. At once. Oh, which of your young gentlemen are you thinking of sending?"

"Doctor Passifern has arranged for Surgeon Lieutenant Kravisky to go with the advance party, sir."

"Never mind that. Who will be the pilot?"

"Er . . . Mr. Grimes, sir."

"Mr. Grimes." The captain switched his attention from the Commander to the Lieutenant. "Mr. Grimes, what experience have you had in the handling of rocket-powered craft?"

"At the Academy, sir. And during my first training cruise."

"And never since. You're like all the rest of the officers aboard this ship, far too used to riding around in comfort with an inertial drive unit tucked away under your backside. Very well, this will be an ideal opportunity for you to gain some experience of *real* spacefaring."

"Yes, sir. See to the boat, sir?"

"Not yet. Commander Griffin is quite capable of that." He walked to the chart desk, beckoned Grimes to follow him. The Navigator had already spread a chart on the flat surface, securing it with spring clips. "This," said Daintree, "was transmitted to us by whatever or whoever passes for Port Control on El Dorado. Mercator's Projection. Here is the spaceport"—his thin, bony fingers jabbed downwards—"by this lake . . ."

"Will the spaceport be suitable for the landing of the rocket boat, sir?" asked Grimes. "After all, if it was designed only to handle inertial drive vessels . . ."

"I've already thought of that point, Mr. Grimes. But our rocket boat is designed to land on water if needs be."

"But . . . but will they be ready for us, sir?"

"This vessel has established electronic radio communication with El Dorado, Mr. Grimes. I shall tell them to be ready for you. After all, we are visiting their planet at their request."

"Yes, sir."

"Very good, then. You may study the chart until it is time for you to take the boat away."

"Yes, sir."

Grimes looked down at the new, as yet unmarked plan of the spaceport and its environs. He would far sooner have spent the time studying the Manual of Spacemanship, with special attention to that section devoted to the handling of rocket-powered re-entry vehicles. But, after all, he was qualified as an atmosphere pilot and had, for some time, been drawing the extra pay to which his certificate entitled him.

As he studied the chart he overheard Captain Daintree talking over the transceiver to somebody, presumably Port Control, on the planet below. "Yes, you heard me correctly. I am sending the advance party down in one of my rocket boats." Came the reply, "But, Captain, our spaceport is not suitable for the reception of such a craft." The voice was as arrogant as Daintree's own but in a different way. It was the arrogance that comes with money (too much money), with inherited titles, with a bloodline traced back to some uncouth robber baron who happened to be a more efficient thief and murderer than his rivals.

"*I* am sending away my rocket boat." One almost expected the acridity of ozone to accompany that quarterdeck snap and crackle.

"I am sorry, Captain—" Port Control didn't sound very sorry— "but that is impossible."

"Do you want our help, or don't you?"

There was a brief silence, then a reluctant "Yes."

"Your spaceport is on the northern shore of Lake Bluewater, isn't it?"

"You have the chart that we transmitted to you, Captain."

"My rocket boat can be put down on water."

"You don't understand, Captain. Lake Bluewater is a very popular resort."

"Isn't that just too bad? Get your kids with their pails and spades and plastic animals off the beaches and out of the water."

Again the silence and then in a voice that shed none of its cold venom over the thousands of miles, "Very well, Captain. But please understand that we shall not be responsible for any accidents to your boat and your personnel."

"And *I*," said Daintree harshly, "refuse to accept responsibility for any picnic or paddling parties who happen to get in the way. The officer in charge of the re-entry vehicle will be using the same frequency as we are using now. He will keep you and me informed of his movements. Over."

"Roger," came the supercilious reply. "Roger. Over and standing by."

"Rocket boat cleared away and ready, sir," said Commander Griffin, who had returned to the control room.

"Very good, Commander. Man and launch. Mr. Grimes, you should have memorized that chart by now, and, in any case, there will be another copy in the boat."

"Yes, sir." Grimes followed the Commander from the control room.

Surgeon Lieutenant Kravisky, his slender body already pressure-suited, his thin, dark face behind the open face plate of his helmet wearing an anxious expression, was already waiting by the boat blister. In each hand he carried a briefcase: one containing ship's papers and the other his uniform. Disgustedly, Grimes stripped to his briefs. If he'd been allowed to take the pinnace instead of this relic from the bad old days, there would have been no need to dress up like a refugee from historical space opera. A rating helped him into his suit, another man neatly folded his shorts and shirt and stowed them, together with his shoes and stockings, into a small case. Being on the Advance Party had its advantages after all,

Grimes decided. At least he would be spared the discomfort of full dress— frock coat, cocked hat and sword—which would be rig of the day when the big ship came in.

"Are you sure that you can drive this thing, John?" asked Kravisky.

"I don't know. I've never tried before." Then, before Commander Griffin could issue a scathing reprimand, he added. "Not this particular one, I mean. But I am qualified."

"That will do, Mr. Grimes," said Griffin. "You know the drill, I hope. After you're down, present yourself to Port Control and make the necessary arrangements for the reception of *Aries*. Don't forget that *you* represent the ship. Comport yourself accordingly. And try to refrain from misguided attempts at humor."

"Ay, ay, sir."

"Then board the boat. Procedure as per Regulations. Bo's'n!"

"Sir!" snapped the petty officer.

"Carry on!"

"Ay, ay, sir."

The inner door to the blister opened, revealing a small airlock. Grimes entered it first, followed by Kravisky, snapping shut his faceplate as he did so. He heard the sighing of the pumps as the air was exhausted from the chamber, watched the needle of the pressure dial drop to Zero. The red light came on. The outer door opened.

Beyond it was the graceless form of the rocket boat, a stubby, flattened dart with venturi and control surfaces; and visible beyond it was black, star-flecked sky and a great, glowing arc that was the limb of El Dorado. Grimes shuffled toward it on his magnetized soles, saw that the cabin door was already open, pulled himself into the vehicle. Then, while Kravisky was stowing the cases in a locker abaft the seats, he pushed the button that shut the door and another that pressurized the compartment. He looked at the dials and meters on the console, saw that the firing chamber had been warmed up and that all was ready for the launch. He strapped himself into his seat and waited until the Surgeon Lieutenant had done likewise. He opened the faceplate of his helmet. The air was breathable enough but carried a stale, canned flavor.

"All systems *Go!*" he said, feeling that the archaic spacemanese matched the archaic means of transportation.

"What was that?" snapped Griffin's voice from the speaker. Then, tiredly, "Oh, all right, Mr. Grimes. Five second count-down. Five . . . four . . . three . . . two . . . one . . . *fire!*"

Smoothly and efficiently the launching catapult threw the rocket boat away and clear from the cruiser. Not very smoothly, but efficiently enough, Grimes actuated the reaction drive, felt the giant hand of acceleration push him back into the padding of his seat.

"Mr. Grimes!" This time it was Captain Daintree's voice that came from the speaker. "Mr. Grimes, you should have been able to fall free all the way to the exosphere. You have no fuel to waste on astrobatics."

"Bloody back-seat drivers!" muttered Grimes, but he held his hand over the microphone as he did so.

∽ Chapter 4 ∽

NONETHELESS he was having his fun, was young Mr. Grimes.

Once he had the feel of his unhandy craft, once he stopped resenting having to worry about such matters as skin temperature, angle of attack, drag, and the rest of the aeronautical esoterica, he began to enjoy himself, to thrill to the sensation of speed as the first wisps of high altitude cirrus whipped by. This was better, after all, than making a slow, dignified descent in the pinnace, with its inertial drive, or in one of the other rocket boats—old-fashioned but not so downright archaic as this re-entry vehicle—in which he had now and again ridden, that cautiously shinnied down, stern first, the incandescent columns of their exhaust gases. He felt confident enough to withdraw his attention from his instruments, to risk a sidewise glance at his companion.

Grimes was happy but Kravisky was not. The Surgeon Lieutenant's face had paled to a peculiar, pale green. He seemed to be swallowing something. *Physician, heal thyself,* thought Grimes sardonically. "I . . . I wish you'd look where you're going," mumbled the young doctor.

"Beautiful view, isn't it?" Grimes glanced through the ports, then at his console. There was nothing to worry about. He had a hemisphere to play around in. By the time he was down, the terminator would be just short of Lake Bluewater. It would be a daylight landing, to save these very casual locals in Port Control the trouble of setting out a flare path. There would be the radio beacon to home upon and at least twenty miles of smooth water for his runway. It was —he searched his memory for the expression used by long ago and faraway pilots of the Royal Air Force; history, especially the history of the ships of Earth's seas and air oceans, was his favorite reading—it was a piece of cake.

"Isn't it . . . isn't it hot in here?" Why couldn't Kravisky relax?

"Not especially. After all, we're sitting in a hot-monococque."

"What's that?" Then, with a feeble attempt at humor, "The remedy sounds worse than the disease . . ."

"Just an airborne thermos flask."

"Oh."

"Like a park, isn't it?" said Grimes. "Even from up here, like a park. Green. No industrial haze. No smog . . ."

"Too . . . tame," said Kravisky, taking a reluctant interest.

"No, I don't think so. They have mountains, and high ones, too. They have seas that must be rough sometimes, even with weather control. If they want to risk life and limb, there'll be plenty of mountaineering and sailing . . ."

"And other sports . . ."

"Yeah." The radio compass seemed to be functioning properly, as were air speed indicator and radio altimeter. The note of the distant beacon was a steady hum. No doubt the El Doradans possessed far more advanced systems that were used by their own aircraft, but the reentry vehicle was not equipped to make use of them. "Yeah," said Grimes again. "Such as?"

"I'm a reservist, you know. But I'm also a ship's doctor in civil life. My last voyage before I was called up for my drill was in the Commission's *Alpha Cepheus* . . . A cruise to Caribbea. Passengers stinking with money and far too much time on their hands . . ."

"What's that to do with sports?"

"You'd be surprised. Or would you?"

No, thought Grimes, he wouldn't. His first Deep Space voyage had been as a passenger, and Jane Pentecost, the vessel's purser, had been very attractive. Where was she now? he wondered. Still in the Commission's ships, or back home, on the Rim?

Damn Jane Pentecost and damn the Rim Worlds. But this planet was nothing like Lorn, Faraway, Ultimo or Thule. He had never been to any of those dreary colonies (and never would go there, he told himself) but he had heard enough about them. Too much.

The air was denser now, and the control column that Grimes had been holding rather too negligently was developing a life of its own. Abruptly the steady note of the beacon changed to a morse A—dot dash, dot dash. Grimes tried to get the re-entry vehicle back on course, overcompensated. It was N now—dash dot, dash dot. The Lieutenant was sweating inside his suit when he had the boat under control again. Flying these antique crates was far too much like work. But he could afford another glance at the scenery.

There were wide fields, some green and some golden-glowing in the light of the afternoon sun, and in these latter worked great, glittering machines, obviously automatic harvesters. There were dense clumps of darker green—the forests which, on this world, had been grown for aesthetic reasons, not as a source of cellulose for industry. But the El Doradans, on the income from their mines alone, could well afford to import anything they needed. Or wanted. And only the odd gods of the Galaxy knew how many billions they had stashed away in the Federation Central Bank on Earth, to say nothing of other banks on other planets.

There were the wide fields and the forests, and towering up at the rim of the world the jagged blue mountains, the dazzlingly white-capped peaks. Rather too dazzling, but that was the glare of the late-afternoon sun, broad on the starboard bow of the rocket boat. Grimes adjusted the viewport polarizer. He could see houses now, large dwellings, even from this altitude, each miles distant from its nearest neighbor, each blending rather than contrasting with the landscape. He could see houses and beyond the huge, gleaming, azure oval that was Lake Bluewater, there were the tall towers of Spaceport Control and the intense, winking red light that was the beacon. Beyond the port again, but distant, shimmered the lofty spires of the city.

All very nice, but what's the air speed? Too high, too bloody high. Cut the rocket drive? Yes. Drag'll slow her down nicely, and there're always the parachute brakes and, in an emergency, the retro-rockets. Still on the beam, according to the beacon. In any case, I can see it plainly enough. Just keep it dead ahead . . .

Getting bumpy now, and mushy . . . What else, in such an abortion of an aircraft? But not to worry. Coming in bloody nicely, though I say it as shouldn't.

Looks like pine trees just inland from the beach. Cleared them all right. Must say that those supercilious drongoes in Port Control might have made some sort of stab at talking me in. All they said, "You may land." Didn't quite say, "Use the servants' entrance . . ."

Parachute brakes? No. Make a big bloody splash in their bloody lake and play hell with their bloody goldfish . . .

Kravisky shouted, screamed almost, and then Grimes, whose attention had been divided between the beacon and the altimeter, saw, cutting across the rocket boat's course, a small surface craft, a scarlet hull skittering over the water in its own, self-generated, double plume of snowy spray. But it would pass clear.

But that slim, golden figure, gracefully poised on a single water ski, would not.

With a curse Grimes released the parachute brakes and, at the same time, yanked back on his control column. He knew that the parachutes would not take hold in time, that before the rocket boat stalled it would crash into the woman. Yet—he was thinking fast, desperately fast—he dared not use either his main rocket drive to lift the boat up and clear, or his retro-rockets. Better for her, whoever she was, to run the risk of being crushed than to face the certainty of being incinerated.

Then there were birds (birds?), great birds that flew headlong at the control cabin, birds whose suicidal impact was enough to slow the boat sufficiently, barely sufficiently, to tip her so that forward motion was transformed to upward motion. The drogues took hold of the water, and that was that. She fell, soggily, ungracefully, blunt stern first, and as she did so Grimes stared stupidly at a broken wing, a broken *metal* wing that had been skewered by the forward antenna.

Chapter 5

NEITHER GRIMES nor Kravisky was hurt—seat padding and safety belts protected them from serious damage—but they were badly shaken. Grimes wondered, as the re-entry craft plunged below the churning surface of the lake, how deep it would sink before it rose again. And then he realized that it would not rise again, ever, or would not do so without the aid of salvage equipment. Aft there was an ominous gurgling that told its own story. Aft? That noise was now in the cabin itself. He looked down. The water was already about his ankles.

"Button up!" he snapped to the Surgeon Lieutenant.

"But what . . . ?" the words trailed off into silence.

"The ejection gear. I hope it works under water."

"But . . ." Kravisky, his faceplate still open, made as though to unsnap his seat belt. "The papers. Our uniforms. I must get them out of the locker . . ."

"Like hell you will. *Button up!*"

Sullenly, Kravisky checked that his belt was still tight, then sealed his helmet. Grimes followed suit. His hand hesitated over the big, red button on the control panel, then slammed down decisively. Even through the thick, resilient padding of his seat he felt the violent kick of the catapulting explosion. He cringed, expecting the skull-crushing impact of his head with the roof of the cabin, the last thing that he would ever feel. But it did not come, although he was faintly aware of the lightest of taps on his shoulder. And then he and the Surgeon Lieutenant, still strapped in their buoyant chairs, were shooting upwards, the sundered shell of the control cabin falling away beneath and below them, soaring to the surface in the midst of a huge bubble of air and other gases. Somehow he found time to look about him. The water was very blue and very clear. And there was a great, goggle-eyed fish staring at them from outside the bubble. It did not look especially carnivorous. Grimes hoped that it wasn't.

The two chairs broke surface simultaneously, bobbing and gyrating. Slowly, their motion ceased. They floated in the middle of a widening circle of discolored water, a spiralling swirl of iridescent oil slicks. And there were more than a few dead fish. Grimes could not repress a chuckle when he saw that they were golden carp. About five hundred yards away, its engine stopped, lay the scarlet power boat. But there was something in the water between it and the astronauts, something that was approaching at a speed that, to the spacemen should have been painfully slow and yet, in this environment, was amazingly fast.

There was a sleek head in a golden helmet—no, decided Grimes, it was hair, not an artificial covering— and there were two slim, golden-brown arms that alternately flashed up and swept down and back. And there was the rest of her, slim and golden-brown all over. Somehow it was suddenly important to Grimes that he see her face. He hoped that it would match what he could already see.

As she neared the floating chairs she reverted to a breaststroke and then, finally, came to a standstill, hanging there, a yard or so distant, just treading water. The spacemen could not help staring at her body through the shimmering transparency, her naked body. It was beautiful. With a sudden start of embarrassment Grimes forced his gaze to slide upwards to her face. It was thin, the cheekbones pronounced, the planes of the cheeks flat. Her mouth was a wide, scarlet slash, parted to reveal perfect white teeth. The eyes were an intense blue, an angry blue. She was saying something, and it was obvious that she was not whispering.

Grimes put up his hand, opened the faceplate of his helmet.

". . . offworld yahoos!" he heard. "My two favorite watchbirds destroyed, thanks to your unspaceman-like antics!" Her voice was not loud but it carried well. It could best be described as an icy soprano.

"Madam," Grimes said coldly. It didn't sound quite right but it would have to do. "Madam, I venture to suggest that the loss of my own boat is of rather greater consequence than the destruction of your . . . pets." (Pets? Watchbirds? That obviously metallic wing skewered on the antenna?) He went on, "Our Captain expressly requested that this lake be cleared as a landing area."

"Your *Captain?*" She made it sound as though the commanding officer of a Zodiac Class cruiser ranked with but below the butler.

"Look here, young woman . . ."

"*What* did you call me?"

"If you aren't a young woman," contributed Kravisky, "you look remarkably like one."

In her fury the girl forgot to tread water. She went down, came up spluttering. Only one word was intelligible and that was "Insolence!" She reached out a long, slender arm, caught hold of a projection at the edge of Grimes' chair. She floated there, maintaining her distance, glaring up at him.

"Now, young lady . . ."

She was mollified but only slightly. "Don't call me that, either," she snapped.

"Then what . . . ?"

"I am the Princess Marlene von Stolzberg. You may call me 'Your Highness'."

"Very well, Your Highness," said Grimes stiffly. "It may interest Your Highness to know that I intend to register a strong complaint with Spaceport Control. Your Highness's lack of ordinary commonsense put Your Highness's life as well as ours in hazard and resulted in the probable total loss of a piece of valuable Survey Service equipment."

"Commonsense?" she sneered. "And what about your own lack of that quality, to say nothing of your appalling spacemanship? You saw me. You must have seen me. And yet *you,* you . . .

offworlder, assumed that *you* had the right to disturb my afternoon's recreation!" She made an explosive, spitting noise.

"Let us be reasonable, Your Highness," persisted Grimes. It cost nothing to play along. "No doubt there was some misunderstanding . . ."

"Misunderstanding?" Her fine eyebrows arced in incredulity. "Misunderstanding? I'll say there was. You come blundering in here like . . . like . . ."

"Like snotty-nosed ragamuffins from the wrong side of the tracks?" asked Grimes sardonically.

Surprisingly, she laughed, tinkling merriment that was not altogether malicious. "How well you put it, my man."

Now was the time to take advantage of her change of mood. "Do you think, Your Highness, that you could call to your friend in the boat so that he can pick us up?"

She laughed again. "My friend in the boat? But I am by myself." She turned her head toward the bright scarlet craft. She called softly, "Ilse! To me, Ilse!"

There was a sudden turbulence at the thing's stern. It turned until it was stem on to the astronauts and the princess. It came in slowly and steadily, turned again until it was broadside on to the girl, brought itself to a smooth halt by an exact application of stern power. A short ladder with handrails extruded itself with a muted click. The Princess Marlene let go of Grimes' chair; two graceful strokes took her to her mechanical servitor. As she climbed on board Grimes saw that she was one of those rare women whose nudity is even more beautiful out of the water than in it; the surprisingly full breasts, deprived of their fluid support, did not sag, and there were no minor blemishes to have been veiled by ripples. He felt a stab of disappointment as she reached down for a robe of spotless white towelling and threw it about her. Still watching her, he made to unsnap his seat belt.

"Not so fast, my man!" she called coldly. "Not so fast. You are not riding in with me. But I shall tow you in." Expertly, she threw the end of a nylon line to Grimes. Not so expertly he caught it in his gloved hand.

"Thank you, Your Highness," he said as nastily as he dared.

The Port Control building, into which the girl finally led them, was deserted. She did not seem to be surprised. "After all," she condescended to explain, "Henri set up the beacon for you and gave you preliminary instructions. He assumed, wrongly, as it turned out, that you were good enough spacemen to find your way in by yourselves. After all, he has better things to do than to sit in this office all day."

"Such as?" asked Grimes. He added hastily, "Your Highness."

"Polo, of course."

"But, damn it all, we have to see *somebody*. We have to arrange for the landing and reception of the ship. We lost our uniforms when the boat went down, so we'd like a change of clothing. Spacesuits aren't very comfortable wear. Your Highness."

"Then take them off. I don't mind."

You wouldn't, thought Grimes. *The aristocrat naked before the serfs, the serfs naked before the aristocrat, what does it matter to the aristocrat?* He said, "The sun is down and it's getting chilly."

"Then keep them on."

"Please, Your Highness . . ." Grimes hated having to beg. He would far sooner have shaken some sense into this infuriating minx. But he was in enough trouble already. He was not looking forward explaining to Captain Daintree the loss of the re-entry vehicle. "Please, Your Highness, can't you help us?"

"Oh, all right. Although why you outworlders have to be so *helpless* is beyond me. Aren't you used to servants on your planets? I suppose not." She walked gracefully, her golden sandals faintly tapping on the polished floor, to what seemed to be, and was, a telephone booth. But there were neither dials nor buttons. She ordered, in her high, clear voice, "Get me the Comte de Messigny."

There was a brief delay, and then the screen on the rear wall of the booth swirled into glowing, three dimensional life. The man looking out from it was tall, clad in white helmet, shirt, riding breeches, and highly polished black boots. He lifted a slim, brown hand to the peak of his headgear in salute. A dazzling grin split the darkly tanned face under the pencil line of the mustache.

"Marlene!"

"Henri. Sorry to trouble you, but I've two lost sheep of spacemen here. They came blundering down in some sort of fire-breathing monstrosity—a dynosoar, would it be?—and cracked up in the lake . . ."

"I did warn you, Marlene."

"There was no risk to me, Henri, although it did cost me my two best watchbirds. But these offworlders, I suppose you'd better do something about them . . ."

"I suppose so. Put them on, please, Marlene."

"Stand where I was standing," the girl said to Grimes. Then, in a voice utterly devoid of interest, "Good evening to you." Then she was gone.

Grimes was conscious of being examined by the unwinking, dark eyes of the man in the screen who, at last, demanded, "Well?"

"Lieutenant Grimes," he replied, adding "sir" to be on the safe side. "Of *Aries,* and this is Surgeon Lieutenant Kravisky. We are the advance landing party . . ."

"You've landed, haven't you?"

"Sir . . ." It hurt to bow and scrape to these civilians, with their absurd, unearned titles. "Sir, we wish to report our arrival. We wish to report, too, that we are in a condition of some distress. Our re-entry vehicle was wrecked and we were badly shaken up. We are unable to establish radio contact with *Aries* so that we may tell our Captain what has happened. Our uniforms were lost in the wreck. We request clothing and food and accommodations." *And a good, stiff drink,* he thought.

"I shall inform your Captain that you are here," said de Messigny. "Meanwhile, the automatic servitors in the hostel have been instructed to obey all reasonable orders. You will find that provisions have been made for your reception and comfort on the floor above the one where you are presently situated."

"Thank you, sir. But when shall we make arrangements for the berthing and reception of *Aries?*"

"Tomorrow, Lieutenant. I shall see you some time tomorrow. Good evening to you."

The screen went blank.

Grimes looked at Kravisky, and Kravisky looked at Grimes. Then they looked around the huge, gleaming hall, beautifully proportioned, opulent in its fittings and furnishings; but, like this entire planet, cold, cold.

☙ Chapter 6 ☙

IF THERE WERE ELEVATORS to the upper floors they must be, thought Grimes, very well concealed. Tiredly, acutely conscious of the discomfort of his clammy spacesuit, he trudged toward the ornamental spiral staircase that rose gracefully from the center of the iridescent, patterned floor. The Surgeon Lieutenant followed him, muttering something that sounded like, and probably was, "Inhospitable bastards!"

But the staircase was more than it seemed. As Grimes put his weight on the first of the treads, there was a subdued humming of machinery, almost inaudible, and he felt himself being lifted. The thing was, in fact, an escalator. For a few seconds Grimes' exhausted brain tried to grapple with the engineering problems involved in the construction of a moving stairway of this design, then gave up. It worked, didn't it? So what?

At the level of the next floor the treads flattened to a track, slid him gently on to the brightly colored mosaic of the landing. He waited there until he was joined by Kravisky. There was a sudden silence as the murmur of machinery ceased. The two men looked around. They were standing in a relatively small hallway, partly occupied by another staircase ascending to yet another level. The walls, covered with what looked like a silken fabric, were featureless. Suddenly a disembodied voice, cultured yet characterless, almost sexless yet male rather than female, spoke. "This way, please."

A sliding door had opened. Beyond it was a room, plainly

furnished but comfortable enough, with two beds, chairs and a table. Apart from its size it could have been a ship's cabin. "Toilet facilities are on your right as you enter," the voice said. "Please leave soiled clothing in the receptacle provided."

"Perhaps a drink first . . ." suggested Kravisky.

"Toilet facilities are on your right as you enter. Please leave soiled clothing in the receptacle provided."

"I never did like arguing with robots," said Grimes. He walked slowly through the open doorway, then through the other door into the bathroom. As he turned, he saw that the main door had slid shut behind Kravisky. There did not seem to be any way of opening it from the inside, but, come to that, neither had there been any way of opening it from the outside. This should have seemed important, but right now the only matter of moment was shucking his stinking suit, clambering out of his sweat-soaked underwear. He pulled off his gloves, then clumsily fumbled with the fastenings of his armour. The protective clothing, fabric and metal with plastic and metal attachments, fell to the floor with an audible clank and rattle. He stepped out of the boots, peeled off his underpants. Kravisky, he saw, was managing quite well and would require no assistance. He started toward one of the two shower stalls.

"Please leave soiled clothing in the receptacle provided," said the annoying voice.

Yes, there was a receptacle, but it had not been designed to accommodate such bulky accoutrements as spacesuits. The underpants went through the hinged flap easily enough, but it was obvious that a full suit of space armour would be beyond its capabilities. In any case, such items of equipment were supposed to be surrendered only to the ship's Armourer for servicing.

"Please leave . . ."

"It won't go in," stated Grimes.

"Please . . ." There was a pause, and then a new voice issued from the concealed speaker. It was still a mechanical one but somehow possessed a definite personality. "Please dispose of your smaller articles of clothing and leave your suits on the floor. They will be collected for dehydration and deodorization later."

By whom? wondered Grimes. *Or by what?* But he could, at least, enjoy his shower now without being badgered. Naked, he stepped into the stall. Before he could raise a hand the curtain slid across the opening, before he could look for controls a fine spray of warm, soapy water came at him from all directions. This was succeeded, after a few minutes, by water with no added detergent and, finally, by a steady blast of hot air. When he was dry, the curtain slid back and, greatly refreshed, he walked out into the main bathroom. He noticed at once that the spacesuits were gone. He shrugged; after all, he had already lost a reentry vehicle. He noticed, too, that two plain, blue robes were hanging inside the door and under each of them, on the floor, was a pair of slippers. He pulled one of the garments on to his muscular body, slid his feet into the soft leather footwear. They fitted as though they had been made for him. He went through into the bed-sitting room, waited for Kravisky. The subtly annoying voice asked, "Would you care for a drink before dinner?"

"Yes," answered Grimes. "We would. Two pink gins, please. Large. With ice."

A faint clicking noise drew his attention. He saw that an aperture had appeared in the center of the polished table top, realized that the stout pillar that was the only support of the piece of furniture must be a supply chute. There was another click and the panel was back in place, and on it were two misted goblets.

"Gin!" complained Kravisky. "Are you mad, John? We could have that aboard the ship. Now's our chance to live it up." He added, "*I* would have ordered Manzanilla."

"Sorry, Doc. I was forgetting that you have personal experience of how the filthy rich live. You can order dinner."

He dropped into one of the chairs at the table, picked up and sipped his drink with appreciation. After all, it wasn't bad gin.

"Please order your meal," said the voice.

Grimes looked at the Surgeon Lieutenant over what remained of his second gin—obviously they were to be allowed no more—and said, "Go ahead, Doc."

Kravisky licked his full lips a little too obviously. "Well . . ." he murmured. "Well . . ." He stared at the ceiling. "Of course, John, I'm a rather old-fashioned type. To my mind there's nothing like good, Terran food, properly cooked, and Terran wines. On a Terraformed planet such as this it must be available."

"Such as?" asked Grimes, knowing, from his own experience, that the foods indigenous to the overcrowded and urbanized home planet were among the most expensive in the Man-colonized Galaxy.

"Please order your meal," said the voice.

"Now . . . Let me see . . . Caviar, I think. Beluga, of course. With *very* thin toast. And unsalted butter. And to follow? I think, John, that after the caviar we can skip a fish course, although Dover sole or blue trout would be good . . . Yes, blue trout. And then? Pheasant under glass, perhaps, with new potatoes and *petit pois*. Then Crepes Suzette. Then fruit—peaches and strawberries should do. Coffee, of course, with Napoleon brandy. And something *good* in the way of an Havana cigar apiece . . ."

"Rather shaky there, aren't you?" commented Grimes.

"In the cruise ships the tucker was for free but the cigars weren't, and even duty free they were rather expensive. But I haven't finished yet. To drink *with* the meal . . . With the caviar, make it vodka. Wolfschmidt. Well chilled. And then a magnum of Pommery . . ."

"I hope that they don't send the bill to Captain Daintree," said Grimes.

The center panel of the table sank from sight. After a very brief delay it rose again. On it were two full plates, two glasses, a carafe of red wine, cutlery and disposable napkins.

"What . . . what's *this*?" almost shouted Kravisky, picking up his fork and prodding the meat on his plate with it. "Steak!" he complained.

"We were instructed to obey all *reasonable* orders," said the mechanical voice coldly.

"But . . ."

"We were instructed to obey all reasonable orders."

"Looks like it's all we're getting," said Grimes philosophically.

"Better start getting used to life in the servants' hall, Doc." He pulled his plate to him, cut off and sampled a piece of the meat. "And, after all, this is not at all bad."

It was, in fact, far better than anything from *Aries'* tissue culture vats and, furthermore, had not been ruined in the cooking by the cruiser's galley staff. Grimes, chewing stolidly, admitted that he was enjoying it more than he would have done the fancy meal that the Doctor had ordered.

Even so, their contemptuous treatment by the robot servitors, and by the robots' masters, rankled.

☙ Chapter 7 ☙

THE TWO MEN slept well in their comfortable beds, the quite sound brandy that had been served with their after-dinner coffee cancelling out the effects of nervous and physical overexhaustion and the strangeness of an environment from which all the noises, of human and mechanical origin, that are so much the manifestation of the life of a ship were missing. It seemed to Grimes that he had been asleep only for minutes when an annoyingly cheerful voice was chanting, "Rise and shine! Rise and shine!" Nonetheless, he was alert at once, opening his eyes to see that the soft, concealed lighting had come back on. He looked at his wrist watch, which he had set to the Zone Time of the spaceport, adjusting it at the same time to the mean rotation of Eldorado before leaving the cruiser. 0700 hours. It was high time that he was up and doing something about everything.

He slid out of the bed. Kravisky, in his own couch, was still huddled under the covers, moaning unhappily, the voice, louder now, was still chanting, "Rise and shine!"

There was a silver tea service on the table. Grimes went to it, poured himself a cup of tea, added milk and plenty of sugar. He sipped it appreciatively. He called to the Surgeon Lieutenant, "Show a leg, you lazy bastard. Come and have your tea while it's hot."

The doctor's rumpled head emerged from under the sheet. "I *never* have tea first thing in the morning," he complained. "I always have coffee."

"You should have made your wishes known before you retired last night," said the robot voice reprovingly. *At least,* thought Grimes, *this was a change from that irritating sing-song.*

"Oh, all right. *All* right." Kravisky got out of bed, pulled his robe about his thin body, joined Grimes at the table. He slopped tea from the pot into the thin, porcelain cup, slopping much of it into the saucer. He grimaced at the first mouthful. Then he asked, "What now, John?"

"Get ourselves cleaned up. The fleet's in port, or soon will be, and not a whore in the house washed."

"How can you be so bloody cheerful?"

"I always wake up this way."

Grimes set down his empty cup, went through to the bathroom. On the shelf under the mirror were two new toothbrushes, toothpaste, a tube of depilatory cream. *Service,* he thought. *But, so far, without a smile.* By the time that he was in the shower the Surgeon Lieutenant was commencing his own ablutions, was still showering when Grimes walked back into the bedroom. The beds, he saw, had been remade. He had heard nothing, decided that they must have been removed and replaced in the same way that the table service operated. On each tautly spread coverlet was fresh clothing: underwear, a shirt, a pair of shorts, sandals. Very gay the apparel looked against the dark, matte blue of the bedspreads—the shirts an almost fluorescent orange, the shorts a rich emerald green.

He said aloud, "Uniform would have been better."

The disembodied voice replied, "We have not the facilities."

"*You* won't have to explain to the Old Man why you aren't wearing the rig of the day," remarked Grimes.

There was silence. Haughty? Hurt? But it was better than some mechanical wisecrack.

"Breakfast," said Kravisky, who had come in from the bathroom.

It was standing there on the table—a coffeepot and cups, cream, sugar, two halves of grapefruit, toast, butter, honey and two covered plates. The Surgeon Lieutenant lifted one of the covers. "The spaceman's delight," he complained. "Ham and eggs."

"What's wrong with that? "

"Nothing. But I would have preferred kidneys and bacon."

"We are not telepathic," said the smug voice.

Breakfast over, the two men dressed. They looked at each other dubiously. "And do we have to face the Old Man like this?" asked Kravisky. "You should have let me save our uniforms, John."

"There wasn't time, Doc. It was all we could do to save ourselves."

"Look. The door's opening."

"Take the escalator to the next upper floor," ordered the robot voice. "You will find the Princess von Stolzberg and the Comte de Messigny awaiting you."

"And wipe the egg off your face," said Grimes to Kravisky.

There was an office on the next floor that, judging by the equipment along two of its walls, was also the spaceport control tower. In one of the big screens swam the image of *Aries,* a silvery, vaned spindle gleaming against the interstellar dark. It was the sight of his ship that first caught Grimes' attention but did not hold it for long. Inevitably his regard shifted to the woman who stood to one side of the screen, the tall woman with her hair braided into a golden coronet, sparkling with jewels, clad in a flowing white tunic of some diaphanous material that barely concealed the lines of her body. He smiled at her but her blue eyes, as she looked back at him, were cold. To her right was the tall man to whom they had talked the previous evening. He was in uniform, black and gold, with four gold bands on the cuffs of his superbly tailored tunic, a stylized, winged rocket gleaming on the left breast. So appareled he was obviously a spaceman, although, as Grimes well knew, it takes far more than gold braid and brass buttons to make an astronaut.

"Henri," said the girl quietly, "these are the two . . . gentlemen from the *Aries.* Mr. Grimes, this is Captain de Messigny."

De Messigny extended his hand without enthusiasm. Grimes shook it. It was like handling a dead fish. Kravisky shook it. The Comte said in a bored voice, "Of course, I am, as it were, only the Acting Harbourmaster. As the senior Master of our own small merchant fleet I was requested to make the arrangements for the landing of your ship." He waved a hand and a hitherto dull screen lit up, displaying what was obviously a plan of the spaceport. "But what is there to arrange? As you see, we can accommodate a squadron. Our own vessels are in their underground hangars, so the apron is absolutely clear. All that your Captain has to do is to set down *Aries* anywhere within the landing area."

"If he's as good a ship-handler as certain of his officers . . ." sneered the girl.

"Now, Marlene, that was quite uncalled for. You did make a small contribution to their crack-up, you know." He waved his hand again, and a triangle of bright red flashing lights appeared on the plan. "Still, I have actuated the beacons. They will serve as a guide."

"Has Captain Daintree been informed, sir?" asked Grimes.

"Of course."

"Has he been informed of the . . . er . . . circumstances of our landing?"

De Messigny smiled. "Not yet, Lieutenant. I told him last night that you were unable to get into direct radio contact with your ship, but no more than that. It will be better if you make your own report on the loss of the re-entry vehicle."

"Yes . . ." agreed Grimes unhappily.

"Very well, then." The tall man made casual gestures with his right hand. Some sort of visual code? wondered Grimes. Or did the controls of this fantastic communications equipment possess built-in psionic capabilities? Anyhow, de Messigny waved his hand and another screen came alive. It depicted the familiar interior of the control room of *Aries* and, in the foreground, the face of the Senior Communications Officer. His eyes lit up with recognition; it was obvious that he could see as well as be seen.

"Captain Daintree," snapped de Messigny. It was more of an order than a request.

"Yes, sir. In a moment."

And then the Old Man was glaring out of the screen. "Mr. Grimes! Mr. Kravisky! Why are you not in uniform?"

"We . . . we lost our uniforms, sir."

"You *lost* your uniforms?" Daintree's voice dropped to a menacing growl. "I am well aware, Mr. Grimes, that things seem to happen to you that happen to no other officer in the ship but, even so . . . Perhaps you will be so good as to explain how you mislaid the not inexpensive clothing with which the Survey Service, in a moment of misguided altruism, saw fit to cover your repulsive nakedness."

"We . . . we lost the re-entry vehicle, sir."

There was a long silence, during which Grimes waited for his commanding officer to reach critical mass. But, surprisingly, when Daintree spoke, his voice was almost gentle.

"But you didn't lose yourselves. Oh, no. That would be too much to hope for. But I shall have to make some sort of report to my Lords Commissioners, Mr. Grimes, and you may care to assist me in this duty by explaining. If you can."

"Well, sir, we were coming in to a landing on the surface of Lake Bluewater. As instructed."

"Yes. Go on."

Grimes looked at the girl, thought that he was damned if he was going to hide behind a woman's skirts. She returned his gaze coldly. He shrugged, no more than a twitch of his broad shoulders. He faced the screen again, saying, "I made an error of judgment, sir."

"An expensive one, Mr. Grimes, both to the Service and to yourself."

And then the Princess Marlene von Stolzberg was standing beside the Lieutenant. "Captain Daintree," she said haughtily, "your officer was not responsible for the loss of your dynosoar. If anybody was, it was I."

Daintree's heavy eyebrows lifted. "*You*, Madam?"

"Yes. It was my hour for water-skiing on the lake, and I saw no reason to cancel my evening recreation because of the proposed landing. I did not think, of course, that any Captain in his right senses would send his advance party down to a planetary surface in such an archaic, unhandy contraption as a dynosoar. Your Mr. Grimes was obliged to take violent evasive action as soon as he saw me cutting across his path. Furthermore, my two watchbirds, seeing that I was in danger, attacked the re-entry vehicle which, in consequence, crashed."

"Oh. Captain de Messigny, is this lady's story true?"

"It is, Captain Daintree."

"Thank you. And may I make a humble request, Captain?"

"You may, Captain."

"Just refrain, if you can, from holding tennis tournaments on the landing field or from converting the apron into a rollerskating rink when I'm on *my* way down. Over," he concluded viciously, "and *out!*"

☙ Chapter 8 ❧

THEY WATCHED *ARIES* come in—de Messigny, the Princess and, a little to one side, Grimes and Kravisky. Grimes had thought it strange that the spaceport control tower should be left unmanned at this juncture, but the two El Doradans, coldly and amusedly, had informed him that the electronic intelligences housed therein were quite capable of handling any normal landing without any human interference. Grimes did not like the way that the Comte slightly stressed the word "normal."

They stood there, the four of them, on the edge of the apron, well clear of the triangle of red lights. Above them, on gleaming wings, wheeled and hovered a quartet of flying things that looked like birds, that must be four of the watchbirds about which Grimes had already heard, which, in fact, he had already encountered. *(And, he thought glumly, there was still the enquiry into the loss of the re-entry vehicle to face.)*

The two El Doradans ignored their mechanical guardians. The Lieutenant could not, wondering what would happen should he make some inadvertent move that would be construed by the electronic brains as an act of hostility. He started to edge a little further away from Marlene von Stolzberg and de Messigny, then, with an audible grunt, stood his ground.

They saw the ship before they heard her—at first a glittering speck in the cloudless, morning sky and then, after only a few seconds,

159

a gleaming spindle. She was well in sight when there drifted down to them the odd, irregular throbbing of an inertial drive unit in operation, no more than an uneasy mutter to begin with but swelling to an ominous, intermittent thunder, the voice of the power that had hurled men out among the stars.

But this was all wrong. On any civilized world, or on any civilized world other than this, there would have been an honor guard, ranks of soldiers, in ceremonial uniform, drawn to rigid attention. There would have been antique cannon with black powder charges to fire a salute to the Captain of a major Terran war vessel. There would have been flags and ceremonial. But here, here there was only one man— and his uniform, after all, was a mercantile one—and one woman. A self-styled Princess, perhaps, but even so . . . *And, thought Grimes, there's also Kravisky and myself, but dressed like beach boys.*

Lower dropped the ship, and lower, the noise of her Drive deafening now, every protrusion, every mast, turret and sponson that broke the smooth lines of her hull visible to the naked eye. From a staff just abaft her sharp stem the ensign of the Survey Service—a golden S on a black field, with the green, blue and gold globe of Earth in the upper canton—was broken out, streamed vertically upwards. Grimes did not have to turn to see that there was no bunting displayed from the masts of the spaceport administration buildings. Perhaps, he thought, there were in the Universe aristocrats sufficiently courteous to put out more flags to celebrate the arrival of snotty-nosed ragamuffins from the wrong side of the tracks, but the only aristocratic quality to be found in abundance on El Dorado was arrogance.

She was down at last, a shining, metallic tower poised between the buttresses of her tripedal landing gear. She was down and until the moment that Captain Daintree cut the Drive, an egg trapped between one of the huge pads and the concrete of the apron would have remained unbroken. And then the sudden silence as the machinery slowed to a halt was broken by the almost inaudible hissings and creakings as the ship's enormous mass adjusted itself to the gravitational field of the planet.

There were other soft noises behind the original reception party. Grimes turned. Three air cars of graceful, almost fragile design were coming in to a smooth landing, each attended by its pair of hovering watch-birds. From the first stepped a fat, bald, yellow-skinned man, his gross body draped in a dark blue robe. From the second emerged a tall, thin individual, black coated, gray trousered, wearing on his head a black hat of antique design. The occupant of the third car was a superbly made Negro, clad in a leopard skin flung carelessly about his body.

Grimes turned again, stiffening to attention, as he heard the bugles. *Aries* had her ramp out now, extending to the ground from the after airlock door. Stiffly, the two Marine buglers marched down it and as they set foot on the apron, raised their gleaming instruments to their lips and sounded another call. Twenty Marines came next, under their Major, and formed two ranks on either side of the foot of the ramp. Then Captain Daintree appeared in the circular door-way, all black and gold and starched white linen, his cocked hat on his head, his ceremonial sword at his side, his decorations gleaming on his breast. He was followed by Surgeon Commander Passifern, looking a little (but only a little) ill at ease in his full dress finery. Marlene von Stolzberg whispered something to her companions and giggled.

Slowly, more like a humanoid robot than a man, Captain Daintree marched towards the waiting group, Passifern keeping step behind him. He glared at Grimes and Kravisky, standing there in their gaudy civilian clothes. His glance flickered over the others. Grimes could almost hear him thinking; who was in authority? Somehow he contrived a salute that included all of them. De Messigny answered it with a casual flip of his hand toward the gold-crusted peak of his cap, then stepped forward. He said, "We have already met at long range, Captain Daintree."

"Yes, M'sieur le Comte."

"Allow me to introduce the Princess Marlene von Stolzberg . . ." Daintree bowed slightly. "And Lord Tarlton of Dunwich, our Physician in Residence . . ." The tall, thin man in the black coat extended a pale hand; Daintree gripped it briefly. "And the Baron

Takada . . ." The fat Oriental hissed and bobbed. "And Hereditary
Chief Lobenga . . ." The big Negro's handshake made Daintree wince
visibly. But his voice was cold and formal as he said, "To complete the
introductions, this is Surgeon Commander Passifern, my Senior
Medical Officer."

There was a long silence, broken by Daintree. He stated, "You
asked for our assistance. Might I suggest that this is hardly the place
to discuss the details. Perhaps Her Highness and you . . . er . . .
gentlemen would care to step aboard my ship. I take it that you are
representative of your government."

"We have no government, Captain Daintree, such as you
understand the word," said de Messigny. "But it was decided that
this little group here was best qualified to meet you. Will it be possible
for you and Commander Passifern to come with us to the city? We
shall provide transport."

"Very well," said Daintree. He looked at Grimes as he added, "I
assume that your own atmosphere fliers are not harassed by careless
sportsmen and sportswomen."

Grimes flushed as he heard Marlene von Stolzberg laugh softly.

❧ Chapter 9 ❧

CAPTAIN DAINTREE could not spare the time for an interview with the two officers of the advance party; he, with Dr. Passifern, was making his preparations and arrangements for the trip to the city, on which he and the Surgeon Commander would be accompanied by the Paymaster Lieutenant who was Daintree's secretary and by the Lieutenant of Marines. But Commander Griffin had time to spare. No sooner had Grimes and Kravisky mounted to the head of the ramp than the public address speakers were blatting their names, ordering them to report at once to the Commander's office.

They would have liked to have changed into more suitable attire, and Kravisky, in fact, did suggest that they do so. But that 'at once' at the end of the announcement had a nasty, peremptory ring to it, and Grimes knew Griffin far better than did the Surgeon Lieutenant. So they hurried through the ship, acutely conscious of the amused glances directed at them by the officers and ratings they encountered in the alleyways. Grimes heard one man mutter to his companion, "These officers don't half have it good! Looks like they've been on a bleeding holiday . . ."

And now the holiday, such as it it had been, was over. Griffin, seated behind his tidy desk, regarded them coldly, his fat face sullen under the sandy hair.

"So," he said. "So." There was an uneasy silence.

"So you lose an expensive re-entry vehicle. Even if it can be salvaged, there will be repairs. So you rejoin the ship looking like a pair of beach bums." His podgy hands shuffled papers. "There will have to be an official report, you know. Or didn't that occur to you?"

"It had occurred to me, sir," replied Grimes.

"I am pleased to hear it, although I was far from pleased with the verbal report you made to the Captain. There is one important thing that you must learn, Mr. Grimes, and that is that although an officer is automatically a gentleman he should not, repeat not, allow chivalry to interfere with his duty. If that woman had not admitted that she was to blame for the loss of the dynosoar, the consequences to you could have been extremely serious, affecting most adversely your future career in this Service. As it is . . ." He grinned suddenly, relaxed visibly. "As it is, I hope that they never salvage that archaic contraption. It's always been a pain in the neck to me. Sit down, both of you." He pushed a box of cigarettes across his desk. "Smoke. And now, before you go away to start putting things down on paper in your best officialese, tell me in your own words just what has been happening to you."

Grimes told the Commander the full story, omitting nothing. Griffin was amused but, at the same time, annoyed. He said, "I gain the impression that everybody on this bloody planet has a title, except the butler. And he's a robot."

"That's the very impression that we gained," Grimes told him. "And even their robot servitors are snobs."

"You can say that again," declared Kravisky, and told again the story of the superb meal that he had ordered but not received.

"And yet they want our help . . ." mused the Commander. "It must have hurt their pride to have to call in outsiders. Whatever sort of a jam they're in, it must be a serious one."

"Have you any idea what it is, sir?" asked Grimes.

"Haven't a clue. Oh, it's something medical, we all know that much. But a world like this must be healthy. This Lord Tarlton of Dunwich, he used to be *the* physician on the planet of that name, although then he was plain Dr. Tarlton. He was the head of their College of Medicine, and we all know how highly a Dunwich degree is regarded throughout the Galaxy. As a diagnostician, he was a recognized genius. It seems incredible that he should be incapable of handling this emergency, whatever it is. What do you think, Kravisky? As a doctor, I mean."

"I think the same as you do, sir."

"And these others . . . I've been doing my homework in the microfiled Encyclopedia Galactica Year Books. Baron Takada. A multimillionaire on his planet of birth, Kobe. Flew the coop when the local income tax collectors got too avaricious. But known as much for his metaphysical researches as for his wealth. Hereditary Chief Lobenga, onetime native, and ruler, of New Katanga. Stinking rich, of course, but made his own world too hot to hold him by his dabbling in the more unsavory varieties of black magic."

"And the Princess?" asked Grimes.

Griffin chuckled. "She seems to have made quite an impression on you. Just a spoiled popsy from Thuringia. Too much money and didn't like to have to plough any of it back into the welfare of the miners and factory hands. Sold out at a pretty profit and bought her way into the El Dorado Corporation. De Messigny? Not even a millionaire but had a name as a space yachtsman and freelance explorer. I suppose that these people wanted somebody who was more or less their breed of cat to captain their merchant ships."

"All these titles . . ." said Kravisky.

"Fair dinkum, most of 'em. I often think that all these stories about effete aristocrats are put out by the aristocrats themselves. After all, *they* have practiced selective breeding for centuries . . ." He leaned back in his chair. "Money snobbery, snobbery of birth . . . It makes a pretty picture, doesn't it? And you two were in the picture. I suppose that we all are, now." His manner stiffened. "But if there's to be any shore leave, which I doubt, I shall impress upon every bastard aboard this ship, every officer, every rating, that he is to wear his uniform with *pride*.

"And, talking of uniforms . . ."

"We'd better get changed, sir," said Grimes.

"You'd better," said Griffin.

~ Chapter 10 ~

CAPTAIN DAINTREE and the officers who had accompanied him returned from the city the following morning, delivered back to the spaceport by one of the graceful flying cars. The captain went straight to his own quarters, accompanied by Griffin, who had received him at the airlock. Dr. Passifern went straight to the ship's well-equipped laboratory, where his own staff was awaiting him. Paymaster Lieutenant Hodge and Lieutenant Lamont, of the Marine Corps, made their way to the wardroom, where all the off-duty officers, including Grimes, were already gathered.

"And what have you to say for yourself, Pusser?" demanded Lieutenant Commander Cooper.

Hodge, a slight, clerkly young man, made a major production of drawing a cup of coffee from the dispenser. He sipped it, made a grimace. He complained, "*They* serve much better espresso than this . . ."

"You did more than drink coffee," stated Cooper.

"We did," said the Marine, stroking the luxuriant mustache that was supposed to give him a martial appearance. "We did. We sat around trying to look intelligent while our lords and masters conferred with all the counts and barons and princes and whatever."

"Any princesses?" asked somebody.

"Yes. There was one, come to think of it. A quite tasty blonde piece. Which reminds me, she gave me a letter for you, young Grimes."

"Never mind Mr. Grime's love life," said Cooper a little jealously. "That can wait. Why were we asked to call here? Or is that classified?"

"It is," Hodge told him primly. "No doubt the Captain will release such information as he sees fit when he feels like it."

"But we weren't told to say nothing of what we *saw*," pointed out Lamont.

"Can I have my letter?" asked Grimes.

"Later, later. It will keep."

"Mr. Grimes!" snapped Cooper, "I will not have the wardroom turned into a beer garden. You will please refrain from laying hands upon the brutal and licentious soldiery. Please continue, Mr. Lamont."

"Well, Pilot, we were taken to the city, as you know. That air car was really posh. Some sort of Inertial Drive but fully automated. There was a girl in charge of it, a Lady Jane Kennelly, one of those really snooty redheads, and she never laid so much as a pinky on the controls, just said in a bored voice, 'Head Office,' and the thing replied—there was a speaker on the console—'Head Office, your ladyship. Certainly, your ladyship.' I felt like saying, 'Home, James, and don't spare the horses,' but the Old Man gave me such a dirty look that I thought better of it.

"She, this Lady Jane, wasn't in a conversational mood and neither was the Old Man, so *nobody* talked. It was only a short flight, anyhow. We passed over what looked like farms, but more like gardens than farms, if you know what I mean. We saw big, specialized machines working in the fields, but never a human being.

"Then we came to the city. Oh, I know that we've all seen it from the air, but you have to be flying through it, below the level of the towers, really to appreciate it. Just towers, spires, rather, and each of them standing in its own park. Not many people around, and nobody looking to be in any sort of a hurry. Quite a few machines like oversized beetles pottering around in the gardens. My own interest in botany doesn't go beyond things you eat and drink, like cauliflowers and hops, but even I could see that just about every species of flower in the whole damn Galaxy must have been in full bloom in those beds.

"We dropped down on to a lawn in front of the really big tower, so tall that the big, golden standard flying from its peak was half-obscured by a wisp of low cloud. And it's not one of those flimsy, reinforced plastic jobs, either. Solid granite, it looked like. Solid granite, and polished, with a bit of gold trim here and there. Not at all gaudy. Like a huge tombstone, a multimillionaire's tombstone, in good taste.

"Lady Jane said, in her cool voice, 'This is the end of the penny section.' She made it quite clear that she'd done her job and that what happened next was none of her concern. The door of the car opened and we got out. The Old Man first, then Doc, then the Pusser's pup, then myself. We were hardly clear of the car when the door shut and it lifted and went whiffling off down the avenue. So we stood there, sort of shuffling our feet and coughing politely. Shuffling our feet? That grass felt good. I'd have loved to have kicked off my boots and walked on it barefooted.

"By this time the Old Man was looking more than somewhat thunderous. He was just about to say something when I saw a big door opening at the base of the tower. And one of those damned mechanical voices that seemed to be coming from nowhere, or everywhere, said, very politely, 'Please to enter, gentlemen.'

"So we entered."

"And then?" pressed Cooper. "And then?"

"I think that's as far as we can take you," Hodge told him severely. "I think we've told you too much already."

"What about my letter?" asked Grimes.

"Shut up!" snarled the Navigator. He turned again to the Marine and Paymaster Lieutenant. "But you must know what it's all about."

"Yes, we know," Hodge told him smugly. "But until we have the Captain's permission we cannot tell you."

Lament looked at the clerical officer with some distaste. Obviously he disliked having his story spoiled by this over-meticulous observance of regulations. He said, "I don't think that I'm contravening the Official Secrets Act or its Survey Service equivalent if I tell you that, although we saw quite a few people in the city, we didn't see a single child. Neither did we see in any of the parks and gardens we flew over anything that looked like a children's playground . . ."

There was a silence while those in the wardroom pondered the implications of Lament's statement. It was broken by Grimes. "And now can I have my letter, Lament?"

"What a one-track mind!" said Cooper, almost admiringly.

"Perhaps it's the right track," Grimes told him.

"Do you think *they* haven't tried it, lover boy?" sneered the Lieutenant Commander.

~ Chapter 11 ~

AS SOON AS he was able Grimes got away from the wardroom, hurried to his spartan dogbox of a cabin. He looked at the letter for quite a long while before he opened it. The envelope was pale blue and conveyed, by appearance and texture, an impression of expensiveness and quality. The address, Grimes decided at last, was typewritten, although he had never either seen or heard of a machine with Gothic characters. He grinned faintly. With that type, *Herr Leutnant* would have looked so much better than the plain, ordinary *Lieutenant.*

There was a tiny tab on the pack of the envelope that made for easier opening. Grimes pulled it and the flap fell away. Immediately he was conscious of a hint of perfume, remembered it as the scent that the princess had worn at the time of their last meeting. He began to feel even more impatient, extracted the sheet of paper and unfolded it. It, too, was pale blue, deckle-edged, luxurious to sight and touch. The letter, apart from the firm, decisive signature, had been written by the same machine as the address. *Dear Mr. Grimes,* he read. *Having met and talked with your Captain I now realize how thoughtless and selfish my behavior was on the occasion of your landing on Lake Bluewater. On this world we are prone to forget that the mores of other planets are different from our own. Perhaps, when Captain Daintree grants shore leave, you would care to be my guest.*

Marlene.

He pursed his lips and whistled softly. *But it means nothing,* he told himself. *Just* noblesse oblige. *Or throw the good doggie a nice bone.* The Universe was full of people who said, "But you must stay with us . . ." And then were surprised and pained when you turned up their front doorstep, suitcase in hand. In any case, it yet remained to be seen whether or not Daintree would allow planet liberty.

The bulkhead speaker burped, then announced, "Attention all! Attention all! This is the Captain speaking. It is my pleasure to announce that the local authorities have agreed to permit shore leave. Arrangements will be made for sightseeing trips and the like. Details will be promulgated by Heads of Departments." There was a pause, then Daintree added, "Mr. Grimes to report to me at once."

So he can tell me that my *leave is stopped,* thought Grimes glumly.

"Sit down, Grimes." Captain Daintree was almost affable.

Grimes sat down.

"Ah, yes, Mr. Grimes. This business of the loss of the re-entry vehicle . . ."

"Sir?"

Surprisingly, the Old Man grinned. "There was a film made of the whole sorry business. One of those damned robots in Spaceport Control records, as a matter of routine, every spaceship arrival and departure. I saw the film." He grinned again. "I must admit that the spectacle of the Princess attired in a single water ski was, shall we say, distracting. An odd woman, Her Highness. But attractive, very attractive . . ."

Come to the point, you old goat, thought Grimes.

"Yes, very attractive and very frank. She freely admits that she was to blame for the bungled landing. Not that I altogether agree with her, but even so . . . As I've already said, an odd woman. With odd tastes. Very odd. Believe it or not, she wants to be your hostess during this vessel's stay on El Dorado." Daintree paused. Grimes decided not to say anything. Daintree went on, "I told her, of course, that your duties toward the ship come first. You have still to write the report on the loss of the dynosoar. You have still to oversee and carry out salvage operations; I declined Comte de Messigny's offer of equipment and robot submarine workers. Then you have to write the report upon the salvage."

"Of course, sir."

"I'm glad that you show some sense of responsibility. But when all these tasks have been completed to my satisfaction, *and not before,* you will be granted leave until the vessel's departure. This Princess von Stolzberg appears to be one of the rulers of this planet, insofar as they have rulers, so it might be advisable to, as it were, humor her."

"Thank you, sir."

"Don't thank me, Mr. Grimes. Thank Her Highness. *When* you get around to meeting her again."

If I ever do, thought Grimes.

Daintree, who had his telepathic moments, laughed. "You will, Mr. Grimes. You will. This medical emergency, I suppose that it could be called that, of theirs is more serious and less straightforward than an epidemic of measles. If *their* quacks can't come up with an answer, I can't see our Dr. Passifern and his aides getting to the bottom of the problem in five seconds flat . . ." He opened the box on his desk. "Smoke, Grimes?"

"My pipe if I may, sir."

"Suit yourself." Daintree tapped the end of his cigarette on his thumbnail to ignite the tobacco, looked thoughtfully at the thin, rising spiral of smoke. "Yes, quite a problem they have, these El Doradans. It all goes to show that money cannot buy happiness . . ."

"But with it, sir," pointed out Grimes, "you can, at least, be miserable in comfort."

"Ha! Very good. I must remember that. But it is a most peculiar situation. As you know, they bought this planet and then, at enormous expense, terraformed it. With improvements. They stocked with all the flora and fauna necessary for sport as well as food. Insofar as the animal and plant kingdoms are concerned the normal cycle of birth, procreation, death has been in operation from the very start. Insofar as the humans are concerned, there are no births. No, that's not quite correct. Some of the women were pregnant when they came here. The youngest of the children born on El Dorado is now a girl of seventeen."

"Something in the air, or the water, sir?"

"Could be, Grimes. Could be. But I'm a spaceman, not a quack. I wouldn't know. If it is, it must be something remarkably subtle. And you'd think that such an . . . agent? would affect the plants and the livestock as well as the people."

Grimes, flattered by the honor of a conversation with the normally unapproachable Captain, ventured another opinion. "Do you think, sir, that they called us in so that we could . . . ? How can I put it? A sort of artificial insemination by donor? Only not so artificial."

"Mr. Grimes!" Daintree at once reverted to his normal manner. "I ask, no, I order, you to put such ideas out of your alleged mind at once. These people, and never forget it, are in their own estimation the aristocrats of the Galaxy. They want children to inherit their wealth, their titles. But they made it quite clear to me that such children must be sired by themselves, not by mongrel outsiders." His face darkened. "I don't mind telling you, Mr. Grimes, that I was furious when I heard that term used. But, bear this in mind, if there are any incidents during this vessel's stay on El Dorado it will go hard, very hard indeed, with those responsible. You will learn, Mr. Grimes, that a senior officer has very often, too often, to subordinate his own true feelings to the well-being of his Service. We are not, repeat not, a drunken, roistering crew of merchant spacemen. We are Survey Service, and every man, from myself to the lowest mess boy, will comport himself like a gentleman."

And one definition of a gentleman, thought Grimes, *is a man who takes his weight on his elbows . . .*

"And this offer of hospitality by the Princess von Stolzberg, it's no more than her way of apologizing to you and to the Survey Service. You'd better not get any false ideas."

"I won't, sir."

"Very well. That will do. See the Commander and ask him for the necessary men and equipment for the salvage of the re-entry vehicle. I have already told him that the entire operation is to be directly under your charge."

"Very good, sir."

Grimes got to his feet, stiffened to attention in salute, turned about smartly and marched towards the door. Daintree's snarl halted him abruptly.

"Mr. Grimes!"

"Sir?"

"I know that I'm only the Captain, but may I point out that it is not correct to take official leave of a senior officer with a pipe stuck in the middle of your cretinous face?"

"Sorry, sir."

"And, Mr. Grimes, may I request that you watch your manners when you are mingling with the aristocracy?"

"I'll do my best, sir."

"Your best, on far too many occasions, has not been good enough. Get out!"

Ears burning, Grimes got out.

≈ Chapter 12 ≈

THE FOLLOWING MORNING Grimes started the salvage operations.

As a unit of the Survey Service fleet, *Aries* was rich in all manner of equipment. She was a fighting ship but, officially at least, her prime function was exploration and survey, and a newly discovered watery world cannot be properly surveyed without underwater gear. Insofar as the raising of the dynosoar was concerned, the engineers' workshop was able to supply, at short notice, what little extra was needed.

Commander Griffin had let Grimes have one of the work boats, a powerful little brute fitted with inertial drive, aboard which the engineers had installed a powerful air compressor. There were coils of tough, plastic hose, together with the necessary valves and connections. There was a submarine welding outfit and a good supply of metal plates of various shapes and sizes. There were scuba outfits for Grimes and for the men who would be working with him.

Shortly after dawn the airlock high on *Aries'* side opened and the work boat, muttering to itself, slid out, wobbled a little in midair and then, with Grimes at the controls, set course for the further end of Lake Bluewater, from the surface of which a light mist, golden in the almost level rays of the morning sun, was lazily rising. The Lieutenant was already in his skin-tight suit, as was the remainder of the working party, but had yet to put on his helmet and flippers. The interior of the boat was crowded with men and gear, and there would have been little room to undress and dress. By his side, similarly attired, sat Chief Petty Officer Anderson, a big man, grossly fat until you looked at him more closely and realized that the fat was solid muscle. Baldheaded, baby-faced, he was peering intently at the submerged metal indicator that had been installed on the work boat's control console. He looked up from the instrument, said, "If I were you, Mr. Grimes, I'd run to the end of the lake and then come back in short sweeps." It was a suggestion, not an order, but when a C. P. O. suggests to even a senior officer the words carry weight.

Grimes replied, cheerfully enough, "I'll do just that, Chief."

He reduced thrust, lost altitude as he approached the beach, so that the boat would make its run barely clear of the surface of the water.

"If I were you, Mr. Grimes, I'd keep her up. That way we get a better spread on the detector beam. Once we've found the wreck we can come down for finer location."

"All right, Chief." *And,* thought Grimes, *what the hell do we have officers for? To carry the can back, that's all.*

Slowly, steadily, the boat grumbled its way out over Lake Bluewater. There were not, Grimes was relieved to see, any early morning swimmers or water-skiers. An audience he could do without, especially when such an audience would have with it a horde of watchbirds. He had good reason to dislike those robotic guardian angels.

To the end of the lake flew Grimes, toward the clump of screw pines that backed the sandy beach. "Anything yet, Chief?" he asked Anderson.

"No, sir." Then, in a reproachful voice, "You should have released the marker buoy, Mr. Grimes."

"I didn't know that we had one."

"I installed it myself, Mr. Grimes." Anderson was the ship's expert, rated and paid as such, in submarine operations.

"Why wasn't it an automatic release?" demanded the Lieutenant.

"Come, sir. You know better than that." The intonation made

it quite clear that in the speaker's opinion Grimes didn't. "What if you make a crash landing on some hostile planet, in the sea, and don't want to give the potential enemy a chance to pinpoint your position? And hadn't you better watch those trees, sir?"

"I am watching them." Slowly Grimes turned the boat, started his sweeps back and forth across the width of the lake.

"Now!" exclaimed Anderson. "That's it, sir, I think. Bring her down, if you don't mind . . . Stop her. Now, back a little. Slowly, sir, slowly. Right a little . . . Stop her again. Cut the drive."

Gently, making only the slightest of splashes, the work boat settled to the surface. With the drive shut down it was suddenly very quiet. The air drifting in through the open windows carried a faint, refreshing tang of early morning mist. One of the ratings in the after compartment muttered, "This is a bit of all right. We should have brought fishing tackle."

Anderson turned his head, "You'll have all the fishing you want, Jones. It's a big, tin fish we've come to catch."

The men who knew what was good for them laughed.

"There are goldfish in the lake," contributed Grimes. His remark was received in silence. He shrugged. "All right, Chief. I'll go down to make the preliminary inspection. I'll let you know when I need help."

"Have you had your antibend shot, sir?" asked Anderson in a way that implied that all officers have to be wet-nursed, junior officers especially.

"Yes, Chief. Now, if somebody will help me on with my helmet . . ."

Anderson himself picked up the transparent sphere, lowered it carefully over Grimes' head, connected up the air pipes to the shoulder tank. The speaker inside the helmet said tinnily, "Testing, sir. Testing. Can you read me?"

"Loud and clear." The Lieutenant eased himself up from his chair, sat on the ledge of the open window, his back to the water. "Flippers," he said.

He saw Anderson speaking into the microphone that somebody had handed him. "If I were you, sir, I'd go down on the line."

"Just what I am doing, Chief. But I'll wear my flippers just the same."

Anderson strapped the large fins on to his bare feet, then made a thumbs-up gesture. Grimes replied in kind, leaned far back and then let himself fall. He knew that this unorthodox method of entering the water would not please the C. P. O. and, even as he hit the surface with a noisy splash, heard, through his helmet speaker, Anderson admonish the men, "Just because an officer does it that way you're not to. See?" The failure to place a hand over the microphone was probably deliberate.

He hit the water and, at once, started to sink. With his equipment and the disposable weights at his belt he had negative buoyancy. He looked up at the shimmering mirror that was the surface, broken by the black hull of the boat. Using his hands and feet he turned about his short axis until he was upright, saw the weighted line, pale-gleaming in the blueness. One tentative kick took him toward it. He grasped the rough-textured cord with one hand and hung there for a little while to get his bearings, to become acclimatized.

"Are you all right, Mr. Grimes?" It was Anderson, giving his famous imitation of a mother hen.

"Of course I'm all right, Chief."

The water was cool, but far from cold. And there was the exhilarating sensation of weightlessness. It was like being Outside in Free Fall but better, much better. There was the weightlessness but not the pressing loneliness, the dreadful emptiness. And the skin-tight suit was almost as good as nudity, but did not, as did space armour, induce the beginnings of claustrophobia.

Grimes looked down.

Yes, there was the wreck, her canopy gaping open like the shell of some monstrous bivalve. Grimes hoped that it was not too badly damaged by the ejection; if it were not so, the task of sealing the ruptured hull would be much easier. Up through the gaping opening drifted a school of gleaming, golden fish. And that was a good sign; it meant that nothing larger and dangerous, even to Man, had taken up residence.

He relaxed his grip on the cord, felt it slide through his hand as he dropped slowly. Then, raising a flurry of fine silt, his flippered feet were on the bottom. He was about three yards from the sunken dynosoar.

"Calling C.P.O. Anderson," he said into the built-in microphone. "Making preliminary inspection." He heard the acknowledgement.

Clumsily at first, he swam the short distance. For several minutes he checked the canopy. Yes, it could be forced back into place and, where too badly buckled, welded over. If necessary, lines could be sent down from the boat to lift the valves to an upright position before their closure. Satisfied, he swam aft, closely inspecting the fuselage as he did so. He could find no damage on the upper surface; the damaged skin must be on the underside, buried in the silt. An air hose to blow the muck clear? Yes, but would it be necessary? After all, when expelled from the hull by air under pressure the water would have to have somewhere to go to, somewhere to get out from, and whatever holes there were in the plating could have been designed for that very purpose.

"Chief!"

"Yes, Mr. Grimes?"

"Tell your men to have the welding gear and the compressor and hoses ready. Then come down yourself as soon as you can."

"Coming, sir."

Something made Grimes look up. The big C. P. O. was already on his way, failing like a stone, weighted by the gear that he was grasping in both of his huge hands. Behind him trailed two of the air hoses and another cable, the power line of the welding equipment. Using his flippered feet only he controlled his descent, made a remarkably graceful landing not far from where Grimes was standing.

"And what do you have in mind, Mr. Grimes?" he asked.

"Get the canopy shut and sealed, Chief. Might run an air hose in at that point. Then blow her out, and up she comes."

"Up she comes you hope, sir. Or she'll blow up, with the internal pressure. Explode, I mean."

"There are holes in the fuselage aft, the holes through which the water entered in the first place."

"Then we have to seal them, Mr. Grimes."

"That shouldn't be necessary, Chief. As far as I can see, they're on the bottom of the hull."

"Very good, sir. But what if she topples? If I were you, I'd seal those holes and fit 'em with non-return valves."

"You aren't me. And don't forget that the brute was designed to fly this way up. Surely she'll *float* this way up."

Stiffly, "I'm not qualified in aerodynamics, sir."

"But you are in hydrodynamics. All right, then. Do you think she'll topple once she starts to lift?"

Anderson, leaving the tool case and the weighted ends of the hoses with Grimes, swam slowly around the wreck. "No," he admitted when he returned. "She shouldn't topple." He stayed by the fore end of the dynosoar, stood in the silt and tried to lift one of the parts of the open canopy. It moved but with extreme reluctance. Grimes heard the man, a massive, black-glistening giant in his suit, grunt with effort.

"I thought of running lines down from the boat," he said.

"And pull the boat over, or under? No, sir. That wouldn't do at all."

No, thought Grimes. It wouldn't. Not if he hoped to get any shore leave on this planet.

"We'll have to cut the flaps and then weld them back into place."

"Now you're talking, sir. With your permission?" he asked, then paused.

"Of course. Carry on, Chief."

"Jones, Willoughby, Antonetti. Down here, on the double. Bring the cutting torches, a bundle of sheeting and that bundle of metal strip. Jump to it!"

"And a spear gun," added Grimes. "If we have one." He had a feeling that the knife at his belt would be inadequate. Helplessly, he looked at the huge, silvery torpedo shape that was approaching them, that was staring at them from glassy eyes as big as dinner plates.

Then, even through his helmet, he heard the muffled whirring of machinery and laughed. "Don't worry, Chief," he said. "Just remember what the Captain told us all and comport yourself like a gentleman. You're on camera."

◈ Chapter 13 ◈

AFTER A WHILE Grimes decided to leave the frogmen to it. It was obvious that Anderson and his team knew what they were doing. The Lieutenant had tried to lend a hand; he had realized quite soon that any attempt at supervision by himself would lead only to confusion, but the C. P. O. had made it quite plain, without actually saying so, that he was just being a bloody nuisance. So he said, in his best offhand manner, "Carry on, Chief. I'll take a dekko at this submarine camera of theirs. Let me know if you want me."

"That'll be the sunny Friday!" he heard somebody mutter. He could not identify the voice.

He put the busy scene—the flaring torches, the exploding bubbles of steam, the roiling clouds of disturbed silt—behind him, swam slowly toward the robot midget submarine. And was it, he wondered, called a watchfish? At first he thought that the thing was ignoring him; its two big eyes remained fixed on the salvage operations. And then he noticed that a small auxiliary lens mounted on a flexible stalk was following his every movement. He thumbed his nose at it, the rude gesture giving him a childish satisfaction.

Then he swam on lazily. He should, he realized, have brought a camera with him. One of Anderson's team had one, he knew; but he knew, too, that all the footage of film would be devoted to the raising of the dynosoar. Shots of the underwater life of this lake would have made an interesting addition to *Aries'* film library. More than a score of worlds must have contributed their share of fresh water fauna. There were graceful shapes, and shapes that were grotesque, and all of them brightly colored. Some were fish and some were arthropods and some—he mentally christened them "magic carpets"—defied classification. And there were plants, too, a veritable subaqueous jungle that he was approaching, bulbous trunks, each crowned with a coronal of spiky branches. If they *were* plants. Grimes decided that he didn't like the look of them, changed course and paddled toward a grove of less menacing appearance, long green ribbons stretching from the muddy bottom to just below the silvery surface. Among the strands and fronds flashing gold and scarlet, emerald and blue, darted schools of the smaller fishes. And there was something larger, much larger, pale and glimmering, making its slow way through the shimmering curtains of waving water weed. The Lieutenant's right hand went to the knife at his belt.

It, whatever it was, was big. And dangerous? It wasn't a fish. It had limbs and was using them for swimming. It undulated gracefully through the last concealing screen of vegetation, swam towards Grimes.

It was a woman.

It was, he saw without surprise (now that the initial surprise had passed) Marlene von Stolzberg.

He looked at her. She was wearing a scuba outfit not unlike his own, with the exception of the skintight suit. Her own golden skin was covering enough. And she was carrying what looked like a spear gun, although it was much stubbier than the weapons of that kind with which he was vaguely familiar.

He said, "Dr. Livingstone, I presume . . ."

He saw a frown darken her mobile features, clearly visible in the transparent helmet. From his own speaker came her voice, "That was neither original nor funny, Mr. Grimes." Then, as she saw his expression of astonishment, "It wasn't much trouble for us to find out what frequency you people are using."

"I suppose not. Your Highness."

"I hope, Mr. Grimes, that you don't mind my engaging in my usual activities. I promise to keep well clear of the salvage operations."

"It's your lake," he said. "And you don't seem to have any watchbirds with you this time."

"No," she agreed. "But . . ." She gestured with a slim arm. Grimes saw, then, that she was not alone, that she was attended by two things like miniature torpedoes. The analogy came into his mind, like a shark with pilot fish. But she was no shark, and pilot fish are mere scavengers.

They hung there in the water, silent for awhile. Grimes found that it was better for his peace of mind to concentrate his regard upon her face. She said at last, "Shouldn't you be looking after your men?"

"Frankly, Your Highness, they can manage better without me. Chief Petty Officer Anderson and his team are experts. I am not."

"You're not very expert in anything, Mr. Grimes, are you?" A grin rather than a smile robbed her words of maliciousness.

"I'm a fairish navigator and a better than average gunnery officer."

"I'll have to take your word for that. Well, Mr. Grimes, since the work seems to be going along very well without you, will you accompany me in a leisurely swim?"

"Cor stiffen the bleedin' crows, Chiefie," remarked an almost inaudible voice, "officers don't half have it good!"

"Watch your welding, Willoughby," came Anderson's reprimand. "That's all that *you're* good for."

There was a gusty sigh, and then, "Well, I suppose we can't *all* be fairish navigators and better than average gunnery officers . . ."

Grimes wished that he were wearing only a breathing mask and not a full helmet. The cool touch of water would have soothed his burning face. He heard the girl's light, tinkling laughter. But he knew that Anderson would deal with matters back at the wreck. And he knew, too, that the petty officer would never report to higher authority that Grimes had wandered away from the work in progress. What was it that he, Anderson, had said once? "You'll be a captain, and higher, while I'm still only a C. P. O. Why should I make enemies?" Then, when asked why he, himself, did not put in for a commission, he had replied, "I like things the way they are.

I enjoy reasonable standards of comfort and authority without responsibility. A junior officer has responsibility without authority."

The Princess Marlene was swimming away now, slowly. She paused, made a beckoning gesture. Should he follow? Yes. To hell with it, he would. He said, "Chief Petty Officer Anderson."

"Sir?"

"One of the . . . er . . . local ladies has offered to take me on an inspection of the lake bottom. It could be useful. Let me know when you want me."

"Very good, sir."

As Grimes followed the girl it was not the lake bottom that he was inspecting.

He caught up with her. One of the silvery miniature torpedoes dashed toward him threateningly, then suddenly (in response to a telepathic command?) sheered away. He said, "You have vicious pets, Your Highness."

"Not vicious, Mr. Grimes. Just faithful."

"That's an odd word to use about machines."

"These, like our watchbirds, are more than mere machines. They have organic brains. These pilot fish of mine, for example, are essentially the small but highly intelligent cetaceans of Algol III with mechanical bodies." She must have read his expression. "Come, come, Lieutenant. There's no need to look so shocked. This is no worse than the dog's brains used by your Psionic Radio Officers as amplifiers. Not so bad, in fact. Our watchbirds and watchdogs and pilot fish have freedom to move about in bodies which, in fact, are rather superior to their original ones."

"It's . . . it's not the same."

She laughed scornfully. "That's what I've been telling you, my good man. One of your poodle's brains in aspic would sell its soul for the motility enjoyed by our guardians."

"Is that what you call them?"

"That is the general term. Yes."

"And their prime function is to protect their owners?"

"Their only function. Yes."

"So if I . . . tried to attack you?"

"It would be the last thing you ever did, Mr. Grimes."

He laughed grimly. "I don't think I'll try it out, Your Highness."

"You'd better not. But would you like a demonstration?"

"Not on me."

She stopped, holding herself stationary in the water with gentle movements of her long, graceful limbs. She pointed with the hand holding the gun. "Look! Do you see the rock ogre?"

"The *what*? I see something that looks like a slime-covered rock."

"That's it. Perhaps the only really dangerous denizen of these waters. Native to Australis. Excellent eating, properly prepared. That's why we introduced it."

"It looks innocent enough."

"But it's not. Keep well back and watch closely."

She swam toward the thing. Then, with explosive suddenness, three triangular flaps sprang back on the top of the rough shell and, uncoiling with lightning rapidity, a thick stalk shot out straight at the girl, a glistening limb tipped with a complexity of writhing tentacles and gnashing mandibles. Grimes cried out in horror and pulled his useless knife, but he was not fast enough, could never have been fast enough.

The pilot fish were there before him, flashing past him at a speed that, even under the water, produced a distinct whine. One of them dived into the orifice from which the stalk had been extruded, the other attacked the ogre's head. It was over almost as soon as it had been begun. Mere flesh and blood, from whatever world, could not withstand the concerted onslaught of the little, armoured monsters. Only seconds had elapsed, and the girl was hanging there in the water, laughing, while the pilot fish frisked around her like dogs demanding an approbatory pat. An unpleasant, brownish mist was seeping up from the base of the stalk and from the debris of torn and severed tentacles, still feebly twitching, and broken mandibles at the head of it.

Grimes was sickened. It was not by the death of a dangerous (and, he had been told) edible creature, life owes its continuance to the destruction of life. It was by the genuine pleasure and amusement in the girl's high, clear laughter. But blood sports, he told himself dourly, have always been the favorite recreation of the so-called aristocracy.

He said, "I must be getting back to work. Your Highness."

He started off in what he thought was the right direction, but the water was heavily befogged by the ichor from the dying rock ogre. He did not see the other rock, the shell, rather, until he was almost on top of it. He screamed and made a frantic effort to avoid the terrifying head that shot out at him. He felt a sharp pain in his side as something grazed his body, heard a dull *thunk* followed by another. The rock ogre seemed to go mad, writhing violently. The thick stalk caught Grimes a flailing blow in the belly, knocking him well clear. He caught a glimpse, vivid, unforgettable, of Marlene, an underwater Artemis, with her gun raised for another shot.

And then the pilot fish swept in to finish the job.

Chapter 14

HE SPRAWLED on the muddy bottom, his hand pressed to the rent in his suit, the rent in his skin. He could feel the warmth of blood. He did not know how badly he was injured, but, at this moment, the imminence of suffocation was of far greater importance than loss of blood. He feared that the pipes from his liquid air tanks to his helmet had been buckled or severed and then, agonisingly, he was able to breathe again. It was the blow to the stomach that had knocked all the air out of his lungs.

She was hanging in the murky water looking at him, her stubby weapon pointing directly at him. A woman with a gun can be a frightening sight; a naked woman with a gun is always clothed in deadly menace.

Grimes whispered hoarsely, "Put that down!"

At first he thought that she had not heard him, then, slowly, she let her hand fall until the muzzle, from which protruded the lethal head of a new dart, was directed downward.

She muttered, "I'm sorry . . ."

Grimes tried to laugh. "What for? You saved my life."

"Yes." There was an odd note of astonishment in her voice. "Yes. I did, didn't I?" She made a swimming motion toward him. "Are you hurt?"

"I don't know how badly. That brute kicked like a mule. And one of your bolts grazed me. At least, I think it was only a graze."

188

"Mr. Grimes, sir," came Anderson's voice. "Mr. Grimes, what's been happening? Shall I send help?"

"Just a slight tussle with the local fauna, Chief. I got a little beaten up, but nothing serious. I'm on my back to the wreck now."

"If I were you, sir, I'd surface and get back into the boat. I'll send Jones up to you. He's qualified in First Aid."

"Better do as the man says," advised the Princess. "I'll see you to your boat. Can you move?"

Grimes worked his arms and legs experimentally. "Yes. Nothing seems to be broken."

He detached the weights from his belt, let his buoyancy carry him upward. The girl floated alongside him. He could not help looking at her. She was beautiful in her nudity, and the few black trappings that she wore accentuated the golden luminosity of her skin. She was beautiful, but he shuddered as he remembered how she had appeared in her moment of bloodthirsty triumph, and how she had stared at him over her aimed weapon.

The silver mirror shattered into a myriad of glittering shards, and then Grimes' head was above the surface. He could not see the boat at first, turned slowly and clumsily in the water until she came into view. She was a long way off. He was, he knew, in no danger of drowning but doubted if he could swim that far in his weakened condition. And he did not know how much blood he was losing, or how fast.

She said softly, "Relax, Mr. Grimes. Let me see . . ."

He felt her alongside him, was conscious of her gently probing fingers, was aware that she had widened and lengthened the tear in his suit.

"Men are such babies," she remarked. "The skin's hardly broken."

He said stiffly, "I hope that your darts aren't poisoned."

"Of course not. And now, just follow me."

He followed her, thinking that it was the first time in his life that he had followed a girl, a naked girl at that, without a sense of pulse quickening anticipation.

〜〜〜〜

He sat there glumly in the boat, dabbing the graze just below the ribs on his right side with antiseptic-soaked cotton wool. The Princess Marlene had helped him to mount the short ladder and then had left him, swimming away toward the further shore, a graceful, golden shape around which sported the two silver pilot fish. His self-administered first aid was interrupted by the man Jones, stocky, competent, revoltingly cheerful, who, as soon as he had clambered inboard, removed his helmet and tanks and then performed a like service for Grimes.

"Now, let's have a look at that, sir. Something bite you? Only a scratch, though. All the same, you'd better have an antibiotic shot. We don't know what microorganisms are in the water, do we? And perhaps whatever it was that attacked you didn't brush his or her teeth this morning. Ha, ha!"

"Ha, ha," echoed Grimes.

"No need to take your suit off for the shot, sir. I'll just pump it in where the fabric's already been torn away." He went to the first aid box and produced a syrette. "Now, sir, just stretch a little . . . Fine. Didn't feel a thing, sir, did you?"

"No," admitted Grimes.

"Then if you're all right, sir, I'll get aft and start the compressor." He reached across the Lieutenant and picked up the microphone. "Jones here, Chiefie. I've seen to Mr. Grimes; he's all right. O. K. to start pumping the air into her?"

"O. K.," came Anderson's voice. "She's all sealed and I think she'll hold. But stand by to stop the compressor at once if I give the word."

"Will do, Chiefie."

Jones left the seat by Grimes' side, made his way toward the stern. After a second or so came the steady throb of the machine; Grimes, looking overside, saw one of the heavy plastic hoses jerking rhythmically, as though alive. It reminded him unpleasantly of a rock ogre's trunk.

"She's holding," announced the Chief Petty Officer. Then, "Mr. Grimes, can I have a word with you, sir?"

"Yes, Chief?" replied Grimes into the microphone.

"She's holding all right. And, as you said, those holes aft are just made to order for blowing the water out of . . . I think she's starting to lift . . . Yes. May I suggest, sir, that you and Jones take in the hose as she comes up, in case she topples . . . Oh, yes, and tell Jones to stop the air pump. Now."

The compressor stopped. Grimes joined the rating where the hoses ran overside, helped him to bring the one that had been used inboard. It was heavy work, and soon both men were sweating uncomfortably under their skintight suits. Then Jones shouted, "There she blows!"

Yes, thought Grimes, she did look something like a whale as she broke surface, although she wasn't blowing. And then, around her, bobbed up the heads of Anderson and his men in their spherical helmets. The Lieutenant saw the petty officer's mouth moving; it seemed odd that his voice should be coming from the speaker in the boat. "Jones! Throw us a line, will you?"

Jones picked up a coil of light nylon cord, with a padded weight spliced to the end, heaved it expertly— and even more expertly Anderson raised a hand to catch it. What followed was a pleasure to watch, was seamanship rather than spacemanship. A heavier line was passed, made fast to a ringbolt that had been welded to the dynosoar's nose, the other end of it taken by Jones to the towing bitts that had been installed at the boat's stern. And then, one by one, the Chief Petty Officer last of all, the salvage crew clambered back on board, stripping off their helmets and flippers, hauling to the surface their tools and other equipment. The competent Anderson insisted on checking every item before he was satisfied. Not until then did he lower his big frame into the seat beside Grimes.

"If I were you, sir, I'd tow her in and beach her by the spaceport."

"I'll do just that, Chief."

"Feel up to handling the boat yourself, sir?"

"Of course. It was only a scratch I got, and a few bruises."

"Right you are, then, Mr. Grimes."

Grimes started up the inertial drive, lifted the boat about a foot clear of the water. He turned her, slowly and carefully, avoiding the imposition of any sudden strain on the towline. He headed for the spaceport beacon inshore from the beach. He realized that he was scanning the water for any sign of the Princess Marlene. But either she had left the lake and gone home—wherever home was—or was still disporting herself in its depths. But she could look after herself, he thought grimly. She could look after herself very well indeed, she and her murderous pilot fish.

He heard Anderson mutter something uncomplimentary and concentrated on his steering; the boat, with that sluggish weight pulling her stern down, was behaving rather oddly. But he got the hang of it and beached the re-entry vehicle without incident.

He sat with Anderson in the boat while the men busied themselves about the stranded dynosoar.

"If I'd been you, sir," said the Chief Petty Officer, "do you know what I'd have done?"

About *what?* wondered Grimes. About the salvage? About the rock ogres? About Her Highness the Princess Marlene von Stolzberg?

"What would you have done?" he snapped.

"I'd have had the engineers waterproof an I. D. unit, complete with power cells, taken it down to the dynosoar, started it up—and Bob's your uncle!"

"He may be yours, Chief. But he's obviously not mine."

"But the way it was was all right, Mr. Grimes. It gave my boys some very useful training."

"Join the Interstellar Survey Service and see the bottom of the sea."

"I must remember that, sir. And that's the way that I wish it always was. But . . . Do you mind if I talk to you man to man, for a little?"

"Do just that."

"I know Captain Daintree. Well. He was an Ensign when I was a rating fourth class, before I started specializing. We've sailed together many a time."

"Go on."

"I won't talk. And the men won't talk. If they did, they'd know that all the Odd Gods of the Galaxy wouldn't be able to save 'em. From me. You officers think that you have power, but"—he slowly opened and then clenched a huge hand—"this is where the real power lies, in any Navy."

"Go on."

"Your report, sir. May I suggest that you tore your suit on a piece of jagged wreckage?"

"But why, Chief?"

"You were supposed to be in charge of the job, Mr. Grimes. The Captain won't like it if he hears that you went off with a girl." Anderson blushed incongruously. "A *naked* girl, at that."

"You've got a dirty mind, Chief."

"*I* haven't," said Anderson virtuously. "But the Old Man, I beg your pardon, sir, the Captain, and some of the other officers mightn't be so broadminded as me . . ."

Grimes chuckled.

"It's not funny, sir."

"Perhaps not. But your double entendre was."

"Yes, it was," admitted the C. P. O. complacently. "I must remember *that,* too . . . But what I'm getting at is that you should edit, or censor, your report on the operations rather carefully. The torn suit, for example, and the jagged projection . . ."

"Thank you, Chief. But no. I can't do it."

"If you knew the bloody liars that I've known that are Admirals now!"

"But they, Chief, didn't have a robot midget submarine sniffing around and recording everything. I've no doubt that whoever sent it will be willing to run the film for Captain Daintree. I'm afraid I have to tell the truth."

Anderson did not look happy. Grimes could imagine what was running through his mind. The petty officer, he knew, was concerned about him, but he would not be human if he were not also concerned about himself. Grimes could almost hear Daintree's voice. "And what were you thinking of, Chief Petty Officer Anderson, to allow a young, inexperienced officer to wander off alone in waters in which all sorts of dangerous creatures might have been—were, in fact—lurking? Not alone, you say? Even worse, then. In the company of a young lady who has already demonstrated her criminal irresponsibility."

"Yes," said Grimes. "I can edit my report."

"But this submarine camera you mentioned, sir . . ."

"We'd started work on the salvage, Chief, and then Her Highness came along and told me about the dangers on the lake bottom, such as the rock ogres. I thought that I'd better see one for myself so that I'd be able to identify them. Not only did she show me one but also persuaded it to give a demonstration of its capabilities. The demonstration was almost too effective . . ."

"Yes, Mr. Grimes. That should do, very nicely." He grinned. "You'll make Admiral yet."

"I hope so," said Grimes.

⇜ Chapter 15 ⇝

SHE CAME to pick up Grimes the following afternoon, her blue and scarlet air car bringing itself down to a perfect landing hard by the main ramp of *Aries*. Daintree, rather to the Lieutenant's surprise, had granted him shore leave, but, at the same time, had made it quite clear that he was doing so only because Grimes had somehow—"and only the Odd Gods of the Galaxy know how!" swore the Captain—contrived to make powerful friends on this strange world. So Grimes, clad in the regulation go-ashore rig that was almost a uniform—slate gray shirt with the golden S embroidered on the breast, matching shorts and stockings, highly polished black shoes—marched down the gangway, a grip in either hand, In the bags, in addition to has toilet gear, he had packed changes of clothing, of some of which Daintree would not have approved. Too, he should have obtained official permission to take from the ship the deadly little Minetti automatic pistol which, together with spare clips of ammunition, was concealed among his shirts. Over his right shoulder was slung a camera, over his left shoulder a tape recorder. "The complete bloody tourist!" Lieutenant Commander Cooper had remarked when he encountered Grimes in the airlock.

But Grimes did not mind. He had decided a long time ago that, much as he liked ships, he did not like big ships. It would be good to get away from *Aries* for a few days or even, with luck, longer. It would be good to eat something better than the mediocre fare

195

served up in the officers' mess. It would be good to be able to wear clothing not prescribed by regulations.

The door of the air car, a fragile-seeming, beautifully designed machine, a gay, mechanical dragonfly, adorned with nonfunctional fripperies, opened as Grimes approached it. The Princess Marlene raised a hand in casual greeting. She was dressed today in a flimsy green tunic, the hem of which came barely to mid-thigh. On her slender feet were rather ornate golden sandals. Her hair was pulled back to a casual (seemingly casual) pony tail. She smiled, said, "Hi!"

"Your Highness," replied Grimes formally.

"Throw your gear in the back, then get in beside me."

"Will your watchbirds mind, Your Highness?" asked Grimes, looking up, rather apprehensively, to the two circling guardian angels.

"Not to worry, Mr. Grimes. They've been told that you're a member of the family, acting, temporary . . ."

"Unpaid?"

She smiled again. "That all depends, doesn't it? But jump in."

Grimes didn't jump in. This contraption seemed of very light construction compared to the ugly, mechanized beetles to which he was accustomed. He got in, watching carefully where he put his feet. He lowered himself cautiously into the cushioned seat. The door slid shut.

"Home," ordered Marlene.

There was a murmur of machinery and the thing lifted, took a wide sweep around the ship, then headed in a direction away from the distant city.

"And now," said the girl, "what do they call you?"

"What do you mean, Your Highness?"

"To begin with, Lieutenant, you can drop the title, as long as you're my guest. And I want to be able to drop yours." In spite of the friendliness of her voice and manner, the "for what it's worth" was implied, although not spoken. "I don't know what planet you were born and dragged up on, but you must have some other name besides Grimes."

"John, Your . . ."

"You may call me Marlene, John. But don't go getting ideas."

I've already got them, thought Grimes. *I got them a long time ago. But I have no desire to be the guest of honor at a lynching party.*

"Cat got your tongue, John?"

"No. I was . . . er . . . thinking."

"Then don't. Too much of it is bad for you. Just relax. You're away from your bloody ship, and all the stiffness and starchiness that are inevitable when the common herd puts on gold braid and brass buttons."

You snobbish bitch! thought Grimes angrily.

"Sorry," she said casually. "But you have to remember that we, on El Dorado, regard ourselves as rather special people."

"That reminds me," said Grimes, "of two famous Twentieth Century writers. Hemingway and Scott Fitzgerald. Fitzgerald said to Hemingway, quite seriously, 'The rich are different from us.' Hemingway replied, 'Yes. They have more money.'"

"So you read, John. You actually read. A spacefaring intellectual. I didn't know that there were any such."

"There are quite a few of us, Marlene. But microfilmed editions aren't the same as *real* books."

"You'll find plenty of real books on this world. Every home has its library."

"You've room here, on this world."

"There's room on every planet but Earth for people to live as they should. But your average colonist, what does he do? He builds cities and huddles in almost exact replicas of Terran slums."

"You aren't average?"

"Too bloody right we're not. And we were determined when we purchased El Dorado that overpopulation would never become one of our problems. But . . ."

"But?"

"But once people start dying, that will be the start of the reverse process . . ." Then a laugh dispelled her somber expression. "However did we get started on this morbid subject? And what sort of hostess am I?" Her voice suddenly became that of the guide of a conducted tour. "Slightly ahead, and to our right, you will see the

Croesus Mines. They constitute the only fully automated mining operation in the Galaxy . . ."

Grimes looked. There was nothing to indicate the nature of the industrial process. There were no roads, no railways, no towering chimneys, no ugly pithead gear. There was only a low, spotlessly white building in a shallow green valley.

"Everything," the girl went on, "is subterranean, including the rail communication with our few factories and with the spaceport. We do not believe in ruining the scenery of our planet while there is ample space underground for industry. Now, coming up on our left, we see the Laredo Ranch. It is not as fully automated as it might be, but you must understand that Senator Crocker, the owner, enjoys the open air life. It irks him, he says, that he must use robot cowboys for his roundups; but that, on this world, is unavoidable . . ."

Grimes, looking out and down, saw a solitary horseman riding toward a herd of red-brown cattle. Crocker, he supposed, making do without his despised mechanical aides.

"Count Vitelli's vineyard. His wines are not bad, although they are only a hobby with him. There is some local consumption and considerable export. Most of *us,* of course, prefer imported vintages."

"You would," said Grimes sharply.

She looked at him in a rather hostile manner, then grinned. "And you, John, would say just that. But this is *our* world. We like it, and we can afford it."

"Money doesn't always bring happiness, Marlene."

"Perhaps not. But we can be miserable in comfort."

"Luxury, you mean."

"All right, luxury. And why the hell not?"

To this there was no answer. Grimes stared ahead, saw on a hilltop a grim, gray castle that was straight out of a book of Teutonic mythology. "Your *Schloss?*" he asked.

"My *what?*" She laughed. "Your pronunciation, my dear. You'd better stick to English. Yes, that is Castle Stolzberg, and in the forests around it I hunt the stag and the boar."

"Is that all you do?"

"Of course not. As you know very well I am fond of aquatic

sports. And I am serving my term on the Committee of Management."

"And who lives there with you?"

"Nobody. I entertain sometimes, but at the moment I have no guests. With the exception, of course, of yourself."

"And you mean to tell me that that huge building is for one person?"

"Isn't it time that you started to lose your petty-bourgeois ideas, John? I warn you, if you start spouting Thorsten Veblen at me on the subject of conspicuous waste I shall lose my temper. And as for Marxism, there just isn't any exploited proletariat on El Dorado, with the exception of the lower deck ratings aboard *your* ship."

"They aren't exploited. Anyhow, what about the people on the other worlds who've contributed to your fantastically high standard of living?"

"They were happy enough to buy us out, and they're happy enough to buy our exports. And, anyhow, you're a spaceman, not a politician or an economist. Just relax, can't you? Just try to be good company while you're my guest, otherwise I'll return you to your transistorized sardine can."

"I'll try," said Grimes. "When in Rome, and all the rest of it. I shall endeavor to be the noblest Roman of them all."

"That's better," she told him.

Slowly, smoothly, the air car drifted down to a landing in the central courtyard, dropping past flagpoles from which snapped and fluttered heavy standards, past turrets and battlemented walls, down to the gray, rough flagstones. From somewhere came the baying of hounds. Then, as the doors slid open, there was a high, clear trumpet call, a flourish of drums.

"Welcome to Schloss Stolzberg," said the girl gravely.

∾ Chapter 16 ∾

"WELCOME TO SCHLOSS STOLZBERG," she said, and suddenly, for no immediately apparent reason, Grimes remembered another girl (and where was she now?) who had told him, "This is Liberty Hall. You can spit on the mat and call the cat a bastard." He could not imagine the Princess Marlene using that expression, no matter how friendly she became. And Castle Stolzberg did not look, could never look like Liberty Hall. If there were no dungeons under the grim (or Grimm, he mentally punned) pile, there should have been.

He got out of his seat, stepped to the ground, then helped the girl down. Her hand was pleasantly warm and smooth in his. She thanked him politely and then turned her head to the car, saying, "We shan't be needing you again. You can put yourself to bed."

A gentle *toot* from somewhere in the vehicle's interior replied, and it lifted smoothly, flew toward a doorway that had suddenly and silently opened in the rough stone wall.

"My bags . . ." said Grimes.

"They will be taken to your room, John. Surely, by this time, you have come to learn how efficient our servitors are."

"Efficient, yes. But they've given *me* enough trouble, Marlene."

"They were doing the jobs for which they were designed. But come."

She put her hand in the crook of his left arm, guided him to a tall, arched doorway. The valves were of some dark timber, iron

200

studded, and as they moved on their ponderous hinges they creaked loudly. Grimes permitted himself a smile. So the robots who ran this place weren't so efficient after all. Even a first trip deck boy would have known enough to use an oil can without being told.

Marlene read his expression and smiled in reply, a little maliciously. "The doors *should* creak," she said. "If they didn't, it would spoil the decor."

"Talking of noises . . . Those rowdy dogs we heard when we landed . . . Also part of the decor, I suppose. And was all that baying a recording?"

"Part of the decor, yes. As for the rest, real hounds in real kennels, I told you that hunting was one of my amusements."

"And where do you keep the vampire bats?"

"You improve with acquaintance, John. But this is not Transylvania."

They were in the main hall now, a huge barn of a place, thought Grimes. But he corrected himself. A barn, when empty, can be a little cheerless; when full its atmosphere is one of utilitarian warmth. This great room was cheerless enough, but far from empty. Only a little daylight stabbed through the high, narrow windows, and the flaring torches and the fire that blazed in the enormous fireplace did little more than cast a multiplicity of confused, flickering shadows. Ranged along the walls were what, at first glance, looked like armoured men standing to rigid attention. But it was not space armour; these suits, if they were genuine (and Grimes felt that they were), had been worn by men of Earth's Middle Ages. By men? By knights and barons and princes, rather; in those days the commonality had gone into battle with only thick leather (if that) as a partial protection. And then had come those equalizers—long bow and crossbow and the first, cumbersome firearms. Grimes wondered if any of this armour had been worn by Marlene's ancestors, and what they would think if they could watch their daughter being squired by a man who, in their day, would have been a humble tiller of the fields or, in battle, a fumbling pikeman fit only to be ridden down by a charge of iron-clad so-called chivalry. *Grimes, you're an inverted snob,* he told himself. He shivered involuntarily as he thought that he saw one of the dark figures move. But it was only the shifting fire and torchlight reflected from dull-gleaming panoply and broadsword. But he looked away from it, nonetheless, to the antique weapons high on the walls, then to the dull, heavy folds of the ancient standards that sagged heavily from their shafts.

He said, "A homey little place you have here."

It was, of course, the wrong thing. Marlene did not think the remark at all funny. She said icily, "Please keep your petty bourgeois witticisms for your ship."

"I'm sorry."

She thawed slightly. "I suppose that the castle *is* home, but never forget that it is history. These stones were shipped from Earth, every one of them."

"I thought that you came from Thuringia."

"Yes, I did. But we're all Terrans, after all, if you go back far enough. And that's not very far."

"I suppose not."

She led him across the hall, past a long, heavy banqueting table with rows of high-backed chairs on either side. She took a seat at the head of it, occupied it as though it were the throne it looked like. In her scanty, flimsy attire she should have struck a note of utter incongruity, but she did not. She was part of the castle, and the castle was part of her. Like some wicked, beautiful queen out of ancient legend she seemed, or like some wicked, beautiful witch. The pale skin of her bare limbs was luminous in the semi-darkness, and her body, scarcely veiled by the diaphanous material of her dress, only slightly less so.

She motioned Grimes to the chair at her right hand. He was amazed to find that it was extremely comfortable, although the wood, at first, was cold on the backs of his legs. He wondered what subtle modifications had been made to the archaic furniture, and at what expense. But he hadn't had to pay the bill. He saw that a decanter of heavy glass had been set out on the table, and with it two glittering, cut crystal goblets. Marlene poured the dark ruby wine with an oddly ceremonial gesture.

She said matter-of-factly, "Angel's blood, from Deneb VII. I hope you like it."

"I've never tried it before." *(And that's not surprising,* he thought, *at the price they charge for it, even on its world of origin.)* "But does it . . . er . . . match the decor?"

Surprisingly she smiled. "Of course, John. In the old days, when the prince and his knights feasted here, there were delicacies from all over the then known world on this table . . ."

Salt beef and beer, thought Grimes dourly, remembering his Terran history.

"To . . ." she started, raising her glass. "To . . . to your stay on this world."

She sipped slowly and Grimes followed suit. The wine was good, although a little too sweet for his taste. It was good but not good enough to warrant a price of forty credits a bottle, Duty Free and with no freight charges.

Away from the gloomy main hall, the rest of the castle was a surprise. Spiral staircases that had been converted into escalators—rather a specialty of El Doradan architectural engineering—spacious apartments, light, color, luxury, all in the best of taste, all in the best of the tastes of at least five score of worlds. At last Marlene showed Grimes into the suite that was to be his. It was a masculine apartment, with no frills or flounces anywhere, almost severe in its furnishings but solidly comfortable. There was a bar, and a playmaster with well-stocked racks of spools and a long shelf with books, real books. Grimes went to it, took from its place one of a complete set of Ian Fleming's novels, handled it reverently. It was old, but dust jacket, cover, binding and pages had been treated with some preservative.

"Not a First Edition," the girl told him, "but, even so, quite authentic Twentieth Century."

"These must be worth a small fortune."

"What's money for if not to buy the things you like?"

There was no answer to that, or no answer that would not lead to a fruitless and annoying argument.

She said, "Make yourself at home. I have a few things to attend to before I change for dinner. We dine, by the way, at twenty hundred hours. In the banqueting hall."

"Where we had the wine?"

"Where else?" She paused in the doorway that had opened for her. "Dress, of course."

Of course, thought Grimes. He decided that in these surroundings his uniform mess dress would be the most suitable. He looked for his bags so that he could unpack. He could not find them anywhere. A disembodied voice said, "Lord, you will find your clothing in the wardrobe in your bedroom."

His clothing was there, hung neatly on hangers, folded away in drawers. But of the Minetti pistol and its ammunition there was no sign.

"Damn it!" he swore aloud, "where the hell's my gun?"

"It will be returned to you, Lord, when you leave the castle. Should Her Highness wish you to accompany her on a boar hunt, a *suitable* weapon will be provided."

Suitable? A Minetti, used intelligently, could kill almost any known life form.

"I'd like my own weapon back," snapped Grimes.

"For centuries, Lord, it has been the rule of this castle that guests surrender their weapons when accepting its hospitality. We are programmed to maintain the old traditions."

"It's a good story," said Grimes. "Stick to it."

In an atmosphere of mutually sulky silence he went to the bar and poured himself a Scotch on the rocks, without too many rocks.

∾ Chapter 17 ∾

SLOWLY, savoring its expensive aroma and smoothness, Grimes finished his Scotch. He poured himself a second glass, being more generous this time with the ice. He let it stand on the glass top of the bar, prowled through the apartment. He considered leaving it to explore the castle, but decided that this would be one sure and certain way of incurring the Princess Marlene's hostility. He found a window that had been concealed by heavy drapes, stared out through it. His quarters were high in the building, must be just under the battlemented roof, but as the casement could not be opened he was not able to stick his head out to confirm this. For long minutes he looked out at the scene—the wooded hills, the green valleys, the silvery streams, over which poured the golden light of the afternoon sun. Earth born and bred as he was, he found himself pining for the sight of another human habitation, of a road with vehicles in motion, of a gleaming airliner in the empty sky.

He returned to the sitting room, examined the catalogue of playmaster spools that stood by the machine. It was comprehensive, fantastically so, putting to shame the collection of taped entertainment available in *Aries'* wardroom, or in any of her recreation rooms. There were the very latest plays and operas, and there were recordings of films that dated back to the dawn of cinematography. There was too much to choose from. Fleming, perhaps? A screened version of one of the 007 novels? Grimes had read them all during his course in English Literature at the Academy and, although his tastes had been considered somewhat odd by his fellow students, had enjoyed them. A title in the catalogue, CASINO ROYALE, caught his eye. He pressed the right sequence of buttons.

The playmaster hummed gently and its wide screen came to glowing life. Grimes stared at the procession of gaudy credits, then at the initial scene depicting the meeting of the two agents in the *pissoir*. Surely this was not James Bond as he had been described by the master storyteller, as he had been imagined by his reader. And then, a little later, there was Sir James Bond, dignified in his mansion with its lion-infested grounds. Grimes gave up, settled down to enjoy himself.

Suddenly, annoyingly, the screen went blank. It was just as Mata Bond had been snatched by the scarlet-uniformed Horse Guardsman, who had galloped with her up the ramp of an odd-looking spacecraft. Grimes got up from his chair to investigate. As he did so, that smug mechanical voice remarked, "Lord, I regret that there is no time for you to witness the end of this entertainment. If you are to perform your ablutions and attire yourself fittingly before escorting Her Highness to dinner, you must commence immediately."

Grimes sighed. After all, he had not become the Princess's guest to spend all his time watching films, no matter how fascinating. He went through to the bedroom, shed his clothing, and then into the bathroom. It operated on the same principle as the one in the space-port's accommodation for transients. When he came out, he found that somebody (something?) had removed the clothes that he had intended to wear from the wardrobe, disposed them neatly on the bed. He resented it rather; why should some complication of printed circuits or whatever take it upon itself to decide that he, a man, would be correctly attired for the occasion only in gold braid, brass buttons and all the trimmings?

He shrugged, thought, *Better play along*. He got into his underwear, his stiff white shirt, his long, black, sharply creased trousers with the thin gold stripe along the outer seams. He carefully knotted the bow tie, wondering who, with the exception of officers in the various services, ever wore this archaic neckwear. The made-up variety lasted far longer and looked just as good, if not better. He put on his light, glistening black shoes. He got into his white waistcoat, with its tiny gilt buttons, and finally into the "bum-freezer" jacket, on the breast of which were three miniature medals. Two of them were for good attendance, the third one really meant something. ("It will be either a medal or a court martial," the Admiral had told him. "The medal is less trouble all round.")

There was a knock at the outer door of the apartment. "Come in!" he called. He was expecting the Princess; surely the mechanical servitors, whatever they looked like (he had imagined something multi-appendaged, like an oversized tin spider) would not knock. The door opened and a man entered. No, not a man. Humanoid, but nonhuman, nonorganic. No attempt had been made to disguise the dull sheen of metal that was obvious on the face and hands. He (it?) was attired in a livery even more archaic than Grimes' uniform: white stockings and knee breeches over silver-buckled shoes, a black, silver-buttoned claw-hammer coat, a froth of white lace at the throat. An elaborately curled white wig completed the ensemble. The face was as handsome as that of a marble statue, and as lifeless. The eyes were little glass beads set in pewter. Nonetheless, the gray lips moved. "Lord, Her Highness awaits you."

"Lead on, MacDuff."

"My name, Lord, is not MacDuff. It is Karl. Furthermore, Lord, the correct quotation is, 'Lay on, MacDuff.'"

"Lead on, anyhow."

"Very well, Lord. Please to follow."

It was like a maze, the interior of the castle. Finally the robot conducted Grimes along a gallery, the walls of which were covered with portraits of long dead and gone von Stolzbergs. Men in armour, men in uniform, they glowered at the spaceman; and those toward the end, those with the Crooked Cross among their insignia, seemed to stir and shift menacingly in their ornate frames. Grimes suddenly remembered his Jewish grandmother and could just imagine that proud old lady staring fiercely and contemptuously back at these arrogant murderers. And there were the von Stolzberg ladies. He didn't mind looking at them, and he had the feeling that they didn't mind looking at him. Although the earlier ones tended to plumpness, many of them had something of the Princess Marlene in their appearance, or she had something of them in hers.

A door at the end of the corridor silently opened. Karl stood to one side, bowing. Grimes went through.

The room beyond it was brightly lit, opulent, but in its furnishings there were glaring incongruities. Weapons, however beautifully designed and finished, look out of place on the satin-covered walls of a lady's *salon*. But they caught Grimes' attention. As a gunnery specialist he could not help looking at the firearms: the heavy projectile rifles, the lighter but possibly deadlier laser guns, the peculiar bell-mouthed weapons that, in a bad light, would have been antique blunderbusses but which, obviously, were not.

"I like to have my toys around me, John," said the Princess.

"Oh, yes. Of course." Grimes felt his ears burn. He turned to face her. "I . . . I must apologize, Marlene. My . . . er . . . professional interest was rather ill-mannered."

"It was, but understandable. Although not many people can appreciate the aesthetic qualities of well-made weaponry." She added, "I'm glad that you can, John."

"Thank you."

"Sit down, unless you would rather stand."

He sat down, looking at his hostess as he did so. She was different, far different, from the naked water nymph of his first acquaintance, but still the heavy folds of her brocaded, long-sleeved, high-necked gown could not quite conceal the fluid beauty of the limbs and body beneath the golden glowing fabric. Her pale hair, platinum rather than gold in this light, was piled high on her head, and in it rather than on it was a bejewelled coronet. Yes, those weapons were beautiful, but she, too, was beautiful.

And in the same way?

"Some sherry, John?"

Her slender hand went to the slim decanter that stood on the lustrous surface of the low table between them, removed the stopper. She poured the pale wine into two glittering, fragile glasses. She raised hers, smiled, inclined her head slightly. It was more of a formal bow than a mere nod.

Grimes did his best to follow suit. They both sipped.

"An excellent Tio Pepe," he commented gravely. She need never know that it was the only wine that he could identify easily.

"Yes," she agreed. "But why put up with second best when you can import the best?"

And was there some hidden meaning in this seemingly innocent remark? But she, of all people, would never admit that any inhabitant of El Dorado was inferior to any offworlder.

"Will you take a second glass with me, John?"

"I shall be pleased to, Marlene."

Again they drank, slowly, gravely. And then, when they were finished, she extended a long, elegant arm toward him. There was an uncomfortable lag until he realized the implication of the gesture. His ears (inevitably) reddening, he got hastily (but not, he congratulated himself too hastily) to his feet, assisted her from her deep chair. Saying nothing, moving with slow grace, she contrived to take charge of the situation. Grimes found himself advancing with her toward the door, her right hand resting in the crook of his left arm. Grimes was sorry that there was not a full-length mirror in which he could see his companion and himself. The doorway gaped open as they approached it. There stood the robot Karl, bowing deeply. There stood four other humanoid robots, in uniform rather than in livery, attired as foot soldiers from some period of Earth's barbaric past. Each of them held aloft a flaring torch. All the other lights in the long corridor had been extinguished.

Slowly, in time to a distant drumbeat, they marched along the gallery—Karl, then two of the torch-bearers, then Grimes and the Princess, then the remaining pair of robots. Past the portraits they marched, past the men in the uniform of the Thuringian Navy (a service that had been disbanded after Federation), past the men in the uniforms of the armed and punitive forces of the Third Reich, past the commanders of mercenaries and the robber barons. There was a sense of uneasy menace. How much of the personality of the sitter survived in the painted likeness? There was a sense of uneasy menace, but the von Stolzberg women smiled encouragingly from within their frames.

They came to a wide stairway. Surely it had not been there before. They came to the broad flight of steps, with ornate wrought-iron balustrades that led down into the fire-lit, torch-lit hall. The drums were louder now, and there was a flourish of trumpets. It was a pity that this effective entrance was wasted on the handful of serving robots that stood to attention around the long table. Grimes wished that his shipmates could witness it.

They descended the stairs, Karl still in the lead, walked slowly to the massive board. Ceremonially, the major-domo saw to the seating of Marlene; one of the lesser serving robots pulled out a chair for Grimes at her right hand. Then, suddenly, all the torches were somehow extinguished, and the only light was that from the blazing fire and from the score of candles set in an elaborately Gothic wrought-iron holder.

There was more wine, poured by Karl.

There was a rich soup served in golden bowls.

"Bisque of rock ogre," said Marlene. "I hope you like it."

Grimes, remembering the monster that had almost killed him, was sure that he would not but, after telling himself that a lobster, or even a prawn, would be a horrendous monstrosity to a man reduced to the size of a mouse, decided to try it. It was good, the flavor not unlike that of crayfish, but different. A hint of squid, perhaps? Or, just possibly, turtle? And then there was a roast of wild boar, and to accompany it a more than merely adequate Montrachet. To conclude the meal there was fresh fruit and a platter of ripe cheeses, with a red wine from Portugal, from grapes grown on the banks of the Douro.

Marlene said, "I like a man who likes *real* food."

Grimes said, "I like a woman who likes *real* food."

The robot Karl filled their coffee cups, offered a box of Panatellas to the Princess, who selected one carefully, and then to Grimes, who took the first one to hand. And then—it was a delightfully outré touch —a jet of intense white flame appeared at the end of Karl's right index finger. He carefully lit the Princess's cigar, and then the spaceman's.

"The brandy, Karl," said Marlene, through a cloud of fragrant smoke.

"The Napoleon, Your Highness? "

"You know as well as I do that it has no more connection with the Emperor of the French than . . . than Lieutenant Grimes has. But . . . Oh, very well, then. The Napoleon."

To Grimes it was just brandy, but he had no cause for complaint.

"And what would you like to do now?" asked the Princess.

Grimes did know but could not muster up the courage to state his desire.

"Oh, yes," said the girl after an uncomfortable pause. "I told you, I think, that I am a member of the Committee of Management. Would you be interested in finding out what that entails? "

"Yes . . ." answered Grimes dubiously.

☙ Chapter 18 ☙

BEFORE its fantastically costly dismantling and transportation Schloss Stolzberg had been well equipped with what, in the Middle Ages, were regarded as finest modern conveniences. Now not even a hole in the ground somewhere in Germany marked the site of these dungeons and torture chambers; where the Castle had once brooded stood a towering block of apartments. But still there were subterranean galleries and spaces: wine cellars, storerooms, and the Monitor Vault.

"It is our obligation as members of the Committee of Management," explained the Princess, "to watch. And we, even during our tenure of office, know that we can be watched . . ."

"You mean that there's no privacy?" asked Grimes, shocked.

"I suppose that you could put it that way."

"But . . . But I thought that this was a society, of . . . aristocratic anarchists."

"That's a good way of putting it, John. And a true way." She lay back in the chair set before the huge screen, relaxed, but with her fine features thoughtful. "But, can't you see?, neither the aristocrat nor the anarchist suffers from false shame. I can conceive of situations in which a petty bourgeois such as yourself would be agonizingly embarrassed if he knew that he was being watched. During copulation, for example or defecation. But *we* . . ." In spite of her almost supine position she managed a delicate shrug. "But *we* . . . We *know* that it doesn't matter."

"But why this body of elected, I suppose that you are elected, Big Brothers? And Big Sisters."

"El Dorado," she told him, "could be a Paradise. But there are snakes in every Eden. When such a snake is found, he is placed aboard a small, one-man spacecraft, with whatever personal possessions he can pack into two suitcases, and a Universal Letter of Credit that will allow him sufficient funds to make a fresh start elsewhere. He is then sent into exile."

"Have there been many such cases?"

"Since the foundation of the colony, several. About a dozen."

"I'm surprised that none of these deportees has talked. Their stories, sold to newspapers and magazines throughout the Galaxy, would bring in enough to maintain them in luxury for the rest of their lives."

She smiled. "Somebody must *know* what happens, but quite a few of us suspect. After all, not much engineering skill would be required to convert a perfectly functioning ship into a perfectly functioning time bomb."

"I suppose not. But tell me, Marlene, just what does anybody have to do to get slung off this, insofar as you all are concerned, perfect world?"

"There was one man who still lusted for power, direct, personal power. Working in secret he tried to form a Party, with himself as Leader, of course, on the same lines as the old Fascist and Communist Parties. . . ." She almost whispered, "I was lucky not to have been involved. Anyhow, *he* went. And there was another man . . . We still have the record. I'll show you."

She made a slight gesture with her right hand. There was the slightest of humming noises, a hesitant click, and then misty forms and colors swirled in the depths of the big screen, slowly coalesced. And there was sound, too, a woman's voice screaming, *"No! Please! No!"*

Horrified, yet obsessed by a fascination of which he was afterwards bitterly ashamed, Grimes stared at the picture. It showed the interior of a cellar, and there was a naked girl, her body dreadfully elongated, stretched out on a rack, and a pale, fat slug of a man, stripped to the waist, in the act of taking a white-hot iron from a glowing brazier.

Suddenly there was an ingress of men and women, all of them armed, one of them carrying a bell-mouthed pistol like the ones Grimes had seen in Marlene's room. The report, when it was fired, was no more than a soft *chuff*. At once the torturer was trapped, enmeshed in a net of metal strands that seemed to be alive, that working with a sort of mechanical intelligence bound his hands and arms and legs and feet, swiftly immobilizing him. He fell against his own brazier, and the others left him there while they attended to his victim. Grimes could see the smoke and the steam that rose from his burning body, could hear his wordless screams (until the net somehow gagged him), thought (although this could have been imagination) that he could smell charred flesh.

The screen went blank.

"And who was that?" asked Grimes, with feeble, cheap humor. "The Marquis de Sade?"

"No. Oddly enough, a Mr. Jones from New Detroit."

"And did he . . . die?"

"Probably. But not on El Dorado."

"And how did you suspect?"

"Oh, we *knew*. But his first victims were collaborators more than martyrs, and he did them no permanent damage. And that girl, for example, was experiencing nothing worse (or better?) than a mild, sexually stimulating whipping. However, the Monitor sees all, knows all, and gave the alarm, but on the rare occasions that arrests are necessary we prefer that they be made by ourselves, not by robots."

"But if your Monitor is so highly efficient, why the human Big Brothers?"

"We monitor the Monitor. That first man I told you about, the would-be dictator, almost succeeded in subverting it."

"I'm not sure that I'd like to live here, Marlene."

"I'm not sure that we'd have you, John, at least not until you've made your first billion or produced cast-iron documentary evidence of a family tree going back to Adam. Or both." But the words were spoken without malice. "And now, John, would you like to see how your lords and masters are behaving themselves?"

"No," he should have said.

"They are guests at the Duchess of Leckhampton's masked ball—the Captain and Surgeon Commander Passifern."

"That sounds innocuous enough," he said, disappointed.

Again there was the languid wave of her slim hand, again there was the coalescing swirl of light and form and color. Again there was sound, distorted at first, that reminded Grimes of Ravel's *Waltz Dream*. But it was not Ravel that poured from the concealed speakers when the picture clarified; it was Strauss, rich, creamy, sensual, unbearably sweet, and to it the dancers swayed and glided over the wide, wide expanse of mirror floor, and in the background there was red plush and gilt, and overhead blazed and sparkled the crystalline electroliers.

Grimes stared, shocked, incredulous.

Crinolines and hussars' uniforms would have added the final touch but not, relieved (accentuated) only by masks and sandals and jewellery, nudity.

And yet . . .

He shifted uneasily in his seat, acutely conscious of his telltale ears. He muttered, "Surely not the Old Man and the Chief Quack . . ."

And then, as though the Monitor had heard his words (perhaps it had), he was looking directly at Captain Daintree and Commander Passifern. The two officers were not among the naked dancers. They were seated at a table against the wall, stiff and incongruous in their dress uniforms. With them was a lady, elderly, elaborately clothed, one of the few people on this world of perpetual youth and near immortality showing her age and not ashamed of it. There was a silver ice bucket, bedewed with condensation; there were three goblets in which the wine sparkled.

Fascinated, Grimes stared at the faces of his superiors. Daintree—he would—was playing the part of the disapproving puritan, his mouth set in a grim line. But his eyes betrayed him, flickering avidly, almost in time to the music, as the nude men and women swirled past. Passifern was more honest, was making no

A. Bertram Chandler

pretence. A shiny film of perspiration covered his plump features. There was more than a suggestion of slobber about his thick lips.

"Your Grace," he muttered, "I . . . I almost wish that I could join them."

The old lady smiled, tapped the Doctor on the arm with her fan. "Naughty, naughty, Commander. You may look but you mustn't touch."

"I wish that I could . . ." sighed Passifern, while Daintree glared at him.

The scene shifted again to an overall view of the ballroom. The scene shifted and, once more, the music seemed to Grimes to carry the subtle discordancies of Ravel's distortion of the traditional Viennese waltz.

The scene faded.

"Decadent," whispered Grimes to himself. "Decadent."

"Do you think so, John?" asked the Princess. She answered herself, "Yes, I suppose that it is. But erotic stimulation carried to extremes is one of the ways that we have tried to deal with our . . . problem. And there are other ways . . ."

Although the screen was still dark, from the speakers drifted a throb and grumble of little drums. Gradually there was light, faint at first then flaring to brilliant reds and oranges. It came from a fire and from torches held aloft by white-robed men and women. It grew steadily brighter, illuminating the clearing in the forest, in the jungle, rather. It shone on the altar, on the squatting, naked drummers, on the rough-hewn wooden cross that stood behind the altar, its arms thrust through the sleeves of a ragged black coat, a band of white cloth, like a clerical collar, where a human neck would have been, the whole surmounted by a battered black hat.

Grimes was an agnostic, but this apparent blasphemy shocked him. He turned to look at the girl. "John!" she whispered, "if you could only see your face! That cross is the symbol of a religion at least as valid as any of the others. It represents Baron Samedi, the Lord of Graveyards. But watch!"

A huge man, black and glistening, was bowing before the altar, before the . . . the idol? He was bowing low before the altar and the frightening effigy of Baron Samedi. He straightened, and Grimes saw that he carried a long, gleaming knife in his right hand. He turned to face the celebrants. His eyes and his teeth were very white in his ebony face. Grimes recognized him, saw that it was the Hereditary Chief Lobenga. Lobenga, the exile from New Katanga, the dabbler in black magic, in voodoo.

The enormous Negro called, his voice a resonant baritone, "De woman! Bring out de woman! Prepare de sacrifice!"

"The woman!" a chorus of voices echoed him. "The woman!"

And while the drums throbbed and muttered, a figure, wrapped in an all-enveloping black cloak and hood, was led to the altar by four of the white-robed worshippers. Their clothing made it impossible for Grimes to determine their sex, but he thought that two of them were men, two of them women. Lobenga faced the victim, towering over her. She seemed to cringe. His left hand went out to her throat, did something, and as the stuttering of the drums rose to a staccato roar, her cloak fell away from her. Beneath it she was naked, her flesh gleaming golden in the fire-lit darkness, her hair reflecting the ruddy flames.

She did not resist. As Lobenga moved to a position directly behind the altar, between it and the cross, she allowed herself to be led forward and then, quite willingly it seemed, lay down upon the dark, gold-embroidered altar cloth. She was beautiful of face, her body perfectly formed. Even in this supine posture her breasts did not sag. She was young, or was she? On this world, thought Grimes, she could be any age at all.

Lobenga had raised his knife. Above the now-muted drums rose the voices of the communicants. "The sacrifice! The sacrifice!"

Grimes was half out of his seat. "Marlene! What's your bloody Monitor doing about it? What are *you* doing?"

"Be quiet, damn you!" she snarled.

"The sacrifice!" cried the people on the screen.

And those about the altar laid hands upon the girl, one to each ankle, one to each-wrist, spread-eagling her.

"The sacrifice!"

"De white goat!" shouted Lobenga, knife upraised.

The white goat . . . the goat without horns . . .

"Marlene!" Grimes' hand was on her arm. "Marlene, we must *do* something. Now. Before it's too late."

She shook him off. "Be quiet!"

And suddenly there *was* a white goat, bleating, struggling. Two men threw the animal on its side to the ground, grasping its feet, lifting it. They set it down on the girl's naked body, its back to her breasts and belly, its head between her legs. The drums throbbed softly, insistently. The priest's knife swept down; the animal's cries ceased in mid-bleat, although its now released limbs kicked spasmodically. The girl, free herself from restraining hands, held the dying body to her.

The drums were clamorous now, ecstatic, yet maintaining a compelling rhythm. All over the clearing men and women were throwing aside their white robes, had begun to dance, to prance, rather, and there was no doubt as to what the outcome would be. Lobenga had lifted the blood-spattered woman off the altar, was carrying her into the darkness. The way that her arms were twined about his neck was proof of her willingness.

"I think," said Grimes, "that I'm going to be sick."

"Karl will escort you to your quarters," said Marlene.

As he walked unsteadily through the doorway of the Monitor Vault he looked back. The girl was still staring raptly into the screen.

≈ Chapter 19 ≈

NOT SURPRISINGLY he dreamed that night, when at last he fell into an uneasy sleep.

There was the nightmare in which naked women and huge white goats, erect on their hind legs, danced to the music of Ravel's *Waltz Dream,* while across the mirror floor, scattering the dancers, stalked Baron Samedi.

There was that other dream, even more frightening.

It seemed that he half woke up but was unable to stir a muscle, to open his eyes more than the merest slit. There was a strange, acridly sweet smell in the air. There were low voices of a man and a woman. He could just see them, standing there by his bed. He thought that, in spite of the darkness, he could recognize them.

"Are you sure?" asked the woman.

"I am sure," replied the man. Although there was now no trace of accent, that deep, rolling baritone was unmistakable. "The white goat."

"The goat without horns." Then, "But I do not like it."

"It must be done."

"Then do it now. Get it over with."

"No. The . . . conditions must be right. You do not know enough about these matters."

"After what I watched on the Monitor, I am not sure that I want to know any more than I know already."

"But you watched."

"Yes. I watched."

"Did he?"

"Some of it."

"Come." The larger of the two figures was already out of range of Grimes' vision.

"All right."

And then both of them were gone, and Grimes slept deeply until morning.

⚞ Chapter 20 ⚟

HE WAS AWAKENED by the inevitable disembodied voice calling softly at first, then louder, "Lord, it is time to arise . . ."

It took a considerable effort to force his gummy eyelids open. His head was fuzzy, his mouth dry and stale-tasting. The uneasy memory of that last nightmare persisted.

There was a condensation-clouded glass on the table beside his bed. He picked it up in a rather shaky hand, drained it gratefully. The chilled, unidentifiable fruit juice was tart and refreshing. After it he began to feel a little better.

"And what's on today, I wonder?" he muttered, more to himself than to any possible listener.

"You will perform your ablutions, Lord," replied the irritating unseen speaker. "Then you will partake of breakfast. And then you will join Her Highness at the hunt." There was a pause. "And would you care to place your order for the meal now?"

"What's on?" asked Grimes, feeling faint stirrings of appetite.

"Anything that you may desire, Lord."

"No stipulations about 'reasonable orders'?"

"Of course not, Lord." The voice was mildly reproachful. "As a guest of Schloss Stolzberg you may command what you will."

"As a Lord, acting, temporary, unpaid, you mean. It was a different story when I was a mere spaceman. But you wouldn't know about that, would you?"

There was the suggestion of a smirk in the reply. "Lord, to the Monitor all things are known."

"Are you part of the Monitor, then?"

"I am not permitted to answer that question, Lord."

"Oh, all right. Skip it. Now, breakfast. A pot of coffee, black, hot and strong. Sugar, but no milk or cream. Two four-minute eggs. Hens' eggs, that is. Plenty of toast. Butter. Honey."

"It will be awaiting you, Lord."

Grimes went through to the bathroom, performed his morning ritual. When he came out, in his dressing gown, he noted that clothing had been laid out on the already made bed. He looked at it curiously; it was nothing that he had brought with him, but he had no doubt that it would prove a perfect fit. His breakfast was waiting on the table in the bedroom, and with it a crisp newspaper. THE ELDORADO CHRONICLE he read as he picked it up. Curious, he skimmed through it over his first cup of coffee. It contained little more than social gossip, although its editor had condescended to notice the presence of *Aries* at the spaceport, and there were even some photographs of the ship's personnel. Grimes chuckled over one of Captain Daintree and Surgeon Commander Passifern at the Duchess of Leckhampton's masked ball, at another one that showed a conducted party of the ship's ratings, looking acutely uncomfortable in their uniforms, at an ocean beach on which the rig of the day was the only sensible one for swimming, and sunbathing. He found a brief item which informed anybody who might be interested that Lieutenant Grimes was the house guest of the Princess Marlene von Stolzberg. On the back page there was Galactic news, but most of it was financial.

Grimes put the paper down and applied himself to his breakfast, which was excellent. After one last cup of coffee he went back to the bedroom and examined curiously the heavy shirt, the tough breeches, the thick stockings and the heavy boots before putting them on. A tweed cap completed the ensemble. He was admiring himself in the mirror when, unannounced, Marlene came in. He removed his hat, turned to look at her. She was dressed as he was, but on her the rough clothing looked extremely feminine.

He said, "Good morning, Marlene."

She said, "Good morning, John." Then, "I trust that you slept well."

"Yes," he lied.

"Good." Her mood seemed to be that of a small girl setting out on a long-promised outing. "Then shall we make a start? The woods are so much better in the morning."

"Your tin butler said something about a hunt."

"Yes. There is a boar, a great, cunning brute that I have promised myself the pleasure of despatching for many a day."

"I don't know anything about hunting."

"But you must. As an officer of an armed service you must, at times, have been a hunter—and, at times, the hunted."

"That's not quite the same."

"No. I suppose it's not. Didn't somebody say once that Man is the most dangerous game of all?"

"But I'm not sure that I approve of blood sports."

She was amusedly contemptuous. "John, John, you typical Terran petty bourgeois! You approved of that roast of wild boar at dinner last night. And that animal was killed by *me,* not in some sterile, allegedly humane abattoir. There is a big difference between killing for sport and mere butchering."

"You could be right."

"Of course I'm right. But come."

She led the way out of Grimes' quarters. He supposed that, given six months or so, he would eventually learn to find his way about this castle, but this morning he certainly needed a guide. At last, several corridors and a couple of escalators later, he followed her into a panelled room at ground level, against the walls of which were stacks of weapons: light and heavy firearms, longbows and, even, spears.

One of these latter she selected, a seven-foot shaft of some dull-gleaming timber, tipped with a wickedly sharp metal head. She tested the point of it on the ball of her thumb, said, "This will do. Select yours."

"A *spear?*" demanded Grimes, incredulous.

"Yes, a spear. What did you expect? A laser cannon? A guided missile with a fusion warhead? Wars were fought with these things, John, once upon a time. Fought and won."

"And fought and lost when the other side came up with bows and arrows."

"The boar only has his tusks. And hooves."

"And he knows how to use them." Grimes deliberately handled his spear clumsily, making it obvious that this was one weapon that *he* did not know how to use.

"Just stay with me," she told him. "You'll be quite safe."

Grimes flushed but said nothing, walked with her out of the castle into the open air.

It was a fine morning, the sun rising in a cloudless sky, the last of the dew still on the grass, the merest suggestion of a pleasantly cool breeze. Grimes found himself remembering the possibly mythical upper-class Englishman who was supposed to have said, "It's a beautiful day. Let's go out and kill something." So it was a beautiful day for killing wild boars, and last night (that memory suddenly flooded back) had been a beautiful night for killing white goats. He shivered a little. A boar hunt would be clean, wholesome by comparison. And, he had to admit, there was a certain glamor about sport of this kind, cruel though some might consider it.

He looked at the hounds, their pelts boldly patterned in ruddy brown and white, streaming ahead of them in a loose pack. They were silent now, although they had belled lustily when released from their kennels. They were part of the countryside, part of this kind of life. And so was Marlene, striding mannishly (but not too mannishly) beside him. Even the two humanoid robots, tricked out in some sort of forester's livery, each carrying a bundle of spears and one of those bell-mouthed net-throwing pistols, were more part of the picture than he, Grimes, was. Even the inevitable pair of watchbirds, hovering and soaring overhead, looked like real birds, fitted in.

There was no need for a path over the grass, something had kept it cropped short. But as they approached the woods Grimes saw that there was a track through the trees, made either by human agency or by wild animals. But the hounds ignored it, split up, each making its own way into the green dimness. They gave voice again, a cacophonous baying that, thought Grimes uneasily, must surely infuriate rather than frighten any large and dangerous animal. But they seemed to know what they were doing, which was more than he did.

He remarked, "Intelligent animals, aren't they?"

"Within their limitations," she replied. "They have been told to find a wild boar, *the* wild boar, rather, and drive him toward us. And they have enough brains to keep out of trouble themselves."

"Which is more than I have."

"You can say that again. Hold your spear at the ready, like this. The way you're handling it he could be on you, ripping your guts out, before you got the point anywhere near him."

"If your watchbirds let him."

"They can't operate in a forest, John." She grinned. "But Fritz and Fredrik"—she made a slight gesture towards the robot foresters—"have very fast reactions."

"I'm pleased to hear that."

They were well into the woods now, on either side of them the ancient oaks (artificially aged? imported as full-grown trees?) and overhead the branches and thick foliage that shut out the blue of the sky. Things rustled in the underbrush. Something burst from the bushes and ran across their path. Instinctively, Grimes raised his spear, lowered it when he saw that the animal was only a rabbit.

"For *them*, John," remarked the Princess chidingly, "we have shotguns."

The baying of the hounds was distant now, muffled by the trees. Perhaps they wouldn't find the boar or, old and cunning as he was, he would not allow himself to be chivvied into the open. Grimes found himself sympathizing with the animal. As Marlene had surmised, he had been in his time both hunter and hunted. He knew (as she did not) what it was like to be at the receiving end.

The baying of the hounds was still distant but, it seemed, a little closer. "Stop," ordered the girl. "Wait here. Let him come to us."

I'd sooner not wait, thought Grimes. *I'd sooner get out of this blasted forest as though I had a Mark XIV missile up my tail.*

"Not long now," said the girl. The tip of her pink tongue moistened her scarlet lips. She looked happy. Grimes knew that he did not. He glanced at the foresters. They were standing there stolidly just behind the humans. They had not bothered to unholster their net-throwing guns. The spaceman muttered something about brass bastards too tired to pull a pistol. "Don't *worry* so, John," the Princess told him. "Relax."

The clamor of the pack was louder and growing louder all the time. It was the only sound in the forest. All the little disturbing rustlings and squeakings and twitterings had ceased. Then there was a new noise, or combination of noises. It was like a medium tank crashing through the undergrowth, squealing as it came. And there was no fear in that high-pitched, nasal screaming, only rage.

"Open up," ordered the Princess. "Give him a choice of targets. It will confuse him."

There was room for them to spread themselves out in the clearing in which they were standing. Marlene, on his right, moved away from him. He could hear, behind him, the feet of the robots shuffling over the dead leaves and coarse grass. He stayed where he was. A shift to the left would bring him too close to the bushes, out of which the enraged animal might emerge at any moment. He thought, *What am I doing here?* He was no stranger to action, but a fire fight at relatively long range is impersonal. This was getting to be too personal for comfort.

And then, ahead of them, the wild boar exploded into the clearing. He stood there for what seemed a long time (it could have been only a second, if that) glaring at them out of his little red eyes. Here was no fat and lazy piglet leading a contented life (but a short one) in the very shadow of the bacon factory. Here was a wild animal, a dangerous animal, one of those animals that are said to be wicked because they defend themselves. The tusks on him, transposed to the upper jaw, would not have been a discredit to a sabre-toothed tiger.

He made his decision, charged at the Princess like a runaway rocket torpedo. She stood her ground, spear extended and ready and then, with a motion as graceful as it was horrible, with the sharp point deftly flicked out the brute's left eye. He was blinded on that side and she had skipped away and clear. He was blind on that side, but his right eye was good, and he could see Grimes and, furthermore, another spear licked out, wielded by one of the robots, not to kill but with the intention of turning him toward the new pain, toward the spaceman.

Grimes wanted to run but knew that he would never be fast enough. (The girl could look after herself, or, if she could not, her faithful automatic servitors would protect her.) He wanted to run, but stubbornness more than any other quality made him remain rooted to the spot. And then—he never knew why—he *threw* his spear. It was not a javelin, was not designed to be used in this manner but, miraculously, sped straight and true, hitting the boar in the left shoulder, missing the bones, plunging through into the fiercely beating heart.

Even so, the animal almost reached him, finally collapsed at his very feet.

Slowly, Grimes turned to look at the others—at the Princess, at the robot foresters, at the grinning, tongue-lolling dogs. He felt betrayed, sensed that only his own luck (rather than skill) had saved him.

Marlene stared back, her eyes and wide mouth very vivid in her pale face. Then she made a tremulous attempt at a smile.

"Third time lucky," she said. "For you."

"What do you mean?"

"That I've shot *my* bolt. Somebody else can do the dirty work."

"What do you mean?"

"Never mind. Let us return to the castle."

In silence they walked back out from the dark woods.

≫ Chapter 21 ≪

THEY LAY, supine and naked, on the velvet grass of the lawn that surrounded the swimming pool, soaking up the warmth and the radiation of the afternoon sun. Grimes raised himself on his shoulders, looked at the perfect body of the girl. He thought, *Yes, you may look, but you mustn't touch.* And he wanted to touch, badly. Hastily he turned over onto his belly.

"What's bothering you, John?" she asked, her voice lazy.

Can't you see? he did not dare to say. Instead, extemporizing, he said, "I'm still puzzled by what you said. After I killed the boar."

"What did I say?"

"Something about third time lucky. And about somebody else having to do the dirty work." He was silent for a little. "And, tell me, was the first time when I brought the dynosoar in to a landing? And was the second time when we had the difference of opinion with the rock ogre?"

"I don't know what you're talking about, John. I can't remember saying anything about third time lucky."

"Can't you?"

"No. You must have imagined it. You were rather badly shaken up." There was a touch of scorn in her voice. "Still, I suppose that it was the first time that you'd ever killed anything at short range."

"Never mind that. Here's another point. I gained the impression that your precious Fritz and Fredrik weren't busting their tin guts to get me out of the jam."

"You hardly gave them time, did you? Also, they are not supposed to intervene until the last possible moment. It's like . . . how shall I put it? It's like the amusement parks you have on most of the overcrowded planets. There are those affairs called . . . roller coasters? Big Dippers? Anyhow, they give their passengers the illusion of danger. We work on the same principle."

"So El Dorado is just one huge amusement park for the very rich?"

She laughed, but without warmth. "You could put it that way." She got up slowly, walked to the battlements. Grimes watched the play of the muscles under her smooth skin, the sway of her round buttocks. *Yes,* he thought, *a huge amusement park, with swimming pools on the roofs of Gothic castles, and the illusion of danger when you want it (and when you don't) and the illusion of glamorous sex. The real thing isn't for snotty-nosed ragamuffins from the wrong side of the tracks.*

She turned to face him. The sun was full on her. She was all golden, the slender length of her, save for the touches of contrasting color that were her eyes, her mouth, her taut nipples and the enameled nails of her fingers and toes.

She said, "You aren't happy here, John." There was regret in her voice.

He said, looking at her, "You're a marvellous hostess. But . . . But I can't help feeling an outsider."

"But you *are,*" she stated simply. "All of you, from your almighty Captain down to the lowest rating, are. We can fraternise with you all, but only within limits."

"And who lays down those limits? Your precious Monitor?" She was shocked. "Of course not. *We* know what those limits are. Normally we just do not mix with those who are not our kind of people. But, as we called your ship in, we realize that we are under an obligation. In *your* case I am trying to make up for the trouble I got you into from the very start."

"And ever since," he said.

"That is not fair, John. You impressed me as being the type of young man who is quite capable of getting himself into trouble without much help or encouragement."

And this young woman has helped me enough, thought Grimes, *nonetheless. Young* woman? But was she? For all he knew she could be old enough to be his grandmother.

"Why are you staring at me, John?"

"A cat can look at a Queen," he quipped. "Or a Princess."

"And many a cat has lost all of its nine lives for doing just that."

Grimes transferred his attention to a tiny, jewelled beetle that was crawling over the grass just under his face.

She said, "If you aren't happy here, John, I'll take you back to your ship."

"Do you want me to go? "

"No," she said at last.

"All right. I'll stay, as long as you'll have me."

"That wasn't very gracious."

"I'm sorry. It was just my proletarian origins showing."

She told him, "Please don't let them show tonight. You must be on your best behavior. I, we, have guests."

"Oh. Anybody I know?"

"Yes. Henri, Comte de Messigny. Hereditary Chief Lobenga and his wife, the Lady Eulalia. The Duchess of Leckhampton. Those whom you have not already met you have seen."

"The Duchess? Yes. I remember now. On the Monitor, at the masked ball. But the Lady Eulalia?"

"At the voodoo ceremony. It was she on the altar."

"His wife?"

"Yes. Lobenga is a very moral man, moral, that is, by your somewhat outdated standards."

And that, thought Grimes, robbed the rites that he had witnessed of much of their sinful glamor. There had been, of course, that revolting business with the white goat but all over the Galaxy, with every passing second, animals were being slaughtered to serve the ends of Man. He, himself, had killed the boar and, quite possibly, sooner or later would enjoy its cooked flesh.

Suddenly he found himself pitying these people with their empty, sterile lives. Messigny, playing at being a spaceman, Lobenga and his wife playing at Black Magic, and the old Duchess casting herself in the role of Grande Dame. And the Princess? *There's nothing wrong with you,* he thought, *that a good roll in the hay wouldn't cure.* And yet, looking at her as she stood there, proud and naked, looking down at him, he knew that she would have to make the first move.

She said, "There is a slight chill in the air. Shall we go down?" She walked to the turret that housed the top of the escalator. He followed her. The robot Karl was awaiting them, helped the girl into a fleecy robe, knelt to slide golden sandals onto her slim feet. Grimes picked up his own robe from where he had left it, got into his footwear unassisted. He knew that had he waited a few seconds Karl would have served him as he served his mistress, but the spaceman was neither used to nor welcomed such attention. The moving stairway took them down into the castle.

Grimes, tricked out once again in his dress uniform, sat watching the screen of the playmaster in his living room, awaiting the summons. He had decided to allow himself just one weak drink, and was sipping a pink gin. He was ready for the knock on the door when it came, drained what was left in his glass and then followed Karl through long corridors that were, once again, strange to him. Finally, he was conducted into a room furnished with baroque splendor, in which Marlene and her guests were already seated.

They broke off their conversation as he came in, and the two men and the Princess got to their feet. "Your Grace," said Marlene formally, "may I introduce Lieutenant John Grimes, of *Aries?*" The Duchess looked him up and down. *If she smiles,* thought Grimes, *the paint will crack and the powder will flake off* . . . But smile she did, thinly, a final touch to the antique elegance already enhanced by an elaborate, white-powdered wig, black beauty spot on the left cheek of her face, black ribbon around the wrinkled neck, gently fluttering fan. She extended a withered hand. Rather to his own surprise, Grimes bowed from the waist to kiss it. She looked at him approvingly.

"Lady Eulalia, may I introduce . . . ?"

Grimes found it hard to believe that this was the naked woman whom he had seen stretched upon the altar, who had participated in the obscene sacrifice, who had been carried into the dark jungle by the giant Negro. She smiled sweetly, demurely almost, up at him. Her skin was hardly darker than Marlene's, and only a certain fullness of the lips betrayed her racial origin. Her auburn-glinting hair was piled high on her narrow head. Her splendid body was clad in a slim sheath of glowing scarlet. The effect was barbaric, and suddenly, credence restored, he could visualize her as she had appeared on the screen. He felt his ears burning.

"We have met before, young Grimes," said de Messigny, shaking his hand. Although the grip was firm, it was cold. The Comte was not in uniform tonight, was sombrely well-dressed in form-fitting black, with a froth of lace at throat and wrists. He, like the Duchess, seemed a survivor from some earlier, more courtly age.

"I remember seeing you at the spaceport, Lieutenant," rumbled Lobenga, a wide, dazzling smile splitting his broad, ebony face. The Hereditary Chief was wearing a white jacket over sharply creased black trousers and, under the white satin butterfly of his necktie, a double row of lustrous black pearls adorned his starched shirt front. "I am pleased with the opportunity to make your acquaintance properly." The hand that crushed Grimes' was the hand that had slain the sacrificial goat.

"Please be seated," ordered Marlene, resuming her own chair. She, tonight, was imperially robed in purple, and an ornate golden brooch—or was it some Order?—gleamed over her left breast. In her hair, as before, was the jewelled coronet. Grimes watched her as she sat down and was suddenly aware that de Messigny was watching him. Glancing sideways, he imagined that he detected jealousy on the tall man's face. *But you've nothing to be jealous of,* he thought.

And then the robot servitors were offering trays of drinks, and the conversation was light and desultory, normal—"And what do you really think of our world, Mr. Grimes?"

"The most beautiful planet I've seen, Your Grace,"—platitudinous, but a welcome change from the platitudes bandied about in *Aries'* wardroom, and after a pleasant enough half hour or so it was time to go down to dinner.

Chapter 22

THEY PARTOOK OF FOOD and wine in the great banqueting hall, waited upon by the silent, efficient serving robots. Grimes—a young man keenly appreciative of the pleasures of the table, although he had yet to acquire discrimination—could never afterwards remember what it was that they ate and drank. There was food and there was wine, and presumably both were palatable and satisfying, but those sitting around the board were of far greater importance than what was set upon it.

Opposite Grimes was Marlene. On her left, darkly glowering, was Lobenga, and to his left was the Duchess. To Grimes' right was the Lady Eulalia, with de Messigny beyond her. The table should have been a little oasis of light and warmth in the huge, dark hall, a splash of color in contrast to the ranged suite of dull-gleaming armour, the sombre folds of the standards that sagged from their inward pointing staffs. It should have been, but it was not. It could have been imagination, but it seemed to Grimes that the candle flames were burning blue, and the fire in the enormous hearth was no more than an ominous smoulder. Somewhere background music was playing, softly, too softly. It could have been the whispering of malign spirits.

De Messigny, speaking diagonally across the table, said abruptly, "And are the ghosts of your Teutonic ancestors walking tonight, Marlene?"

She stared back at him, her face grave, shadows under her high cheekbones, what little light there was reflected from the jewels in her coronet, an unhappy princess out of some old German fairy story. She said at last, "The ghosts of Schloss Stolzberg stayed on Earth, Henri."

"Unfortunately," added Lobenga, his low rumble barely audible.

"And was the Castle haunted?" asked Grimes, breaking the uneasy hush.

They all turned to stare at him—the Princess gravely, Lobenga sullenly, the Duchess with a birdlike maliciousness. On his right Eulalia laughed softly and coldly, and de Messigny glared at him down his long, thin nose.

"Yes," said Marlene at last. "It *was* haunted. There was the faithless Princess Magda, who used to run screaming through the corridors, the hilt of her husband's dagger still protruding from between her breasts. There was Butcher Hermann, who met his end in the torture chamber at the hands of his own bastard son. There was S. S. General von Stolzberg, roasted in this very fireplace by his slave-labor farm workers when the Third Reich collapsed . . ."

"We could do without *them*, "de Messigny stated.

"Hermann and the General, perhaps," cackled the Duchess. "But Magda would have been at home here." As she said this she ceased to be the Grande Dame, looked more, thought Grimes, like the Madam of a whorehouse.

"Yes," agreed the Comte. "She would have been." Had he not looked so long and hard at Marlene as he said it, the remark would have been inoffensive.

Eulalia laughed again. "I have often wondered why some men persist in attaching such great importance to the supremely unimportant." She shrugged her slim, elegant shoulders. "But, of course, Lobenga has no cause to worry about me. Not even on this world. Perhaps, Henri, we could enroll you in a course of study in the so-called Black Arts."

"That filth!" exploded this Comte.

"Sir," the huge Negro told him gravely, "it is not filth. We have seen, on this planet, what happens when Man gets too far away from the mud and blood of his first beginnings. Every member of the Committee of Management, with the exception of Lord Tarlton . . ."

"That *materialist!*" interjected his wife.

". . . agrees that we are on the right track. There is disagreement regarding which method to employ. Her Grace, for example, pins her faith in super-civilized but decadent orgies . . ."

"Thank you, Lobenga," said the old woman sardonically.

"On the other hand, Her Highness concurs with me that a sacrifice is necessary."

"Then," put in de Messigny, "why were not such few criminals as we have discovered on El Dorado executed *here,* instead of being sent to their deaths somewhere in outer space?"

"You heard what was said about Hermann von Stolzberg and his descendant, the S. S. General. We can do without such raw material."

"Rubbish!" The Comte's normally pale face was flushed. "Marlene carries in her veins the blood of her murderous ancestors. We all of us carry in our veins the blood of ancestors guilty of every crime—yes, and of every sin—known to Man."

"There has been a certain refining process," the Duchess told him.

"Perhaps that's the trouble. Perhaps we are all too refined. Or perhaps we have culminated in a new species of Mankind that is sterile."

The Duchess cackled. "That from you, Henri? I recall, just the other day, that you were telling me about your illegitimate children on Caribbea and Austral." Then, maliciously, "But are you sure that they are yours?"

"There is a strong family resemblance," he snapped.

"And so, Henri, you alone on El Dorado are capable of the act of procreation. Why don't you . . ."

"I didn't mean it that way, Honoria."

"We have a guest," Marlene reminded the others.

"And so we have," agreed de Messigny, tossing down almost a full glass of wine. "Or so *you* have. But we must not offend Mr.

Grimes' delicate susceptibilities, although I am sure that an officer of the Survey Service will be able to take the rough with the smooth." He managed to make the last word sound obscene.

"Henri. You know very well that that would be entirely contrary to the rules by which we live."

"You have always made your own rules, Marlene. As we all, at this table, know."

"As we all know," stated Lobenga.

"That is my privilege," she said. "As it is the privilege of all on El Dorado."

"But you told us," complained the Duchess, "that you would, for the good of us all, cooperate. Cooperate, did I say? As I recall it, you were to play a leading part in one of the schemes."

"I did," said Marlene. "I did. But we von Stolzberg's have a family tradition. Shall I tell you? Try to do something, and fail. Try a second time, and fail. Try a third time, and fail. Try a fourth time, and the consequences are unforeseen and disastrous."

"Superstition," growled the Hereditary Chief.

"This from *you,* Lobenga . . ." murmured the Princess.

"The Old Religion is *not* superstition!" flared Eulalia. "If we had been allowed to do things *our* way . . ."

"We still can," said her husband.

"But not," stated the Princess, "in Schloss Stolzberg. I am fully conscious of the obligations of a host."

"Mr. Grimes!" It was the Duchess of Leckhampton addressing him. Then, sharply, "Mr. Grimes!"

He turned to her, still bewildered by the conversation in which he had played no part, but of which he appeared to have been the subject. "Your Grace?"

She was very much the great lady again, and she spoke with hauteur. "Mr. Grimes, I shall apologize to you, even if these others will not. It must be embarrassing for an outsider to be the witness to what, in effect, is a family quarrel. Yes, we are a family here on El Dorado, even though we are of diverse races and origins. But I must commend you, Mr. Grimes, for having the good sense and the courtesy not to take sides."

He tried to make a joke of his reply. "I didn't know whose side to take, Your Grace."

"Didn't you, Mr. Grimes?" sneered de Messigny.

"No," said Grimes. He allowed his indignation to take charge. "Damn it all, you people are the upper crust of the entire bloody Galaxy, or think that you are. But I tell you that such squabbling at table would not be tolerated in the Fourth Class Ratings' messroom, let alone the wardroom of a ship."

"That will do, Grimes!" snapped the Count.

"That will do, Henri!" almost snarled the Princess. "John was right in what he said."

"*John?*" echoed de Messigny, with a sardonic lift of his black eyebrows. "But I was forgetting, Marlene. After all, you have Karl and Fritz and Fredrik and Augustin and Johann . . . Although John has the advantage of being flesh and blood, not metal."

"De Messigny . . ." Lobenga's voice was an ominous rumble. "De Messigny, you will be silent." His strange yellow eyes swept the table. "You will all of you be silent, until I have had my say." Then he addressed the Lieutenant directly. "Mr. Grimes, what has happened should never have happened. What has been said should never have been said. But there are forces loose tonight in this old castle. Perhaps, even though there are no ghosts, the centuries of bloodstained history that these walls have seen have left a record of some kind on the very stones. There has been a clash of personalities. There has been sexual jealousy, and so the record has been played back. It was in this very hall, I am told, that Her Highness's forebear, Magda, died of her wounds.

"Be that as it may, Mr. Grimes, too much has been said in your hearing. You know too much, and too little. But I, we, feel that you have the right to know more. Do we have your word, as an officer and a gentleman, that what we shall tell you will never be divulged?"

Grimes' head was buzzing. Could it have been the effects of too much wine, or of something in the wine? And those yellow eyes staring into his were strangely hypnotic.

"Do we have your word?" asked Lobenga.

"Yes," he whispered.

"Is this wise?" asked Eulalia.

"Shut yo' mouf, woman." The deliberate lapse into the archaic dialect was frightening rather than ludicrous. This was the High Priest speaking, not the cultured Negro gentleman. "Shut yo' mouf, all of yo', until Ah is done.

"Mr. Grimes," he went on, "I can tell you that you were to have been honored, greatly honored. But circumstances now are such that, after your stay here, you will be allowed to return to your ship."

"Honored?" asked Grimes. "How?"

"You were to have been the white goat, the goat without horns." Grimes stared around the table in horror rather than in disbelief.

"It is true," said Marlene.

Chapter 23

"YES," said Lobenga, breaking the heavy silence, "you are entitled to an explanation."

"You can say that again," Grimes told him.

The Hereditary Chief ignored this. "You are aware, Mr. Grimes," he went on, "of the nature of our problem on this planet."

"Yes." The spaceman was deliberately flippant. "You miss the pitterpatter of little feet and all the rest of it."

"Crudely put, sir. Crudely put, but true. Even though our lives are enormously prolonged, even though our system of safeguards almost obviates the possibility of accidental death, or death by any kind of violence, we are not immortal. And what use is great wealth if you have nobody to whom to leave it? What comfort is a bloodline stretching back to antiquity if it dies out with yourself?"

"Those," said Grimes, "are worries that I'm never likely to have."

"But you are not one of us," stated Marlene.

Lobenga continued. "All we ask, sir, is to be able to live our own kind of life on the planet of our choice. But for this one, but dreadfully important, factor we have no complaints. We are neither impotent nor frigid. Our sex lives are normal, better than normal. But are sterile, even though our finest medical practitioners assure us that there are no physical abnormalities or deficiencies."

"I was told," said Grimes, "that the women who were already pregnant when they came here were successfully brought to term and that their children lived and are now adults."

"That is correct."

"And I learned tonight that Captain de Messigny has fathered offspring on other planets."

"So he tells us," said Lobenga, adding, before the Comte could flare up, "and I have no reason to doubt his word. Furthermore, the Comte de Messigny has, on occasion, acted as procurer, bringing young men of good family to El Dorado for a vacation. Women with wealth and family lines of their own entertained them. But even though de Messigny's friends could, like himself, offer proof of their capacity for parenthood, they achieved nothing here."

"And what is the explanation?" asked Grimes. "Something in the air, or the water? Some virus or radiation?"

"According to Lord Tarlton and his colleagues, no. And we adherents to the Old Religion, in its various forms, are in agreement with the materialists."

"Then have *you* a theory?"

"We have, sir. If you will be patient I shall try to explain it to you. But, first of all, I shall ask a question. What is life?"

"I . . . I don't know. Growth? But a crystal does that. Metabolism? Motility? The ability to reproduce? We have inorganic machines that can do all these things."

"Perhaps *soul* would be the correct word," said Lobenga. "Not used in its conventional sense but, nonetheless, soul. Something indefinable, intangible that makes the difference between the organic and the inorganic, between the warm, soupy primordial seas, the lifeless fluids rich in minerals held in solution, cloudy with suspended matter, and the first viruses. And with those humble and simple beginnings the cycle was started. How did the poet put it? *Birth, procreation, death—and there's an end to it.* But as long as there's death, there's no end to it."

"And somebody or something," cackled the Duchess, "has put a spoke in the wheel of the cycle."

"Yes, Your Grace," agreed Lobenga. "*We* have. We have interrupted the natural sequence."

"But how?" asked Grimes.

"Imagine, if you can," said the Negro, "a reservoir of soul-stuff, of life-essence on every inhabited planet. Imagine, too, that *soul* has evolved, just as physical form has evolved. Visualize the act of conception—the coupling of humans, of dogs, cats, fishes, even the pollenization of a flower—and try to see that before the process of growth can commence there has to be a third factor involved, a priming of the pump, as it were. A drop has to be withdrawn from the reservoir and that reservoir is always kept topped up by the process of death."

"I begin to see."

"Good. Now this world, as you know, was utterly sterile when we purchased it, before we terraformed it, with improvements. We brought in our plant life, our animals, ourselves. Insofar as the plants and animals are concerned the normal cycle was resumed in a matter of months, at the outside. There were the inevitable deaths, the equally inevitable births. Insofar as *we* are concerned, the normal cycle has never been initiated."

"But it could have been," said Grimes. "That is, if your theory is correct."

"How, sir?"

"You, even you, have had criminals. I have seen pictures from the Monitor's memory bank. These criminals, I am informed, were arrested and sent into exile, although it was hinted that they would not live to make planetfall on another world. If, Mr. Lobenga, these men had been executed on El Dorado, surely your pump would have been primed."

"Do you think that we have not thought of that?" asked Lobenga. "There are two valid reasons why this has never been done. To begin with, we have always taken great pains to impress upon the Monitor the sanctity of the lives of all members of the El Dorado Corporation, and have always striven to maintain the Master/Servant relationship, with ourselves, of course, as the Masters. Secondly, if you were going to top up a reservoir of any kind, would you use polluted fluids?"

"Our own souls were dipped out of dirty buckets," chuckled the Duchess of Leckhampton. "Marlene's not the only one here with a murky family past."

"But we have *evolved*," Lobenga explained patiently.

"Hah! "exploded the old lady sardonically.

"Then," said Grimes, "there is another solution."

"You are a veritable mine of information, John," the Princess told him.

"I was taught," he said, "that spacemanship is only applied commonsense. And commonsense can be applied to more things than the handling of ships. All right. We *know* that women who had conceived before coming to El Dorado bore their children here. We have reason to believe that Captain de Messigny has fathered children on other worlds. Then why, *why*, WHY shouldn't all of you who feel the urge to parenthood do your breeding off-planet?"

"Because," said Lobenga sombrely, "we have too much to lose. Because we are cowards. Because we are like the rich men mentioned, time after time in the Christian Bible, who would not give up their worldly possessions for an assured place in the Kingdom of Heaven. There is always risk involved in travelling off-planet. On El Dorado the Monitor protects us from all possible harm. On other worlds we are liable to death from disease, accident, premeditated violence. Oh, there have been couples who have taken the risk. None of them have returned. The Bernsteins both' drowned in a boating accident on Atlantia. Dom Pedro da Silva and his wife, *he* was executed on Waverley for the murder of her lover. She committed suicide. I could go on. It seems that a malign fate pursues us once we lift beyond the limits of our own atmosphere . . ." He paused. "It seems that all the risks that we avoid by living here accumulate, as it were, and once we are away from the protection of the Monitor topple, and crush us beneath their weight."

"Captain de Messigny is still with you," observed Grimes.

"Yes," said the Comte coldly. "I am still around. But before I became a member of the Corporation I led an adventurous life. And, furthermore, I could never remain planetbound for long. *That* would kill me, Monitor or no Monitor. But even I am reluctant to leave the safety of my ship in strange ports and, furthermore, do all my entertaining on board."

"Yet another solution," put forward Grimes happily. "Build a passenger vessel, with accommodation for fifty or a hundred couples. Make a landing on a world with a well-topped-up reservoir and then breed like rabbits."

"And do you think that we haven't tried it?" the Comte asked. "The ship was half-way back to El Dorado when, inexplicably, her micro-pile went critical. I need not tell you that there were no survivors."

"So," asked Grimes, "where does the white goat come into it? Where do *I* come in?"

"We are a moral people," said Lobenga

The Duchess snorted.

"We are a moral people," he stated firmly. "It would have been relatively easy for us to have arranged an accident that would have destroyed your *Aries* and all her crew when she was coming in for a landing. But, apart from the question of morality, there would have been a full scale investigation by the Survey Service. In the same way, it would be possible to stage an accident that would wipe out one of the parties of sightseers from your ship presently touring our planet. But, once again, it would be a needless sacrifice of life and, furthermore, your Captain Daintree is no fool. Too, those of us who are practitioners of what are loosely called the Black Arts resorted to various methods or divination; even Her Grace is an expert manipulator of the Tarot pack. Each and every one of us came up with the same prognostication, the same conclusion. This was that the first offworlder to make a landing would be the bringer of new life to El Dorado. And that first offworlder was you."

"It is expedient for one man to die for the good of the people," quoted Grimes bitterly.

"Yes. And it would have been in an accident costing only one life, or, in the case of the crash-landing of your dynosoar, only two lives. There would have been no investigation."

"But why can't one of *you* prime the pump?" almost shouted Grimes. "You're always saying what a wonderful world you have here. Hasn't any one of you the guts to make a sacrifice for it? "

"Not *that* sacrifice. Mr. Grimes, I do not ask you for your sympathy, your pity, but I do ask for some measure of understanding.

Only a man who has known great possessions knows how hard it is to give them up."

"And so you'd cheerfully slaughter an innocent outsider just so that you can enjoy a few more years in your sterile Eden."

"Not cheerfully, Mr. Grimes. Not cheerfully. And tell me, sir, have *you* ever slaughtered innocent outsiders?"

"No."

"Not yet, you should have said. As an officer of the armed forces of the Federation you will inevitably do so. You *will,* I said. Because, Mr. Grimes, you will live to take part in punitive expeditions, in raids upon commerce, in all the unsavory operations that are always fully justified by the historians of the winning side. We have reread the cards and the cups and the entrails, we have cast the bones. Your lifeline is a long one, but I shall not tell you the surprising turns that it will take.

"You have our word for it, Mr. Grimes. You are safe from us. Neither you nor anybody from your ship is destined to become the white goat, the goat without horns."

"You have our word," echoed the others solemnly.

He believed them. He almost said thank you, but why should he thank them for giving back to him what was not theirs to give, his life?

The Princess Marlene rose to her feet, and her guests followed suit. She said, "We are all tired, I suggest that we retire."

Robot servitors led the humans to their quarters. Grimes, entering his bedroom, saw something small and dull gleaming in the center of the coverlet of his bed. It was his Minetti automatic pistol, and beside it was the carton of spare ammunition.

And now that I shan't need it, he thought, *they give it back to me.*

≈ Chapter 24 ≈

NONETHELESS, he was not sorry to have the deadly little weapon back in his own possession. If there were to be any more hunting of large and dangerous animals, he would prefer to have something with which he was familiar to defend himself with. His successful use of that absurd spear against the wild boar had been nothing but luck, and he knew it.

He slept well, with the pistol under his pillow. Lobenga and the others had given their words that he was safe insofar as they were concerned, but what if they were not the only parties involved in the scheme to set the normal cycle of death and birth running on El Dorado? That gun of his own, loaded and ready to hand, gave him a sense of security that otherwise would have been lacking.

He was called in the morning in the usual manner. After he had freshened up, he found that clothing similar to that which he had worn for the boar hunt had been laid out on the remade bed. The Minetti slipped easily into the right-hand side pocket of the breeches. He practiced drawing. He would never be the Fastest Gun in the West or anywhere else, but he was sure that he would be able to defend himself adequately given only a little warning.

He enjoyed his breakfast of beautifully grilled kidneys, bacon and sausages, skimmed through the morning paper. As before, it was mainly social news and gossip. He noted that the Duchess of Leckhampton, the Comte de Messigny, the Hereditary Chief

Lobenga and the Lady Eulalia were guests of the Princess Von Stolzberg, as was, still, Lieutenant John Grimes. And Captain Daintree and Surgeon Commander Passifern, together with other officers, had been present at Count Vitelli's wine tasting. Passifern, at least, would have enjoyed himself.

Karl entered silently, made a metallic cough to attract Grimes' attention. "Lord, Her Highness awaits you in the gun room."

The gun room? It took a second or so for Grimes' mind to orient itself. Aboard a ship the gun room is to cadets and midshipmen (if such are carried) what the wardroom is to commissioned officers. *The gun room?* The robot must mean that paneled chamber with its racks of assorted weaponry.

"And what's on today?" asked the spaceman through a mouthful of buttered toast dripping with honey. "Another wild boar hunt? Or are we going out for tigers or rogue elephants?"

"None of them, Lord." (Robots are apt to be humorless.) "Today you are shooting Denebian fire pheasants." There was a touch of envy in the mechanical voice. "I am told that they are very good eating, as well as affording excellent sport."

"How so? Are they the size of corvettes, heavily armed and armoured, and vicious when aroused?"

"No, Lord. They are relatively small creatures, brilliantly plumaged, but when put up their flight is extremely fast and erratic."

"Then they should be safe enough from me."

"I was informed, Lord, that you are a gunnery specialist."

"Shooting at large targets, Karl, with a shipful of electronic aids to do all the work for me." He finished his coffee, patted his lips with the napkin (if the supercilious tin butler had not been watching, he would have wiped them) and followed the robot through the doorway.

Marlene was waiting in the gun room. With the Duchess, Lobenga and his wife, and the Comte de Messigny. Grimes noted that only the Princess was dressed for rough outdoor activities, the others were in light, comfortable attire, suitable for lounging about indoors or in the garden. They all seemed in a cheerful mood but for de Messigny whose handsome features were darkened by what was almost a scowl.

"Good morning, John," the Princess greeted him. "It's a fine day for a shoot."

"I always think that it's a pity," said the Duchess, "to destroy those beautiful birds."

"You enjoy them when they appear on the table," Marlene told her.

"Yes, my dear. Yes. And you enjoy blasting them out of the sky, so each of us has her pleasures."

"Blood sports," said the Comte, "are primitive." He permitted himself a sneer. "No doubt they are very much to the taste of a Survey Service gunnery officer, although he may find a shotgun a little small after the weapons that he is used to."

"You are a spaceman yourself, Henri," said Marlene.

"Yes. And a good one. But I'm a merchant spaceman, and before that I was a yachtsman."

"And your ship, as you have said to me, packs the armament of a light cruiser."

"Defensive, Marlene. Defensive. It is the right of any shipmaster or of any man to use any and every means available to defend his own ship, property or whatever."

"I have never liked guns," stated Lobenga, more or less changing the subject. "A hunt in which spears are used—that is to my taste."

"Not to mine," said Grimes.

He took the weapon that Marlene handed him, examined it curiously. It was a shotgun, twin-barreled, light, but with just enough heft to it. Carefully keeping it pointed at the floor, he inspected the action, soon got the hang of it. "Two shots only," he commented, "and then you reload. Wouldn't an automatic weapon be better?"

"Yes," said the Princess, "if all you want to do is kill things. But it would take away the necessity for real skill, would destroy any element of sport."

"But I thought that the whole idea of hunting was to kill things."

"You, John," she told him, "are the sort of man who would use grenades in a trout stream."

"However did you guess?" he countered.

"Mr. Grimes," sneered de Messigny, "is obviously unacquainted with the *mystique* of huntin', shootin' and fishin'. But I have no doubt, Marlene, that under your expert tutelage he will acquire a smattering."

"No doubt," she agreed coldly. "Now, John, you have your gun. I shouldn't need to tell you about safety catches, pointing it at people and all the rest of it. Here's your bag of cartridges." Grimes took it, slung it over his shoulder. "A miniwagon will accompany us to bring in the game we shoot and will also carry our refreshments. Are you ready?"

"Yes," he said.

He followed her out of the gun room.

"Good huntin'!" called the Duchess ironically.

As before, it was a beautiful morning. They strode out over the dew-spangled grass, the sunlight warm on their faces, the grim pile of the castle behind them. To one side and a little back trundled the miniwagon, a vehicle little more than a rectangular box on balloon tired wheels. No doubt it possessed a rudimentary intelligence as well as hidden capabilities. Overhead soared the watchbirds, and ahead, trotting sedately, was a pair of beautiful dogs, red- rather than brown-coated, their plumed tails upraised and waving.

They left the relatively short grass of the fields for rougher ground, gently undulating, with outcroppings of chalky rock (but limestone, thought Grimes, could not exist on this planet), with clumps of golden-blossoming gorse, of purple-flowered heather. The warm air was full of spicy scent, and the stridulation of unseen insects was a pleasant monotone.

Suddenly the Princess stopped, broke her gun, snapped two cartridges into the breech, clicked the weapon into a state of readiness. A little clumsily, Grimes followed suit. Then Marlene gave an order in a language with which Grimes was not familiar, and both dogs yelped softly in acknowledgment. They were away then, running between the boulders and the gorse clumps, tails in a rigid line with their bodies. They were away, something almost serpentine in their smooth, fluid motion, vanishing up the hillside.

There was an outburst of yapping, a surprisingly loud clatter of wings. Two gaudy birds rocketed up, levelled off and flew toward Grimes and the Princess. They were fast, fantastically fast, and their line of flight was unpredictable. The butt of Marlene's gun was to her shoulder and the twin barrels twitched gently as she lined up, leading the birds. There was a report, dull rather than sharp, and, a microsecond later, another one. Two bundles of ruined feathers fell to the ground. The miniwagon rolled toward them, extended a long, thin tentacle, picked up the bodies and dropped them into a receptacle at its rear.

"Nice shooting," said Grimes. He felt that it was expected of him.

"Yes," she agreed, without false modesty. "With the next pair we shall see how you can do."

Again the dogs gave voice, and again a couple of fire pheasants took to the air. Grimes was used to taking snapshots with a pistol, but never with a weapon like the one that he was holding now. But it was so well designed and balanced that it was almost part of him. He let go with his left barrel, felt the satisfaction of seeing a little explosion of scarlet and orange feathers as the shot struck home. But he was too slow with his right, and the surviving bird was darting away and clear before he could pull the trigger.

But it was coming back, flying straight toward him, steadily this time. Grimes fired, was sure that he had scored a hit, but the thing still came on steadily. Hastily, but without fumbling, he ejected and reloaded, fired again, both barrels in quick succession.

Damn it! he thought, *the brute must be armour-plated!*

Again the ejection and the reloading but before he could bring the gun up to his shoulder, the Princess put out a hand to stop him.

"What the hell are you playing at?" she blazed. "First you smash my watchbirds with your bloody dynosoar, and now you try to shoot them!"

"A . . . a watchbird?"

"What else?"

Yes, it was one of the watchbirds; now that he was no longer looking into the sun Grimes could see that. It circled them, its machinery humming, a few feet above their heads, then hovered there. From it came a voice, and some humorist had endowed the thing with a psittacoid squawk.

"Your Highness," it began.

"Yes. What is it?"

"Danger, Your Highness. The Monitor has informed me that a new model of protective avian, still in the experimental stage, has gotten out of control and is heading this way. It is liable to kill any human being on sight."

The Princess laughed. "Yes: I have heard of this new model. A fire pheasant's brain has been incorporated and with it, perhaps, a certain resentment toward ourselves. But it will not be long before it is rounded up and destroyed."

"Hadn't we better return to the Castle?" asked Grimes.

"If you're afraid, yes."

"I am," he said frankly. "And shouldn't we ride in the miniwagon?"

"No. We can walk as fast and run, if we must, faster."

"Your Highness," screeched the watchbird. "It approaches. We go to intercept."

And then a metallic flash in the almost still air and it was gone. Marlene shrugged, whistled the dogs and then, when they came bounding up, told Grimes, "All right. We beat a retreat. But we'd better be ready to fight a rearguard action."

～ Chapter 25 ～

THEY WALKED BACK toward the castle in silence, the miniwagon trundling along to their right, the setters to heel. Somehow, it seemed to Grimes, there was a sudden chill in the air, although the climbing sun still shone brightly, although there was only the gentlest of breezes. *And the dogs,* he thought, *feel something too.* He looked back at the two animals. They were padding along in a cowed manner, their tails drooping.

Marlene said suddenly, angrily, "This is absurd!"

"How so?" asked Grimes.

"Running from a watchbird. They are designed to protect us, not to attack us."

"But you heard what *your* watchbird said. 'It is liable to kill any human being on sight'."

"Any offplanet human being it must have meant. Such as you." She shrugged. "Well, you are my guest, after all. I am responsible for you."

"I've managed to look after myself, so far."

"Thank you. A truly gracious guest."

"And I want to look after you," he said.

She looked full at him then. Momentarily, the harsh lines of her face softened and then she smiled. "I believe that you mean that, John. In any case, some of that incredible luck of yours might rub off on me . . ." She paused, then went on. "Yes, you are lucky. But how will it end? You recall that story I told you about our family

251

superstition, the consequences that always ensued if something is tried, stubbornly, for a fourth time? Well, I was not quite truthful. The *third* attempt is the crucial one."

"It's that way with me and with most people."

"Is it? Anyhow, three times I tried to bring about your accidental death and failed. I'm glad I failed. But something is bound to happen to me now. With that third failure some cataclysmic sequence of events was set in motion."

"Don't be so bloody cheerful."

"This is a morbid conversation, isn't it? As for what's happening now, or what's liable to happen, I have no doubt that my own two watchbirds will be able to deal with the rogue."

Grimes wished that he could share her confidence. After all, he had been instrumental in destroying two of the things. On the other hand, there had been a certain disparity in size and weight, two relatively flimsy, miniature flying machines against a re-entry vehicle.

One of the dogs whined. Grimes stopped, looked back and down. The animals had turned, around, had stiffened in the classic pointing posture. He stared in the direction toward which they were staring, at first saw nothing. And then he could make out three distant specks in the clear sky, three dots apparently in frantic orbital motion about each other.

"Take these," said Marlene. She had got two pairs of binoculars from somewhere in the miniwagon, gave Grimes one of them. He slung his gun, lifted the high-powered glasses to his eyes. A mere touch of his finger sufficed to focus them.

It was like something from one of the History of Warfare films that the cadets had been shown at the Academy. It reminded him of an aerial dogfight over the battlefields of Flanders in the Kaiser's War. There was the rogue, larger than its assailants, brilliantly enameled in orange and scarlet. There were Marlene's two watchbirds, metallically glittering in the sunlight. They were diving and feinting, soaring up and away, diving again. All that was missing was the rattle of machine-gun fire. Contemptuously, the experimental model bore on, ignoring its smaller adversaries. And then one of them, coming up from below while its companion drove in from above, struck the rogue at the juncture of starboard wing with body, oversetting it. It fell out of control, almost to the ground, and then with a frantic fluttering of gaudy pinions somehow made a recovery. There was a burst of bright flame at its tail, a puff of smoke. It went up, almost vertically, like a rocket.

It was a rocket, a rocket with a brain and with the instincts of a bird of prey . . . and with the armament, miniaturized but still deadly, of a minor warship.

The two watchbirds, which had gained altitude, plunged to meet it. From the nose of the rogue came an almost invisible flicker, and the nearer of the airborne guardians burst at once into flames, exploded in blinding blue fire. The other one was hit, too, but only part of its tail was shorn away. It dived, racing its burning companion to the surface, recovered and came up again. The rogue spread its wings and turned in the air to meet the attack.

The watchbird climbed slowly, slowly, unsteadily. It must have been damaged more than superficially by the slashing blade of radiation that had almost missed it. But still it climbed, and the rogue just hung there, waiting, swinging about its short axes, deliberately sighting.

There was another flicker from the vicinity of its beak, and its crippled antagonist was no more (and no less) than a bundle of coruscating, smoking wreckage drifting groundwards.

"Laser . . ." whispered Grimes. "The bloody thing's got laser!"

"We must run!" For the first time there was fear in Marlene's voice, the fear of one who has seen her impregnable defenses fall before superior, overwhelming fire power. Grimes knew how she must feel. He had felt the same way himself, as everybody has felt when faced with the failure of foolproof, *everything* proof mechanisms. "We must run!"

"Where to? That thing'll pick us off faster than you picked off the fire pheasants." He grabbed her arm before she could stumble away in panic flight. "Cover!" he shouted. "That's the answer."

"The miniwagon!" So she was thinking again.

"No." He could visualize the thing's machinery exploding as the mechanism of the watchbirds had exploded. He pulled her to one of the outcroppings of rock, about five feet high. It wasn't very good but it was better than nothing. He and the girl dropped behind it as the rogue screamed over, using its rocket drive, firing its laser gun. There was an explosion of smoke and dust and splinters from the top of the boulder.

"Quick!" cried Grimes. "Before it can turn!" He got to his feet, yanked the girl to hers, dragged her around to the other side of the outcropping. He unslung his gun. His pistol would not have been a better weapon, it didn't have the range or the spread. There was always the chance that the shotgun pellets would find some vital spot. It was a slim one, he knew, but . . .

The rogue seemed to be having trouble in turning. It came round at last, lined up for the natural fortification (such as it was). It drove in, its laser beam scoring a smoldering furrow in the turf. Unless it lifted its sights, Grimes knew that he was safe until the last moment, or he *hoped* that he was safe. He stood his ground.

Now!

A left and a right, the noise of the explosions deafening and he dropped to the ground, his ears still ringing, but he was able to hear the sharp *crack* of riven rock, felt a gust of heat.

He scrambled to his feet. This time he did not have to help the girl up. Together they ran around the clump of weatherworn boulders. Grimes half-tripped over something soft, which yelped. The dogs were still with them.

He stood there, reloading.

From the ground Marlene said, "You hit it, John."

"Yes. I hit it. Like hitting a dreadnaught with a peashooter. Keep down. Here comes the bastard again!"

It seemed to be slower this time and erratic in its flight. The wavering laser beam started a flaring, crackling fire in the gorse. But it straightened up toward the finish of its run, came in fast. Grimes let fly with both barrels at once and dropped hastily. The Princess snatched the smouldering cap off his head.

"John! John! Are you . . .?"

"I'm all right. My brains are no more addled than usual. Come on!"

Like a game of musical chairs, he thought. *And, somebody has to be the loser . . .*

This last time it came in slowly, using wings and not reaction drive. And its laser seemed to be out of action. It came in slowly, a mechanical bird of prey, climbing, finally hanging directly above the man and the girl and the two cringing dogs, high, but not too high to be a good target.

As we, thought Grimes, *are good targets for its bombs, if it carries any.*

Standing, he could not bring his gun to bear, so lay supine, the weapon aimed directly upwards. The air in the shallow hollow was blue with acrid smoke and the turf was littered with empty shells as Grimes fired again and again and again, as the Princess matched him shot for shot. Something hot stung his cheek; it was a pellet from his own gun or from Marlene's. They must be falling all over this circumscribed area like a metallic hail.

One of the dogs cried out sharply; it must have been hit and hurt by the fall of shot. Yelping, its tail between its legs, it dashed out from the barely adequate shelter of the outcropping. Its companion followed it. Then, screaming, the rogue dived. Grimes scrambled erect somehow, kept the butt of the shotgun to his shoulder, led the thing as it plunged and let it have both barrels.

Perhaps he hit again, perhaps he did not, but it made no difference. The killer bird swooped down upon the leading dog, and its long, straight beak (rapier as well as laser gun) skewered the hapless animal just behind the ribs, hooked it up from the ground, shrieking, and then with a peculiar midair twisting motion tossed it up and away. The body, its legs still running in nothingness, fell against a rock with an audible *crunch,* and then was still.

The other setter howled dismally, kept on running, but it could never be as fast as the rogue. It almost made the protection of a clump of gorse, and then the murderous machine was on it. This time it did not use its blood-dripping beak. It banked, like an old-fashioned aircraft, and the leading edge of one stiff wing slashed the animal across the hindquarters. Howling still, it tried to drag itself along with its forelegs.

Marlene was saying something. "I must go, John. I must put him out of his misery."

He caught her arm. "No. Don't be a fool."

She shook him off. "I *must.* Cover me."

She was running out over the uneven turf, slipping and staggering. Grimes dropped his shotgun, pulled the pistol from his pocket, started after her. The rogue reached her before he did. She screamed as the deadly beak grazed her shoulder, tearing a ragged square of fabric out of her shirt; she fell to her hands and knees. But she was up again, still staggering toward her dying dog, then knocked sprawling by buffeting metal wings. Again there was the thrust of the rapier beak, and this time most of the back of her upper garment was carried away on the point of it.

I must fire, thought Grimes, *before it gets too close to her. In case it blows up.* The rattle of the Minetti set on full automatic, was startlingly loud, and the butt vibrated in the moist palm of his hand. The rogue, obligingly, was making a good target of itself (it *must* have been damaged by all the shotgun fire) slowly turning broadside on before coming in for another attack.

Grimes ejected the empty clip, put in a full one. He was firing more slowly and carefully now, in short bursts. Then, anticlimactically, the rogue fluttered slowly to the ground. There was no explosion, only a thin trickle of blue smoke. He watched it for a second, then hurried to Marlene. She was sitting up now, only a few shreds of ruined shirt clinging to her torso. There was a trickle of blood from her right shoulder.

She waved him away, pointing. "Bruno. First you must . . . do what is necessary for him . . ."

He did it. A single shot from the Minetti sufficed. Then he walked slowly back to her, fell on his knees beside her.

"Marlene! You're hurt . . ."

"Only a scratch. But for you I . . . I could have been killed."

And when you're a near-immortal, he thought, *death can be important.* But, for the first time perhaps, he could see her point of view, could feel with her and for her. Suddenly there was a warmth between them, a warmth that, until now, had been lacking. It could be that it was shared fear that brought them together, shared peril. It could be that, at last, there was the admission of a common humanity.

But her arms were about him and her face, grimy and tear-stained was lifted to his, and his arms were about her, and her mouth on his was soft and warm and moist, and suddenly all barriers were down, scattered like the clothing that littered the turf around them, and the sun was warm on their naked bodies, although never as warm as the heat of their own mutual generating . . .

Almost, Grimes did not hear the sharp *plop*.

Almost he did not hear it, but he felt the metal strands writhing about his bare skin, biting into his limbs, binding himself and Marlene together in a ghastly parody, an obscene exhibition of physical love.

Into his limited range of vision, still further obscured by the tangle of the girl's blonde hair, stepped de Messigny. In his hand he held one of the bell-mouthed net-throwing pistols.

"A pretty picture!" he sneered. "A very pretty picture." In spite of the deliberate coldness of his voice, it was obvious that he was struggling to contain his fury. "As for you, Marlene, you slut! An affair with one of us I could have tolerated, but for you to give yourself to a lowbred outworlder!"

Her voice, in reply, was muffled. Grimes could feel her lips moving against his face. "I'm not property, Henri. I'm not *your* property."

"I would not want you now, you bitch."

Grimes saw that the man had pulled a knife from the sheath at his belt. He struggled to get his mouth clear, after an effort was able to mumble, "Put that thing away."

"Not yet, Mr. Grimes. Not yet."

"But this is not Marlene's fault, de Messigny."

"I have come here neither as judge nor as executioner, Mr. Grimes, although Marlene will be most appropriately punished for what *she* has done. I have come, only to sacrifice Lobenga's white goat, and the white goat is *you*."

Grimes waited for the descent of the blade. Stab or slash, what did it matter? Although a stab might be faster. And then de Messigny uttered a choking cry, seemed to be trying to contort himself so that he could strike with the blade at something behind him. Wound tightly about his neck there was a thin, metal tentacle. He was jerked out of sight.

Grimes heard the threshing sounds of the Comte's struggles slowly diminish. They finally ceased.

"The miniwagon . . ." whispered Marlene, "and only a carryall but it has intelligence of sorts, and it's supposed to protect its mistress to the best of its ability. But it's slow. It was almost too slow . . ."

"It . . . it got here in time."

"Only . . . just."

She was close to him, even closer then she had been before de Messigny cast his net. Suddenly he was acutely conscious of her, all of her. And he had some freedom, not much, but a little, enough.

"Can you. . . .?" she murmured. Then, "After all, as the old saying has it, we might as well be hung for sheep as lambs . . ."

"I can . . ." he muttered.

He did.

And then, only then, did Marlene give careful orders to the dim-witted machine, telling it to pick up the pistol with its tentacle, telling it how to set the weapon so that a pulse of radiation would cause the net to loose its hold. Neither of them could see what was happening, and Grimes feared that the stupid thing would well-meaningly pick up and fire the Minetti at them.

But it did not, and each of them felt a brief tingling sensation, and then they were free. Marlene wept again over her slaughtered dogs, stared at the purple-faced, contorted body of de Messigny without expression. She resumed her clothing. Grimes resumed his.

They clambered into the miniwagon, let it carry them in silence back to the Castle.

～ Chapter 26 ～

THEY WERE WAITING for Grimes and Marlene in the castle courtyard—Lobenga, the Lady Eulalia, and the Duchess of Leckhampton. They were an oddly assorted trio: the Negro in his leopard skin, with a necklace of bones (animal? human?) and with a hide bag, containing who knew what disgusting relics slung at his waist; his wife robed in spotless white, with a gold circlet about her dark hair; the Duchess in gaudy finery, flounced skirt boldly striped in black and scarlet, sequined lemon-yellow blouse, a blue, polka dotted kerchief as a head covering. The clay pipe that she was smoking with obvious enjoyment should have been incongruous, but it suited her.

Before them was a large box, a three dimensional viewing screen. To one side was the grim effigy of Baron Samedi, the wooden cross in its scarecrow clothing. It should have looked absurd in broad daylight, in these surroundings, but it did not.

Witch doctor, priestess and fortune teller . . . thought Grimes bewilderedly.

"What is this?" demanded Marlene. "What are you doing here?"

"We had to come outside, Princess," Lobenga told her. "There is magic soaked into the very stones of your castle, but it is the wrong sort of magic."

"Magic!" her voice was contemptuous. "That?" She gestured to the extension of the Monitor, in the screen of which the dead man, the dead dogs and the crumpled wreckage of the rogue were still visible. "Or *that?*" Her arm pointed rigidly at the clothed cross.

"Or both? "asked the Duchess quietly.

"You watched?"

"We watched," confirmed Lobenga.

"Everything?"

"Everything."

"And you did nothing to help?"

"It was all in the cards," said the Duchess.

"And you watched, everything. And you felt a vicarious thrill, just as you do at those famous masked balls of yours, Your Grace. There is nothing more despicable than a *voyeur,* especially one who spies upon her friends."

"We were obliged to watch," said Lobenga.

"By whom? By what?"

"The bones were cast," almost sang Eulalia, "the cards were read. But still there was the possibility of the unforeseen, the unforeseeable, some malign malfunction of the plan. We had to be ready to intervene."

"There were quite a few times when you could have intervened," growled the spaceman. "When you *should* have intervened."

"No," said Lobenga. "No, Mr. Grimes. The entire operation went as planned."

"What a world!" snarled the Lieutenant. "What a bloody world! I'm sorry, Marlene, but I can't stay in this castle a second longer. I don't like your friends. Call me a taxi, or whatever you do on this planet, so that I can get back to the ship. Tell that tin butler of yours to pack my bags."

"John!"

"I mean it, Marlene."

"Let him go," said Eulalia. "He has played his part."

"As I have," whispered the princess.

"Yes."

"As Henri did."

"Yes."

She flared, "What sort of monsters are you? "

"Not monsters, Marlene," said Lobenga gently. "Just servants of a higher power."

"Of the Monitor?" she sneered. "Or of Baron Samedi?"

"Or both?" asked Eulalia.

"Things went a little too far," said the Duchess.

"You mean Henri's death?" queried Marlene. "But somebody had to die."

"I do not mean Henri's death. I mean what happened afterwards. But it does not matter. After all, the English aristocracy has always welcomed an occasional infusion of fresh blood. And, my dear, in a way the child, if there is one, will be Henri's."

"That," said Marlene, her voice expressionless, "is a comforting thought."

"I'm glad that you see it that way." The Duchess sucked on her pipe, blew out a cloud of smoke that was acrid rather than fragrant. "You know, my dear, the cards were really uncanny. The Hanged Man kept turning up." For Grimes' benefit she explained, "That is one of the cards of ill-omen in the Tarot pack." She went on, "Of course, we were expecting a death, a violent death, but not in so literal a manner."

"Must we go into all this, Honoria?" asked Marlene.

"If you would rather not, my dear, we will not. But. . ."

"But what?"

"Poor Henri was addicted to the use of archaic slang but, oddly enough, only when he was talking to me. Just before he went out to play Vulcan to your Venus and Mars he said that he was going to fix your wagon." She deliberately took her time refilling and relighting her short pipe. "But your wagon fixed him."

"Let us leave these ghouls," said Marlene disgustedly. Grimes fell rather than jumped out of the miniwagon, then helped the girl to the ground. Together they walked into the castle.

"Yes, John," said Marlene. "It is better that return to your ship. You have played your part, more than your part."

Grimes looked at the girl's grave face. There was nothing in it for him any more. He looked past her to the shining weapons incongruously displayed on the wall of her boudoir. He thought, *I know more about guns than women.*

He said, "I'm sorry it happened."

"Don't be a liar, John. You wanted me from the very first moment that you saw me, and you finally got me."

"Are you sorry it happened?"

For the first time since their return to the castle, she showed signs of emotion.

"That is a hard question to answer, John. But, no, I am not sorry that it happened. I am not even sorry that it happened the way that it did. What I am sorry about is the humiliation. And, of course, Henri's death." Her features suddenly contorted into a vicious mask. "But he deserved it!"

"And somebody, as everybody here has been telling me, had to die."

"And better, I suppose, one of us than one of you. It keeps it all in the family, doesn't it? Very neat, very tidy." There were the beginnings of hysteria in her voice.

"Marlene!"

"No. *Don't touch me!*"

"All right. But I thought . . ."

"Don't think. It's dangerous."

"Marlene, what about the child, if there is one?"

"What about it?"

"Well . . . it could be . . . embarrassing. Will you marry me?"

She laughed then but it was not hysterical laughter. It was not altogether contemptuous. "Oh, John, John . . . The perfect petty bourgeois to the very last. Offering to make an honest woman of me, *me*, and on a world which can boast the finest medical brains in the Galaxy. Not that our physicians have had much practice in terminating pregnancies. Marry *you*, John, a penniless Survey Service Lieutenant? Oh; I appreciate it, appreciate the offer, but it just wouldn't work out. You aren't our sort of people and we aren't yours. I'd sooner have married Henri, and he asked me often enough, with all his faults."

"We could marry," he pressed doggedly, "and then divorce."

"No. This is El Dorado, not some lower middle-class slum of a planet. And furthermore, John, I shall be a heroine. I shall go down in history. The first woman to conceive on this world."

"You don't know that you have."

"But I do. I . . . *I felt it.*"

He got slowly to his feet. "I'll see if Karl has packed my bags."

She said, "You don't have to go."

He asked, "Do you want me to?"

Her expression softened almost imperceptibly. "What if I told you that Lobenga, Eulalia and the Duchess have already left the castle? They have done what they had to do."

"And have they? Left, I mean."

"Yes."

He felt the weakening of his resolution. Those other guests had witnessed what had happened between Marlene and himself but, as servants of the Monitor, there was much that they must have witnessed. Now that he would no longer be obliged to meet them socially . . .

"You will stay?" she asked.

"Why?" he queried bluntly.

"Because . . ."

"Because what?"

"Because I want to be sure."

"You told me that you were."

She quoted, "Only two things in life are certain, death and taxes. Death, John, not Birth. But, together, we can bring some degree of certainty to the fact of conception."

He said, "You are a cold-blooded bitch."

"But I'm not, John, I'm not." She was on her feet, her body gleaming golden through the translucent green wrap that she had changed into, her slender arms slightly away from her sides. He took a step toward her, and another, until she was pressed against him. Her hands went up, clasped at the back of his neck, pulled his mouth down to hers.

There was a discreet, metallic cough.

The princess pulled away from Grimes, asked coldly, "Yes, Karl?"

"I must apologize, Your Highness. But a call has come through by way of the Monitor for all personnel of the cruiser *Aries*. It seems that the ship is urgently required to help quell an insurrection on Merganta, which world, as you know, is only two light years from El Dorado. Lieutenant Grimes' bags are already in the air car."

She said, "You have to go."

He said, "Yes."

"Good bye."

"I'll be back."

"Will you?" she asked, her face suddenly hard, "Will you?" Her laugh was brittle. "Yes, John, come back when you have your first billion credits."

He could think of nothing more to say, turned abruptly on his heel and followed the robot to the waiting air car.

~ Chapter 27 ~

THERE WAS the insurrection on Merganta, a bloody affair, in the suppression of which *Aries* did all that was demanded of her, but no more. Many of her officers and most of her crew felt more than a little sympathy for the rebels. It was Grimes, in command of one of the cruiser's armed pinnaces, who intervened to stop the mass executions of three hundred women, wives of leading insurgents, turning his weapons on the government machine gunners. For this he was reprimanded, officially, by Captain Daintree, who, later, in a stormy interview with the planetary president, used such phrases as "an overly zealous officer" and "mistaken identity," adding coldly that Lieutenant Grimes naturally assumed that it was not the forces of law and order who were about to commit cold-blooded murder.

There was the mutiny aboard the Dog Star Line's freighter *Corgi* and the long chase, almost clear out to the Rim, before the merchantman was overhauled and boarded. The mutineers did not put up a fight, for which Grimes, in charge of the boarding party, was profoundly thankful. He had seen enough of killing.

There was the earthquake that destroyed Ballantrae, the capital of Ayr, one of the planets of the Empire of Waverley. *Aries,* the only major vessel in the vicinity, hastened to the stricken city, performed nobly in the rescue work and then, from her generators supplied power for essential services until the work of reconstruction was well under way.

All in all, it was an eventful voyage, and a long one, with the movements of the ship unpredictable. The married men, those who were pining for letters from home, were far from sorry when, at last, *Aries* was recalled to Lindisfarne Base.

Almost all the officers were in the wardroom when the mail came on board. They waited impatiently. Finally Hodge, the Paymaster Lieutenant, came in, followed by a rating carrying a large hamper of packages. "Gentlemen," he announced. "Cupid's messenger, in person. Sweethearts and wives, all in the same basket. What am I bid?"

"Cut the cackle, Hodge!" snarled Lieutenant Commander Cooper. "Deal 'em out, although mine'll be only bills and please explains as usual."

"As you say, sir, Lieutenant Commander, sir. Roll up, roll up, for the lucky dip!"

"Get on with it, Hodge!" snapped the Navigator. He was not the only one becoming impatient. Luckily the mail had already been sorted, so there was little delay in its distribution. Most of the officers, as soon as they had received their share, retired to the privacy of their own cabins to read it.

Grimes looked at his, recognizing handwriting, typescript styles, postage stamps. A letter from faraway . . . From Jane? Nice of her to write after all these years. One from Caribbea. That would be from Susanna. And a parcel, a little, cubical parcel. The address typed, with oddly Gothic lettering. And the stamp in the likeness of a gold coin, and it probably was embossed gold leaf at that . . .

Surgeon Commander Passifern was demanding attention. "This is interesting," he declaimed. "This is *really* interesting. You remember how we were called in to El Dorado so that I could help their top doctor, Lord Tarlton of Dunwich, with his problem. I worked with him and his people—they've some brilliant men there, too—quite closely. 'Diet,' I said to him. 'Diet, Tarlton, that's the answer. Cut out fancy, mucked-up food of yours, get back to the simple life. Don't over-eat. Don't drink.'"

"Physician, heal thyself . . ." muttered Cooper.

Passifern ignored this, "And it worked. This—" he waved the sheet of expensive looking paper—"is a letter from Lord Tarlton. In it he thanks me—well, *us,* actually, but he's just being polite to the ship—for our help. Since we left there have been no fewer than four hundred and twenty-five births."

"Did he . . ." began Grimes, "did he say who the mothers were?"

"Hardly, young Grimes. Not in a short note."

"At least," put in Cooper, "we know that none of us were the fathers."

Grimes left the wardroom then. He found himself resenting the turn that the conversation had taken. He went to his cabin, shut the door behind him, then sat down on his bunk. He found the little tab on the seal of the parcel, pulled it sharply. The wrapping fell away.

Inside it was a solidograph. From its depths smiled a blonde woman, Marlene, a more mature Marlene, a matronly Marlene, looking down at the infant in her arms.

Grimes had been amused more than once by the gushing female friends of young mothers with their fatuous remarks: "Oh, he's got his mother's eyes," or "He's got his Uncle Fred's nose," or "He's got his Auntie Kate's mouth . . ."

But there was, he admitted now, something in it. This child, indubitably, had his father's ears.

Suddenly he felt very sorry that he would never make that billion credits.

THE
HARD WAY
UP

~ With Good Intentions ~

PATHFINDER was not a happy ship.

Pathfinder's Captain was not a happy man, and made this glaringly obvious.

Young Lieutenant Grimes, newly appointed to the Survey Service cruiser, was also far from happy. During his few years in Space he had served under strict commanding officers as well as easy going ones, but never under one like Captain Tolliver.

"You must make allowances, John," Paymaster Lieutenant Beagle told him as the two young men were discussing matters over a couple or three drinks in Grimes's cabin.

"Make allowances?" echoed Grimes. "I don't know what's biting him—but I know what's biting me. Him, that's what."

"All the same, you should make allowances."

"It's all very well for you to talk, Peter—but you idlers can keep out of his way. We watchkeepers can't."

"But he's a Worrallian," said Beagle. "Didn't you know?"

"No," admitted Grimes. "I didn't."

He knew now. He knew, too, that there were only a hundred or so Worrallians throughout the entire Galaxy. Not so long ago the population of Worrall had been nudging the thirty million mark. Worrall had been a prosperous planet—also it had been among the few Man-colonized worlds of the Interstellar Federation upon which the concepts of race and nationality had been allowed to take hold and develop. "It makes for healthy competition," had been the claim of the Worrallian delegations—three of them—whenever the subject came up at the meetings of the Federation Grand Council. And so they had competed happily among themselves on their little ball of mud and rock and water—North Worrall, and South Worrall, and Equatorial Worrall—until all three nations laid simultaneous claim to a chain of hitherto worthless islands upon which flourished the stinkbird colonies. The stinkbird—it was more of a flying reptile really, although with certain mammalian characteristics—had always been regarded as more unpleasant than useful, and if anybody had wanted those barren, precipitous rocks lashed by the perpetually stormy seas the stinkbird would soon have gone the way of many another species unlucky enough to get in Man's way. The stinkbird—along with everything and everybody else on Worrall—finally was unlucky, this being when a bright young chemist discovered that a remarkably effective rejuvenating compound was secreted by certain glands in its body. Worrall, although a prosperous enough closed economy, had always been lacking, until this time, in exports that would fetch high prices on the interstellar market.

So there was a squabble—with words at first, and then with weapons. In its ultimate stage somebody pushed some sort of button—or, quite possibly, three buttons were pushed. The only Worrallians to survive were those who were elsewhere at the time of the button-pushing.

And Captain Tolliver was a Worrallian.

Grimes sighed. He felt sorry for the man. He could visualize, but dimly, what it must be like to have no place in the entire Galaxy to call home, to know that everything, but everything, had been vaporized in one hellish blast of fusion flame—parents, friends, lovers, the house in which one was brought up, the school in which one was educated, the bars in which one used to drink. Grimes shuddered. But he still felt sorry for himself.

Grimes realized that Captain Tolliver had come into the control room. But, as the commanding officer had not announced his presence, the young man went on with what he was doing—the mid-watch check of the ship's position. Carefully, trying hard not to fumble, Grimes manipulated the Carlotti Direction Finder—an instrument with which he was not yet familiar—lining up the antenna, an elliptical Mobius Strip rotating about its long axis, with the Willishaven beacon, finally jotting down the angle relative to the fore-and-aft line of the ship. Then, still working slowly and carefully, he took a reading on Brownsworld and, finally, on Carlyon. By this time he was perspiring heavily and his shirt was sticking to his body, and his prominent ears were flushed and burning painfully. He swiveled his chair so that he could reach the chart tank, laid off the bearings. The three filaments of luminescence intersected nicely, exactly on the brighter filament that marked *Pathfinder's* trajectory. Decisively Grimes punched the keys that caused the time of the observation, in tiny, glowing figures, to appear alongside the position.

"Hrrmph."

Grimes simulated a start of surprise, swung round in his chair to face the Captain. "Sir?"

Tolliver was a tall, gangling scarecrow of a man, and even though his uniform was clean and correct in every detail it hung on him like a penitent's sackcloth and ashes. He stared down at his officer from bleak grey eyes. He said coldly, "Mr. Grimes, I checked the time it took you to put a position in the tank. It was no less than eleven minutes, forty-three point five seconds. Objective speed is thirty-five point seven six lumes. Over what distance did this ship travel from start to finish of your painfully slow operations?"

"I can work it out, sir . . ." Grimes half got up from his chair to go to the control room computer.

"Don't bother, Mr. Grimes. Don't bother. I realize that watch-keepers have more important things with which to exercise their tiny minds than the boresome details of navigation—the girl in the last port, perhaps, or the girl you hope to meet in the next one . . ."

More than Grimes's ears was flushed now. A great proportion of his watch had been spend reminiscing over the details of his shore leave on New Capri.

"This cross of yours looks suspiciously good. I would have

expected an inexpert navigator such as yourself to produce more of a cocked hat. I suppose you did allow for distance run between bearings?"

"Of course, sir."

"Hrrmph. Well, Mr. Grimes, we will assume that this fix of yours is reasonably accurate. Put down a D.R. from it for 1200 hours, then lay off a trajectory from there to Delta Sextans."

"Delta Sextans, sir?"

"You heard me."

"But aren't we bound for Carlyon?"

"We were bound for Carlyon, Mr. Grimes. But—although it may well have escaped your notice—the arm of our lords and masters in Admiralty House is a long one, extending over many multiples of light years. For your information, we have been ordered to conduct a survey of the planetary system of Delta Sextans."

"Will there be landings, sir?" asked Grimes hopefully.

"Should it concern you, Mr. Grimes, you will be informed when the time comes. Please lay off the trajectory."

Lieutenant Commander Wanger, the ship's Executive Officer, was more informative than the Captain had been. Convening off-duty officers in the wardroom he gave them a run-down on the situation. He said, "No matter what the biologists, sociologists and all the rest of 'em come up with, population keeps on exploding. And so we, as well as most of the other survey cruisers presently in commission, have been ordered to make more thorough inspections of habitable planets which, in the past, were filed away, as it were, for future reference.

"Delta Sextans has a planetary family of 10 worlds. Of these, only two—Delta Sextans IV and Delta Sextans V—could possibly meet our requirements. According to Captain Loveil's initial survey IV could be rather too hot, and V more than a little too cold. Both support oxygen-breathing life forms, although V, with its mineral wealth, has greater industrial potential than IV. In any case it is doubtful if IV will be selected as the site for the Delta Sextans colony; Captain Lovell said that in his opinion, and in that of his biologists, at least one of the indigenous species comes into the third category."

"And what is that?" asked a junior engineer.

"Any being in the third category," explained the Executive Officer, "is considered capable of evolving into the second category."

"And what is the second category?" persisted the engineer.

"The likes of us. And the first category is what we might become—or, if we're very unlucky, run into. Anyhow, the ruling is that third category beings may be observed, but not interfered with. And taking somebody else's world is classed as interference. Will somebody pour me some more coffee?"

Somebody did, and after lubricating his throat Wanger went on. "The drill will be this. We establish a camp of observers on IV— according to the initial surveys there's nothing there that could be at all dangerous to well-equipped humans—and then the ship shoves off for V to get on with the real work. There's no doubt that V will be selected for the new colony—but it will be as well if the colonists know something about their next-door neighbors."

"Any idea who'll be landed on IV?" asked Grimes.

"Haven't a clue, John. There'll be a team of biologists, ethologists, cartographers, geologists, and whatever. If the Old Man abides by Regulations—and he will—there'll be an officer of the military branch officially in charge of the camp. Frankly, it's not a job that I'd care for—I've had experience of it. Whoever goes with the boggins will soon find that he's no more than chief cook and bottle washer— quite literally."

Nonetheless, Grimes was pleased when he was told, some days later, that he was to be in charge of the landing party.

Pathfinder hung in orbit about Delta Sextans IV until the boat was safely down, until Grimes reported that the camp was established. To start with, Grimes enjoyed his authority and responsibility—then found that once the turbulent atmospheric approach had been negotiated and the landing craft was sitting solidly and safely on the bank of a river it was responsibility only. The scientists—not at all offensively—soon made it clear that once they were away from the ship gold braid and brass buttons meant less than nothing. When the stores and equipment were unloaded each of them was concerned only with his own treasures. They cooperated, after a fashion, in setting up the inflatable tents that were living quarters and laboratory. Reluctantly they agreed to defer their initial explorations until the following morning. (The boat, following the Survey Service's standard practice, had landed at local dawn, but by the time that Grimes had things organized to his liking the sun, a blur of light and heat heavily veiled by the overcast, was almost set.)

It was Grimes who cooked the evening meal—and even though the most important tool employed in its preparation was a can opener he rather resented it. Three of the six scientists were women, and if anybody had ever told them that a woman's place is in the kitchen they had promptly forgotten it. He resented it, too, when nobody showed any appreciation of his efforts. His charges gobbled their food without noticing what it was, intent upon their shop talk. The only remark addressed to Grimes was a casual suggestion that he have the flitters ready for use at first light.

The Lieutenant left the surveying party, still talking nineteen to the dozen, in the mess tent, hoping that they would eventually get around to stacking the dishes and washing up. (They didn't.) Outside it was almost dark and, in spite of the heat of the past day, there was a damp chill in the air. Something was howling in the forest of cabbage-like trees back from the river bank, and something else flapped overhead on wide, clattering wings. There were insects, too—or things analogous to insects. They did not bite, but they were a nuisance. They were attracted, Grimes decided, by his body heat. He muttered to himself, "If the bastards like warmth so much, why the hell can't they come out in the daytime?"

He decided to switch on the floods. With this perpetual overcast he might have trouble recharging the batteries during the hours of daylight, but they should hold out until *Pathfinder's* return. He was able to work easily in the harsh glare and made a thorough check of the alarm system. Anything trying to get into the camp would either be electrocuted or get a nasty shock, according to size. (The same applied, of course, to anything or anybody trying to get out—but he had warned the scientists.) Finally he opened the boxes in which the flitters were stowed, started to assemble the first of the machines. He did not like them much himself—they were flimsy, one-person helicopters, with a gas bag for greater lift—but he doubted that he would get the chance to use one. Already he could see that he would be confined to camp for the duration of the party's stay on IV.

With the camp secure for the night and the flitters assembled he returned to the mess tent—to find that the scientists had retired to their sleeping tents and left him with all the washing up.

Came the dawn, such as it was, and Grimes was rudely awakened by Dr. Kortsoff, one of the biologists. "Hey, young Grimes," shouted the bearded, burly scientist. "Rise and shine! What about some breakfast? Some of us have to work for our livings, you know!"

"I know," grumbled Grimes. "That's what I was doing most of last night."

He extricated himself from his sleeping bag, pulled on yesterday's shirt and shorts (still stiff with dried sweat, but they would have to do until he got *himself* organized) and thrust his feet into sandals, stumbled out of his tent—and was surrounded by a mob of naked women. There were only three of them, as a matter of fact, but they were making enough noise for a mob. One of them, at least—the red-haired Dr. Margaret Lazenby—possessed the sort of good looks enhanced by anger, but Grimes was not in an appreciative mood.

"Mr. Grimes!" she snapped. "Do you want to *kill* us?"

"What do you mean, Dr. Lazenby?" he asked meekly.

"That bloody force field of yours, or whatever it is. When we were trying to go down to the river for our morning swim Jenny and I were nearly electrocuted. Turn the bloody thing off, will you?"

"I warned you last night that I'd set it up . . ."

"We never heard you. In any case, there aren't any dangerous animals here . . ."

"Never take anything for granted . . .!" Grimes began.

"You can say that again, Grimes. Never take it for granted, for example, that everybody knows all about the odd things you do during the night when sensible people are sleeping. Setting up force fields on a world where there's nothing more dangerous than a domestic cat!"

"What about some *coffee*, Mr. Grimes?" somebody else was yelling.

"I've only one pair of hands," muttered Grimes as he went to switch off the force field. . And so it went on throughout the day—fetch this, fix that, do this, don't do that, lend a hand here, there's a good fellow . . . Grimes remembered, during a very brief smoke, what Maggie Lazenby had told him once about the pecking order, claiming that what was true for barnyard fowls was also true for human beings. "There's the boss bird," she had said, "and she's entitled to peck everybody. There's the number two bird—and she's pecked by the boss, and pecks everybody else. And so on, down the line, until we come to the poor little bitch who's pecked by *everybody*."

"But that doesn't apply to humans," Grimes had demurred. "Doesn't it just, duckie! In schools, aboard ships . . . I've nothing to do with the administration of this wagon—thank all the Odd Gods of the Galaxy!—but even I can see now that poor Ordinary Spaceman Wilkes is bullied by everybody . . ."

Grimes had never, so far as he knew, bullied that hapless rating—but he found himself wishing that the man were here. As he was not, Grimes was bottom bird in the pecking order. There was no malice about it—or no conscious malice. It was just that Grimes was, by the standards of the scientific party, only semi-literate, his status that of a hewer of wood, a drawer of water. He was in an environment where his qualifications counted for little or nothing, where the specialists held sway. And these same specialists, Grimes realized, must have resented the very necessary discipline aboard the ship. Although they would never have admitted it to themselves they were dogs having their day.

The next day wasn't so bad. Six of the flitters were out—which meant that Grimes had the camp to himself. Two by two the scientists had lifted from the camp site, ascending into the murk like glittering, mechanical angels. Carrying a portable transceiver—and a projectile pistol, just in case—Grimes went for a stroll along the river bank. He felt a little guilty about deserting his post, but should any of his charges get into trouble and yell for help he would know at once. He decided that he would walk to the first bend in the wide stream, and then back.

Delta Sextans IV was not a pretty world. The sky was grey, with a paler blur that marked the passage of the hot sun across it. The river was grey. The fleshy-leaved vegetation was grey, with the merest hint of dull green. There was little distinction between blossom and foliage as far as a non-botanist like Grimes was concerned.

But it was good to get away from the camp, from that huddle of plastic igloos, and from the multitudinous chores. It was good to walk on the surface of a world unspoiled by Man, the first time that Grimes had done so. Captain Loveil's survey had been, after all, a very superficial effort and so, thought Grimes, there was a chance that he, even he, would find something, some plant or animal, that would be named after him. He grinned wryly. If any Latin tags were to be affixed to local fauna and flora his own name would be the last to be considered.

He came to the bend in the river, decided to carry on for just a few yards past it. *Well,* he thought with a glow of pleasure, *I have found* something—*something which the others, flapping around on their tin wings, have missed* . . . The something was an obvious game trail leading through the jungle to the water's edge. But why in this particular spot? Grimes investigated. Elsewhere the bank was steep—here there was a little bay, with a gently shelving beach. Here, too, growing in the shallow water, was a clump of odd-looking plants—straight, thick stems, each a few feet high, each topped by a cluster of globules varying in size from grape to orange. And here, too, something had died or been killed. Only the bones were left—yellowish, pallidly gleaming. There was a rib cage, which must have run the entire length of a cylindrical body. There was a skull, almost spherical. There were jaws, with teeth—the teeth of a herbivore, thought Grimes. The beast, obviously, had been a quadruped, and about the size of a Terran Shetland pony.

Suddenly Grimes stiffened. Something was coming along that trail through the jungle—something that rustled and chattered. As he backed away from the skeleton he pulled out his pistol, thumbed back the safety catch. He retreated to the bend of the river and waited there, ready to fight or run—but curious as to what sort of animal would appear.

There were more than one of them. They spilled out on to the river bank—about a dozen grey, shaggy brutes, almost humanoid. Mostly they walked upright, but now and again dropped to all fours. They chattered and gesticulated. They varied in size from that of a small man to that of a young child—but somehow Grimes got the idea that there were no children among them.

They had not come to drink. They went straight to the plants, started tearing the largest—the ripest?—fruit from the stems, stuffing them into their wide mouths, gobbling them greedily. There was plenty for all—but, inevitably, there was one who wasn't getting any. It was not that he was the smallest of the tribe—but neither was he the largest. Even so, his trouble seemed to be psychological rather than physical; he seemed to be hampered by a certain diffidence, a reluctance to join in the rough and tumble scramble.

At last, when all his mates were busy gorging themselves, he shambled slowly through the shallows to the fruit plants. Glancing timorously around to see that nobody was watching he put out a hand, wrenched one of the spheroids from its stem. He was not allowed to even taste it. A hairy paw landed on the side of his head with a loud *thunk,* knocking him sprawling into the muddy water. The brute who had attacked him snatched the fruit from his hand, bit into it, spat and grimaced and threw it out into the river. No less than three times there was a roughly similar sequence of events—and then, as though in response to some inaudible signal, the troop scampered back into the jungle, the victim of the bullies looking back wistfully to the fruit that he had not so much as tasted.

That evening Grimes told the scientists about his own minor exploration, but none of them was interested. Each was too engrossed in his own project—the deposit of rich, radioactive ores, the herds of food animals, the villages of the simian-like creatures.

Maggie Lazenby did say that she would accompany Grimes as soon as she had a spare five minutes—but that would not be until her real work had been tidied up. And then, after dinner, Grimes was left with the washing up as usual.

That night he set an alarm to wake him just before sunrise, so that he was able to switch off the force fields to allow the women to leave the camp for their morning swim, to make coffee and get breakfast preparations under way. After the meals he was left to himself again.

He was feeling a certain kinship with the native who was bottom bird in the pecking order. He thought smugly: "If Maggie were right, I'd kick him around myself. But I'm civilized." This time he took with him a stun-gun instead of a projectile pistol, setting the control for minimum effect.

The natives had not yet arrived at the little bay when he got there. He pulled off his shoes and stockings, waded out through the shallow water to where the fruit-bearing plants were growing. He plucked two of the largest, ripest-seeming globes. He didn't know whether or not they would be dangerous to the human metabolism, and was not tempted to find out. Even with their tough skins intact they stank. Then he retired a few yards from the end of the trail, sat down to wait.

At almost exactly the same time the gibbering, gesticulating troop debouched from the jungle. As before, the timid member hung back, hovering on the outskirts of the scrum, awaiting his chance—his slim chance—to get some fruit for himself. Grimes got slowly to his feet. The primitive humanoids ignored him, save for the timorous one—but even he stood his ground. Grimes walked carefully forward, the two ripe fruit extended in his left hand. He saw a flicker of interest, of greed, in the creature's yellow eyes, the glisten of saliva at the corners of the wide, thin-lipped mouth. And then, warily, the thing was shambling towards him. "Come and get it," whispered Grimes. "Come and get it."

Was the native telepathic? As soon as he was within snatching distance of the spaceman he snatched, his long nails tearing the skin of Grimes's left hand. Were his fellows telepathic? Growling, the leader of the troop dropped the fruit that he had been guzzling, scampered through the shallows and up the bank towards the recipient of Grimes's gift. That miserable being whined and cringed, extended the fruit towards the bully in a placatory gesture.

Grimes growled too. His stun-gun was ready, and aiming it was a matter of microseconds. He pressed the stud. The bully gasped, dropped to the ground, twitching. "Eat your bloody fruit, damn you!" snarled Grimes. This time the timorous one managed a couple of bites before another bully—number two in the pecking order?— tried to steal his meal. By the time the fruit were finished no less than half a dozen bodies were strewn on the moss-like ground-covering growth. They were not dead, Grimes noted with some relief. As he watched the first two scrambled unsteadily to their feet, stared at him reproachfully and then shambled away to feed on what few ripe fruit were left. Characteristically they did not pluck these for themselves but snatched them from the weaker members of the troop. Oddly enough they made no attempt to revenge themselves on Grimes's protégé.

The next day Grimes continued his experiment. As before, he plucked two tempting—but not to him—fruit. As before, he presented them to Snuffy. (It was as good a name as any.) This time, however, he was obliged to use his stun-gun only once. Grimes thought that it was the troop leader—again—who was least capable of learning by experience. The third day he did not have to use the weapon at all, and Snuffy allowed him to pat him, and patted him back. The fourth day he did not think that he would be using the gun—and then one of the smaller humanoids, one who had taken Snuffy's place as tribal butt, screamed angrily and flew at Snuffy, all claws and teeth. Snuffy dropped his fruit and tried to run—and then the whole troop was on him, gibbering and hitting and kicking. Grimes—the gun set on wide beam, shocked them all into unconsciousness. When they recovered all of them scampered back into the jungle.

On the fifth day Grimes was all ready for the next stage of his experiment. He was glad that the scientists were still fully occupied with their own games; he suspected that they—especially Maggie Lazenby—would want to interfere, would want things done their way, would complicate an essentially simple situation. It was all so glaringly obvious to the young Lieutenant. Snuffy would have to be taught to defend himself, to protect his own rights.

He picked the two fruits as usual. He used the stun-gun to deter the bullies—and then he used the weapon on Snuffy, giving him another shock every time that he showed signs of regaining consciousness. He realized that the creature—as he had hoped would be the case—was not popular with his troop fellows; when the time came for them to return to their village or whatever it was they vanished into the jungle without a backward glance. Grimes lifted Snuffy—he wasn't very heavy—and carried him to where the skeleton of the horse-like animal lay on the bank like the bones of a wrecked and stranded ship. He felt a tickling on his skin under his shirt, was thankful that he had thought to make a liberal application of insect-repellent before leaving the camp. He deposited the hairy body on the thick moss, then went to work on the skeleton. Using his knife to sever the dry, tough ligaments he was able to detach the two thigh bones. They made good clubs—a little too short and too light for a man's use, but just right for a being of Snuffy's size. Finally he picked some more fruit—there were a few ripe ones that had been missed by the troop.

At last Snuffy came round, making his characteristic snuffling sound. He stared at Grimes. Grimes looked calmly back, offered him what he had come to think of as a stink-apple. Snuffy accepted it, bit into it. He belched. Grimes regretted that he was not wearing a respirator. While the humanoid was happily munching, Grimes juggled with one of the thigh bones. Snuffy finally condescended to notice what he was doing, to evince some interest. With a sharp *crack* Grimes brought his club down on the skeleton's rib cage. Two of the ribs were broken cleanly in two.

Snuffy extended his hands toward the club. Grimes gave it to him, picking up the other one.

The native was a good pupil. Finally, without any prompting from the spaceman, he was flailing away at the skull of the dead animal, at last cracking it. Grimes looked guiltily at his watch. It was time that he was getting back to the camp to get the preparations for the evening meal under way. Still feeling guilty, he wondered how Snuffy would make it back to his own living place, what his reception would be. But he was armed now, would be able to look after himself—Grimes hoped.

And then it became obvious that the native had no intention of going home by himself. Still carrying his bone club he shambled along at Grimes's side, uttering an occasional plaintive *eek*. He would not be chased off, and Grimes was reluctant to use the stun-gun on him. But there was a spare tent that would be used eventually for the storage of specimens. Snuffy would have to sleep there.

To Grimes's surprise and relief the native did not seem to mind when he was taken into the plastic igloo. He accepted a bowl of water, burying his wrinkled face in it and slurping loudly. Rather dubiously he took a stick of candy, but once he had sampled it it soon disappeared. (Grimes had learned from the scientists that anything eaten by the life form of Delta Sextans IV could be handled by the human metabolism; it was logical to suppose that a native of IV could eat human food with safety.) More water, and more candy—and Snuffy looked ready to retire for the night, curling up on the floor of the tent in a fetal posture. Grimes left him to it.

He did not sleep at all well himself. He was afraid that his . . . guest? prisoner? would awake during the hours of darkness, would awaken the whole camp by howling or other anti-social conduct. Grimes was beginning to have an uneasy suspicion that the scientists would not approve of his experiments. But the night was as silent as night on Delta Sextans IV ever was, and after their usual early break-fast the scientific party flapped off on its various occasions.

Grimes went to the spare tent, opened the flap. The stench that gusted out made him retch, although Snuffy did not seem to be worried by it. The native shambled into the open on all fours, and then, rising to an approximately erect posture, went back inside for his previous club. With his free hand he patted Grimes on the arm, grimacing up at him and whining. Grimes led him to where a bucket of water was standing ready, and beside it two candy bars.

The spaceman, fighting down his nausea, cleaned up the interior of the tent. It had been bad enough washing up after the scientists—but this was too much. From now on Snuffy would have to look after himself. He had no occasion to change his mind as the aborigine followed him around while he coped with the camp chores. The humanoid displayed an uncanny genius for getting in the way.

At last, at long last, it was time to get down to the river. Grimes strode along smartly, Snuffy shuffling along beside him, swinging his club. Their arrival at the little bay coincided with that of the troop of humanoids. Snuffy did not hang back. He got to the fruit before the others did. The troop leader advanced on him menacingly. For a moment it looked as though Snuffy were going to turn and run—then he stood his ground, seeming suddenly to gain inches in stature as he did so. Clumsily he raised his club, and even more clumsily brought it crashing down. More by luck than otherwise the blow fell on the bully's shoulder. The second blow caught him squarely on the side of the head, felling him. Grimes saw the glisten of yellow blood in the grey, matted fur.

Snuffy screamed—but it was not a scream of fear. Brandishing the club he advanced on those who had been his tormentors. They broke and ran, most of them. The two who did not hastily retreated after each had felt the weight of the primitive weapon.

Grimes laughed shakily. "That's my boy," he murmured. "That's my boy . . ."

Snuffy ignored him. He was too busy stuffing himself with the pick of the ripe fruit.

When you have six people utterly engrossed in their own pursuits and a seventh person left to his own devices, it is easy for that seventh person to keep a secret. Not that Grimes even tried to do so. More than once he tried to tell the scientists about his own experiment in practical ethology, and each time he was brushed aside. Once Maggie Lazenby told him rather tartly, "You're only our bus driver, John. Keep to your astronautics and leave real science to us."

Then—the time of *Pathfinder's* return from Delta Sextans V was fast approaching—Grimes was unable to spend much, if any, time on the river bank. The preliminaries to shutting up shop were well under way with specimens and records and unused stores to be packed, with the propulsion unit of the landing craft to be checked. Nonetheless, Grimes was able to check up now and again on Snuffy's progress, noted with satisfaction that the native was making out quite well.

In all too short a time the cruiser signaled that she was establishing herself in orbit about IV, also that the Captain himself would be coming down in the pinnace to inspect the camp. Grimes worked as he had never worked before. He received little help from the others— and the scientists were such untidy people. There should have been at least six general purpose robots to cope with the mess, but there was only one. Grimes. But he coped.

When the pinnace dropped down through the grey overcast the encampment was as near to being shipshape and Bristol fashion as it ever could be. Grimes barely had time to change into a clean uniform before the boat landed. He was standing to attention and saluting smartly when Captain Tolliver strode down the ramp.

Tolliver, after acknowledging the salute, actually smiled. He said, "You run a taut shore base, Mr. Grimes. I hope that when the time comes you will run a taut ship."

"Thank you, sir."

Grimes accompanied the Captain on his rounds of the encampment, the senior officer grunting his approval of the tidiness, the neatly stacked items all ready to be loaded into the landing craft and the pinnace in the correct order. And the scientists—thank the Odd Gods of the Galaxy!—were no longer their usual slovenly selves. Just as the camp was a credit to Grimes, so were they. Maggie Lazenby winked at him when Captain Tolliver was looking the other way. Grimes smiled back gratefully.

Said Tolliver, "I don't suppose that you've had time for any projects of your own, Mr. Grimes. Rather a pity . . ."

"But he has found time, sir," said the Ethologist.

"Indeed, Dr. Lazenby. What was it?"

"Er . . . We were busy ourselves, sir. But we gained the impression that Mr. Grimes was engaged upon research of some kind."

"Indeed? And what was it, Mr. Grimes?"

Grimes looked at his watch. It was almost time. He said, "I'll show you, sir. If you will come this way. Along the river . . ."

"Lead the way, Mr. Grimes," ordered Tolliver jovially. In his mind's eye Grimes saw the glimmer of that half ring of gold braid that would make him a Lieutenant Commander. Promotions in the Survey Service were the result of Captain's Reports rather than seniority.

Grimes guided Tolliver along the river bank to where the trail opened from the jungle to the little bay. "We wait here, sir," he said. He looked at his watch again. It shouldn't be long. And then, quite suddenly, Snuffy led the way out of the jungle. He was proudly carrying his bone club, holding it like a sceptre. He was flanked by two smaller humanoids, each carrying a crude bone-weapon, followed by two more, also armed. He went to the fruit plants, tore at them greedily, wasted more than he ate. The others looked on hungrily. One tried to get past the guards, was clubbed down viciously. Grimes gulped. In a matter of only three days his experiment was getting out of hand.

"I have studied Captain Loveil's films of these beings," said Tolliver in a cold voice. "Are *you* responsible for this?"

"Yes, sir. But . . ."

"You will be wise to apply for a transfer, Mr. Grimes. Should you continue in the Service, which is doubtful, I sincerely hope that you discover the legendary fountain of youth."

"Why, sir?"

"Because it's a bloody pity that otherwise you won't be around to see the end results of what you started," said Tolliver bitterly.

✍ The Subtracter ✍

THE FEDERATION'S SURVEY Service Cruiser *Pathfinder* returned to Lindisfarne Base, and Lieutenant Grimes was one of the officers who was paid off there. He was glad to leave the ship; he had not gotten on at all well with Captain Tolliver. Yet he was far from happy. What was going to happen to him? Tolliver—who, for all his faults, was a just man—had shown Grimes part of the report that he had made on *Pathfinder's* officers, and this part of the report was that referring to Grimes.

"Lieutenant Grimes shows initiative," Tolliver had written, "and has been known to be zealous. Unfortunately his initiative and zeal are invariably misdirected."

Grimes had decided not to make any protest. There had been occasions, he knew very well, when his initiative and zeal had not been misdirected—but never under Tolliver's command. But the Captain, as was his right—his duty—was reporting on Grimes as *he* had found him. His report was only one of many. Nonetheless Grimes was not a little worried, was wondering what his next appointment would be, what his future career in the Survey Service (if any) would be like.

Dr. Margaret Lazenby had also paid off *Pathfinder,* at the same time as Grimes. (Her Service rank was Lieutenant Commander, but she preferred the civilian title.) As old shipmates, with shared experiences, she and Grimes tended to knock about in each other's company whilst they were on Lindisfarne. In any case, the Lieutenant liked the handsome red-haired ethologist, and was pleased that she liked him. With a little bit of luck the situation would develop favorably, he thought. Meanwhile, she was very good company, even though she would permit nothing more than the briefest goodnight kiss.

One night, after a drink too many in the almost deserted B.O.Q. wardroom, he confided his troubles to her. He said, "I don't like it, Maggie . . ."

"What don't you like, John?"

"All this time here, and no word of an appointment. I told you that I'd seen Tolliver's report on me . . ."

"At least six times. But what of it?"

"It's all right for you, Maggie. For all your two and a half rings you're not a space woman. *You* don't have to worry about such sordid details as promotion. I do. I'm just a common working stiff of a spaceman, a trade school boy. Space is all I know."

"And I'm sure you know it well, duckie." She laughed. "But not to worry. Everything will come right in the end. Just take Auntie Maggie's word for it."

"Thank you for trying to cheer me up," he said. "But I can't help worrying. After all, it's *my* career."

She grinned at him, looking very attractive as she did so. "All right. I'll tell you. Your precious Captain Tolliver wasn't the only one to put in a report on your capabilities. Don't forget that the Delta Sextans IV survey was carried out by the Scientific Branch. You, as the spaceman, were officially in command, but actually it was *our* show. Dr. Kortsoff—or Commander Kortsoff if you'd rather call him that—was the real head of our little expedition. *He* reported on you too."

"I can imagine it," said Grimes. "I can just imagine it. 'This officer, with no scientific training whatsoever, took it upon himself to initiate a private experiment which, inevitably, will disastrously affect the ecology, ethology, zoology and biology of the planet.' Have I missed any 'ologies' out?"

"We all liked you," said the girl. "I still like you, come to that.

Just between ourselves, we all had a good laugh over your 'private experiment.' You might have given your friend Snuffy and his people a slight nudge on to the upward path—but no more than a slight nudge. Sooner or later—sooner rather than later, I think—they'd have discovered weapons by themselves. It was bound to happen.

"Do you want to know what Dr. Kortsoff said about you?"

"It can't be worse than what Captain Tolliver said."

"'This officer,'" quoted Maggie Lazenby, "'is very definitely command material.'"

"You're not kidding?" demanded Grimes.

"Most certainly not, John."

"Mphm. You've made me feel a little happier."

"I'm glad," she said.

And so Grimes, although he did not get promotion, got command. The Survey Service's Couriers, with their small crews, were invariably captained by two ringers, mere lieutenants. However, as the twentieth century poet Gertrude Stein might have said, "a captain is a captain is a captain . . ." The command course which Grimes went through prior to his appointment made this quite clear.

There was one fly in the ointment, a big one. His name was Damien, his rank was Commodore, his function was Officer Commanding Couriers. He knew all about Grimes; he made this quite clear at the first interview. Grimes suspected that he knew more about Grimes than he, Grimes, did himself.

He had said, toying with the bulky folder on the desk before him, "There are so many conflicting reports about you, Lieutenant. Some of your commanding officers are of the opinion that you'll finish up as the youngest Admiral ever in the Service, others have said that you aren't fit to be Third Mate in Rim Runners. And then we have the reports from high-ranking specialist officers, most of whom speak well of you. But these gentlemen are not spacemen.

"There's only one thing to do with people like you, Lieutenant. We give you a chance. We give you the command of something small and relatively unimportant—and see what sort of a mess you make of it. I'm letting you have *Adder*. To begin with you'll be just a galactic errand boy, but if you shape well, *if* you shape well, you will be entrusted with more important missions.

"Have I made myself clear?"

"Yes, sir."

"Then try to remember all that we've tried to teach you, and try to keep your nose clean. That's all."

Grimes stiffened to attention, saluted, and left Damien's office.

Grimes had come to love his first command, and was proud of her, even though she was only a little ship, a Serpent Class Courier, lightly armed and manned by a minimal crew. In addition to Grimes there were two watch-keeping officers, both Ensigns, an engineering officer, another one ringer, and two communications officers, Lieutenants both. One was in charge of the vessel's electronic equipment, but could be called upon to stand a control room watch if required. The other was the psionic radio officer, a very important crew member, as *Adder* had yet to be fitted with the Carlotti Deep Space Communications and Direction Finding System. In addition to crew accommodation there was more than merely adequate passenger accommodation; one function of the Couriers is to get V.I.P.s from Point A to Point B in a hurry, as and when required.

"You will proceed," said Commodore Damien to Grimes, "from Lindisfarne Base to Doncaster at maximum speed, but considering at all times the safety of your vessel."

"And the comfort of my passenger, sir?" asked Grimes.

"That need not concern you, Lieutenant." Damien grinned, his big teeth yellow in his skull-like face. "Mr. Alberto is . . . tough. Tougher, I would say, than the average spaceman."

Grimes's prominent ears flushed. The Commodore had managed to imply that he, Grimes, was below average. "Very well, sir," he said. "I'll pile on the Gees and the Lumes."

"Just so as you arrive in one piece," growled Damien. "That's all that our masters ask of you. Or, to more exact, just so as Mr. Alberto arrives in one piece, and functioning." He lifted a heavily sealed envelope off his desk, handed it to Grimes. "Your Orders, to be opened after you're on trajectory. But I've already told you most of it." He grinned again. "On your bicycle, spaceman!"

Grimes got to his feet, put on his cap, came stiffly to attention. He saluted with his free right hand, turned about smartly and marched out of the Commodore's office.

This was his first Sealed Orders assignment. Clear of the office, Grimes continued his march, striding in time to martial music audible only to himself. Then he paused, looking towards the docking area of the spaceport. There was his ship, already positioned on the pad, dwarfed by a huge *Constellation* Class cruiser to one side of her, a *Planet* Class transport to the other. But she stood there bravely enough on the apron, a metal spire so slender as to appear taller than she actually was, gleaming brightly in the almost level rays of the westering sun. And she was *his*. It did not matter that officers serving in larger vessels referred to the couriers as flying darning needles.

So he strode briskly to the ramp extruded from the after airlock of his flying darning needle, his stocky body erect in his smart—but not too smart—uniform. Ensign Beadle, his First Lieutenant, was there to greet him. The young man threw him a smart salute. Grimes returned it with just the right degree of sloppiness.

"All secure for lift off—Captain!"

"Thank you, Number One. Is the passenger aboard?"

"Yes, sir. And his baggage."

Grimes fought down the temptation to ask what he was like. Only when one is really senior can one unbend with one's juniors. "Very well, Number One." He looked at his watch. "My lift off is scheduled for 1930 hours. It is now 1917. I shall go straight to Control, Mr. Beadle . . ."

"Mr. von Tannenbaum and Mr. Slovotny are waiting for you there, sir, and Mr. McCloud is standing by in the engine room."

"Good. And Mr. Deane is tucked safely away with his poodle's brain in aspic?"

"He is, sir."

"Good. Then give Mr. Alberto my compliments, and ask him if he would like to join us in Control during lift off."

Grimes negotiated the ladder in the axial shaft rapidly, without losing breath. (The *Serpent* Class couriers were too small to run to an elevator.) He did not make a stop at his own quarters. (A courier captain was supposed to be able to proceed anywhere in the Galaxy, known or unknown, at a second's notice.) In the control room he found Ensign von Tannenbaum ("The blond beast") and Lieutenant Slovotny (just "Sparks") at their stations. He buckled himself into his own chair. He had just finished doing so when the plump, lugubrious Beadle pulled himself up through the hatch. He addressed Grimes. "I asked Mr. Alberto if he'd like to come up to the office, Captain . . ."

"And is he coming up, Number One,?" Grimes looked pointedly at the clock on the bulkhead.

"No, Captain. He said . . ."

"Out with it man. It's time we were getting up them stairs."

"He said, 'You people look after your job, and I'll look after mine.'"

Grimes shrugged. As a courier captain he had learned to take V.I.P.s as they came. Some—a very few of them—he would have preferred to have left. He asked, "Are Mr. Alberto and Mr. Deane secured for lift off?"

"Yes, Captain, although Spooky's not happy about the shock-proof mount for his amplifier . . ."

"He never is. Clearance, Sparks . . ."

"Clearance, Captain." The wiry little radio officer spoke quietly into his microphone. "Mission 7DKY to Tower. Request clearance."

"Tower to Mission 7DKY. You have clearance. Bon voyage."

"Thank him," said Grimes. He glanced rapidly around the little control room. All officers were strapped in their acceleration chairs. All tell-tale lights were green. "All systems *Go* . . ." he muttered, relishing the archaic expression.

He pushed the right buttons, and *went*.

It was a normal enough courier lift off. The inertial drive developed maximum thrust within microseconds of its being started. Once his radar told him that the ship was the minimum safe altitude above the port, Grimes cut in his auxiliary rockets. The craft was built to take stresses that, in larger vessels, would have been dangerous. Her personnel prided themselves on their toughness.

And the one outsider, the passenger. Grimes would have grinned had it not been for the acceleration flattening his features. Commodore Damien had said that Mr. Alberto was tough—so Mr. Alberto would just have to take the G's and like it.

The ship drove up through the last, high wisps of cirrus, into the darkling purple sky, towards the sharply bright, unwinking stars. She plunged outward through the last, tenuous shreds of atmosphere, and the needles of instruments flickered briefly as she passed through the van Allens. She was out and clear now, out and clear, and Grimes cut both inertial and reaction drives, used his gyroscopes to swing the sharp prow of the ship onto the target star, the Doncaster sun, brought that far distant speck of luminosity into the exact center of his spiderweb sights. Von Tannenbaum, who was Navigator, gave him the corrections necessitated by Galactic Drift; it was essential to aim the vessel at where the star was *now*, not where it was some seventy-three years ago.

The Inertial Drive was restarted, and the ever-precessing rotors of the Mannschenn Drive were set in motion. There was the usual brief queasiness induced by the temporal precession field, the usual visual shock as colors sagged down the spectrum, as the hard, bright stars outside the viewports became iridescent nebulosities. Grimes remained in his chair a few minutes, satisfying himself that all was as it should be. Slowly and carefully he filled and lit his foul pipe, ignoring a dirty look from Beadle who, in the absence of a Bio-Chemist, was responsible for the ship's air-regeneration system.

Then, speaking through a swirl of acrid smoke, he ordered. "Set Deep Space watches, Number One. And tell Mr. Deane to report to Lindisfarne Base that we are on trajectory for Doncaster."

"E.T.A. Doncaster, Captain?" asked Beadle.

Grimes pulled the sealed envelope from the pouch at the side of his chair, looked at it. He thought, *For Your Eyes Only. Destroy By Fire Before Reading.* He said, "I'll let you know after I've skimmed through this bumf." After all, even in a small ship informality can be allowed to go only so far. He unbuckled himself, got up from his seat, then went down to his quarters to read the Orders.

There was little in them that he had not already been told by

Commodore Damien. Insofar as the E.T.A. was concerned, this was left largely to his own discretion, although it was stressed that the courier was to arrive at Doncaster not later than April 23, Local Date. And how did the Doncastrian calendar tally with that used on Lindisfarne? Grimes, knowing that the Blond Beast was now on watch, called Control and threw the question on to von Tannenbaum's plate, knowing that within a very short time he would have an answer accurate to fourteen places of decimals, and that as soon as he, Grimes, made a decision regarding the time of arrival the necessary adjustment of velocity would be put in hand without delay. Von Tannenbaum called back. "April 23 on Doncaster coincides with November 8 on Lindisfarne. I can give you the exact correlation, Captain . . ."

"Don't bother, Pilot. My orders allow me quite a bit of leeway. Now, suppose we get Mr. Alberto to his destination just three days before the deadline . . . It will give him time to settle in before he commences his duties, whatever they are, in the High Commissioner's office. As far as I can gather, we're supposed to stay on Doncaster until directed elsewhere—so an extra three days in port will do us no harm."

"It's a pleasant planet, I've heard, Captain." There was a pause, and Grimes could imagine the burly, flaxen-headed young man running problems through the control room computer, checking the results with his own slipstick. "This calls for a reduction of speed. Shall I do it by cutting down the temporal precession rate, or by reducing actual acceleration?"

"Two G *is* a little heavy," admitted Grimes.

"Very well, Captain. Reduce to 1.27?"

"That will balance?"

"It will balance."

"Then make it so."

Almost immediately the irregular throbbing of the Inertial Drive slowed. Grimes felt his weight pressing less heavily into the padding of his chair. He did not need to glance at the accelerometer mounted among the other tell-tale instruments on the bulkhead of his cabin. Von Tannenbaum was a good man, a good officer, a good navigator.

There was a sharp rap on his door.

"Come in," called Grimes, swiveling his seat so that he faced the caller. This, he realized, would be his passenger, anticipating the captain's invitation to an introductory drink and talk.

He was not a big man, this Mr. Alberto, and at first he gave an impression of plumpness, of softness. But it was obvious from the way that he moved that his bulk was solid muscle, not fat. He was clad in the dark grey that was almost a Civil Service uniform—and even Grimes, who knew little of the niceties of civilian tailoring, could see that both the material and the cut of Alberto's suit were superb. He had a broad yet very ordinary looking face; his hair was black and glossy, his eyes black and rather dull. His expression was petulant. He demanded rather then asked, "Why have we slowed down?"

Grimes bit back a sharp retort. After all, he was only a junior officer, in spite of his command, and his passenger probably piled on far more G's than a mere lieutenant. He replied, "I have adjusted to a comfortable actual velocity, Mr. Alberto, so as to arrive three days, local, before the deadline. I trust that this suits your plans."

"Three days . . ." Alberto smiled—and his face was transformed abruptly from that of a sulky baby to that of a contented child. It was, Grimes realized, no more than a deliberate turning of charm—but, he admitted to himself, it was effective. "Three days . . . That will give me ample time to settle down, Captain, before I start work. And I know, as well as you do, that overly heavy acceleration can be tiring."

"Won't you sit down, Mr. Alberto? A drink, perhaps?"

"Thank you, Captain. A dry sherry, if I may . . ."

Grimes grinned apologetically. "I'm afraid that these Couriers haven't much of a cellar. I can offer you gin, scotch, brandy . . ."

"A gin and lime, then."

The Lieutenant busied himself at his little bar, mixed the drinks, gave Alberto his glass, raised his own in salute. "Here's to crime!"

Alberto smiled again. "Why do you say that, Captain?"

"It's just one of those toasts that's going the rounds in the Service. Not so long ago it was, 'Down the hatch!' Before that it was, 'Here's mud in yer eye' . . ."

"I see." Alberto sipped appreciatively. "Good gin, this."

"Not bad. We get it from Van Diemen's Planet." There was a brief silence. Then, "Will you be long on Doncaster, Mr. Alberto? I rather gained the impression that we're supposed to wait there until you've finished your . . . business."

"It shouldn't take long."

"Diplomatic?"

"You could call it that." Again the smile—but why should those white teeth look so carnivorous? *Imagination,* thought Grimes.

"Another drink?"

"Why, yes. I like to relax when I can."

"Yours is demanding work?"

"And so is yours, Captain."

The brassy music of a bugle drifted into the cabin through the intercom.

"Mess call," said Grimes.

"You do things in style, Captain."

Grimes shrugged. "We have a tape for all the calls in general use. As for the tucker . . ." He shrugged again. "We don't run to a cook in a ship of this class. Sparks—Mr. Slovotny—prepares the meals in space. As a chef he's a good radio officer . . ."

"Do you think he'd mind if I took over?" asked Alberto. "After all, I'm the only idler aboard this vessel."

"We'll think about it," said Grimes.

"You know what I think, Captain . . ." said Beadle.

"I'm not a telepath, Number One," said Grimes. "Tell me."

The two men were sitting at ease in the Courier's control room. Each of them was conscious of a certain tightness in the waistband of his uniform shorts. Grimes was suppressing a tendency to burp gently. Alberto, once he had been given a free hand in the galley, had speedily changed shipboard eating from a necessity to a pleasure. (He insisted that somebody else always do the washing up, but this was a small price to pay.) This evening, for example, the officers had dined on *saltimbocca,* accompanied by a rehydrated rough red that the amateur chef had contrived, somehow, to make taste like real wine. Nonetheless he had apologized—actually apologized!—for the meal. "I should have used *prosciutto,* not any old ham. *And fresh* sage leaves, not dried sage . . ."

"I think" said Beadle, "that the standard of the High Commissioner's entertaining has been lousy. Alberto must be a *cordon bleu* chef, sent out to Doncaster to play merry hell in the High Commissioner's kitchen."

"Could be," said Grimes. He belched gently. "Could be. But I can't see our lords and masters laying on a ship, even a lowly *Serpent* Class Courier, for a cook, no matter how talented. There must be cooks on Doncaster just as good."

"There's one helluva difference between a chef and a cook."

"All right. There must be chefs on Doncaster."

"But Alberto is *good.* You admit that."

"Of course I admit it. But one can be good in quite a few fields and still retain one's amateur status. As a matter of fact, Alberto told me that he was a mathematician . . ."

"A mathematician?" Beadle was scornfully incredulous. "You know how the Blond Beast loves to show off his toys to anybody who'll evince the slightest interest. Well, Alberto was up in the control room during his watch; you'll recall that he said he'd fix the coffee maker. Our Mr. von Tannenbaum paraded his pets and made them do their tricks. He was in a very disgruntled mood when he handed over to me when I came on. How did he put it? 'I don't expect a very high level of intelligence in planetlubbers, but that Alberto is in a class by himself. I doubt if he could add two and two and get four twice running . . ."

"Did he fix the machinetta?"

"As a matter of fact, yes. It makes beautiful coffee now."

"Then what are you complaining about, Number One?"

"I'm not complaining, Captain. I'm just curious."

And so am I, thought Grimes, *so am I.* And as the commanding officer of the ship he was in a position to be able to satisfy his curiosity. After Mr. Beadle had gone about his multifarious duties Grimes called Mr. Deane on the telephone. "Are you busy, Spooky?" he asked.

"I'm always busy, Captain," came the reply. This was true enough. Whether he wanted it or not, a psionic radio officer was on duty all the time, sleeping and waking, his mind open to the transmitted thoughts of other telepaths throughout the Galaxy. Some were powerful transmitters, others were not, some made use, as Deane did, of organic amplifiers, others made do with the unaided power of their own minds. And there was selection, of course. Just as a wireless operator in the early days of radio on Earth's seas could pick out his own ship's call sign from the babble and Babel of Morse, could focus all his attention on an S.O.S. or T.T.T, so the trained telepath could "listen" selectively. At short ranges he could, too, receive the thoughts of the non-telepaths about him—but, unless the circumstances were exceptional, he was supposed to maintain the utmost secrecy regarding them.

"Can you spare me a few minutes, Spooky? After all, you can maintain your listening watch anywhere in the ship, in my own quarters as well as in yours."

"Oh, all right, Captain. I'll be up. I already know what you're going to ask me."

You would, thought Grimes.

A minute or so later, Mr. Deane drifted into his day cabin. His nickname was an apt one. He was tall, fragile, so albinoid as to appear almost translucent. His white face was a featureless blob.

"Take a pew, Spooky," ordered Grimes. "A drink?"

"Mother's ruin, Captain."

Grimes poured gin for both of them. In his glass there was ice and a generous sprinkling of bitters. Mr. Deane preferred his gin straight, as colorless as he was himself.

The psionic radio officer sipped genteelly. Then: "I'm afraid that I can't oblige you, Captain."

"Why not, Spooky?"

"You know very well that we graduates of the Rhine Institute have to swear to respect privacy."

"There's no privacy aboard a ship, Spooky. There cannot be."

"There can be, Captain. There must be."

"Not when the safety of the ship is involved."

It was a familiar argument—and Grimes knew that after the third gin the telepath would weaken. He always did.

"We got odd passengers aboard this ship, Spooky. Surely you remember that Waldegren diplomat who had the crazy scheme of seizing her and turning her over to his Navy . . ."

"I remember, Captain." Deane extended his glass which, surprisingly, was empty. Grimes wondered, as he always did, if its contents had been teleported directly into the officer's stomach, but he refilled it.

"Mr. Alberto's another odd passenger," he went on.

"But a Federation citizen," Deane told him.

"How do we know? He could be a double agent. Do *you* know?"

"I don't." After only two gins Spooky was ready to spill the beans. This was unusual. "I don't know *anything*."

"What do you mean?"

"Usually, Captain, we have to shut our minds to the trivial, boring thoughts of you psionic morons. No offense intended, but that's the way we think of you. We get sick of visualizations of the girls you met in the last port and the girls you hope to meet in the next port." He screwed his face up in disgust, made it evident that he did, after all, possess features. "Bums, bellies and breasts! The Blond Beast's a tit man, and *you* have a thing about *legs* . . ."

Grimes's prominent ears reddened, but he said nothing.

"And the professional wishful thinking is even more nauseating. *When do I get my half ring? When do I get my brass hat? When shall I make Admiral?*"

"Ambition . . ." said Grimes.

"Ambition, shambition! And of late, of course, *I wonder what Alberto's putting on for breakfast? For lunch? For dinner?*"

"What *is* he putting on for dinner?" asked Grimes. "I've been rather wondering if our tissue culture chook could be used for *Chicken Cacciatore* . . ."

"I don't know."

"No, you're not a chef. As well we know, after the last time that you volunteered for galley duties."

"I mean, I don't know what the menus will be." It was Deane's turn to blush. "As a matter of fact, Captain, I *have* been trying to get previews. I have to watch my diet . . ."

Grimes tried not to think uncharitable thoughts. Like many painfully thin people, Deane enjoyed a voracious appetite.

He said, "You've been *trying* to eavesdrop?"

"Yes. But there are non-telepaths, you know, and Alberto's one of them. *True* non-telepaths, I mean. Most people transmit, although they can't receive. Alberto doesn't transmit."

"A useful qualification for a diplomat," said Grimes. "If he is a diplomat. But could he be using some sort of psionic jammer?"

"No. I'd know if he were."

Grimes couldn't ignore that suggestively held empty glass any longer. He supposed that Deane had earned his third gin.

The Courier broke through into normal space-time north of the plane of Doncaster's ecliptic. In those days, before the Carlotti Beacons made FTL position fixing simple, navigation was an art rather than a science—and von Tannenbaum was an artist. The little ship dropped into a trans-polar orbit about the planet and then, as soon as permission to land had been granted by Aerospace Control, descended to Port Duncannon. It was, Grimes told himself smugly, one of his better landings. And so it should have been; conditions were little short of ideal. There was no cloud, no wind, not even any clear air turbulence at any level. The ship's instruments were working perfectly, and the Inertial Drive was responding to the controls with no time lag whatsoever. It was one of those occasions on which the Captain feels that his ship is no more—and no less—than a beautifully functioning extension of his own body. Finally, it was morning Local Time, with the sun just lifting over the verdant, rolling hills to the eastward, bringing out all the color of the sprawling city a few miles from the spaceport, making it look, from the air, like a huge handful of gems spilled carelessly on a green carpet.

Grimes set the vessel down in the exact center of the triangle marked by the blinkers, so gently that, until he cut the drive, a walnut under the vaned landing gear would not have been crushed. He said quietly, "Finished with engines."

"Receive boarders, Captain?" asked Beadle.

"Yes, Number One." Grimes looked out through the viewport to the ground cars that were making their way from the Administration Block. Port Health, Immigration, Customs . . . The Harbormaster paying his respects to the Captain of a visiting Federation warship . . . And the third vehicle? He took a pair of binoculars from the rack, focused them on the flag fluttering from the bonnet of the car in the rear. It was dark blue, with a pattern of silver stars, the Federation's colors. So the High Commissioner himself had come out to see the ship berth. He wished that he and his officers had dressed more formally, but it was too late to do anything about it now. He went down to his quarters, was barely able to change the epaulettes of his shirt, with their deliberately tarnished braid, for a pair of shining new ones before the High Commissioner was at his door.

Mr. Beadle ushered in the important official with all the ceremony that he could muster at short notice. "Sir, this is the Captain, Lieutenant Grimes. Captain, may I introduce Sir William Willoughby, Federation High Commissioner on Doncaster?"

Willoughby extended a hand that, like the rest of him was plump. "Welcome aboard, Captain. Ha, ha. I hope you don't mind my borrowing one of the favorite expressions of you spacefaring types!"

"We don't own the copyright, sir."

"Ha, ha. Very good."

"Will you sit down, Sir William?"

"Thank you, Captain, thank you. But only for a couple of minutes. I shall be out of your hair as soon as Mr. Alberto has been cleared by Port Health, Immigration and all the rest of 'em. Then I'll whisk him off to the Residence." He paused, regarding Grimes with eyes that, in the surrounding fat, were sharp and bright. "How did you find him, Captain?"

"Mr. Alberto, sir?" What was the man getting at? "Er . . . He's a very good cook . . ."

"Glad to hear you say it, Captain. That's why I sent for him. I have to do a lot of entertaining, as you realize, and the incompetents

I have in my kitchens couldn't boil water without burning it. It just won't do, Captain, it just won't do, not for a man in my position."

"So he *is a* chef, sir."

Again those sharp little eyes bored into Grimes's skull. "Of course. What else? What did you think he was?"

"Well, as a matter of fact we were having a yarn the other night, and he sort of hinted that he was some sort of a mathematician . . ."

"Did he?" Then Willoughby chuckled. "He was having you on. But, of course, a real chef *is* a mathematician. He has to get his equations just right—this quantity, that quantity, this factor, that factor . . ."

"That's one way of looking at it, Sir William."

Beadle was back then, followed by Alberto. "I must be off, now, Captain," said the passenger, shaking hands. "Thank you for a very pleasant voyage."

"Thank *you*," Grimes told him, adding, "We shall miss you."

"But you'll enjoy some more of his cooking," said the High Commissioner genially. "As officers of the only Federation warship on this world you'll have plenty of invitations—to the Residence as well as elsewhere. Too, if Mr. Alberto manages to train my permanent staff in not too long a time you may be taking him back with you."

"We hope so," said Grimes and Beadle simultaneously.

"Good day to you, then. Come on, Mr. Alberto—it's time you started to show my glorified scullions how to boil an egg!"

He was gone, and then the Harbormaster was at the door. He was invited in, took a seat, accepted coffee. "Your first visit to Doncaster," he announced rather than asked.

"Yes, Captain Tarran. It looks a very pleasant planet."

"Hphm." That could have meant either "yes" or "no."

"Tell me, sir, *is* the cooking in the High Commissioner's Residence as bad as he makes out?"

"I wouldn't know, Captain. I'm just a merchant skipper in a shore job, I don't get asked to all the posh parties, like you people." The sudden white grin in the dark, lean face took the rancor out of the words. "And I thank all the Odd Gods of the Galaxy for that!"

"I concur with your sentiments, Captain Tarran. One never

seems to meet any *real* people at the official bunstruggle . . . it's all stiff collars and best behavior and being nice to nongs and drongoes whom normally you'd run a mile to avoid . . ."

"Still," said Mr. Beadle, "the High Commissioner seems to have the common touch . . ."

"How so?" asked Grimes.

"Well, coming out to the spaceport in person to pick up his chef . . ."

"Cupboard love," Grimes told him. "Cupboard love."

There were official parties, and there were unofficial ones. Tarran may not have been a member of the planet's snobocracy, but he knew people in all walks of life, in all trades and professions, and the gatherings to which, through him, Grimes was invited were far more entertaining affairs than the official functions which, now and again, Grimes was obliged to attend. It was at an informal supper given by Professor Tolliver, who held the Chair of Political Science at Duncannon University, that he met Selma Madigan.

With the exception of Tarran and Grimes and his officers all the guests were university people, students as well as instructors. Some were human and some were not. Much to his surprise Grimes found that he was getting along famously with a Shaara Princess, especially since he had cordially detested a Shaara Queen to whom he had been introduced at a reception in the Mayor's Palace. ("And there I was," he had complained afterwards to Beadle, "having to say nice things to a bedraggled old oversized bumblebee loaded down with more precious stones than this ship could lift . . . and with all that tonnage of diamonds and the like she couldn't afford a decent voice box; it sounded like a scratched platter and a worn-out needle on one of those antique record players . . .") This Shreen was—beautiful. It was an inhuman beauty (of course), that of a glittering, intricate mobile. By chance or design—design thought Grimes—her voice box produced a pleasant, almost seductive contralto, with faintly buzzing undertones. She was an arthroped, but there could be no doubt about the fact that she was an attractively female member of her race.

She was saying, "I find you humans so fascinating, Captain.

There is so much similarity between yourselves and ourselves, and such great differences. But I have enjoyed my stay on this planet . . ."

"And will you be here much longer, Your Highness?"

"Call me Shreen, Captain," she told him.

"Thank you, Shreen. My name is John. I shall feel honored if you call me that." He laughed. "In any case, my real rank is only Lieutenant."

"Very well, Lieutenant John. But to answer your question. I fear that I shall return to my own world as soon as I have gained my degree in Socio-Economics. Our Queen Mother decided that this will be a useful qualification for a future ruler. The winds of change blow through our hives, and we must trim our wings to them." *And very pretty wings, too,* thought Grimes.

But Shreen was impossibly alien, and the girl who approached gracefully over the polished floor was indubitably human. She was slender, and tall for a woman, and her gleaming auburn hair was piled high in an intricate coronal. Her mouth was too wide for conventional prettiness, the planes of her thin face too well defined. Her eyes were definitely green. Her smile, as she spoke, made her beautiful.

"Another conquest, Shreen?" she asked.

"I wish it were, Selma," replied the Princess. "I wish that Lieutenant John were an arthroped like myself."

"In that case," grinned Grimes, "I'd be a drone."

"From what I can gather," retorted the human girl, "that's all that spaceship captains are anyhow."

"Have you met Selma?" asked Shreen. Then she performed the introductions.

"And are you enjoying the party, Mr. Grimes?" inquired Selma Madigan.

"Yes, Miss Madigan. It's a very pleasant change from the usual official function—but don't tell anybody that I said so."

"I'm glad you like us. We try to get away from that ghastly Outposts of Empire atmosphere. Quite a number of our students are like Shreen here, quote aliens unquote . . ."

"On *my* world *you* would be the aliens."

"I know, my dear, and I'm sure that Mr. Grimes does too. But all intelligent beings can make valuable contributions to each other's cultures. No one race has a sacred mission to civilize the Galaxy."

"I wish you wouldn't *preach*, Selma." It was amazing how much expression the Princess could get out of her mechanical voice box. "But if you must, perhaps you can make a convert out of Lieutenant John." She waved a thin, gracefully articulated forelimb and was away, gliding off to join a group composed of two human men, a young Hallichek and a gaudy pseudo-saurian from Dekkovar.

Selma Madigan looked directly at Grimes. "And what do you think of our policy of integration?" she asked.

"It has to come, I suppose."

"It has to come," she mimicked. "You brassbound types are all the same. You get along famously with somebody like Shreen, because she's a real, live Princess. But the Shaara royalty isn't royalty as we understand it. The Queens are females who've reached the egg-laying stage, the Princesses are females who are not yet sexually developed. Still—Shreen's a Princess. You have far less in common with her, biologically speaking, than you have with Oona—but you gave Oona the brush-off and fawned all over Shreen."

Grimes flushed. "Oona's a rather smelly and scruffy little thing like a Terran chimpanzee. Shreen's—beautiful."

"Oona has a brilliant mind. Her one weakness is that she thinks that Terrans in pretty, gold-braided uniforms are wonderful. You snubbed her. Shreen noticed. I noticed."

"As far as I'm concerned," said Grimes, "Oona can be Her Imperial Highness on whatever world she comes from, but I don't *have* to like her."

Professor Tolliver, casually clad in a rather grubby toga, smoking a pipe even fouler than Grimes's, joined the discussion. He remarked, "Young Grimes has a point . . . "

"Too right I have," agreed Grimes. "As far as I'm concerned, people are people—it doesn't matter a damn if they're humanoid, arachnoid, saurian or purple octopi from the next galaxy but three. If they're our sort of people, I like 'em. If they ain't—I don't."

"Oona's our sort of people," insisted Selma.

"She doesn't smell like it."

The girl laughed. "And how do you think *she* enjoys the stink of your pipe—and, come to that, Peter's pipe?"

"Perhaps she does enjoy it," suggested Grimes.

"As a matter of fact she does," said Professor Tolliver.

"*Men . . .*" muttered Selma Madigan disgustedly.

Tolliver drifted off then, and Grimes walked with the girl to the table on which stood a huge punchbowl. He ladled out drinks for each of them. He raised his own glass in a toast. "Here's to integration!"

"I wish that you really meant that."

"Perhaps I do . . ." murmured Grimes, a little doubtfully. "Perhaps I do. After all, we've only one Universe, and we all have to live in it. It's not so long ago that blacks and whites and yellows were at each other's throats on the Home Planet—to say nothing of the various subdivisions within each color group. Von Tannenbaum—that's him over there, the Blond Beast we call him. He's an excellent officer, a first class shipmate, and a very good friend. But *his* ancestors were very unkind to mine, on my mother's side. And mine had quite a long record of being unkind to other people. I could be wrong—but I think that much of Earth's bloody history was no more—and no less—than xenophobia carried to extremes . . ."

"Quite a speech, John." She sipped at her drink. "It's a pity that the regulations of your Service forbid you to play any active part in politics."

"Why?"

"You'd make a very good recruit for the new Party we're starting. LL . . ."

"LL . . . ?"

"The obvious abbreviation. The League of Life. You were talking just now of Terran history. Even when Earth's nations were at war there were organizations—religions, political parties, even fraternal orders—with pan-national and pan-racial memberships. The aim of the League of Life is to build up a membership of all intelligent species."

"Quite an undertaking."

"But a necessary one. Doncaster could be said to be either unfortunately situated, or otherwise, according to the viewpoint. Here we are, one Man-colonized planet on the borders of no less than two . . . yes, I'll use that word, much as I dislike it . . . no less than two alien empires. The Hallichek Hegemony, the Shaara Super-Hive. We know that Imperial Earth is already thinking of establishing Fortress Doncaster, converting this world into the equivalent of a colossal, impregnably armored and fantastically armed dreadnought with its guns trained upon both avian and arthroped, holding the balance of power, playing one side off against the other and all the rest of it. But there are those of us who would sooner live in peace and friendship with our neighbors. That's why Duncannon University has always tried to attract non-Terran students—and that's why the League of Life was brought into being." She smiled. "You could, I suppose call it enlightened self-interest."

"Enlightened," agreed Grimes.

He liked this girl. She was one of those women whose physical charm is vastly enhanced by enthusiasm. She did far more to him, for him, than the sort of female equally pretty or prettier, whom he usually met.

She said, "I've some literature at home, if you'd like to read it."

"I should—Selma."

She took the use of her given name for granted. Was that a good sign, or not?

"That's splendid—John. We could pick it up now. The party can get along without us."

"Don't you . . . er . . . live on the premises?"

"No. But it's only a short walk from here. I have an apartment in Heathcliff Street."

When Grimes had collected his boat cloak and cap from the cloakroom she was waiting for him. She had wrapped herself in a green academic gown that went well with her hair, matched her eyes. Together they walked out into the misty night. There was just enough chill in the air to make them glad of their outer garments, to make them walk closer together than they would, otherwise— perhaps—have done. As they strode over the damp-gleaming cobblestones Grimes was conscious of the movements of her body against his. *Political literature,* he thought with an attempt at cynicism. *It makes a change from etchings.* But he could not remain cynical for long. He had already recognized in her qualities of leadership, had no doubt in his mind that she would achieve high political rank on the world of her birth. Nonetheless, this night things could happen between them, probably would happen between them, and he, most certainly, would not attempt to stem the course of Nature. Neither of them would be the poorer; both of them, in fact, would be the richer. Meanwhile, it was good to walk with her through the soft darkness, to let one's mind dwell pleasurably on what lay ahead at the end of the walk.

"Here we are, John," she said suddenly.

The door of the apartment house was a hazy, golden-glowing rectangle in the dimness. There was nobody in the hallway—not that it mattered. There was an elevator that bore them swiftly upwards, its door finally opening on a richly carpeted corridor. There was another door—one that, Grimes noted, was opened with an old-fashioned metal key. He remembered, then, that voice-actuated locks were not very common on Doncaster.

The furnishing of her living room was austere but comfortable. Grimes, at her invitation, removed his cloak and cap, gave them to her to hang up somewhere with her own gown, sat down on a well-sprung divan. He watched her walk to the window that ran all along one wall, press the switch that drew the heavy drapes aside, press another switch that caused the wide panes to sink into their housing.

She said, "The view of the city is good from here—especially on a misty night. And I like it when you can smell the clean tang of fog in the air . . ."

"You're lucky to get a clean fog," said Grimes, Earth-born and Earth-raised. He got up and went to stand with her. His arm went about her waist. She made no attempt to disengage it. Nonetheless, he could still appreciate the view. It was superb; it was like looking down at a star cluster enmeshed in a gaseous nebula . . .

"Smell the mist . . ." whispered Selma.

Dutifully, Grimes inhaled. *Where did that taint of garlic come from?* It was the first time that he had smelled it since Alberto ceased to officiate in the ship's galley. *It must come from a source in the room with them . . .*

Grimes could act fast when he had to. He sensed rather than saw that somebody was rushing at him and the girl from behind. He let go of her, pushed her violently to one side. Instinctively he fell into a crouch, felt a heavy body thud painfully into his back. He dropped still lower, his arms and the upper part of his torso hanging down over the windowsill. What followed was the result of luck rather than of any skill on the spaceman's part—good luck for Grimes, the worst of bad luck for his assailant. The assassin slithered over Grimes's back, head down, in an ungraceful dive. The heel of a shoe almost took one of the Lieutenant's prominent ears with it. And then he was staring down, watching the dark figure that fell into the luminous mist with agonizing slowness, twisting and turning as it plunged, screaming. The scream was cut short by a horridly fluid *thud.*

Frantically, Selma pulled Grimes back to safety.

He stood there, trembling uncontrollably. The reek of garlic was still strong in the air. He broke away from her, went back to the window and was violently sick.

"There are lessons," said Commodore Damien drily, "that a junior officer must learn if he wishes to rise in the Service. One of them is that it is unwise to throw a monkey wrench into the machinations of our masters."

"How was I to know, sir?" complained Grimes. He flushed. "In any case, I'd do it again!"

"I'm sure that you would, Mr. Grimes. No man in his right senses submits willingly to defenestration—and no gentleman stands by and does nothing while his companion of the evening is subjected to the same fate. Even so . . ." He drummed on his desk top with his skeletal fingers. "Even so, I propose to put you in the picture, albeit somewhat belatedly.

"To begin with, the late Mr. Alberto was criminally careless.

Rather a neat play on words, don't you think? Apparently he officiated as usual in the High Commissioner's kitchen on the night in question, and Sir William had, earlier in the day, expressed a wish for *pasta* with one of the more redolent sauces. As a good chef should, Alberto tasted, and tasted, and tasted. As a member of his *real* profession he should have deodorized his breath before proceeding to Miss Madigan's apartment—where, I understand, he concealed himself in the bathroom, waiting until she returned to go through her evening ritual of opening the window of her living room. He was not, I think, expecting her to have company—not that it would have worried him if he had . . ."

"What happened served the bastard right," muttered Grimes.

"I'm inclined to agree with you, Lieutenant. But we are all of us no more than pawns insofar as Federation policy is concerned. Or, perhaps, Alberto was a knight—in the chess sense of the word, although the German name for that piece, *springer,* would suit him better.

"Alberto was employed by the Department of Socio-Economic Science, and directly responsible only to its head, Dr. Barratin. Dr. Barratin is something of a mathematical genius, and uses a building full of computers to extrapolate from the current trends on all the worlds in which the Federation is interested. Doncaster, I need hardly tell you, is such a world, and the League of Life is a current trend. According to the learned Doctor's calculations, this same League of Life will almost certainly gain considerable influence, even power, in that sector of the Galaxy, under the leadership of your Miss Madigan . . ."

"She's not *my* Miss Madigan, sir. Unfortunately."

"My heart fair bleeds for you. But, to continue. To Dr. Barratin the foreign and colonial policies of the Federation can all be worked out in advance like a series of equations. As you will know, however, equations are apt, at times, to hold undesirable factors. Alberto was employed to remove such factors, ensuring thereby that the good Doctor's sums came out. He was known to his employers as the Subtracter . . ."

"Very funny," said Grimes. "Very funny. Sir."

"Isn't it?" Damien was laughing unashamedly. "But when things went so very badly wrong on Doncaster, Barratin couldn't see the joke, even after I explained it to him. "You see, Grimes, that *you* were a factor that wasn't allowed for in the equation. Alberto travelled to Doncaster in *your* ship, a Serpent Class Courier. *You* were with Miss Madigan when Alberto tried to . . . subtract her.

"And you were captain of the *Adder!*"

⚘ The Tin Messiah ⚘

"I'M AFRAID, LIEUTENANT," said Commodore Damien, "that your passenger, this trip, won't be able to help out in the galley."

"As long as he's not another assassin, he'll do me," said Grimes. "But I've found, sir, that anybody who likes to eat also likes now, and again, to prepare his own favorite dishes . . ."

"This one does. All the time."

Grimes looked at his superior dubiously. He suspected the Commodore's sense of humor. The older man's skull-like face was stiffly immobile, but there was a sardonic glint in the pale grey eyes.

"If he wants galley privileges, sir, it's only fair that he shares, now and again, what he hashes up for himself."

Damien sighed. "I've never known officers so concerned about their bellies as you people in the *Adder*. All you think about is adding to your weight . . ." Grimes winced—as much because of the unfairness of the imputation as in reaction to the pun. The Couriers—little, very fast ships—did not carry cooks, so their officers, obliged to cook for themselves, were more than usually food-conscious. *Adder's* crew was no exception to this rule. Damien went on, "I've no doubt that Mr. Adam would be willing to share his . . . er . . . nutriment with you, but I don't think that any of you, catholic as your tastes may be, would find it palatable. Or, come to that, nourishing. But who started this particularly futile discussion?"

"You did, sir," said Grimes.

"You'll never make a diplomat, Lieutenant. It is doubtful that you'll ever reach flag rank in this Service, rough and tough spacemen though we be, blunt and outspoken to a fault, the glint of honest iron showing through the work-worn fabric of our velvet gloves . . . H'm. Yes. Where was I?"

"Talking about iron fists in velvet gloves, sir."

"Before you side-tracked me, I mean. Yes, your passenger. He is to be transported from Lindisfarne Base to Delacron. You just dump him there, then return to Base forthwith." The Commodore's bony hand picked up the heavily sealed envelope from his desk, extended it. "Your Orders."

"Thank you, sir. Will that be all, sir?"

"Yes. Scramble!"

Grimes didn't exactly scramble; nonetheless he walked briskly enough to where his ship, the Serpent Class Courier *Adder,* was berthed. Dwarfed as she was by the bigger vessels about her she still stood there, tall, proud and gleaming. Grimes knew that she and her kind were referred to, disparagingly, as "flying darning needles," but he loved the slenderness of her lines, would not have swapped her for a hulking dreadnought. (In a dreadnought, of course, he would have been no more than one of many junior officers.) She was *his.*

Ensign Beadle, his First Lieutenant, met him at the airlock ramp, saluted. He reported mournfully (nobody had ever heard Beadle laugh, and he smiled but rarely), "All secure for lift off, Captain."

"Thank you, Number One."

"The . . . the passenger's aboard . . ."

"Good. I suppose we'd better extend the usual courtesy. Ask him if he'd like the spare seat in Control when we shake the dust of Base off our tail vanes."

"I've already done so, Captain. It says that it'll be pleased to accept the invitation."

"*It*, Number One. *It!* Adam is a good Terran name."

Beadle actually smiled. "Technically speaking, Captain, one could not say that Mr. Adam is of Terran birth. But he is of Terran manufacture."

"And what does he eat?" asked Grimes, remembering the Commodore's veiled references to the passenger's diet. "A.C. or D.C.? Washed down with a noggin of light lubricating oil?"

"How did you guess, Captain?"

"The Old Man told me, in a roundabout sort of way. But . . . A passenger, not cargo . . . There must be some mistake."

"There's not, Captain. It's intelligent, all right, and it has a personality. I've checked its papers, and officially it's a citizen of the Interstellar Federation, with all rights, privileges and obligations."

"I suppose that our masters know best," said Grimes resignedly.

It was intelligent, and it had a personality, and Grimes found it quite impossible to think of Mr. Adam as "it." This robot was representative of a type of which Grimes had heard rumors, but it was the first one that he had ever seen. There were only a very few of them in all the worlds of the Federation—and most of that few were of Earth itself. To begin with, they were fantastically expensive. Secondly, their creators were scared of them, were plagued by nightmares in which they saw themselves as latter day Frankensteins. Intelligent robots were not a rarity—but intelligent robots with imagination, intuition, and initiative were. They had been developed mainly for research and exploration, and could survive in environments that would be almost immediately lethal to even the most heavily and elaborately armored man.

Mr. Adam sat in the spare chair in the control room. There was no need for him to sit, but he did so, in an astonishingly human posture. Perhaps, thought Grimes, he could sense that his hosts would feel more comfortable if something that looked like an attenuated knight in armor were not looming tall behind them, peering over their shoulders. His face was expressionless—it was a dull-gleaming ovoid with no features to be expressive with—but it seemed to Grimes that there was the faintest flicker of luminosity behind the eye lenses that could betoken interest. His voice, when he spoke, came from a diaphragm set in his throat.

He was speaking now. "This has been very interesting, Captain. And now, I take it, we are on trajectory for Delacron." His voice was a pleasant enough baritone, not quite mechanical.

"Yes, Mr. Adam. That is the Delacron sun there, at three o'clock from the center of the cartwheel sight."

"And that odd distortion, of course, is the resultant of the temporal precession field of your Drive . . ." He hummed quietly to himself for a few seconds. "Interesting."

"You must have seen the same sort of thing on your way out to Lindisfarne from Earth."

"No, Captain. I was not a guest, ever, in the control room of the cruiser in which I was transported." The shrug of his gleaming, metal shoulders was almost human. "I . . . I don't think that Captain Grisby trusted me."

That, thought Grimes, was rather an odd way of putting it. But he knew Grisby, had served under him. Grisby, as a naval officer of an earlier age, on Earth's seas, would have pined for the good old days of sail, of wooden ships and iron men—and by "iron men" he would not have meant anything like this Mr. Adam . . .

"Yes," the robot went on musingly, "I find this not only interesting, but amazing . . ."

"How so?" asked Grimes.

"It could all be done—the lift off, the setting of trajectory, the delicate balance between acceleration and temporal precession—so much . . . faster by one like myself . . ."

You mean "better" rather than faster, thought Grimes, *but you're too courteous to say it.*

"And yet . . . and yet . . . You're flesh and blood creatures, Captain, evolved to suit the conditions of just one world out of all the billions of planets. Space is not your natural environment."

"We carry our environment around with us, Mr. Adam." Grimes noticed that the other officers in Control—Ensign von Tannenbaum, the Navigator, Ensign Beadle, the First Lieutenant, and Lieutenant Slovotny, the radio officer—were following the conversation closely and expectantly. He would have to be careful. Nonetheless, he had to keep his end up. He grinned. "And don't forget," he said, "that Man, himself, is a quite rugged, self-maintaining, self-reproducing, all-purpose robot."

"There are more ways than one of reproducing," said Mr. Adam quietly.

"I'll settle for the old-fashioned way!" broke in von Tannenbaum.

Grimes glared at the burly, flaxen-headed young man—but too late to stop Slovotny's laughter. Even Beadle smiled.

John Grimes allowed himself a severely rationed chuckle. Then: "The show's on the road, gentlemen. I'll leave her in your capable hands. Number One. Set Deep Space watches. Mr. Adam, it is usual at this juncture for me to invite any guests to my quarters for a drink and a yarn . . ."

Mr. Adam laughed. "Like yourself, Captain, I feel the occasional need for a lubricant. But I do not make a ritual of its application. I shall, however, be very pleased to talk with you while you drink."

"I'll lead the way," said Grimes resignedly.

In a small ship passengers can make their contribution to the quiet pleasures of the voyage, or they can be a pain in the neck. Mr. Adam, at first, seemed pathetically eager to prove that he could be a good shipmate. He could talk—and he did talk, on anything and everything. Mr. Beadle remarked about him that he must have swallowed an encyclopedia. Mr. McCloud, the Engineering Officer, corrected this statement, saying that he must have been built around one. And Mr. Adam could listen. That was worse than his talking— one always had the impression of invisible wheels whirring inside that featureless head, of information either being discarded as valueless or added to the robot's data bank. He could play chess (of course)—and on the rare occasions that he lost a game it was strongly suspected that he had done so out of politeness. It was the same with any card game.

Grimes sent for Spooky Deane, the psionic communications officer. He had the bottle and the glasses ready when the tall, fragile young man seeped in through the doorway of his day cabin, looking like a wisp of ectoplasm decked out in Survey Service uniform. He sat down when invited, accepted the tumbler of neat gin that his captain poured for him.

"Here's looking up your kilt," toasted Grimes coarsely.

"'A *physical* violation of privacy, Captain," murmured Deane. "I see nothing objectionable in that."

"And just what are you hinting at, Mr. Deane?"

"I know, Captain, that you are about to ask me to break the Rhine Institute's Privacy Oath. And this knowledge has nothing to do with my being a telepath. Every time that we carry passengers it's the same. You always want me to pry into their minds to see what makes them tick."

"Only when I feel that the safety of the ship might be at stake." Grimes refilled Deane's glass, the contents of which had somehow vanished.

"You are . . . frightened of our passenger?" Grimes frowned. "Frightened" was a strong word. And yet mankind has always feared the robot, the automaton, the artificial man. A premonitory dread? Or was the robot only a symbol of the machines—the *mindless* machines—that with every passing year were becoming more and more dominant in human affairs?

Deane said quietly, "Mr. Adam is not a mindless machine."

Grimes glared at him. He almost snarled, "How the hell do you know what I'm thinking?"—then thought better of it. Not that it made any difference.

The telepath went on, "Mr. Adam has a mind, as well as a brain."

"That's what I was wondering."

"Yes. He broadcasts, Captain, as all of you do. The trouble is that I haven't quite got his . . . frequency."

"Any . . . hostility towards us? Towards humans?"

Deane extended his empty glass. Grimes refilled it. The telepath sipped daintily, then said, "I . . . I don't think so, but, as I've already told you, his mind is not human. Is it contempt he feels? No . . . Not quite. Pity? Yes, it could be. A sort of amused affection? Yes . . ."

"The sort of feelings that we'd have towards—say—a dog capable of coherent speech?"

"Yes."

"Anything else?"

"I could be wrong, Captain. I most probably am. This is the first time that I've eavesdropped on a non-organic mind. There seems to be a strong sense of . . . mission . . ."

"*Mission?*"

"Yes. It reminds me of that priest we carried a few trips back— the one who was going out to convert the heathen Tarvarkens . . ."

"A dirty business," commented Grimes. "Wean the natives away from their own, quite satisfactory local gods so that they stop lobbing missiles at the trading post, which was established without their consent anyhow . . ."

"Father Cleary didn't look at it that way."

"Good for him. I wonder what happened to the poor bastard?"

"Should you be talking like this, Captain?"

"I shouldn't. But with you it doesn't matter. You know what I'm thinking, anyhow. But this Mr. Adam, Spooky. A missionary? It doesn't make sense."

"That's just the *feeling* I get."

Grimes ignored this. "Or, perhaps, it does make sense. The robots of Mr. Adam's class are designed to be able to go where Man himself cannot go. In our own planetary system, for example, they've carried out explorations on Mercury, Jupiter, and Saturn. A robot missionary on Tarvark would have made sense, being impervious to poisoned arrows, spears, and the like. But on Delacron, an Earth colony? No."

"But I still get that *feeling*," insisted Deane.

"There are feelings *and* feelings," Grimes told him. "Don't forget that this is non-organic mind that you're prying into. Perhaps you don't know the code, the language . . ."

"Codes and languages don't matter to a telepath." Deane contrived to make his empty glass obvious. Grimes refilled it. "Don't forget, Captain, that there are machines on Delacron, *intelligent* machines. Not a very high order of intelligence, I admit, but . . . And you must have heard of the squabble between Delacron and its nearest neighbor, Muldoon . . ."

Grimes had heard of it. Roughly midway between the two planetary systems was a sun with only one world in close orbit about it—and that solitary planet was a fantastic treasure house of radioactive ores. Both Delacron and Muldoon had laid claim to it. Delacron wanted the rare metals for its own industries, the less highly industrialized Muldoon wanted them for export to other worlds of the Federation.

And Mr. Adam? Where did he come into it? Officially, according to his papers, he was a programmer, on loan from the Federation's Grand Council to the Government of Delacron. A programmer . . . A teacher of machines . . . An intelligent machine to teach other intelligent machines . . . To teach other intelligent machines *what?*

And who had programmed *him*—or had he just, as it were, happened?

A familiar pattern—vague, indistinct, but nonetheless there— was beginning to emerge. It had all been done before, this shipping of revolutionaries into the places in which they could do the most harm by governments absolutely unsympathetic towards their aspirations . . .

"Even if Mr. Adam had a beard," said Deane, "he wouldn't *look* much like Lenin . . ."

And Grimes wondered if the driver who brought that train into the Finland Station knew what he was doing.

Grimes was just the engine driver, and Mr. Adams was the passenger, and Grimes was tied down as much by the Regulations of his Service as was that long ago railwayman by the tracks upon which his locomotive ran. Grimes was blessed—or cursed—with both imagination and a conscience, and a conscience is too expensive a luxury for a junior officer. Those who can afford such a luxury all too often decide that they can do quite nicely without it.

Grimes actually wished that in some way Mr. Adam was endangering the ship. Then he, Grimes, could take action, drastic action if necessary. But the robot was less trouble than the average human passenger. There were no complaints about monotonous food, stale air and all the rest of it. About the only thing that could be said against him was that he was far too good a chess player, but just about the time that Grimes was trying to find excuses for not playing with him he made what appeared to be a genuine friendship, and preferred the company of Mr. McCloud to that of any the other officers.

"Of course, Captain," said Beadle, "they belong to the same clan."

"What the hell do you mean, Number One?"

Deadpan, Beadle replied, "The Clan MacHinery."

Grimes groaned, then, with reluctance, laughed. He said, "It makes sense. A machine will have more in common with our Engineering Officer than the rest of us. Their shop talk must be fascinating." He tried to initiate McCloud's accent. "An' tell me, Mr. Adam, whit sorrt o' lubricant d'ye use on yon ankle joint?"

Beadle, having made his own joke, was not visibly amused. "Something suitable for heavy duty I should imagine, Captain."

"Mphm. Well, if Mac keeps him happy, he's out of our hair for the rest of the trip."

"He'll keep Mac happy, too, Captain. He's always moaning that he should have an assistant."

"Set a thief to catch a thief," cracked Grimes. "Set a machine to . . . to . . ."

"Work a machine?" suggested Beadle.

Those words would do, thought Grimes, but after the First Lieutenant had left him he began to consider the implications of what had been discussed. McCloud was a good engineer—but the better the engineer, the worse the psychological shortcomings. The Machine had been developed to be Man's slave—but ever since the twentieth century a peculiar breed of Man had proliferated that was all too ready and willing to become the Machine's servants, far too prone to sacrifice human values on the altar of Efficiency. Instead of machines being modified to suit their operators, men were being modified to suit the machines. And McCloud? He would have been happier in industry than in the Survey Service, with its emphasis on officer-like qualities and all the rest of it. As it was, he was far too prone to regard the ship merely as the platform that carried his precious engines.

Grimes sighed. He didn't like what he was going to do. It was all very well to snoop on passengers, on outsiders—but to pry into the minds of his own people was not gentlemanly.

He got out the gin bottle and called for Mr. Deane.

"Yes, Captain?" asked the telepath.

"You know what I want you for, Spooky."

"Of course. But I don't like it."

"Neither do I." Grimes poured the drinks, handed the larger one to Deane. The psionic communications officer sipped in an absurdly genteel manner, the little finger of his right hand extended. The level of the transparent fluid in his glass sank rapidly.

Deane said, his speech ever so slightly slurred, "And you think that the safety of the ship is jeopardized?"

"I do." Grimes poured more gin—but not for himself.

"If I have your assurance, Captain, that such is the case . . ."

"You have."

Deanne was silent for a few seconds, looking through rather than at Grimes, staring at something . . . elsewhere. Then: "They're in the computer room. Mr. Adam and the Chief. I can't pick up Adam's thoughts—but I feel a sense of . . . rightness? But I can get into Mac's mind . . ." On his almost featureless visage the grimace of extreme distaste was startling. "I . . . I don't understand . . ."

"You don't understand what, Spooky?"

"How a man, a human being, can regard a hunk of animated ironmongery with such reverence . . ."

"You're not a very good psychologist, Spooky, but go on."

"I . . . I'm looking at Adam through Mac's eyes. He's bigger, somehow, and he seems to be self-luminous, and there's a sort of circle of golden light around his head . . ."

"That's the way that Mac sees him?"

"Yes. And his voice. Adam's voice. It's not the way that *we* hear it. It's more like the beat of some great engine . . . And he's saying, 'You believe, and you will serve.' And Mac has just answered, 'Yes, Master. I believe, and I will serve.'"

"What are they *doing!*" demanded Grimes urgently.

"Mac's opening up the computer. The memory bank, I think it is. He's turned to look at Adam again, and a panel over Adam's chest is sliding away and down, and there's some sort of storage bin in there, with rows and rows of pigeonholes. Adam has taken something out of one of them . . . A ball of greyish metal or plastic, with connections all over its surface. He's telling Mac where to put it in the memory bank, and how to hook it up . . ."

Grimes, his glass clattering unheeded to the deck, was out of his chair, pausing briefly at his desk to fling open a drawer and to take from it his .50 automatic. He snapped at Deane, "Get on the intercom. Tell every officer off duty to come to the computer room, armed if possible." He ran through the door out into the alleyway, then fell rather than clambered down the ladder to the next deck, and to the next one, and the next. At some stage of his descent he twisted his ankle, painfully, but kept on going.

The door to the computer room was locked, from the inside—but Grimes, as Captain, carried always on his person the ship's master key. With his left hand—the pistol was in his right—he inserted the convoluted sliver of metal into the slot, twisted it. The panel slid open.

McCloud and Adam stared at him, at the weapon in his hand. He stared back. He allowed his gaze to wander, but briefly. The cover plate had been replaced over the memory bank—but surely that heavily insulted cable leading to and through it was something that had been added, was an additional supply of power, too much power, to the ship's electronic bookkeeper.

McCloud smiled—a vague sort of smile, yet somehow exalted, that looked odd on his rough-hewn features. He said, "You and your kind are finished, Captain. You'd better tell the dinosaurs, Neanderthal Man, the dodo, the great auk, and all the others to move over to make room for you."

"Mr. McCloud," ordered Grimes, his voice (not without effort on his part) steady, "switch off the computer, then undo whatever it is that you have done."

It was Adam who replied. "I am sorry, genuinely sorry, Mr. Grimes, but it is too late. As Mr. McCloud implied, you are on the point of becoming extinct."

Grimes was conscious of the others behind him in the alleyway. "Mr. Beadle?"

"Yes, Captain?"

"Take Mr. Slovetny with you down to the engine room. Cut off all power to this section of the ship."

"You can try," said Mr. Adam. "But you will not be allowed. I give notice now; I am the Master."

"You are the Master," echoed McCloud.

"Mutiny," stated Grimes.

"Mutiny?" repeated Adam, iron and irony in his voice. He stepped towards the Captain, one long, metallic arm upraised.

Grimes fired. He might as well have been using a pea-shooter. He fired again, and again. The bullets splashed like pellets of wet clay on the robot's armor. He realized that it was too late for him to turn and run; he awaited the crushing impact of the steel fist that would end everything.

There was a voice saying, "No . . . *No* . . ."

Was it his own? Dimly, he realized that it was not.

There was the voice saying, "No!"

Surprisingly Adam hesitated—but only for a second. Again he advanced—and then, seemingly from the computer itself, arced a crackling discharge, a dreadful, blinding lightning. Grimes, in the fleeting instant before his eyelids snapped shut, saw the automaton standing there, arms outstretched rigidly from his sides, black amid the electric fire that played about his body. Then, as he toppled to the deck, there was a metallic crash.

When, at long last, Grimes regained his eyesight he looked around the computer room. McCloud was unharmed—physically. The engineer was huddled in a corner, his arms over his head, in a fetal position. The computer, to judge from the wisps of smoke still trickling from cracks in its panels, was a total write-off. And Adam, literally welded to the deck, still in that attitude of crucifixion, was dead.

Dead . . . thought Grimes numbly. *Dead* . . . Had he ever been alive, in the real sense of the word?

But the ship, he knew, had been briefly alive, had been aware, conscious, after that machine which would be God had kindled the spark of life in her electronic brain. And a ship, unlike other machines, always has personality, a pseudo-life derived from her crew, from the men who live and work, hope and dream within her metal body.

This vessel had known her brief minutes of full awareness, but her old virtues had persisted, among them loyalty to her rightful captain.

Grimes wondered if he would dare to put all this in the report that he would have to make. It would be a pity not to give credit where credit was due.

✒ The Sleeping Beauty ✒

COMMODORE DAMIEN, Officer Commanding Couriers, was not in a very good mood. This was not unusual—especially on the occasions when Lieutenant Grimes, captain of the Serpent Class Courier *Adder,* happened to be on the carpet.

"Mr. Grimes . . ." said the Commodore in a tired voice.

"Sir!" responded Grimes smartly.

"Mr. Grimes, you've been and gone and done it *again.*"

The Lieutenant's prominent ears reddened. "I did what I could to save my ship and my people, sir."

"You destroyed a *very* expensive piece of equipment, as well as playing merry hell with the Federation's colonial policy. My masters—who, incidentally, are also *your* masters—are not, repeat not, amused."

"I saved my ship," repeated Grimes stubbornly.

The Commodore looked down at the report on his desk. A grim smile did little, if anything, to soften the harsh planes of his bony face. "It says here that your ship saved you."

"She did," admitted Grimes. "It was sort of mutual . . ."

"And it was your ship that killed—I suppose that 'kill' is the right word to use regarding a highly intelligent robot—Mr. Adam . . . H'm. A *slightly* extenuating circumstance. Nonetheless, Grimes, were it not for the fact that you're a better than average spaceman you'd be O-U-bloody-T, trying to get a job as Third Mate in Rim

326

Runners or some such outfit." He made a steeple of his skeletal fingers, glared at the Lieutenant coldly over the bony erection. "So, in the interests of all concerned, I've decided that your *Adder* will not be carrying any more passengers for a while—at least, not with you in command of her. Even so, I'm afraid that you'll not have much time to enjoy the social life—such as it is—of Base . . ."

Grimes sighed audibly. Although a certain Dr. Margaret Lazenby was his senior in rank he was beginning to get on well with her.

"As soon as repairs and routine maintenance are completed, Mr. Grimes, you will get the hell off this planet."

"What about my officers, sir? Mr. Beadle is overdue for Leave . . ."

"My heart fair bleeds for him."

"And Mr. McCloud is in hospital . . ."

"Ensign Vitelli, your new Engineering Officer, was ordered to report to your vessel as soon as possible, if not before. The work of fitting a replacement computer to *Adder* is already well in hand." The Commodore looked at his watch. "It is now 1435. At 1800 hours you will lift ship."

"My Orders, sir . . ."

"Oh, yes, Grimes. Your Orders. A matter of minor importance, actually. As long as you get out of *my* hair that's all that matters to me. But I suppose I have to put you in the picture. The Shaara are passing through a phase of being nice to humans, and we, of the Federation, are reciprocating. There's a small parcel of *very* important cargo to be lifted from Droomoor to Brooum, and for some reason or other our arthropedal allies haven't a fast ship of their own handy. Lindisfarne Base is only a week from Droomoor by Serpent Class Courier. So . . ."

So *Viper, Asp and Cobra have all been in port for weeks,* thought Grimes bitterly, *but I get the job.*

The Commodore had his telepathic moments. He smiled again, and this time there was a hint of sympathy. He said, "I want you off Lindisfarne, young Grimes, before there's too much of a stink raised over this Mr. Adam affair. You're too honest. I can bend the truth better than you can."

"Thank you, sir," said Grimes, meaning it.

"Off you go, now. Don't forget these." Grimes took the heavily sealed envelope. "And try not to make too much of a balls of this assignment."

"I'll try, sir."

Grimes saluted, marched smartly out of the Commodore's office, strode across the apron to where his "flying darning needle," not yet shifted to a lay-up berth (not that she would be now), was awaiting him.

Mr. Beadle met him at the airlock. He rarely smiled—but he did so, rather smugly, when he saw the Orders in Grimes' hand. He asked casually, "Any word of my relief, Captain?"

"Yes. You're not getting it, Number One," Grimes told him, rather hating himself for the pleasure he derived from being the bearer of bad tidings. "And we're to lift off at 1800 hours. Is the new engineer aboard yet?"

Beadle's face had resumed its normal lugubrious case. "Yes," he said. "But stores, Captain . . . Repairs . . . Maintenance . . ."

"Are they in hand?"

"Yes, but . . ."

"Then if we aren't ready for space, it won't be our fault." But Grimes knew—and it made him feel as unhappy as his first lieutenant looked—that the ship would be ready.

Adder lifted at precisely 1800 hours. Grimes, sulking hard— he had not been able to see Maggie Lazenby—did not employ his customary, spectacular getting-upstairs-in-a-hurry technique, kept his fingers off the auxiliary reaction drive controls. The ship drifted up and out under inertial drive only, seemingly sharing the reluctance to part of her officer. Beadle was slumped gloomily in his chair, von Tannenbaum, the navigator, stared at his instruments with an elaborate lack of interest, Slovotny, the electronic communications officer, snarled every time that he had occasion to hold converse with Aerospace Control.

And yet, once the vessel was clear of the atmosphere, Grimes began to feel almost happy. *Growl you may,* he thought, *but go you must*. He had gone. He was on his way. He was back in what he regarded as his natural element. Quite cheerfully he went through the motions of lining *Adder* up on the target star, was pleased to note that von Tannenbaum was cooperating in his usual highly efficient manner. And then, once trajectory had been set, the Mannschenn Drive was put into operation and the little ship was falling at a fantastic speed through the warped Continuum, with yet another mission to be accomplished.

The captain made the usual minor ritual of lighting his pipe. He said, "Normal Deep Space routine, Number One."

"Normal Deep Space routine, sir."

"Who has the watch?"

"Mr. von Tannenbaum, Captain."

"Good. Then come to see me as soon as you're free."

When Beadle knocked at his door Grimes had the envelope of instructions open. He motioned the first lieutenant to a chair, said, "Fix us drinks, Number One, while I see what's in this bumf . . ." He extended a hand for the glass that the officer put into it, sipped the pink gin, continued reading. "Mphm. Well, we're bound for Droomoor, as you know . . ."

"As well I know." Beadle then muttered something about communistic bumblebees.

"Come, come, Mr. Beadle. The Shaara are our brave allies. And they aren't at all bad when you get to know them."

"I don't want to get to know them. If I couldn't have my leave I could have been sent on a mission to a world with real human girls and a few bright lights . . ."

"Mr. Beadle, you shock me. By your xenophobia as well as by your low tastes. However, as I was saying, we are to proceed to Droomoor at maximum velocity consistent with safety. There we are to pick up a small parcel of very important cargo, the loading of which is to be strictly supervised by the local authorities. As soon as possible thereafter we are to proceed to Brooum at maximum velocity etc. etc."

"Just delivery boys," grumbled Beadle. "That's us."

"Oh, well," Grimes told him philosophically, "it's a change from being coach drivers. And after the trouble we've had with passengers of late it should be a welcome one."

Droomoor is an Earth-type planet, with the usual seas, continents, polar icecaps and all the rest of it. Evolution did not produce any life-forms deviating to any marked degree from the standard pattern; neither did it come up with any fire-making, tool-using animals. If human beings had been the first to discover it, it would have become a Terran colony. But it was a Shaara ship that made the first landing, so it was colonized by the Shaara, as was Brooum, a very similar world.

Grimes brought *Adder* in to Port Sherr with his usual competence, receiving the usual cooperation from the Shaara version of Aerospace Control. Apart from that, things were not so usual. He and his officers were interested to note that the aerial traffic which they sighted during their passage through the atmosphere consisted of semirigid airships rather than heavier-than-air machines. And the buildings surrounding the landing apron at the spaceport were featureless, mud-colored domes rather than angular constructions of glass and metal. Beadle mumbled something about a huddle of bloody beehives, but Grimes paid no attention. As a reasonably efficient captain he was interested in the lay-out of the port, was trying to form some idea of what facilities were available. A ship is a ship is a ship, no matter by whom built or by whom manned—but a mammal is a mammal and an arthroped is an arthroped, and each has its own separate requirements.

"Looks like the Port Officials on their way out to us," remarked von Tannenbaum.

A party of Shaara had emerged from a circular opening near the top of the nearer dome. They flew slowly towards the ship, their gauzy wings almost invisible in the sunlight. Grimes focused his binoculars on them. In the lead was a Princess, larger than the others, her body more slender, glittering with the jeweled insignia of her rank. She was followed by two drones, so hung about with precious stones and metal that it was a wonder that they were able to stay airborne. Four upper caste workers, less gaudily caparisoned than the drones, but with sufficient ornamentation to differentiate them from the common herd, completed the party.

"Number One," said Grimes, "attend the airlock, please. I shall receive the boarding party in my day cabin."

He went down from the control room to his quarters, got out the whisky—three bottles, he decided, should be sufficient, although the Shaara drones were notorious for their capacity.

The Princess was hard, businesslike. She refused to take a drink herself, and under her glittering, many-faceted eyes the workers dared not accept Grimes's hospitality, and even the drones limited themselves to a single small glass apiece. She stood there like a gleaming, metallic piece of abstract statuary, motionless, and the voice that issued from the box strapped to her thorax was that of a machine rather than of a living being.

She said, "This is an important mission, Captain. You will come with me, at once, to the Queen Mother, for instructions."

Grimes didn't like being ordered around, especially aboard his own ship, but was well aware that it is foolish to antagonize planetary rulers. He said:

"Certainly, Your Highness. But first I must give instructions to my officers. And before I can do so I must have some information. To begin with, how long a stay do we have on your world?"

"You will lift ship as soon as the consignment has been loaded." She consulted the jeweled watch that she wore strapped to a forelimb. "The underworkers will be on their way out to your vessel now." She pointed towards the four upper caste working Shaara. "These will supervise stowage. Please inform your officers of the arrangements."

Grimes called Beadle on the intercom, asked him to come up to his cabin. Then, as soon as the First Lieutenant put in an appearance, he told him that he was to place himself at the disposal of the supervisors and to ensure that *Adder* was in readiness for instant departure. He then went through into his bedroom to change into a dress uniform, was pulling off his shirt when he realized that the Princess had followed him.

"What are you doing?" she asked coldly.

"Putting on something more suitable, Your Highness," he told her.

"That will not be necessary, Captain. *You* will be the only human in the presence of Her Majesty, and everybody will know who and what you are."

Resignedly Grimes shrugged himself back into his uniform shirt, unadorned save for shoulder boards. He felt that he should be allowed to make more of a showing, especially among beings all dressed up like Christmas trees themselves, but his orders had been to cooperate fully with the Shaara authorities. And, in any case, shorts and shirt were far more comfortable than long trousers, frock coat, collar and tie, fore-and-aft hat and that ridiculous ceremonial sword. He hung his personal communicator over his shoulder, put on his cap and said, "I'm ready, Your Highness."

"What is that?" she asked suspiciously. "A weapon?"

"No, Your Highness! A radio transceiver. I must remain in touch with my ship at all times."

"I suppose it's all right," she said grudgingly.

When Grimes walked down the ramp, following the princess and her escorting drones, he saw that a wheeled truck had drawn up alongside *Adder* and that a winch mounted on the vehicle was reeling in a small airship, a bloated gasbag from which was slung a flimsy car, at the after end of which a huge, two-bladed propeller was still lazily turning. Workers were scurrying about on the ground and buzzing between the blimp and the truck.

"Your cargo," said the Princess. "And your transport from the spaceport to the palace."

The car of the airship was now only a foot above the winch. From it the workers lifted carefully a white cylinder, apparently made from some plastic, about four feet long and one foot in diameter. Set into its smooth surface were dials, and an indicator light that glowed vividly green even in the bright sunlight. An insulated lead ran from it to the airship's engine compartment where, thought Grimes, there must be either a battery or a generator. Yes, a battery it was. Two

workers, their wings a shimmering transparency, brought it out and
set it down on the concrete beside the cylinder.

"You will embark," the princess stated.

Grimes stood back and assessed the situation. It would be easy
enough to get on to the truck, to clamber on top of the winch and
from there into the car—but it would be impossible to do so
without getting his white shorts, shirt and stockings filthy. Insofar as
machinery was concerned the Shaara believed in lubrication, and
plenty of it.

"I am waiting," said the Princess.

"Yes, Your Highness, but . . ."

Grimes did not hear the order given—the Shaara communicated
among themselves telepathically—so was somewhat taken aback
when two of the workers approached him, buzzing loudly. He
flinched when their claws penetrated the thin fabric of his clothing
and scratched his skin. He managed to refrain from crying out when
he was lifted from the ground, carried the short distance to the
airship and dumped, sprawling, on to the deck of the open car. The
main hurt was to his dignity. Looking up at his own vessel he could
see the grinning faces of von Tannenbaum and Slovotny at the
control room viewports.

He scrambled somehow to his feet, wondering if the fragile
decking would stand his weight. And then the Princess was with
him, and the escorting drones, and the upper caste worker in
command of the blimp had taken her place at the simple controls
and the frail contraption was ballooning swiftly upwards as the
winch brake was released. Grimes, looking down, saw the end of the
cable whip off the barrel. He wondered what would happen if the
dangling wire fouled something on the ground below, then decided
that it was none of his business. These people had been playing
around with airships for quite some years and must know what they
were about.

The Princess was not in a communicative mood, and obviously
the drones and the workers talked only when talked to—by her—
although all of them wore voice boxes. Grimes was quite content with
the way that things were. He had decided that the Shaaran was a bossy

female, and he did not like bossy females, mammalian, arthropedal or whatever. He settled down to enjoy the trip, appreciating the leisurely—by his standards—flight over the lush countryside. There were the green, rolling hills, the great banks of flowering shrubs, huge splashes of color that were vivid without being gaudy. Thousands of workers were busily employed about the enormous blossoms. There was almost no machinery in evidence—but in a culture such as this there would be little need for the machine, workers of the lower grades being no more than flesh-and-blood robots.

Ahead of them loomed the city.

Just a huddle of domes it was, some large, some small, with the greatest of all of them roughly in the center. This one, Grimes saw as they approached it, had a flattened top, and there was machinery there—a winch, he decided.

The airship came in high, but losing altitude slowly, finally hovering over the palace, its propeller just turning over to keep it stemming the light breeze. Two workers flew up from the platform, caught the end of the dangling cable, snapped it on to the end of another cable brought up from the winch drum. The winch was started and, creaking in protest, the blimp was drawn rapidly down. A set of wheeled steps was pushed into position, its upper part hooked on to the gunwale of the swaying car. The princess and her escort ignored this facility, fluttering out and down in a flurry of gauzy wings. Grimes used the ladder, of course, feeling grateful that somebody had bothered to remember that he was a wingless biped.

"Follow me," snapped the Princess.

The spaceman followed her, through a circular hatch in the platform. The ramp down which she led him was steep and he had difficulty in maintaining his balance, was unable to gain more than a confused impression of the interior of the huge building. There was plenty of light, luckily, a green-blue radiance emanating from clusters of luminescent insects hanging at intervals from the roof of the corridor. The air was warm, and bore an acrid but not unpleasant tang. It carried very few sounds, however, only a continuous, faintly sinister rustling noise. Grimes missed the murmur of machinery. Surely—apart from anything else—a vast structure such as this would need mechanical ventilation. In any case, there was an appreciable air flow. And then, at a junction of four corridors, he saw a group of workers, their feet hooked into rings set in the smooth floor, their wings beating slowly, maintaining the circulation of the atmosphere.

Down they went, and down, through corridors that were deserted save for themselves, through other corridors that were busy streets, with hordes of workers scurrying on mysterious errands. But they were never jostled; the lower caste Shaara always gave the Princess and her party a respectfully wide berth. Even so, there seemed to be little, if any curiosity; only the occasional drone would stop to stare at the Earthman with interest.

Down they went, and down . . .

They came, at last, to the end of a long passageway, closed off by a grilled door, the first that Grimes had seen in the hive. On the farther side of it were six workers, hung about with metal accoutrements. Workers? No, Grimes decided, soldiers, Amazons. Did they, he wondered, have stings, like their Terran counterparts? Perhaps they did—but the laser pistols that they held would be far more effective.

"Who comes?" asked one of them in the sort of voice that Grimes associated with sergeant-majors.

"The Princess Shrla, with Drones Brrynn and Drryhr, and Earth-Drone-Captain Grrimes."

"Enter, Princess Shrla, Enter, Earth-Drone-Captain Grrimes."

The grille slid silently aside, admitting Grimes and the Princess, shutting again, leaving the two drones on its further side. Two soldiers led the way along a tunnel that, by the Earthman's standards, was very poorly illuminated, two more brought up the rear. Grimes was pleased to note that the Princess seemed to have lost most of her arrogance.

They came, then, into a vast chamber, a blue-lit dimness about which the shapes of the Queen-Mother's attendants rustled, scurried and crept. Slowly they walked over the smooth, soft floor—under Grimes's shoes it felt unpleasantly organic—to the raised platform on which lay a huge, pale shape. Ranged around the platform were screens upon which moved pictures of scenes all over the planet—one of them showed the spaceport, with *Adder* standing tall slim and gleaming on the apron—and banks of dials and meters. Throne-room this enormous vault was, and nursery, and the control room of a world.

Grimes's eyes were becoming accustomed to the near-darkness. He looked with pity at the flabby, grossly distended body with its ineffectual limbs, its useless stubs of wings. He did not, oddly enough, consider obscene the slowly moving belt that ran under the platform, upon which, at regular intervals, a glistening, pearly egg was deposited, neither was he repelled by the spectacle of the worker whose swollen body visibly shrank as she regurgitated nutriment into the mouth of the Shaara Queen—but he was taken aback when that being spoke to him while feeding was still in progress. He should not have been, knowing as he did that the artificial voice boxes worn by the Shaara have no connection with their organs of ingestion.

"Welcome, Captain Grimes," she said in deep, almost masculine tones.

"I am honored, Your Majesty," he stammered.

"You do us a great service, Captain Grimes."

"That is a pleasure as well as an honor, Your Majesty."

"So . . . But, Captain Grimes, I must, as you Earthmen say, put you in the picture." There was a short silence. "On Brooum there is crisis. Disease has taken its toll among the hives, a virus, a mutated virus. A cure was found—but too late. The Brooum Queen-Mother is dead. All Princesses not beyond fertilization age are dead. Even the royal eggs, larvae and pupae were destroyed by the disease.

"We, of course, are best able to afford help to our daughters and sisters on Brooum. We offered to send a fertilizable Princess to become Queen-Mother, but the Council of Princesses which now rules the colony insists that their new monarch be born, as it were, on the planet. So, then, we are dispatching, by your vessel, a royal pupa. She will tear the silken sheath and emerge, as an imago, into the world over which she will reign."

"Mphm . . ." grunted Grimes absentmindedly. "Your Majesty," he added hastily.

The Queen-Mother turned her attention to the television screens. "If we are not mistaken," she said, "the loading of the refrigerated canister containing the pupa has been completed. Princess Shrla will take you back to your ship. You will lift and proceed as soon as is practicable." Again she paused, then went on. "We need not tell you, Captain Grimes, that we Shaara have great respect for Terran spacemen. We are confident that you will carry out your mission successfully. We shall be pleased, on your return to our planet, to confer upon you the Order of the Golden Honeyflower.

"On your bicycle, spaceman!"

Grimes looked at the recumbent Queen dubiously. Where had she picked up *that* expression? But he had heard it said—and was inclined to agree—that the Shaara were more human than many of the humanoids throughout the Galaxy.

He bowed low—then, following the Princess, escorted by the soldiers, made his way out of the throne-room.

It is just three weeks, Terran Standard, from Droomoor to Brooum as the Serpent Class Courier flies. That, of course, is assuming that all systems are Go aboard the said Courier. All systems were not Go insofar as *Adder* was concerned. This was the result of an unfortunate combination of circumstances. The ship had been fitted with a new computer at Lindisfarne Base, a new Engineering Officer—all of whose previous experience had been as a junior in a Constellation Class cruiser—had been appointed to her, and she had not been allowed to stay in port long enough for any real maintenance to be carried out.

The trouble started one evening, ship's time, when Grimes was discussing matters with Spooky Deane, the psionic communications officer. The telepath was, as usual, getting outside a large, undiluted gin. His captain was sipping a glass of the same fluid, but with ice cubes and bitters as additives.

"Well, Spooky," said Grimes, "I don't think that we shall have any trouble with *this* passenger. She stays in her cocoons—the home-grown one and the plastic outer casing—safe and snug and

hard-frozen, and thawing her out will be up to her loyal subjects. By
that time we shall be well on our way . . ."

"She's alive, you know," said Deane.

"Of course she's alive."

"She's conscious, I mean. I'm getting more and more attuned to
her thoughts, her feelings. It's always been said that it's practically
impossible for there to be any real contact of minds between human
and Shaara telepaths, but when you're cooped up in the same ship
as a Shaara, a little ship at that . . ."

"Tell me more," ordered Grimes.

"It's . . . fascinating. You know, of course, that race memory
plays a big part in the Shaara culture. The princess, when she
emerges as an imago, will *know* just what her duties are, and what
the duties of those about her are. She *knows* that her two main
functions will be to rule and to breed. Workers exist only to serve
her, and every drone is a potential father to her people . . ."

"Mphm. And is she aware of us?"

"Dimly, Captain. She doesn't know, of course, who or what we
are. As far as she's concerned we're just some of her subjects, in
close attendance upon her . . ."

"Drones or workers?"

Spooky Deane laughed. "If she were more fully conscious, she'd
be rather confused on that point. Males are drones, and drones
don't work . . ."

Grimes was about to make some unkind remarks about his
officers when the lights flickered. When they flickered a second time
he was already on his feet. When they went out he was halfway
through the door of his day cabin, hurrying towards the control
room. The police lights came on, fed from the emergency batteries—
but the sudden cessation of the noise of pumps and fans, the cutting
off in mid-beat of the irregular throbbing of the inertial drive, was
frightening. The thin, high whine of the Mannschenn Drive Unit
deepened as the spinning, precessing gyroscopes slowed to a halt,
and as they did so there came the nauseating dizziness of temporal
disorientation.

Grimes kept going, although—as he put it, later—he didn't

know if it was Christmas Day or last Thursday. The ship was in Free Fall now, and he pulled himself rapidly along the guide rail, was practically swimming in air as he dived through the hatch into Control.

Von Tannenbaum had the watch. He was busy at the auxiliary machinery control panel. A fan restarted somewhere, but a warning buzzer began to sound. The navigator cursed. The fan motor slowed down and the buzzer ceased.

"What's happened, Pilot?" demanded Grimes.

"The Phoenix Jennie I *think*, Captain. Vitelli hasn't reported yet . . ."

Then the engineer's shrill, excited voice sounded from the intercom speaker. "Auxiliary engine room to Control! I have to report a leakage of deuterium!"

"What pressure is there in the tank?" Grimes asked.

"The gauges still show 20,000 units. But . . ."

"But what?" Grimes snapped.

"Captain, the tank is empty."

Grimes pulled himself to his chair, strapped himself in. He looked out through the viewports at the star-begemmed blackness, each point of light hard and sharp, no longer distorted by the temporal precession fields of the Drive, each distant sun lifetimes away with the ship in her present condition. Then he turned to face his officers—Beadle, looking no more (but no less) glum than usual, von Tannenbaum, whose normally ruddy face was now as pale as his hair, Slovotny, whose dark complexion now had a greenish cast, and Deane, ectoplasmic as always. They were joined by Vitelli, a very ordinary looking young man who was, at the moment, more than ordinarily frightened.

"Mr. Vitelli," Grimes asked him. "This leakage—is it into our atmosphere or outside the hull?"

"Outside, sir."

"Good. In that case . . ." Grimes made a major production of filling and lighting his battered pipe. "Now I can think. Mphm. Luckily I've not used any reaction mass this trip, so we have ample fuel for the emergency generator. Got your slipstick ready, Pilot?

Assuming that the tanks are full, do we have enough to run the inertial and interstellar drives from here to Brooum?"

"I'll have to use the computer, Captain."

"Then use it. Meanwhile, Sparks and Spooky, can either of you gentlemen tell me what ships are in the vicinity?"

"The Dog Star Line's *Basset*," Slovotny told him. "The cruiser *Draconis*" added Deane.

"Mphm." It would be humiliating for a Courier Service Captain to have to call for help, but *Draconis* would be the lesser of two evils. "Mphm. Get in touch with both vessels, Mr. Deane. I'm not sure that we can spare power for the Carlotti, Mr. Slovotny. Get in touch with both vessels, ask their positions and tell them ours. But don't tell them anything else."

"*Our* position, sir, is . . . ?"

Grimes swiveled his chair so that he could see the chart tank, rattled off the coordinates, adding, "Near enough, until we get an accurate fix . . ."

"I can take one now, Captain," von Tannenbaum told him.

"Thank you, Pilot. Finished your sums?"

"Yes." The navigator's beefy face was expressionless. "To begin with, we have enough chemical fuel to maintain all essential services for a period of seventy-three Standard days. *But* we do not have enough fuel to carry us to Brooum, even using Mannschenn Drive only. We could, however, make for ZX1797—Sol-type, with one Earth-type planet, habitable but currently uninhabited by intelligent life forms . . ."

Grimes considered the situation. If he were going to call for help he would be better off staying where he was, in reasonable comfort.

"Mr. Vitelli," he said, "you can start up the emergency generator. Mr. Deane, as soon as Mr. von Tannenbaum has a fix you can get a message out to *Basset* and *Draconis* . . . "

"But she's properly awake," Deane muttered. "She's torn open the silk cocoon, and the outer canister is opening . . ."

"What the hell are you talking about?" barked Grimes.

"The Princess. When the power went off the refrigeration unit stopped. She . . ." The telepath's face assumed an expression of rapt devotion. "We must go to her . . ."

"We must go to her . . ." echoed Vitelli.

"The emergency generator!" almost yelled Grimes. But he, too, could feel that command *inside* his brain, the imperious demand for attention, for . . . love. Here, at last, was something, somebody whom he could serve with all the devotion of which he was, of which he ever would be capable. And yet a last, tattered shred of sanity persisted.

He said gently, "We must start the emergency generator. *She* must not be cold or hungry."

Beadle agreed. "We must start the emergency generator. *For her.*"

They started the emergency generator and the ship came back to life—of a sort. She was a small bubble of light and warmth and life drifting down and through the black immensities.

The worst part of it all, Grimes said afterwards, was *knowing* what was happening but not having the willpower to do anything about it. And then he would add, "But it was educational. You can't deny that. I always used to wonder how the Establishment gets away with so much. Now I know. If you're a member of the Establishment you have that inborn . . . arrogance? No, not arrogance. That's not the right word. You have the calm certainty that everybody will do just what you want. With *our* Establishment it could be largely the result of training, of education. With the Shaara Establishment no education or training is necessary.

"Too, the Princess had it easy—almost as easy as she would have done had she broken out of her cocoon in the proper place at the proper time. Here she was in a little ship, manned by junior officers, people used to saluting and obeying officers with more gold braid on their sleeves. For her to impose her will was child's play. Literally child's play in this case. There was a communication problem, of course, but it wasn't a serious one. Even if she couldn't actually speak, telepathically, to the rest of us, there was Spooky Deane. With him she could dot the i's and cross the t's.

"And she did."

And she did.

Adder's officers gathered in the cargo compartment that was now the throne-room. A table had been set up, covered with a cloth that was, in actuality, a new Federation ensign from the ship's flag locker. To it the Princess—the Queen, rather—clung with her four posterior legs. She was a beautiful creature, slim, all the colors of her body undimmed by age. She was a glittering, bejeweled piece of abstract statuary, but she was alive, very much alive. With her great, faceted eyes she regarded the men who hovered about her. She was demanding something. Grimes knew that, as all of them did. She was demanding something—quietly at first, then more and more insistently.

But what?

Veneration? Worship?

"She hungers," stated Deane.

She hungers . . . thought Grimes. His memory was still functioning, and he tried to recall what he knew of the Shaara.

He said, "Tell her that her needs will be satisfied."

Reluctantly yet willingly he left the cargo compartment, making his way to the galley. It did not take him long to find what he wanted, a squeeze bottle of syrup. He hurried back with it.

It did not occur to him to hand the container to the Queen. With his feet in contact with the deck he was able to stand before her, holding the bottle in his two hands, squeezing out the viscous fluid, drop by drop, into the waiting mouth. Normally he would have found that complexity of moving parts rather frightening, repulsive even—but now they seemed to possess an essential rightness that was altogether lacking from the clumsy masticatory apparatus of a human being. Slowly, carefully he squeezed, until a voice said in his mind, *Enough. Enough.*

"She would rest now," said Deane.

"She shall rest," stated Grimes.

He led the way from the cargo compartment to the little wardroom.

∽∾∽∾∽

In a bigger ship, with a larger crew, with a senior officer in command who, by virtue of his rank, was a member of the Establishment himself, the spell might soon have been broken. But this was only a little vessel, and of her personnel only Grimes was potentially a rebel. The time would come when this potentiality would be realized—just as, later, the time of compromise would come—but it was not yet. He had been trained to obedience—and now there was aboard *Adder* somebody whom he obeyed without question, just as he would have obeyed an Admiral.

In the wardroom the officers disposed of a meal of sorts, and when it was over Grimes, from force of habit, pulled his pipe from his pocket, began to fill it.

Deane admonished him, saying, "*She* wouldn't like it. It taints the air."

"Of course," agreed Grimes, putting his pipe away.

Then they sat there, in silence, but uneasily, guiltily. They should have been working. There was so much to be done about the Hive. Von Tannenbaum at last unbuckled himself from his chair and, finding a soft rag, began, unnecessarily, to polish a bulkhead. Vitelli muttered something about cleaning up the engine room and drifted away, and Slovotny, saying that he would need help, followed him. Beadle took the dirty plates into the pantry—normally he was one of those who washes the dishes *before a* meal.

"She is hungry," announced Deane.

Grimes went to the galley for another bottle of syrup.

So it went on, for day after day, with the Queen gaining strength and, if it were possible, even greater authority over her subjects. And she was learning. Deane's mind was open to her, as were the minds of the others, but to a lesser degree. But it was only through Deane that she could speak.

"She knows," said the telepath, "that supplies in the Hive are limited, that sooner or later, sooner rather than later, we shall be without heat, without air or food. She knows that there is a planet within reach. She orders us to proceed there, so that a greater Hive may be established on its surface."

"Then let us proceed," agreed Grimes.

He knew, as they all knew, that a general distress call would bring help—but somehow was incapable of ordering it made. He knew that the establishment of a Hive, a colony on a planet of ZX1797 would be utterly impossible—but that was what *she* wanted.

So Adder awoke from her sleeping state, vibrating to the irregular rhythm of the inertial drive and, had there been an outside observer, flickered into invisibility as the gyroscopes of the Mannschenn Drive unit precessed and tumbled, falling down and through the warped continuum, pulling the structure of the ship with them.

Ahead was ZX1797, a writhing, multi-hued spiral, expanding with every passing hour.

It was von Tannenbaum who now held effective command of the ship—Grimes had become the Queen's personal attendant, although it was still Deane who made her detailed wishes known. It was Grimes who fed her, who cleansed her, who sat with her hour after hour in wordless communion. A part of him rebelled, a part of him screamed soundlessly and envisaged hard fists smashing those great, faceted eyes, heavy boots crashing through fragile chitin. A part of him rebelled—but was powerless—and *she* knew it. She was female and he was male and the tensions were inevitable, and enjoyable to one if not to the other.

And then Deane said to him, "She is tiring of her tasteless food."

She would be, thought Grimes dully. And then there was the urge to placate, to please. Although he had never made a deep study of the arthropedal race he knew, as did all spacemen, which Terran luxuries were appreciated by the Shaara. He went up to his quarters, found what he was looking for. He decanted the fluid from its own glass container into a squeeze bottle. Had it been intended for human consumption this would not have been necessary, now that the ship was accelerating, but Shaara queens do not, ever, feed themselves.

He went back to the throne-room. Deane and the huge arthroped watched him. The Queen's eyes were even brighter than usual. She lifted her forelimbs as though to take the bottle from

Grimes, then let them fall to her side. Her gauzy wings were quivering in anticipation.

Grimes approached her slowly. He knelt before her, holding the bottle before him. He raised it carefully, the nippled end towards the working mandibles. He squeezed, and a thin, amber stream shot out. Its odor was rich and heavy in the almost still air of the compartment.

More! the word formed itself in his mind. *More!*

He went on squeezing.

But . . . You are not a worker . . . You are a drone . . .

And that word "drone" denoted masculinity, not idleness.

You are a drone . . . You shall be the first father of the new Hive . . .

"Candy is dandy, but liquor is quicker . . ." muttered Deane, struggling to maintain a straight face.

Grimes glared at the telepath, What was so funny about this? He was feeling, strongly, the stirrings of desire. *She* was female, wasn't she? She was female, and she was beautiful, and he was male. She was female—and in his mind's eye those flimsy wings were transparent draperies enhancing, not concealing, the symmetry of the form of a lovely woman—slim, with high, firm breasts, with long, slender legs. She wanted him to be her mate, her consort.

She wanted him.

She . . .

Suddenly the vision flickered out.

This was no woman spread in alluring, naked abandon.

This was no more than a repulsive insect sprawled in drunken untidiness, desecrating the flag that had been spread over the table that served it for a bed. The wings were crumpled, a dull film was over the faceted eyes. A yellowish ichor oozed from among the still-working mandibles.

Grimes retched violently. To think that he had almost . . .

"Captain!" Deane's voice was urgent. "She's out like a light! She's drunk as a fiddler's bitch!"

"And we must keep her that way!" snapped Grimes. He was himself again. He strode to the nearest bulkhead pick-up. "Attention, all hands! This is the Captain speaking. Shut down inertial and interstellar drive units. Energize Carlotti transceiver. Contact any and all shipping in the vicinity, and request aid as soon as possible. Say that we are drifting, with main engines inoperable due to fuel shortage." He turned to Deane. "I'm leaving you in charge, Spooky. If she shows signs of breaking surface, you know what to do." He looked sternly at the telepath. "I suppose I can trust you . . ."

"You can," the psionic communications officer assured him. "You can. Indeed you can, captain. I wasn't looking forward at all, at all, to ending my days as a worker in some *peculiar* Terran-Shaara Hive!" He stared at Grimes thoughtfully. "I wonder if the union *would* have been fertile?"

"That will do, Mr. Deane," growled Grimes.

"Fantastic," breathed Commodore Damien. "Fantastic. Almost, Mr. Grimes, I feel a certain envy. The things you get up to . . ."

The aroma of good Scotch whisky hung heavily in the air of the Commodore's office. Damien, although not an abstainer, never touched the stuff. Grimes's tastes were catholic—but on an occasion such as this he preferred to be stone cold sober.

"It is more than fantastic," snarled the Shaara Queen-Emissary, the special envoy of the Empress herself. Had she not been using a voice-box her words would have been slurred. "It is . . . disgusting. Reprehensible. This officer *forced* liquor down the throat of a member of *our* Royal family. He . . ."

"He twisted her arm?" suggested the Commodore.

"I do not understand. But she is now Queen-Mother of Brooum. A drunken, even alcoholic Queen-Mother."

"I saved my ship and my people," stated Grimes woodenly.

Damien grinned unpleasantly. "Isn't this where we came in, Lieutenant? But no matter. There are affairs of far more pressing urgency. Not only do I have to cope with a direct complaint from the personal representative of Her Imperial Majesty . . ."

Even though she was wearing a voice-box, the Queen-Emissary contrived to hiccough. And all this, Grimes knew, was going down on tape. It was unlikely that he would ever wear the ribbon of the

Order of the Golden Honeyflower, but it was equally unlikely that he would be butchered to make a Shaara holiday.

"He *weaned* her on Scotch . . ." persisted the Queen-Emissary.

"Aren't you, perhaps, a little jealous?" suggested Damien. He switched his attention back to Grimes. "Meanwhile, Lieutenant, I am being literally bombarded with Carlottigrams from Her not-so-Imperial Majesty on Brooum demanding that I dispatch to her, as soon as possible if not before, the only drone, in the Galaxy with whom she would dream of mating . . ."

"No!" protested Grimes. "*NO!*"

"Yes, mister. Yes. For two pins I'd accede to her demands." He sighed regretfully. "But I suppose that one must draw some sort of a line somewhere . . ." He sighed again—then, "Get out, you *drone!*" he almost shouted. It was a pity that he had to spoil the effect by laughing.

"We are not amused," said the Shaara Queen.

❧ The Wandering Buoy ❧

IT SHOULDN'T have been there.

Nothing at all should have been there, save for the sparse drift of hydrogen atoms that did nothing at all to mitigate the hard vacuum of interstellar space, and save for the Courier *Adder*, proceeding on her lawful occasions.

It shouldn't have been there, but it was, and Grimes and his officers were pleased rather than otherwise that something had happened to break the monotony of the long voyage.

"A definite contact, Captain," said von Tannenbaum, peering into the spherical screen of the mass proximity indicator.

"Mphm . . ." grunted Grimes. Then, to the Electronic Communications Officer. "You're quite sure that there's no traffic around, Sparks?"

"Quite sure, Captain," replied Slovotny. "Nothing within a thousand light years."

"Then get Spooky on the intercom, and ask him if *he's* been in touch with anybody—or anything."

"Very good, Captain," said Slovotny rather sulkily. There was always rivalry, sometimes far from friendly, between electronic and psionic communications officers.

Grimes looked over the Navigator's shoulder into the velvety blackness of the screen, at the tiny, blue-green spark that lay a little to one side of the glowing filament that was the ship's extrapolated trajectory. Von Tannenbaum had set up the range and bearing markers, was quietly reading aloud the figures. He said, "At our present velocity we shall be up to it in just over three hours."

"Spooky says that there's no psionic transmission at all from it, whatever it is," reported Slovotny.

"So if it's a ship, it's probably a derelict," murmured Grimes.

"Salvage . . ." muttered Beadle, looking almost happy.

"You've a low, commercial mind, Number One," Grimes told him. *As I have myself,* he thought. The captain's share of a fat salvage award would make a very nice addition to his far from generous pay. "Oh, well, since you've raised the point you can check towing gear, spacesuits and all the rest of it. And you, Sparks, can raise Lindisfarne Base on the Carlotti. I'll have the preliminary report ready in a couple of seconds . . ." He added, speaking as much to himself as to the others, "I suppose I'd better ask permission to deviate, although the Galaxy won't grind to a halt if a dozen bags of mail are delayed in transit . . ." He took the message pad that Slovotny handed him and wrote swiftly, *To Officer Commanding Couriers. Sighted unidentified object coordinates A1763.5 x ZU97.75 x J222.0 approx. Request authority investigate. Grimes.*

By the time that the reply came Grimes was on the point of shutting down his Mannschenn Drive and initiating the maneuvers that would match trajectory and speed with the drifting object.

It read, *Authority granted, but please try to keep your nose clean for a change. Damien.*

"Well, Captain, we can *try,*" said Beadle, not too hopefully.

With the Mannschenn Drive shut down radar, which gave far more accurate readings than the mass proximity indicator, was operable. Von Tannenbaum was able to determine the elements of the object's trajectory relative to that of the ship, and after this had been done the task of closing it was easy.

At first it was no more than a brightening blip in the screen and then, at last, it could be seen visually as *Adder's* probing searchlight caught it and held it. To begin with it was no more than just another star among the stars, but as the ship gained on it an appreciable disc was visible through the binoculars, and then with the naked eye.

Grimes studied it carefully through his powerful glasses. It was spherical, and appeared to be metallic. There were no projections on it anywhere, although there were markings that looked like painted letters or numerals. It was rotating slowly.

"It could be a mine . . ." said Beadle, who was standing with Grimes at the viewport.

"It could be . . ." agreed Grimes. "And it could be fitted with some sort of proximity fuse . . ." He turned to address von Tannenbaum. "You'd better maintain our present distance off, Pilot, until we know better what it is." He stared out through the port again. Space mines are a defensive rather than offensive weapon, and *Adder* carried six of the things in her own magazine. They are a dreadfully effective weapon when the conditions for their use are ideal—which they rarely are. Dropped from a vessel being pursued by an enemy they are an excellent deterrent—provided that the pursuer is not proceeding under interstellar drive. Unless there is temporal synchronization there can be no physical contact.

Out here, thought Grimes, in a region of space where some sort of interstellar drive *must* be used, a mine just didn't make sense. On the other hand, it never hurt to be careful. He recalled the words of one of the Instructors at the Academy. "There are old spacemen, and there are bold spacemen, but there aren't any old, bold spacemen."

"A sounding rocket . . ." he said.

"All ready, Captain," replied Beadle.

"Thank you, Number One. After you launch it, maintain full control throughout its flight. Bring it to the buoy or the mine or whatever it is *very* gently—I don't want you punching holes in it. Circle the target a few times, if you can manage it, and then make careful contact." He paused. "Meanwhile, restart the Mannschenn Drive, but run it in neutral gear. If there is a big bang we might be able to start precessing before the shrapnel hits us." He paused again, then, "Have any of you gentlemen any bright ideas?"

"It might be an idea," contributed Slovotny, "to clear away the laser cannon. Just in case."

"Do so, Sparks. And you, Number One, don't launch your rocket until I give the word."

"Cannon trained on the target," announced Slovotny after only a few seconds.

"Good. All right, Number One. Now you can practice rocket-ship handling."

Beadle returned to the viewport, with binoculars strapped to his eyes and a portable control box in his hands. He pressed a button, and almost at once the sounding rocket swam into the field of view, a sleek, fishlike shape with a pale glimmer of fire at its tail, a ring of bright red lights mounted around its midsection to keep it visible at all times to the aimer. Slowly it drew away from the ship, heading towards the enigmatic ball that hung in the blaze of the searchlight. It veered to one side to pass the target at a respectable distance, circled it, went into orbit about it, a miniscule satellite about a tiny primary.

Grimes started to get impatient. He had learned that one of the hardest parts of a captain's job is to refrain from interfering—even so . . . "Number One," he said at last, "don't you think you could edge the rocket in a little closer?"

"I'm trying, sir," replied Beadle. "But the bloody thing won't answer the controls."

"Do you mind if I have a go?" asked Grimes.

"Of course not, Captain." Implied but not spoken was, "And you're bloody welcome!"

Grimes strapped a set of binoculars to his head, then took the control box. First of all he brought the sounding rocket back towards the ship, then put it in a tight turn to get the feel of it. Before long he was satisfied that he had it; it was as though a tiny extension of himself was sitting in a control room in the miniature spaceship. It wasn't so very different from a rocket-handling simulator.

He straightened out the trajectory of the sounding rocket, sent it back towards the mysterious globe and then, as Beadle had done, put it in orbit. So far, so good. He cut the drive and the thing, of course, continued circling the metallic sphere. A brief blast from a braking jet—that should do the trick. With its velocity drastically reduced the missile should fall gently towards its target. But it did not—as von Tannenbaum, manning the radar, reported.

There was something wrong here, thought Grimes. The thing

had considerable mass, otherwise it would never have shown so strongly in the screen of the MPI. The greater the mass, the greater the gravitational field. But, he told himself, there are more ways than one of skinning a cat. He actuated the steering jets, tried to nudge the rocket in towards its objective. "How am I doing, Pilot?" he asked.

"What are you trying to do, Captain?" countered von Tannenbaum. "The elements of the orbit are unchanged."

"Mphm." Perhaps more than a gentle nudge was required. Grimes gave more than a gentle nudge—and with no result whatsoever. He did not need to look at Beadle to know that the First Lieutenant was wearing his best I-told-you-so expression.

So . . .

So the situation called for brute strength and ignorance, a combination that usually gets results.

Grimes pulled the rocket away from the sphere, almost back to the ship. He turned it—and then, at full acceleration, sent it driving straight for the target. He hoped that he would be able to apply the braking jets before it came into damaging contact—but the main thing was to make contact, of any kind.

He need not have worried.

With its driving jet flaring ineffectually the rocket was streaking back towards *Adder,* tail first. The control box was useless. "Slovotny!" barked Grimes. "Fire!"

There was a blinding flare, and then only a cloud of incandescent but harmless gases, still drifting towards the ship.

"And what do we do now, Captain?" asked Beadle. "Might I suggest that we make a full report to Base and resume our voyage?"

"You might, Number One. There's no law against it. But we continue our investigations."

Grimes was in a stubborn mood. He was glad that *Adder* was not engaged upon a mission of real urgency. These bags of Fleet Mail were not important. Revised Regulations, Promotion Lists, Appointments . . . If they never reached their destination it would not matter. But a drifting menace to navigation was important.

Perhaps, he thought, it would be named after him. Grimes's Folly . . . He grinned at the thought. There were better ways of achieving immortality.

But what to do?

Adder hung there, and the *thing* hung there, rates and directions of drift nicely synchronized, and in one thousand seven hundred and fifty-three Standard years they would fall into or around Algol, assuming that Grimes was willing to wait that long—which, of course, he was not. He looked at the faces of his officers, who were strapped into their chairs around the wardroom table. They looked back at him. Von Tannenbaum—the Blond Beast—grinned cheerfully. He remarked, "It's a tough nut to crack, Captain—but I'd just hate to shove off without cracking it." Slovotny, darkly serious, said, "I concur. And I'd like to find out how that repulsor field works." Vitelli, not yet quite a member of the family, said nothing. Deane complained, "If the thing had a mind that I could read it'd all be so much easier . . ."

"Perhaps it's allergic to metal . . ." suggested von Tannenbaum. "We could try to bring the ship in towards it, to see what happens . . ."

"Not bloody likely, Pilot," growled Grimes. "Not yet, anyhow. Mphm . . . you might have something. It shouldn't be too hard to cook up, with our resources, a sounding rocket of all-plastic construction . . ."

"There has to be metal in the guidance system . . ." objected Slovotny.

"There won't be any guidance systems, Sparks. It will be a solid fuel affair, and we just aim it and fire it, and see what happens . . ."

"*Solid* fuel?" demurred Beadle. "Even if we had the formula we'd never be able to cook up a batch of cordite or anything similar . . ."

"There'd be no need to, Number One. We should be able to get enough from the cartridges for our projectile small arms. But I don't intend to do that."

"Then what do you intend, Captain?"

"We have graphite—and that's carbon. We've all sorts of fancy chemicals in our stores, especially those required for the maintenance of our hydroponics system. Charcoal, sulphur, saltpeter . . . Or we could use potassium chlorate instead of that . . ."

"It *could* work," admitted the First Lieutenant dubiously.

"Of course it will work," Grimes assured him.

It did work—although mixing gunpowder, especially in Free Fall conditions, wasn't as easy as Grimes had assumed that it would be. To begin with, graphite proved to be quite unsuitable, and the first small sample batch of powder burned slowly, with a vile sulphurous stench that lingered in spite of all the efforts of the air conditioner. But there were carbon water filters, and one of these was broken up and then pulverized in the galley food mixer—and when Grimes realized that the bulkheads of this compartment were rapidly acquiring a fine coating of soot he ordered that the inertial drive be restarted. With acceleration playing the part of gravity things were a little better.

Charcoal 13 percent, saltpeter 75 percent, sulphur 12 percent . . . That, thought Grimes, trying hard to remember the History of Gunnery lectures, was about right. They mixed a small amount dry, stirring it carefully with a wooden ladle. It was better than the first attempt, using graphite, had been—but not much. And it smelled as bad. Grimes concluded that there was insufficient space between the grains to allow the rapid passage of the flame.

"Spooky," he said in desperation. "Can you read my mind?"

"It's against Regulations," the telepath told him primly.

"Damn the Regulations. I sat through all those Gunnery Course lectures, and I'm sure that old Commander Dalquist went into the history of gunnery *very* thoroughly, but I never thought that the knowledge of how to make black powder would be of any use at all to a modern spaceman. But it's all there in my memory—if I could only drag it out!"

"Relax, Captain." Spooky Deane told him in a soothing voice. "Relax. Let your mind become a blank. You're tired, Captain. You're very tired. Don't fight it. Yes, sit down. Let every muscle go loose . . ."

Grimes lay back in the chair. Yes, he *was* tired . . . but he did not like the sensation of cold, clammy fingers probing about inside his brain. But he trusted Deane. He told himself very firmly that he *trusted* Deane . . .

"Let yourself go back in Time, Captain, to when you were a midshipman at the Academy . . . You're sitting there, on a hard bench, with the other midshipmen around you . . . And there, on his platform before the class, is old Commander Dalquist . . . I can see him, with his white hair and his white beard, and his faded blue eyes looking enormous behind the spectacles . . . And I can see all those lovely little models on the table before him . . . The culverin, the falcon, the carronade . . . He is droning on, and you are thinking, *How can he make anything so interesting so boring?* You are wondering, *What's on for dinner tonight?* You are hoping that it won't be boiled mutton *again* . . . Some of the other cadets are laughing. You half heard what the Commander was saying. It was that the early cannoneers, who mixed their own powder, maintained that the only possible fluid was a wine drinker's urine, their employer to supply the wine . . . And if the battle went badly, because of misfires the gunners could always say that it was due to the poor quality of the booze . . . But you are wondering now if you stand any chance with that pretty little Nurse . . . You've heard that she'll play. You don't know what it's like with a woman, but you want to find out . . ."

Grimes felt his prominent ears turning hot and scarlet. He snapped into full wakefulness. He said firmly, "That will do, Spooky. You've jogged my memory sufficiently. And if any of you gentlemen think I'm going to order a free wine issue, you're mistaken. We'll use plain water, just enough to make a sort of mud, thoroughly mixed, and then we'll dry it out. No, we'll not use heat, not inside the ship. Too risky. But the vacuum chamber should do the job quite well . . ."

"And then?" asked Beadle, becoming interested in spite of himself.

"Then we crush it into grains."

"Won't that be risky?"

"Yes. But we'll have a plastic bowl fitted to the food mixer, and the Chief can make some strong, plastic paddles. As long as we avoid the use of metal we should be safe enough."

They made a small batch of powder by the method that Grimes had outlined. Slovotny fitted a remote control switch to the food mixer in the galley, and they all retired from that compartment while the cake was being crushed and stirred. The bowlful of black, granular matter looked harmless enough—but a small portion of it transferred to a saucer—and taken well away from the larger amount remaining in the bowl—burned with a satisfying *whoof!* when ignited.

"We're in business!" gloated Grimes. "*Adder* Pyrotechnics, Unlimited!"

They were in business, and while Grimes, Beadle and von Tannenbaum manufactured a large supply of gunpowder Slovotny and Vitelli set about converting a half-dozen large plastic bottles into rocket casings. They were made of thermoplastic, so it was easy enough to shape them as required, with throat and nozzle. To ensure that they would retain the shape after firing they were bound about with heavy insulating tape. After this was finished, there was a rocket launcher to make—a tube of the correct diameter, with a blast shield and with the essential parts of a projectile pistol as the firing mechanism.

Then all hands joined forces in filling the rockets. Tubes of stiff paper, soaked in a saturated solution of saltpeter and allowed to dry, were inserted into the casing and centered as accurately as possible. The powder was poured around them, and well tamped home.

While this was being done Spooky Deane—who, until now, had played no part in the proceedings—made a suggestion. "Forgive me for butting in, Captain, but I remember—with *your* memory—the models and pictures that the Instructor showed the class. Those old chemical rockets had sticks or vanes to make them fly straight . . ."

For a moment this had Grimes worried. Then he laughed. "Those rockets, Spooky, were used in the atmosphere. Sticks or vanes would be utterly useless in a vacuum." But he couldn't help wondering if vanes set actually in the exhaust would help to keep the missiles on a straight trajectory. But unless he used metal there was no suitable material aboard the ship—and metal was out.

Grimes went outside, with von Tannenbaum, to do the actual firing. They stood there on the curved shell plating, held in place by the magnetic soles of their boots. Each of them, too, was secured by lifelines. Neither needed to be told that to every action there is an equal and opposite reaction. The backblast of the home-made rockets would be liable to sweep them from their footing.

Grimes held the clumsy bazooka while the Navigator loaded it, then he raised it slowly. A cartwheel sight had been etched into the transparent shield. Even though the weapon had no weight in Free Fall it still had inertia, and it was clumsy. By the time that he had the target, gleaming brightly in the beam of *Adder's* searchlight, in the center of the cartwheel, he was sweating copiously. He said into his helmet microphone, "Captain to *Adder*. I am about to open fire."

"*Adder* to Captain. Acknowledged," came Beadle's voice in reply.

Grimes's right thumb found the firing stud of the pistol. He recoiled involuntarily from the wash of the orange flame that swept over the blast shield—and then he was torn from his hold on the hull plating, slammed back to the full extent of the lifeline. He lost his grip on the rocket launcher, but it was secured to his body by stout, fireproof cords. Somehow he managed to keep his attention on the fiery flight of the rocket. It missed the target, but by a very little. To judge by the straight wake of it, it had not been deflected by any sort of repulsor field.

"It throws high . . ." commented Grimes.

He pulled himself back along the line to exactly where he had been standing before. Von Tannenbaum inserted another missile into the tube. This time, when he aimed, Grimes intended to bring the target to just above the center of the cartwheel. But there was more delay; the blast shield was befogged by smoke. Luckily this eventuality had been foreseen, and von Tannenbaum cleaned it off with a soft rag.

Grimes aimed, and fired.

Again the blast caught him—but this time he hung in an untidy tangle facing the wrong way, looking at nothingness. He heard somebody inside the ship say, "It's blown up!"

What had blown up?

Hastily Grimes got himself turned around. The mysterious globe was still there, but between it and *Adder* was an expanding cloud of smoke, a scatter of fragments, luminous in the searchlight's glare. So perhaps the nonmetallic missiles weren't going to work after all—or perhaps this missile would have blown up by itself, anyhow.

The third rocket was loaded into the bazooka. For the third time Grimes fired—and actually managed to stay on his feet. Straight and true streaked the missile. It hit, and exploded in an orange flare, a cloud of white smoke which slowly dissipated.

"Is there any damage?" asked Grimes at last. He could see none with his unaided vision, but those on the control room had powerful binoculars at hand.

"No," replied Beadle at last. "It doesn't seem to be scratched."

"Then stand by to let the Pilot and myself back into the ship. We have to decide what we do next."

What they did next was a matter of tailoring rather than engineering. *Adder* carried a couple of what were called "skin-divers' suits." These were, essentially, elasticized leotards, skin-tight but porous, maintaining the necessary pressure on the body without the need for cumbersome armor. They were ideal for working in or outside the ship, allowing absolute freedom of movement—but very few spacemen liked them. A man feels that he should be armored, well armored, against an absolutely hostile environment. Too, the conventional spacesuit has built-in facilities for the excretion of body wastes, has its little tank of water and its drinking tube, has its container of food and stimulant pellets. (Grimes, of course, always maintained that the ideal suit should make provision for the pipe smoker . . .) A conventional spacesuit is, in fact, a spaceship in miniature.

Now these two suits had to be modified. The radio transceivers, with their metallic parts, were removed from the helmets. Plastic air bottles were substituted for the original metal ones. Jointures and seals between helmet and shoulder pieces were removed, and replaced by plastic.

While this was going on Beadle asked, "Who are you sending, Captain?"

"I'm *sending* nobody, Number One. I shall be going myself, and if any one of you gentlemen cares to volunteer . . . No, not you. You're second in command. You must stay with the ship."

Surprisingly it was Deane who stepped forward. "I'll come with you, Captain."

"*You*, Spooky?" asked Grimes, not unkindly.

The telepath flushed. "I . . . I feel that I should. That . . . That *thing* out there is awakening. It was as though that rocket was a knock on the door . . ."

"Why didn't you tell us?"

"I . . . I wasn't sure. But the feeling's getting stronger. There's something there. Some sort of intelligence."

"Can't you get in touch with it?"

"I've been trying. But it's too vague, too weak. And I've the feeling that there has to be actual contact. Physical contact, I mean."

"Mphm."

"In any case, Captain, you *need* me with you."

"Why, Spooky?"

Deane jerked his head towards the watch on Grimes's wrist. "We'll not be allowed to take any metal with us. How shall we know when we've been away long enough, that we have to get back before our air runs out?"

"How shall we know if you're along?"

"Easy. Somebody will have to sit with Fido, and clock watch all the time, really concentrating on it. At that short range Fido will pick up the thoughts even of a non-telepath quite clearly. I shall remain *en rapport* with Fido, of course."

"Mphm," grunted Grimes. Yes, he admitted to himself, the idea had its merits. He wondered whom he should tell off for the clock-watching detail. All spacemen except psionic radio officers hate the organic amplifiers, the so-called "dogs' brains in aspic," the obscenely naked masses of canine thinking apparatus floating in their spherical containers of circulating nutrient fluid.

Slovotny liked dogs. He'd be best for the job.

Slovotny was far from enthusiastic, but was told firmly that communications are communications, no matter how performed.

The Inertial Drive was restarted to make it easier for Grimes and Deane to get into their suits. Each, stripped to brief, supporting underwear, lay supine on his spread-out garment. Carefully they wriggled their hands into the tight-fitting gloves—the gloves that became tighter still once the fabric was in contact with the skin. They worked their feet into the bootees, aided by Beadle and von Tannenbaum, acting as dressers. Then, slowly and carefully, the First Lieutenant and the Navigator drew the fabric up and over arms and legs and bodies, smoothing it, pressing out the least wrinkle, trying to maintain an even, all-over pressure. To complete the job the seams were welded. Grimes wondered, as he had wondered before, what would happen if that fantastic adhesive came unstuck when the wearer of the suit was cavorting around in hard vacuum. It hadn't happened yet—as far as he knew—but there is always a first time.

"She'll do," said Beadle at last.

"She'd better do," said Grimes. He added, "If you're after promotion, Number One, there are less suspect ways of going about it."

Beadle looked hurt.

Grimes got to his feet, scowling. If one is engaged upon what might be a perilous enterprise armor is so much more appropriate than long underwear. He said, "All right. Shut down inertial drive as soon as we've got our helmets on. Then we'll be on our way."

They were on their way.

Each man carried, slung to his belt, a supply of little rockets—Roman candles, rather—insulated cardboard cylinders with friction fuses. They had flares, too, the chemical composition of such making them combustible even in a vacuum.

The Roman candles functioned quite efficiently, driving them across the gap between ship and sphere. Grimes handled himself well, Deane not so well. It was awkward having no suit radio; it was impossible to give the telepath any instructions. At the finish Grimes came in to a perfect landing, using a retro blast at the exact split second. Deane came in hard and clumsily. There was no air to transmit the *clang*, but Grimes felt the vibration all along and through his body.

He touched helmets. "Are you all right, Spooky?"

"Just . . .winded, Captain."

Grimes leading, the two men crawled over the surface of the sphere, the adhesive pads on gloves, knees, elbows and feet functioning quite well—rather too well, in fact. But it was essential that they maintain contact with the smooth metal. Close inspection confirmed distant observation. The 100-foot-diameter globe was utterly devoid of protuberances. The markings—they were no letters or numerals known to the Earthmen—could have been painted on, but Grimes decided that they were probably something along the lines of an integrated circuit. He stopped crawling, carefully made contact with his helmet and the seamless, rivetless plating. He listened. Yes, there was the faintest humming noise. Machinery?

He beckoned Deane to him, touched helmets. He said, "There's something working inside this thing, Spooky."

"I know, Captain. And there's something alive in there. A machine intelligence, I think. It's aware of us."

"How much time have we?"

Deane was silent for a few seconds, reaching out with his mind to his psionic amplifier aboard *Adder*. "Two hours and forty-five minutes."

"Good. If we could only find a way to get into this oversized beach ball . . ."

Deane jerked his head away from Grimes's. He was pointing with a rigid right arm. Grimes turned and looked. Coming into view in the glare of the searchlight, as the ball rotated, was a round hole, an aperture that expanded as they watched it. Then they were in shadow, but they crawled towards the opening. When they were in the light again they were almost on top of it. They touched helmets again. "Will you come into my parlor . . . ?" whispered Grimes.

"I . . . I feel that it's safe . . ." Deane told him.

"Good. Then we'll carry on. Is that an airlock, I wonder? There's only one way to find out . . ."

It was not an airlock. It was a doorway into cavernous blackness, in which loomed great, vague shapes, dimly visible in the reflected beam of *Adder's* searchlight—then invisible as this hemisphere of the little, artificial world was swept into night. Grimes was falling; his gloves could get no grip on the smooth, slippery rim of the hole. He was falling, and cried out in alarm as something brushed against him. But it was only Deane. The telepath clutched him in an embrace that, had Deane been of the opposite sex, might have been enjoyable.

"Keep your paws off me, Spooky!" ordered Grimes irritably. Yet he, too, was afraid of the dark, was suffering the primordial fear. The door through which they had entered must be closed now, otherwise they would be getting some illumination from *Adder's* searchlight. The dense blackness was stifling. Grimes fumbled at his belt, trying to find a flare by touch. The use of one of the little rockets in this confined space could be disastrous. But there had to be light. Grimes was not a religious man, otherwise he would have prayed for it.

Then, suddenly, there was light.

It was a soft, diffused illumination, emanating from no discernible source. It did not, at first, show much. The inner surface of the sphere was smooth, glassy, translucent rather than transparent. Behind it hulked the vague shapes that they had glimpsed before their entry. Some were moving slowly, some were stationary. None of them was like any machine or living being that either of the two men had ever seen.

Helmets touched.

"It's aware of us. It knows that we need light . . ." whispered Deane.

"What is It?"

"I . . . I dare not ask. It is too . . . big?"

And Grimes, although no telepath, was feeling it too, awe rather than fear, although he admitted to himself that he was dreadfully afraid. It was like his first space walk, the first time that he had been out from the frail bubble of light and warmth, one little man in the vastness of the emptiness between the worlds. He tried to take his mind off it by staring at the strange machinery—if it was machinery—beyond that glassy inner shell, tried to make out what these devices were, what they were doing. He focused his attention on what seemed to be a spinning wheel of rainbow luminescence. It was a mistake.

He felt himself being drawn into that radiant eddy—not physically, but psychically. He tried to resist. It was useless.

Then the pictures came—vivid, simple.

There was a naked, manlike being hunkered down in a sandy hollow among rocks. Manlike? It was Grimes himself. A flattish slab of wood was held firmly between his horny heels, projecting out and forward, away from him. In his two hands he gripped a stick, was sawing away with it, to and fro on the surface of the slab, in which the pointed end of it had already worn a groove. (Grimes *could feel* that stick in his hands, could feel the vibration as he worked it backwards and forwards.) There was a wisp of blue smoke from the groove, almost invisible at first, but becoming denser. There was a tiny red spark that brightened, expanded. Hastily Grimes let go of the fire stick, grabbed a handful of dried leaves and twigs, dropped them on top of the smolder. Carefully he brought his head down, began to blow gently, fanning the beginnings of the fire with his breath. There was flame now—feeble, hesitant. There was flame, and a faintly heard crackle as the kindling caught. There was flame—and Grimes had to pull his head back hastily to avoid being scorched.

The picture changed.

It was night now—and Grimes and his family were squatting around the cheerful blaze. One part of his mind that had not succumbed to the hypnosis wondered who that woman was. He decided wryly that she—big-bellied, flabby-breasted—was not his cup of tea at all. But he *knew* that she was his mate, just as he *knew* that those almost simian brats were his children.

It was night, and from the darkness around the camp came the roars and snarls of the nocturnal predators. But they were afraid of fire. He, Grimes, had made fire. Therefore those beasts of prey should be afraid of him. He toyed with the glimmerings of an idea. He picked up a well-gnawed femur—that day he had been lucky enough to find a not-too-rotten carcass that had been abandoned by the original killer and not yet discovered by the other scavengers— and hefted it experimentally in his hand. It seemed to belong there. From curiosity rather than viciousness he brought it swinging around, so that the end of it struck the skull of the woman with a sharp *crack*. She squealed piteously. Grimes had no language with which to think, but he knew that a harder blow could have killed her. Dimly he realized that a hard blow could kill a tiger . . .

He . . .

He was outside the sphere, and Deane was with him. Coming towards him was a construction of blazing lights. He was afraid— and then he snapped back into the here-and-now. He was John Grimes, Lieutenant, Federation Survey Service, Captain of the courier *Adder*. That was his ship. His home. He must return to his home, followed by this Agent of the Old Ones, so that observation and assessment could be made, and plans for the further advancement of the race.

The ship was no longer approaching.

Grimes pulled a Roman candle from his belt, motioned to Deane to do likewise. He lit it, jetted swiftly towards *Adder*. He knew, without looking around, that the sphere was following.

Although blinded by the searchlight he managed to bring himself to the main airlock without mishap, followed by Deane. The two men pulled themselves into the little compartment. The outer door shut. Atmospheric pressure built up. Grimes removed the telepath's helmet, waited for Deane to perform a like service for him.

Deane's face was, if possible, even paler than usual. "Captain," he said, "we got back just in time. We've no more than a few minutes' air in our bottles."

"Why didn't you tell me?"

Deane laughed shakily. "How could I? I was being . . . educated. If it's any use to me or to anybody else, I know how to make wheels out of sections of tree trunk . . ."

Beadle's voice crackled from an intercom bulkhead speaker. "Captain! Captain! Come up to Control! It's . . . vanished!"

"What's vanished?" demanded Grimes into the nearest pick-up.

"That . . . that sphere . . ."

"We're on our way," said Grimes.

Yes, the sphere had vanished. It had not flickered out like a snuffed candle; it had seemed to recede at a speed approaching that of light. It was gone, and no further investigation of its potentialities and capabilities would be possible.

It was Deane who was able to give an explanation of sorts. He said, "It was an emissary of the Old Ones. All intelligent races in this Galaxy share the legends—the gods who came down from the sky, bearing gifts of fire and weaponry, setting Man, or his local equivalent, on the upward path . . ."

"I played God myself once," said Grimes. "I wasn't very popular. But go on, Spooky."

"These Old Ones . . . Who were they? We shall never know. What were their motivations? Missionary zeal? Altruism? The long-term development of planets, by the indigenes, so that the Old Ones could, at some future date, take over?

"Anyhow, I wasn't entirely under Its control. I was seeing the things that It meant me to see, feeling the things that It meant me to feel—but, at the same time, I was picking up all sorts of outside impressions. It was one of many of Its kind, sent out—how long ago?—on a missionary voyage. It was a machine, and—as machines do—it malfunctioned. Its job was to make a landing on some likely world and to make contact with the primitive natives, and to initiate their education. It was programmed, too, to get the hell out if It landed on a planet whose natives already used fire, who were already metal workers. That was why It, although not yet awakened from Its long sleep, repelled our metallic sounding rocket. That was why you, Captain, got this odd hunch about a nonmetallic approach.

"Your plastic rocket woke It up properly. *It* assumed that we, with no metal about us, were not yet fire-making, tool-using animals. It did what It was built to do—taught us how to make fire, and tools and weapons. And then It followed us home. It was going to keep watch over us, from generation to generation, was going to give us an occasional nudge in the right direction. Possibly It had another function—to act as a sort of marker buoy for Its builders, so that They, in Their own good time, could find us, to take over.

"But even It, with Its limited intelligence, must have realized, at the finish, that we and It were in airless space and not on a planetary surface. It must have seen that we, using little rocket-propulsion units, were already sophisticated fire-users. And then, when we entered an obviously metallic spaceship, the penny must finally have dropped, with a loud clang.

"Do you want to know what my last impression was, before It shoved off?"

"Of course," said Grimes.

"It was one of hurt, of disillusion, of bewilderment. It was the realization that It was at the receiving end of a joke. The thing was utterly humorless, of course—but It could still hate being laughed at."

There was a silence, broken by Beadle. "And Somewhere," he said piously, "at Some Time, Somebody must have asked, 'Where is my wandering buoy tonight?'"

"I sincerely hope," Grimes told him, "that this Somebody is not still around, and that He or It never tries to find out."

～ The Mountain Movers ～

OLGANA—Earth-type, revolving around a Sol-type primary—is a backwater planet. It is well off the main Galactic trade routes, although it gets by quite comfortably by exporting meat, butter, wool and the like to the neighboring, highly industrialized, Mekanika System. Olgana was a Lost Colony, one of those worlds stumbled upon quite by chance during the First Expansion, settled in a spirit of great thankfulness by the personnel of a hopelessly off-course, completely lost emigrant lodejammer. It was rediscovered—this time with no element of chance involved—by the Survey Service's *Trail Blazer,* before the colonists had drifted too far from the mainstream of human culture. Shortly thereafter there were legal proceedings against these same colonists, occupying a few argumentative weeks at the Federation's Court of Galactic Justice in Geneva, on Earth; had these been successful they would have been followed by an Eviction Order. Even in those days it was illegal for humans to establish themselves on any planet already supporting an intelligent life form. *But*—and the colonists' Learned Counsel made the most of it—that law had not been in existence when *Lode Jumbuk* lifted off from Port Woomera on what turned out to be her last voyage. It was only a legal quibble, but the aborigines had no representation at Court—and, furthermore, Counsel for the Defense had hinted, in the right quarters, that if he lost this case he would bring suit on behalf of his clients against the Interstellar Transport

Commission, holding that body fully responsible for the plights of *Lode Jumbuk's* castaways and their descendants. ITC, fearing that a dangerous and expensive precedent might be established, brought behind-the-scenes pressure to bear and the case was dropped. Nobody asked the aborigines what they thought about it all.

There was no denying that the Olganan natives—if they were natives—were a backward race. They were humanoid—to outward appearances human. They did not, however, quite fit into the general biological pattern of their world, the fauna of which mainly comprised very primitive, egg-laying mammals. The aborigines were mammals as highly developed as Man himself; although along slightly different lines. There had been surprisingly little research into Olganan biology, however; the Colony's highly competent biologists seemed to be entirely lacking in the spirit of scientific curiosity. They were biological engineers rather than scientists, their main concern being to improve the strains of their meat-producing and wool-bearing animals, descended in the main from the spermatozoa and ova which *Lode Jumbuk*—as did all colonization vessels of her period— had carried under refrigeration.

To Olgana came the Survey Service's Serpent Class Courier *Adder,* Lieutenant John Grimes commanding. She carried not-very-important dispatches for Commander Lewin, Officer-in-Charge of the small Federation Survey Service Base maintained on the planet. The dispatches were delivered and then, after the almost mandatory small talk, Grimes asked, "And would there be any Orders for me, Commander?"

Lewin—a small, dark, usually intense man—grinned. "Of a sort, Lieutenant. Of a sort. You must be in Commodore Damien's good books. When *I* was a skipper of a Courier it was always a case of getting from Point A to Point B as soon as possible, if not before, with stopovers cut down to the irreducible minimum . . . Well, since you ask, I received a Carlottigram from Officer Commanding Couriers just before you blew in. I am to inform you that there will be no employment for your vessel for a period of at least six weeks local. You and your officers are to put yourselves at my disposal . . ." The Commander grinned again. "I find it hard enough to find jobs enough to keep my own personnel as much as half busy. So . . . enjoy yourselves. Go your merry ways rejoicing, as long as you carry your personal transceivers at all times. See the sights, such as they are. Wallow in the fleshpots—such as *they* are." He paused. "I only wish that the Commodore had loved me as much as he seems to love you."

"Mphm," grunted Grimes, his prominent ears reddening. "I don't think that it's quite that way, sir." He was remembering his last interview with Damien. *Get out of my sight!* the Commodore had snarled. *Get out of my sight, and don't come back until I'm in a better temper, if ever . . .*

"Indeed?" with a sardonic lift of the eyebrows.

"It's this way, Commander. I don't think that I'm overly popular around Lindisfarne Base at the moment . . ."

Lewin laughed outright. "I'd guessed as much. Your fame, Lieutenant, has spread even to Olgana. Frankly, I don't want you in *my* hair, around *my* Base, humble though it be. The administration of this planet is none of my concern, luckily, so—you and your officers can carouse to your hearts' content as long as it's not in *my* bailiwick."

"Have you any suggestions, sir?" asked Grimes stiffly.

"Why yes. There's the so-called Gold Coast. It got started after the Trans-Galactic Clippers started calling here on their cruises."

"Inflated prices," grumbled Grimes. "A tourist trap . . ."

"How right you are. But not every TG cruise passenger is a millionaire. I could recommend, perhaps, the coach tour of Nevernever. You probably saw it from Space on your way in—that whacking great island continent in the Southern Hemisphere."

"How did it get its name?"

"The natives call it that—or something that sounds almost like that. It's the only continent upon which the aborigines live, by the way. When *Lode Jumbuk* made her landing there was no intelligent life at all in the Northern Hemisphere."

"What's so attractive about this tour?"

"Nevernever is the only unspoiled hunk of real estate on the planet. It has been settled along the coastal fringe by humans, but the Outback—which means the Inland and most of the country north of Capricorn—is practically still the way it was when Men first came here. Oh there're sheep and cattle stations, and a bit of mining, but there won't be any real development, with irrigation and all the rest, until population pressure forces it. And the aborigines— well, most of them—still live in the semi-desert the way they did before *Lode Jumbuk* came." Lewin was warming up. "Think of it, Lieutenant, an opportunity to explore a primitive world whilst enjoying all mod. cons.! *You* might never get such a chance again."

"I'll think about it," Grimes told him.

He thought about it. He discussed it with his officers. Mr. Beadle, the First Lieutenant, was not enthusiastic. In spite of his habitual lugubrious mien he had a passion for the bright lights, and made it quite clear that he had enjoyed of late so few opportunities to spend his pay that he could well afford a Gold Coast holiday. Von Tannenbaum, Navigator, Slovotny, Electronic Communications, and Vitelli, Engineer, sided with Beadle. Grimes did not try to persuade them—after all, he was getting no commission from the Olganan Tourist Bureau. Spooky Deane, the psionic communications officer, asked rather shyly if he could come along with the Captain. He was not the companion that Grimes would have chosen—but he was a telepath, and it was just possible that his gift would be useful.

Deane and Grimes took the rocket mail from Newer York to New Melbourne, and during the trip Grimes indulged in one of his favorite gripes, about the inability of the average colonist to come up with really original names for his cities. At New Melbourne—a drab, oversized village on the southern coast of Nevernever—they stayed at a hotel which, although recommended by Trans-Galactic Clippers, failed dismally to come up to Galactic standards, making no attempt whatsoever to cater for guests born and brought up on worlds with widely differing atmospheres, gravitational fields and dietary customs. Then there was a day's shopping, during which the two spacemen purchased such items of personal equipment as they had been told would be necessary by the office of Nevernever Tours. The following morning, early, they took a cab from their hotel to the Never-Never Coach Terminus. It was still dark, and it was cold, and it was raining.

They sat with the other passengers, all of whom were, like themselves, roughly dressed, in the chilly waiting room, waiting for something to happen. To pass the time Grimes sized up the others. Some were obviously outworlders—there was a TG Clipper in at the spaceport. Some—their accent made it obvious—were Olganans, taking the opportunity of seeing something of their own planet. None of them, on this dismal morning, looked very attractive. Grimes admitted that the same could be said about Deane and himself; the telepath conveyed the impression of a blob of ectoplasm roughly wrapped in a too gaudy poncho.

A heavy engine growled outside, and bright lights stabbed through the big windows. Deane got unsteadily to his feet. "Look at that, Captain!" he exclaimed. "Wheels, yet! I expected an inertial drive vehicle, or at least a hoverbus!"

"You should have read the brochure, Spooky. The idea of this tour is to see the country the same way as the first explorers did, to get the *feel* of it."

"I can get the feel of it as well from an aircraft as from that archaic contraption!"

"We aren't all telepaths . . ."

Two porters had come in and were picking up suitcases, carrying them outside. The tourists, holding their overnight grips, followed, watched their baggage being stowed in a locker at the rear of the coach. From the p.a. system a voice was ordering, "All passengers will now embus! All passengers will now embus!"

The passengers embussed, and Grimes and Deane found themselves seated behind a young couple of obviously Terran origin, while across the aisle from them was a pair of youngish ladies who could be nothing other than schoolteachers. A fat, middle-aged man, dressed in a not very neat uniform of grey coveralls, eased himself into the driver's seat. "All aboard?" he asked. "Anybody who's not, sing out!" The coach lurched from the terminus on to the rain-wet street, was soon bowling north through the dreary suburbs of New Melbourne.

Northeast they ran at first, and then almost due north, following the coast. Here the land was rich, green, well-wooded, with apple orchards, vineyards, orange groves. Then there was sheep country, rolling downland speckled with the white shapes of the grazing animals. "It's wrong," Deane whispered to Grimes. "It's all wrong . . ."

"What's wrong, Spooky?"

"I can feel it—even if you can't. The . . . the resentment . . ."

"The aborigines, you mean?"

"Yes. But even stronger, the native animals, driven from their own pastures, hunted and destroyed to make room for the outsiders from beyond the stars. And the plants—what's left of the native flora in these parts. Weeds to be rooted out and burned, so that the grapes and grain and the oranges may flourish . . ."

"You must have felt the same on other colonized worlds, Spooky."

"Not as strongly as here. I can almost put it into words . . . *The First Ones* let us alone."

"Mphm," grunted Grimes. "Makes sense, I suppose. The original colonists, with only the resources of *Lode Jumbuk* to draw upon, couldn't have made much of an impression. But when they had all the resources of the Federation to draw upon . . ."

"I don't think it's quite that way . . . " murmured Deane doubtfully.

"Then what *do* you think?"

"I . . . I don't know Captain . . ."

But they had little further opportunity for private talk. Slowly at first, and then more rapidly, the coachload of assorted passengers was thawing out. The driver initiated this process—he was, Grimes realized, almost like the captain of a ship, responsible for the well-being, psychological as well as physical, of his personnel. Using a fixed microphone by his seat he delivered commentaries on the places of interest that they passed, and, when he judged that the time was ripe, had another microphone on a wandering lead passed among the passengers, the drill being that each would introduce himself by name, profession and place of residence.

Yes, they were a mixed bag, these tourists. About half of them

were from Earth—they must be, thought Grimes, from the TG Clipper
Cutty Sark presently berthed at the spaceport. Public Servants, lawyers,
the inevitable Instructors from universities, both major and minor,
improving their knowledge of the worlds of the Federation in a
relatively inexpensive way. The Olganans were similarly diversified.

When it came to Grimes's turn he said, "John Grimes, spaceman. Last place of permanent residence St. Helier, Channel Islands,
Earth."

Tanya Lancaster, the young and prettier of the two teachers
across the aisle, turned to him. "I thought you were a Terry, John.
You don't mind my using your given name, do you? It's supposed to
be one of the rules on this tour . . ."

"I like it, Tanya."

"That's good. But you can't be from the *Cutty Sark*. I should
know all the officers, at least by sight, by this time."

"And if I were one of *Cutty Sark's* officers," said Grimes gallantly
(after all, this Tanya wench was not at all bad looking, with her
chestnut hair, green eyes and thin, intelligent face), "I should have
known you by this time."

"Oh," she said, "you must be from the Base."

"Almost right."

"You are making things awkward. Ah, I have it. You're from
that funny little destroyer or whatever it is that's berthed at the
Survey Service's end of the spaceport."

"She's not a funny little destroyer," Grimes told her stiffly.
"She's a Serpent Class Courier."

The girl laughed. "And she's *yours*. Yes, I overheard your friend
calling you 'Captain' . . ."

"Yes. She's mine . . ."

"And now, folks," boomed the driver's amplified voice, "how
about a little singsong to liven things up? Any volunteers?"

The microphone was passed along to a group of young Olganan
students. After a brief consultation they burst into song.

"When the jolly *Jumbuk* lifted from Port Woomera
  Out and away for Altair Three

Glad were we all to kiss the tired old Earth good-bye—
Who'll come a-sailing in *Jumbuk* with me?

Sailing in *Jumbuk,* sailing in *Jumbuk,*
Who'll come a-sailing in *Jumbuk* with me?
Glad were we all to kiss the tired old Earth good-bye—
You'll come a-sailing *in Jumbuk* with me!

Then there was Storm, the Pile and all the engines dead—
Blown out to Hell and gone were we!
Lost in the Galaxy, falling free in sweet damn all—
Who'll come a-sailing *Jumbuk* with me?

Sailing in *Jumbuk,* sailing in *Jumbuk,*
Who'll come a-sailing in *Jumbuk* with me?
Lost in the Galaxy, falling free in sweet damn all—
You'll come a-sailing *in Jumbuk* with me!

Up jumped the Captain, shouted for his Engineer,
'Start me the diesels, one, two, three!
Give me the power to feed into the Ehrenhafts—
You'll come a-sailing in *Jumbuk* with me!'"

"But that's *ours!*" declared Tanya indignantly, her Australian accent suddenly very obvious. "It's our *Waltzing Matilda!*"

"*Waltzing Matilda* never was yours," Grimes told her. "The words—yes, but the tune, no. Like many another song it's always having new verses tacked on to it."

"I suppose you're right. But these comic lyrics of theirs—what are they all about?"

"You've heard of the Ehrenhaft Drive, haven't you?"

"The first FTL Drive, wasn't it?"

"I suppose you could call it that. The Ehrenhaft generators converted the ship, the lodejammer, into what was, in effect, a huge magnetic particle. As long as she was on the right tramlines, the right line of magnetic force, she got to where she was supposed to get to in a relatively short time. But a magnetic storm, tangling the lines of force like a bowl of spaghetti, would throw her anywhere—or nowhere. And these storms also drained the micropile of all energy. In such circumstances, all that could be done was to start up the emergency diesel generators, to supply electric power to the Ehrenhaft generators. After this the ship would stooge along hopefully, trying to find a habitable planet before the fuel ran out . . ."

"H'm." She grinned suddenly. "I suppose it's more worthy of being immortalized in a song than our sheep-stealing Jolly Swagman. But I still prefer the original." And then aided by her friend, Moira Stevens—a fat and cheerful young woman—she sang what she still claimed was the original version. Grimes allowed himself to wonder what the ghost of the Jolly Swagman—still, presumably, haunting that faraway billabong—would have made of it all. . . .

That night they reached the first of their camping sites, a clearing in the bush, on the banks of a river that was little more than a trickle, but with quite adequate toilet facilities in plastic huts. The coach crew—there was a cook as well as the driver—laid out the pneumatic pup tents in three neat rows, swiftly inflated them with a hose from the coach's air compressor. Wood was collected for a fire, and folding grills laid across it. "The inevitable steak and billy tea," muttered somebody who had been on the tour before. "It's *always* steak and billy tea . . ."

But the food, although plain, was good, and the yarning around the fire was enjoyable and, finally, Grimes found that the air mattress in his tent was at least as comfortable as his bunk aboard *Adder.* He slept well, and awoke refreshed to the sound of the taped *Reveille.* He was among the first in the queue for the toilet facilities and, dressed and ready for what the day might bring, lined up for his eggs and bacon and mug of tea with a good appetite. Then there was the washing up, the deflation of mattresses and tents, the stowing away of these and the baggage—and, very shortly after the bright sun had appeared over the low hills to the eastward, the tour was on its way again.

On they drove, and on, through drought-stricken land that showed few signs of human occupancy, that was old, old long before the coming of Man. Through sun-parched plains they drove, where scrawny cattle foraged listlessly for scraps of sun-dried grass, where tumbleweed scurried across the roadway, where dust-devils raised their whirling columns of sand and light debris. But there was life, apart from the thirsty cattle, apart from the grey scrub that, with the first rains of the wet season, would put forth its brief, vivid greenery, its short-lived gaudy flowers. Once the coach stopped to let a herd of sausagekine across the track—low-slung, furry quadrupeds, wriggling like huge lizards on their almost rudimentary legs. There was a great clicking of cameras. "We're lucky, folks," said the driver. "These beasts are almost extinct. They were classed as pests until only a couple of years ago—now they've been reclassed as protected fauna . . ." They rolled past an aboriginal encampment where gaunt, black figures, looking arachnoid rather than humanoid, stood immobile about their cooking fires. "Bad bastards those," announced the driver. "Most of the others will put on shows for us, will sell us curios—but not that tribe . . ."

Now and again there were other vehicles—diesel-engined tourist coaches like their own, large and small hovercraft and, in the cloudless sky, the occasional high-flying inertial drive aircraft. But, in the main, the land was empty, the long, straight road seeming to stretch to infinity ahead of them and behind them. The little settlements—pub, general store and a huddle of other buildings—were welcome every time that one was reached. There was a great consumption of cold beer at each stop, conversations with the locals, who gathered as though by magic, at each halt. There were the coach parks—concentration camps in the desert rather than oases, but with much appreciated hot showers and facilities for washing clothing.

On they drove, and on, and Grimes and Deane teamed up with Tanya and Moira. But there was no sharing of tents. The rather disgruntled Grimes gained the impression that the girl's mother had told her, at an early age, to beware of spacemen. Come to that, after the first two nights there were no tents. Now that they were in regions where it was certain that no rain would fall all hands slept in their sleeping bags only, under the stars.

And then they came to the Cragge Rock reserve. "Cragge Rock," said the driver into his microphone, "is named after Captain Cragge, Master of the *Lode Jumbuk,* just as the planet itself is named after his wife, Olga." He paused. "Perhaps somewhere in the Galaxy there's a mountain that will be called Grimes Rock—but with all due respect to the distinguished spaceman in our midst he'll have to try hard to find the equal to Cragge Rock! The Rock, folks is the largest monolith in the known Universe—just a solid hunk of granite. Five miles long, a mile across, half a mile high." He turned his attention to Tanya and Moira. "Bigger than *your* Ayers Rock, ladies!" He paused again for the slight outburst of chuckles. "And to the north, sixty miles distant, there's Mount Conway, a typical mesa. Twenty miles to the south there's Mount Sarah, named after Chief Officer Conway's wife. It's usually called 'the Sallies,' as it consists of five separate domes of red conglomerate. So you see that geologically Cragge Rock doesn't fit in. There're quite a few theories, folks. One is that there was a submarine volcanic eruption when this was all part of the ocean bed. The Rock was an extrusion of molten matter from the core of the planet. It has been further shaped by millions of years of erosion since the sea floor was lifted to become this island continent."

As he spoke, the Rock was lifting over the otherwise featureless horizon. It squatted there on the skyline, glowering red in the almost level rays of the westering sun, an enormous crimson slug. It possessed beauty of a sort—but the overall impression was one of strength.

"We spend five full days here, folks," went on the driver. "There's a hotel, and there's an aboo settlement, and most of the boos speak English. They'll be happy to tell you *their* legends about the Rock—Wuluru they call it. It's one of their sacred places, but they don't mind us coming here as long as we pay for the privilege. That, of course, is all taken care of by the Tourist Bureau, but if you want any curios you'll have to fork out for them. See the way that the Rock's changing color as the sun gets lower? And once the sun's down it'll slowly fade like a dying ember. . . ."

The Rock was close now, towering above them, a red wall

against the darkening blue of the cloudless sky. Then they were in its shadow, and the sheer granite wall was purple, shading to cold blue . . . Sunlight again, like a sudden blow, and a last circuit of the time-pocked monolith, and a final stop on the eastern side of the stone mountain.

They got out of the coach, stood there, shivering a little, in the still, chilly air. "It has something. . . ." whispered Tanya Lancaster.

"It has something . . ." agreed Moira Stevens.

"Ancestral memory?" asked Deane, with unusual sharpness.

"You're prying!" snapped the fat girl.

"I'm not, Moira. But I couldn't help picking up the strong emanation from your minds."

Tanya laughed. "Like most modern Australians we're a mixed lot—and, in our fully integrated society, most of us have some aboriginal blood. But . . . Why should Moira and I feel so at home here, both at home and hopelessly lost?"

"If you let me probe . . ." suggested Deane gently.

"No," flared the girl. "No!"

Grimes sympathized with her. He knew, all too well, what it is like to have a trained telepath, no matter how high his ethical standards, around. But he said, "Spooky's to be trusted. I know."

"You might trust him, John. I don't know him well enough."

"He knows *us* too bloody well!" growled Moira.

"I smell steak," said Grimes, changing the subject.

The four of them walked to the open fire, where the evening meal was already cooking.

Dawn on the Rock was worth waking up early for. Grimes stood with the others, blanket-wrapped against the cold, and watched the great hulk flush gradually from blue to purple, from purple to pink. Over it and beyond it the sky was black, the stars very bright, almost as bright as in airless Space. Then the sun was up, and the Rock stood there, a red island in the sea of tawny sand, a surf of green brush breaking about its base. The show was over. The party went to the showers and toilets and then, dressed, assembled for breakfast.

After the meal they walked from the encampment to the Rock.

Tanya and Moira stayed in the company of Grimes and Deane, but their manner towards the two spacemen was distinctly chilly; they were more interested in their guidebooks than in conversation. On their way they passed the aboriginal village. A huddle of crude shelters it was, constructed of natural materials and battered sheets of plastic. Fires were burning, and gobbets of unidentifiable meat were cooking over them. Women—naked, with straggling hair and pendulous breasts, yet human enough—looked up and around at the well-clothed, well-fed tourists with an odd, sly mixture of timidity and boldness. One of them pointed to a leveled camera and screamed, "First gibbit half dollar!"

"You'd better," advised the driver. "Very commercial minded, these people . . ."

Men were emerging from the primitive huts. One of them approached Grimes and his companions, his teeth startlingly white in his coal-black face. He was holding what looked like a crucifix. "Very good," he said, waving it in front of him. "Two dollar."

"I'm not religious . . ." Grimes began, to be cut short by Tanya's laugh.

"Don't be a fool, John," she told him. "It's a throwing weapon."

"A throwing weapon?"

"Yes. Like our boomerangs. Let me show you." She turned to the native, held out her hand. "Here. Please."

"You throw, missie?"

"Yes. I throw."

Watched by the tourists and the natives she held the thing by the end of its long arm, turned until she was facing about forty-five degrees away from the light, morning breeze, the flat surfaces of the cross at right angles to the wind. She raised her arm, then threw, with a peculiar flick of her wrist. The weapon left her hand, spinning, turned so that it was flying horizontally, like a miniature helicopter. It travelled about fifty yards, came round in a lazy arc, faltered, then fell in a flurry of fine sand.

"Not very good," complained the girl. "You got better? You got proper one?"

The savage grinned. "*You* know?"

"Yes. I know."

The man went back into his hut, returned with another weapon. This one was old, beautifully made, and lacking the crude designs that had been burned into the other with red-hot wire. He handed it to Tanya, who hefted it approvingly. She threw it as she had thrown the first one—and the difference was immediately obvious. There was no clumsiness in its flight, no hesitation. Spinning, it flew, more like a living thing than a machine. Its arms turned more and more lazily as it came back—and Tanya, with a clapping motion, deftly caught it between her two hands. She stood admiring it—the smooth finish imparted by the most primitive of tools, the polish of age and of long use.

"How much?" she asked.

"No for sale, missie." Again the very white grin. "But I give."

"But you can't. You mustn't."

"You take."

"I shouldn't, but . . ."

"Take it, lady," said the driver. "This man is Najatira, the Chief of these people. Refusing his gift would offend him." Then, businesslike, "You guide, Najatira?"

"Yes. I guide." He barked a few words in his own language to his women, one of whom scuttled over the sand to retrieve the first fallen throwing weapon. Then, walking fast on his big, splayed feet he strode towards the rock. Somehow the two girls had ranged themselves on either side of him. Grimes looked on disapprovingly. Who was it who had said that these natives were humanoid only? This naked savage, to judge by his external equipment, was all too human. Exchanging disapproving glances, the two spacemen took their places in the little procession.

"Cave," said Najatira, pointing. The orifice, curiously regular, was exactly at the tail of the slug-shaped monolith. "Called, by my people, the Hold of Winds. Story say, in Dream Time, wind come from there, wind move world . . . Before, world no move. No daytime, no nighttime . . ."

"Looks almost like a venturi, Captain," Deane marked to Grimes.

"Mphm. Certainly looks almost too regular to be natural. But erosion does odd things. Or it could have been made by a blast of gases from the thing's inside . . ."

"Precisely," said Deane.

"But you don't think . . . ? No. It would be impossible."

"I don't know what to think," admitted Deane.

Their native guide was leading them around the base of the Rock. "This Cave of Birth. Tonight ceremony. We show you . . . And there—look up. What we call the fishing net. In Dream Time caught big fish . . ."

"A circuit . . ." muttered Grimes. "Exposed by millennia of weathering . . ." He laughed. "I'm getting as bad as you, Spooky. Nature comes up with the most remarkable imitations of Man-made things . . ."

So it went on, the trudge around the base of the monolith, under the hot sun, while their tireless guide pointed out this and that feature. As soon as the older members of the party began to show signs of distress the driver spoke into his wrist transceiver, and within a few minutes the coach came rumbling over the rough track and then, with its partial load, kept pace with those who were still walking. Grimes and Deane were among these hardy ones, but only because Tanya and Moira showed no signs of flagging, and because Grimes felt responsible for the women. After all, the Survey Service had been referred to as the Policemen of the Galaxy. It was unthinkable that two civilized human females should fall for this unwashed savage—but already he knew that civilized human females are apt to do the weirdest things.

At last the tour came to an end. Najatira, after bowing with surprising courtesy, strode off towards his own camp. The tourists clustered hungrily around the folding tables that had been set up, wolfed the thick sandwiches and gulped great draughts of hot, sweet tea.

During the afternoon there were flights over the Rock and the countryside for those who wished them, a large blimp having come in from the nearest airport for that purpose. This archaic transport was the occasion for surprise and incredulity, but it was explained that such aircraft were used by *Lode Jumbuk's* people for their initial explorations.

"The bloody thing's not safe," complained Deane as soon as they were airborne.

Grimes ignored him. He was looking out and down through the big cabin windows. Yes, the Rock did look odd, out of place. It was part of the landscape—but it did not belong. It had been there for millions of years—but still it did not belong. Mount Conway and Mount Sarah were natural enough geological formations—*but,* he thought, *Cragge Rock was just as natural.* He tried to envision what it must have looked like when that up-welling of molten rock thrust through the ocean bed.

"It wasn't like that, Captain," said Deane quietly.

"Damn you, Spooky! Get out of my mind."

"I'm sorry," the telepath told him, although he didn't sound it. "It's just that this locality is like a jigsaw puzzle. I'm trying to find the pieces, and to make them fit." He looked around to make sure that none of the others in the swaying, creaking cabin was listening. "Tanya and Moira . . . The kinship they feel with Najatira . . ."

"Why don't you ask them about it?" Grimes suggested, jerking his head towards the forward end of the car, where the two girls were sitting. "Is it kinship, or is it just the attraction that a woman on holiday feels for an exotic male?"

"It's more than that."

"So you're prying."

"I'm trying not to." He looked down without interest at Mount Conway, over which the airship was slowly flying. "But it's hard not to."

"You could get into trouble, Spooky. And you could get the ship into trouble . . ."

"And you, Captain."

"Yes. And me." Then Grimes allowed a slight smile to flicker over his face. "But I know you. You're on to something. And as we're on holiday from the ship I don't suppose that I can give you any direct orders . . ."

"I'm not a space-lawyer, so I'll take your word for that."

"Just be careful. And keep me informed."

While they talked the pilot of the blimp, his voice amplified, had been giving out statistics. The conversation had been private enough.

That night there was the dance.

Flaring fires had been built on the sand, in a semi-circle, the inner arc of which faced the mouth of the Cave of Birth. The tourists sat there, some on the ground and some on folding stools, the fires at their backs, waiting. Overhead the sky was black and clear, the stars bitterly bright.

From inside the cave there was music—of a sort. There was a rhythmic wheezing of primitive trumpets, the staccato rapping of knocking sticks. There was a yelping male voice—Najatira's—that seemed to be giving orders rather than singing.

Grimes turned to say something to Tanya, but she was no longer in her place. Neither was Moira. The two girls must have gone together to the toilet block; they would be back shortly. He returned his attention to the black entrance to the Cave.

The first figure emerged from it, crouching, a stick held in his hands. Then the second, then the third . . . There was something oddly familiar about it, something that didn't make sense, or that made the wrong kind of sense. Grimes tried to remember what it was. Dimly he realized that Deane was helping him, that the telepath was trying to bring his memories to the conscious level. Yes, that was it. That was the way that the Marines disembarked on the surface of an unexplored, possibly hostile planet, automatic weapons at the ready . . .

Twelve men were outside the Cave now, advancing in a dance-like step. The crude, tree-stem trumpets were still sounding, like the plaint of tired machinery, and the noise of the knocking sticks was that of the cooling metal. The leader paused, stood upright. With his fingers in his mouth he gave a piercing whistle.

The women emerged, carrying bundles, hesitantly, two steps forward, one step back. Grimes gasped his disbelief. Surely that was Tanya, as naked as the others—and there was no mistaking Moira.

He jumped to his feet, ignoring the protests of those behind him, trying to shake off Deane's restraining hand. "Let go!" he snarled.

"Don't interfere, Captain!" The telepath's voice was urgent. "Don't you see? They've gone native—no, that's not right. But they've reverted. And there's no law against it."

"I can still drag them out of this. They'll thank me after." He turned around and shouted, "Come on, all of you! We must put a stop to this vile performance!"

"Captain Grimes!" This was the coach driver, his voice angry. "Sit down, sir! This sort of thing has happened before, and it's nothing to worry about. The young ladies are in no danger!"

"It's happened before," agreed Deane, unexpectedly. "With neurotic exhibitionists, wanting to have their photographs taken among the savages. But not *this* way!"

Then, even more unexpectedly, it was Deane who was running out across the sand, and it was Najatira who advanced to meet him, not in hostility but in welcome. It was Grimes who, unheeded, yelled, "Come back, Spooky! Come back here!"

He didn't know what was happening, but he didn't like it. First of all those two silly bitches, and now one of his own officers. What the hell was getting into everybody? Followed by a half-dozen of the other men he ran towards the cave mouth. Their way was barred by a line of the tribesmen, holding their sticks now like spears (which they were)—not like make-believe guns. Najatira stood proudly behind the armed men, and on either side of him stood the two girls, a strange, arrogant pride in every line of their naked bodies. And there was Deane, a strange smile on his face. His face, too, was strange, seemed suddenly to have acquired lines of authority.

"Go back, John," he ordered. "There is nothing that you can do." He added softly, "But there is much that I can do."

"What the hell are you talking about, Spooky?"

"I'm an Australian, like Moira and Tanya here. Like them, I have the Old Blood in my veins. Unlike them, I'm a spaceman. Do you think that after all these years in the Service I, with my talent, haven't learned how to handle and navigate a ship, any ship? I shall take my people back to where they belong."

And then Grimes *knew*. The knowledge came flooding into his mind, from the mind of Deane, from the minds of the others, whose ancestral memories had been awakened by the telepath. But he was still responsible. He must still try to stop this craziness.

"Mr. Deane!" he snapped as he strode forward firmly. He brushed aside the point of the spear that was aimed at his chest. He saw Tanya throw something, and sneered as it missed his head by inches. He did not see the cruciform boomerang returning, was aware of it only as a crashing blow from behind, as a flash of crimson light, then darkness.

He recovered slowly. He was stretched out on the sand beside the coach. Two of the nurses among the passengers were with him.

He asked, as he tried to sit up, "What happened?"

"They all went back into the cave," the girl said. "The rock . . . The rock closed behind them. And there were lights. And a voice, it was Mr. Deane's voice, but loud, loud, saying, 'Clear the field! Clear the field! Get back, everybody. Get well back. Get well away!' So we got well back."

"And what's happening now?" asked Grimes. The nurses helped him as he got groggily to his feet. He stared towards the distant Rock. He could hear the beat of mighty engines and the ground was trembling under the monolith. Even with the knowledge that Deane had fed into his mind he could not believe what he was seeing.

The Rock was lifting, its highest part suddenly eclipsing a bright constellation. It was lifting, and the skin of the planet protested as the vast ship, that for so long had been embedded in it, tore itself free. Tremors knocked the tourists from their feet, but somehow Grimes remained standing, oblivious to the shouts and screams. He heard the crash behind him as the coach was overturned, but did not look. At this moment it was only a minor distraction.

The Rock was lifting, had lifted. It was a deeper blackness against the blackness of the sky, a scattering of strange, impossible stars against the distant stars, a bright cluster (at first) that dimmed and diminished, that dwindled, faster and faster, and then was gone, leaving in its wake utter darkness and silence.

The silence was broken by the coach driver. He said slowly, "I've had to cope with vandalism in my time, but nothing like this. What the Board will say when they hear that their biggest tourist attraction has gone I hate to think about . . ." He seemed to cheer up slightly. "But it was one *of your* officers, Captain Grimes, from *your* ship, that did it. I hope you enjoy explaining it!"

Grimes explained, as well as he was able, to Commander Lewin.

He said, "As we all know, sir, there are these odd races, human rather than humanoid, all through the Galaxy. It all ties in with the Common Origin of Mankind theories. I never used to have much time for them myself, but now . . ."

"Never mind that, Grimes. Get on with the washing."

"Well, Deane was decent enough to let loose a flood of knowledge into my mind just before that blasted Tanya clonked me with her boomerang. It seems that millions of years ago these stone spaceships, these hollowed out asteroids, were sent to explore this Galaxy. I got only a hazy idea of their propulsive machinery, but it was something on the lines of our Inertial Drive, and something on the lines of our Mannschenn Drive, with auxiliary rockets for maneuvering in orbit and so forth. They were never meant to land, but they could, if they had to. Their power? Derived from the conversion of matter, any matter, with the generators or converters ready to start up when the right button was pushed—but the button had to be pushed psionically. Get me?"

"Not very well. But go on."

"Something happened to the ship, to the crew and passengers of this ship. A disease, I think it was, wiping out almost all the adults, leaving only children and a handful of not very intelligent ratings. Somebody—it must have been one of the officers just before he died—got the ship down somehow. He set things so that it could not be re-entered until somebody with the right qualifications came along."

"The right qualifications?"

"Yes. Psionic talents, more than a smattering of astronautics, and descended from the Old People . . ."

"Like your Mr. Deane. But what about the two girls?"

"They had the old Blood. And they were highly educated. And they could have been latent telepaths . . ."

"Could be." Lewin smiled without much mirth. "Meanwhile, Lieutenant, I have to try to explain to the Olganan Government, with copies to Trans-Galactic Clippers *and* to our own masters, including *your* Commodore Damien. All in all, Grimes, it was a fine night's work. Apart from the Rock, there were two TG passengers *and* a Survey Service officer . . ."

"*And* the tribe . . ."

"The least of the Olganan Government's worries, and nothing at all to do with TG or ourselves. Even so . . ." This time his smile was tinged with genuine, but sardonic, humor.

"Even so?" echoed Grimes.

"What if those tribesmen and women decided to liberate—I suppose that's the right word—those other tribespeople, the full-blooded ones who're still living in the vicinity of the other stone spaceship? What if the Australians realize, one sunny morning, that their precious Ayers Rock has up and left them?"

"I know who'll be blamed," said Grimes glumly.

"How right you are," concurred Lewin.

❧ What You Know ❧

LIEUTENANT JOHN GRIMES, captain of the Serpent Class Courier *Adder*, was in a bitter and twisted mood. He had his reasons. To begin with, he had just been hauled over the coals by Commodore Damien, Officer Commanding Couriers, and still resented being blamed for the disappearance of Cragge Rock from Olgana. Then he had been told that his ship's stay at Lindisfarne Base was to be a very short one—and Dr. Maggie Lazenby, with whom he hoped to achieve something warmer than mere friendship, was off planet and would not be returning until after his own departure. Finally, he had seen the latest Promotion List and had noted that officers junior to himself had been given their half rings, were now Lieutenant Commanders. And some of those same officers, in Grimes's words, wouldn't be capable of navigating a plastic duck across a bathtub.

Ensign Beadle, his first lieutenant, was sympathetic. He said, "But it isn't what you do, Captain. It isn't what you know, even. It's whom you know . . ."

"You could be right, Number One," admitted Grimes. "But in my case I'm afraid that it boils down to who knows me . . . Did you ever see that book, *How to Win Friends and Influence People?* I often think that I must have read the wrong half, the second half . . ."

Beadle made a noncommittal noise. Then, "We're ready to lift ship, Captain. Mechanically, that is. Mr. Hollister, the new

388

psionic radio officer, has yet to join—and, of course, there are the passengers . . ." Grimes allowed himself a sardonic smile. "I wonder what the Commodore has against *them!*"

Beadle took the question literally. "We're the only Courier in port, Captain, and it's essential that the Commissioner reaches Dhartana as soon as possible . . ."

" . . . if not before," finished Grimes. "Mphm. All right, Number One. Is the V.I.P. suite swept and garnished?"

"I . . . I've been busy with the *important* preparations for space, Captain . . ."

Grimes scowled. "I sincerely hope, Number One, that Mrs. Commissioner Dalwood never hears you implying that she's unimportant. We'll make a tour of the accommodation *now.*"

Followed by Beadle he strode up the ramp into the airlock of his little ship, his "flying darning needle." The V.I.P. suite took up almost the entire compartment below the officers' flat. As he passed through the sliding door into the sitting room Grimes's prominent ears reddened; with him it was a sign of anger as well as of embarrassment. "Damn it all, Number One," he exploded, "don't you realize that this woman is one of the civilian big wheels on the Board of Admiralty? You may not want promotion—but I do. Look at that table top! Drinking glass rings—and it must have been something sweet and sticky!—and bloody nearly an inch of cigarette ash! And the ashtrays! They haven't been emptied since Christ was a pup!"

"The suite hasn't been used since we carried Mr. Alberto . . ."

"I know that. Am I to suppose that you've kept it the way he left it in loving memory of him?"

"You did say, sir, that bearing in mind the circumstances of his death we should leave everything untouched in case his department wanted to make a thorough investigation . . ."

"And his department did check just to make sure that he'd left nothing of interest on board when he disembarked on Doncaster. But that was months ago. And this bedroom . . . The way it is now I wouldn't put a dog into it. Get on the blower at once to Maintenance, ask them? no, *tell* them—to send a cleaning detail here immediately."

Grimes became uncomfortably aware that there was somebody behind him. He turned slowly, reluctantly, looked into the hard, steel-grey eyes of the woman who was standing just inside the doorway. She returned his stare coldly. She was tall, and she was handsome, with short-cut platinum blonde hair, wearing a beautifully tailored grey costume that looked like a uniform but wasn't, that looked more like a uniform than a deliberately casual rig of the day affected by Grimes and Beadle in common with all Courier Service officers. Her figure seemed to be that of a girl—but her face, although unlined, was old. There were no physical marks of age, but it was somehow obvious that she had seen too much, experienced too much. Grimes thought, *If she smiles, something will crack.*

She didn't smile.

She said—and her voice, although well modulated, was hard as the rest of her—"Mr. Grimes . . ."

"Ma'am?"

"I am Commissioner Dalwood."

She did not extend her hand. Grimes bowed stiffly. "Honored to have you aboard, Ma'am."

"The honor is all yours, Mr. Grimes. Tell me, is the rest of your ship like this pigsty?"

"We're having the suite put to rights, Mrs. Dalwood."

"Pray do not put yourself out on my behalf, Mr. Grimes. My lady's maid and my two robot servants are at this moment bringing my baggage aboard. The robots are versatile. If you will let them have the necessary cleaning gear they will soon have these quarters fit for human occupancy."

"Mr. Beadle," ordered Grimes, "belay that call to Maintenance. See that Mrs. Dalwood's servants are issued with what they need."

"Very good, sir," replied Beadle smartly, glad of the chance to make his escape.

"And now, Mr. Grimes, if I may sit down somewhere in less squalid surroundings . . ."

"Certainly, Ma'am. If you will follow me . . ."

Grimes led the way out of the suite. The two humanoid robots, with expensive-looking baggage piled at their feet, stared at him impassively. The maid—small, plump, pert, and darkly brunette—allowed a flicker of sympathy to pass over her rosy face. Grimes thought that she winked, but couldn't be sure. On the way up to his own quarters Grimes was relieved to see that Beadle had kept the rest of the ship in a reasonably good state of cleanliness, although he did hear one or two disapproving sniffs from his passenger. His own day cabin was, he knew, untidy. He liked it that way. He was not surprised when Mrs. Dalwood said, "Your *desk,* Mr. Grimes. Surely some of those papers are of such a confidential nature that they should be in your safe."

Grimes said, "Nobody comes in here except by invitation. I trust my officers, Ma'am."

The Commissioner smiled thinly. Nothing cracked. She said, "What a child you are, Lieutenant. One of the first lessons I learned in politics was never to trust anybody."

"In space, aboard ship, you have to trust people, Ma'am."

She sat down in Grimes's easy chair, extending her long, elegant legs. Grimes suspected that she looked at her own limbs with brief admiration before returning her regard to him. Her laugh was brittle. "How touching, Lieutenant. And that is why ships are lost now and again."

"Can I offer you refreshment, Ma'am?" Grimes said, changing the subject.

"And do *you* drink, Lieutenant?"

I know damn well that I'm only a two ringer, Grimes thought, *but I do like being called* Captain *aboard my own ship . . .* He said, "Never on departure day, Mrs. Dalwood."

"Perhaps I shall be wise if I conform to the same rule. I must confess that I am not used to travelling in vessels of this class, and it is possible that I shall need all my wits about me during lift off. Might I ask for a cup of coffee?"

Grimes took from its rack the thermos container, which he had refilled from the galley coffee maker that morning. After he had removed the cap he realized that he had still to produce a cup, sugar bowl, spoon and milk. His tell-tale ears proclaiming his embarrassment, he replaced the container, conscious of the woman's coldly amused scrutiny. At last he had things ready, finally filling the jug from a carton of milk in his refrigerator.

She said. "The milk should be warmed."

"*Yes,* Mrs. Dalwood. Of course. If you wouldn't mind waiting . . ."

"If I took my coffee white I should mind. But I prefer it black, and unsweetened."

Grimes poured out, remembering that the coffee maker was long overdue for a thorough cleaning. *Adder's* coffee had a tang of its own. Her people were accustomed to it. The Commissioner was not. After one cautious sip she put her cup down, hard. She asked, "And what is the food like aboard this ship?"

"Usually quite good. Ma'am. We carry no ratings or petty officers, so we take it by turns cooking. Mr. Beadle—he's my First Lieutenant—makes an excellent stew." Grimes babbled on. "It's a sort of a curry, actually, but not quite, if you know what I mean . . ."

"I don't, Lieutenant. Nor do I wish to. As I have already told you, my robots are versatile. Might I suggest that they take over galley duties, first of all thoroughly cleaning all vessels and implements, starting with your coffee maker? Apart from anything else it will mean that your officers will have more time to devote to their real duties."

"If you want it that way, Mrs. Dalwood . . ."

"I do want it that way."

To Grimes's intense relief the intercom phone buzzed. He said to the Commissioner, "Excuse *me,* Ma'am," and then into the speaker/microphone, "Captain here."

"First Lieutenant, Captain. Mr. Hollister, the new P.C.O., has just boarded. Shall I send him up to report to you?"

"Yes, Mr. Beadle. Tell him that I'll see him in the Control Room. Now." He turned to Mrs. Dalwood. "I'm afraid I must leave you for a few minutes, Ma'am. There are cigarettes in that box, and if you wish more coffee . . ."

"I most certainly do not. And, Mr. Grimes, don't you think that you had better put those papers away in your safe before you go about your pressing business?" She allowed herself another thin smile. "After all, you haven't asked yet to see *my* identification. For all you know I could be a spy."

And if you are, thought Grimes, *I hope I'm the officer commanding the firing squad.* He said, "You are very well known, Ma'am." He swept his desk clean, depositing the pile of official and private correspondence on the deck, then fumbled through the routine of opening his safe. As usual the door stuck. Finally he had the papers locked away. He bowed again to Mrs. Dalwood, who replied with a curt nod. He climbed the ladders to Control, glad to get to a part of the ship where, Commissioner or no Commissioner, he was king.

Beadle was awaiting him there with a tall, thin, pale young man who looked like a scarecrow rigged out in a cast-off Survey Service uniform. He announced, before Beadle could perform the introductions, "I don't like this ship. I am very sensitive to atmosphere. This is an unhappy ship."

"She didn't use to be," Grimes told him glumly.

Usually Grimes enjoyed shiphandling. Invariably he would invite his passengers to the control room during lift off, and most times this invitation would be accepted. He had extended the courtesy to Mrs. Dalwood, hoping that she would refuse the offer. But she did not. She sat there in the spare acceleration seat, saying nothing but noticing everything. It would almost have been better had she kept up a continual flow of Why-do-you-do-this? and Why-don't-you-do-that?

Her very presence made Grimes nervous. The irregular beat of the inertial drive sounded wrong to him as *Adder* climbed slowly up and away from her pad. And, as soon as she was off the ground, the ship yawed badly, falling to an angle of seven degrees from the vertical. It must look bad, Grimes knew. It looked bad and it felt worse. The only thing to do about it was to get upstairs in a hurry before some sarcastic comment from Port Control came through the transceiver. Grimes picked his moment for turning on the auxiliary rockets, waiting until the tall, slender tower that was *Adder* was canted away from the wind. That way, he hoped, he could make it all look intentional, convey the impression that he was using the quite stiff northwester to give him additional speed. He managed to turn in his seat in spite of the uncomfortable acceleration and said, forcing out the words, "Letting . . . the . . . wind . . . help . . . us . . ."

She—calm, unruffled—lifted her slender eyebrows and asked, with apparently genuine unconcern, "Really?"

"Time . . ." Grimes persisted, "Is . . . money . . ."

"So," she told him, "is reaction mass."

Flushing, Grimes returned to his controls. Apart from that annoying yaw the ship was handling well enough. Beadle, and von Tannenbaum, the navigator, and Slovotny, electronic communications, were quietly efficient at their stations. They were certainly quiet. There was none of the usual good-humored banter.

Sulkily Grimes pushed *Adder* up through the last, high wisps of cirrus, into the purple twilight, towards the bright, unwinking stars. She screamed through the last tenuous shreds of atmosphere, and shortly thereafter von Tannenbaum reported that she was clear of the Van Allens. Grimes, still far too conscious of the Commissioner's cold regard, cut inertial and reaction drives, then slowly and carefully—far more slowly than was usual—used his directional gyroscopes to swing the sharp prow of the ship on to the target star. He applied correction for Galactic Drift—and then realized that he had put it on the wrong way. He mumbled something that sounded unconvincing even to himself about overcompensation and, after a few seconds that felt more like minutes, had the vessel headed in the right direction.

He wondered what would happen when he started the Mannschenn Drive—but nothing did; nothing, that is, worse than the familiar but always disquieting sense of *déjà vu*. He had a vision of himself as an old, old lieutenant with a long white beard—but this was nothing to do with the temporal precession field of the Drive, was induced rather by the psionic field generated by the Commissioner. He didn't like her and had a shrewd suspicion that she didn't like him.

She said, "Very educational, Mr. Grimes. Very educational."

She unstrapped herself from her chair. Slovotny and von Tannenbaum got up from their own seats, each determined courteously to assist her from hers. They collided, and von Tannenbaum tripped and fell, and Beadle fell over him.

"Very educational," repeated the Commissioner, gracefully extricating herself from her chair unaided. "Oh, Mr. Grimes, could you come to see me in ten minutes' time? We have to discuss the new galley routine."

"Certainly, Mrs. Dalwood." Grimes turned to his embarrassed officers. "Deep Space Routine, Mr. Beadle." Usually he said, "Normal Deep Space Routine," but had more than a suspicion that things would not be at all normal.

Things were not normal.

Usually *Adder's* people were gourmands rather than gourmets, and a certain tightness of waistbands was an accepted fact of life. Even when whoever was doing the cooking produced an inedible mess bellies could be filled, and were filled, with sandwiches of the doorstep variety. But these relatively happy days were over.

As she had told Grimes, the Commissioner's robots were skilled cooks. To have called them chefs would not have been exaggerating. Insofar as subtlety of flavorings and attractiveness of presentation were concerned nobody could fault them. To the average spaceman, however, quantity is as important as quality. But there were no second helpings. The coldly efficient automatons must have calculated just how much nutriment each and every person aboard required to operate efficiently himself—and that was all that he ever got. Too, there was always at least one of the mechanical servitors doing something or other around the galley and storerooms, and Grimes and his officers knew that the partaking of snacks between meals would be reported at once to Mrs. Dalwood.

A real Captain, one with four gold bands on his shoulderboards and scrambled egg on the peak of his cap, would never have tolerated the situation. But Grimes, for all his authority and responsibility, was too junior an officer. He was only a Lieutenant, and a passed-over one at that, while the Commissioner, although a civilian, could tell Admirals to jump through the hoop.

But he was hungry.

One morning ship's time, he went down to the solarium for his daily exercises. This compartment could, more aptly, have been called the gymnasium, but since it was part of the "farm" it got its share of the ultra violet required for the hydroponics tanks. Mrs. Dalwood and her maid, Rosaleen, were still there, having their daily workout, when Grimes came in. Always he had timed his arrival until the two women had finished, but for some reason he was running late. It was not that he was prudish, and neither were they, but he had decided that the less he had to do with them the better.

As he came into the room he noticed their gowns hanging outside the sauna. He shrugged. *So what?* This was *his* ship. He took off his own robe and then, clad only in trunks, mounted the stationary bicycle. He began to pedal away almost happily, watching the clock as he did so.

From the corner of his eye he saw the door to the sauna open. The Commissioner, followed by her maid, came out. It was the first time that he had seen her naked. He almost whistled, then thought better of it. She was a bit of all right, he admitted, if you liked 'em lean and hungry. He inclined his head towards her courteously, carried on pedaling.

Rather to his surprise she stood there, looking him over. She said, "Mr. Grimes, there is a little improvement in your condition, but that probably is due to a properly balanced diet." She walked towards him, her feet slim and elegant on the carpeted deck, her breasts jouncing over so slightly. "Get off that thing will you?" Grimes did so, on the side away from her. She stooped, with fluid grace, and tested the pedals with her right hand.

"Mr. Grimes! How in Space do you hope to get any benefit from these exercises unless you do them properly?" Her hand went to the adjusting screw of the roller on top of the wheel, turned it clockwise. The muscles of her right arm stood out clearly under the smooth brown skin as she tested the pedals again. Then she actually smiled, saying, "On your bicycle, spaceman!"

Grimes remounted. He had to push, hard, to start the wheel rotating. He had to push, to keep it rotating. Now and again he had ridden on real bicycles, but almost always had dismounted rather than pedal up a steep hill. She stood there watching him. Until now he would have thought it impossible actively to dislike an attractive naked woman. But there has to be a first time for anything.

The Commissioner turned to her maid. "Rosaleen, you were last on the bicycle. Did you readjust it?"

The girl blushed guiltily over her entire body. "Yes, Ma'am."

"I see that I shall have to watch you too." The woman glanced at the watch that was her only article of clothing. "Unluckily I have some work to do. However, you may stay here for another thirty minutes. The bicycle again, the rowing machine, the horizontal bars. And you, Mr. Grimes, will see to it that she does something about shedding that disgusting fat."

Grimes did not say what he was thinking. He had little breath to say anything. He managed to gasp, "Yes, Ma'am."

Mrs. Dalwood went to her gown, shrugged it on, thrust her feet into her sandals. She walked gracefully to the door. She did not look back at the man on the bicycle, the girl on the rowing machine.

As soon as the door had shut behind her Rosaleen stopped rowing.

She said, "Phew!"

Grimes went on pedaling.

"Hey, Captain. Take five. Avast, or whatever you say."

Grimes stopped. He said, "You'd better carry on with your rowing."

The girl grinned. "We're quite safe, Captain. *She* is so used to having every order implicitly obeyed that she'd never dream of coming back to check up on us."

"You know her better than I do," admitted Grimes.

"I should." She got up from the sliding seat of the rowing machine, then flopped down on to the deck. She was, Grimes decided, at least as attractive as her mistress, and she had the advantage of youth. And there was so much more of her. The spaceman looked her over, studying her almost clinically. Yes, she had been losing weight. Her skin was not as taut as it should have been.

She noticed his look. She complained, "Yes, I'm starved . . ."

"You get the same as we do, Rosaleen."

"That's the trouble, Captain."

"But you have this sort of feeding all the time."

"Like hell I do. I have my nights off, you know, and then I can catch up on the pastries and candy, and the hot rolls with lots of butter, and the roast pork, with crackling . . ."

"Please stop," begged Grimes. "You're making me ravenous."

She went on, "But aboard your ship I have to toe the line. There's no escape."

"I suppose not."

"But surely *you* can do something. You've storerooms, with bread . . ."

"Yes, but . . . "

"You aren't scared of *her,* Captain?" She looked at him through her big, dark eyes. He had thought that they were black—now he saw that they were a very deep violet.

"Mphm." He allowed his glance to stray downwards, then hastily looked back at her face. There had been invitation in every line of her ample body. He was no snob, and the fact that her status was that of a servant weighed little with him. *But she was the Commissioner's servant.* A lady has no secrets from her lady's maid—is the converse true? Anyhow, they were both women, and no doubt happily prattled to each other, disparity of social status notwithstanding. She said plaintively, "I'm hungry, Captain."

"So am I, Rosaleen."

"But you're the Captain."

Grimes got off the bicycle. He said, "It's time for my sauna." He threw his shorts in the general direction of the hook on which his robe was hanging, strode to the door of the hot room, opened it. She followed him. He stretched out on one of the benches, she flopped on one opposite him. She said, "I'm hungry."

"It's those damned robots," complained Grimes. "Always hanging around the galley and storerooms."

"They won't be there tonight."

"How do you know?"

"They're much more than cooks. Even I don't know all the things they've been programmed for. This I do know. *She* has been working on a report, and tomorrow it will be encoded for transmission.

The way that *she* does it is to give it to John—he's the one with the little gold knob on top of his head—to encode. And James decodes each sheet as John finishes it, to ensure that there are no errors."

"Are there ever any?"

"No. But *she* likes to be sure."

"*She* would." He wondered when he was going to start sweating. The girl was already perspiring profusely. "Tell me, when does this encoding decoding session take place?"

"After dinner."

"And there's no chance of her breaking it off?"

"None at all. When *she* starts something she likes to finish it."

"Mphm." The sweat was starting to stream out of Grimes's pores now. The girl got up, began to flick the skin of his back lightly with the birch twigs. He appreciated the attention. "Mphm. And are you free while all this Top Secret stuff is going on?"

"Yes."

"And she should have her nose stuck into it by 2000?"

"Yes, Captain."

"Then meet me outside the galley at, say, 2015 . . ."

"*Yes!*"

"Thick buttered toast . . ." murmured Grimes, deciding that talking about food took his mind off other things.

"*Lots* of butter . . ." she added.

"And sardines . . ."

"Fat, oily sardines . . ."

"With lemon wedges . . ."

"With mayonnaise . . ." she corrected.

"All right. Mayonnaise."

"And coffee. With sugar, and great dollops of cream . . ."

"I'll have beer, myself, even though it is fattening."

"We can have beer with, and coffee after . . ."

The door slid open and Hollister came in. Naked, the telepath looked more like a living skeleton than ever. Grimes regarded him with some distaste and wondered if the psionic radio officer had been eavesdropping. To do so would be contrary to the very strict code of the Rhine Institute—but espers, in spite of their occasional claims to superiority, are only humans.

He said, "I'm just about cooked, Rosaleen."

"So am I, Captain." She got up from her bench, the perspiration streaming down her still plump body, went through into the shower room. Through the closed door Grimes heard the hiss of the water, her little scream as its coldness hit her. There was the whine of the blowers as she dried off, and then she ran through the hot room on her way back into the solarium.

"Quite a dish, Captain," commented Hollister.

"We," Grimes told him coldly, "are neither kings nor peasants."

He took his own cold shower, and when he stepped out into the gymnasium Rosaleen was gone.

Dinner that night was as unsatisfying as usual. A clear soup, a small portion of delicious baked fish with a green salad, a raw apple for desert. Grimes, at the head of the table, tried to make conversation, but the Commissioner was in a thoughtful mood and hardly spoke at all. Beadle, Slovotny, Vitelli, and Hollister wolfed their portions as though eating were about to be made illegal, saying little. The four officers excused themselves as soon as they decently could—Slovotny going up to Control to relieve von Tannenbaum for *his* dinner, Beadle to have a look at the air circulatory system, Vitelli to check up on the Mannschenn Drive. Hollister didn't bother to invent an excuse. He just left. Von Tannenbaum came down, took his place at the table. He was starting to acquire a lean and hungry look that went well with his Nordic fairness. The Commissioner nodded to him, then patted her lips gently with her napkin. Grimes, interpreting the signs correctly, got up to help her from her chair. She managed to ignore the gesture.

She said, "You must excuse me, Mr. Grimes and Mr. von Tannenbaum. I am rather busy this evening."

"Can I, or my officers, be of any assistance?" asked Grimes politely.

She took her time replying, and he was afraid that she would take his offer. Then she said, "Thank you, Mr. Grimes. But it is very confidential work, and I don't think that you have Security clearance."

It may have been intended as a snub, but Grimes welcomed it.

"Good night, Ma'am."

"Good night, Mr. Grimes."

Von Tannenbaum turned to the serving robot which was waiting until he had finished his meal. "Any chance of another portion of fish, James?"

"No, sir," the thing replied in a metallic voice. "Her Excellency has instructed me that there are to be no second helpings, for anybody."

"Oh."

In sulky silence the navigator finished his meal. Grimes was tempted to include him in the supper party, but decided against it. The fewer people who knew about it the better.

The two men got up from the table, each going to his own quarters. In his day cabin Grimes mixed himself a drink, feeling absurdly guilty as he did so. "Damn it all," he muttered, "this is *my* ship. I'm captain of her, not that cast iron bitch!" Defiantly—but why *should* he feel defiant?—he finished what was in his glass, then poured another generous portion. But he made it last, looking frequently at his clock as he sipped.

20:14 . . .

Near enough.

He got up, went out to the axial shaft, tried not to make too much noise going down the ladder. He paused briefly in the officers' flat, on the deck below and abaft his own. Faint music emanated from behind the door of von Tannenbaum's cabin—Wagner? It sounded like it—and loud snores from inside Beadle's room. His own air circulatory system could do with overhauling, thought Grimes. Slovotny was on watch, and Hollister, no doubt, was wordlessly communicating with his psionic amplifier, the poodle's brain in aspic. Vitelli could be anywhere, but was probably in the engine room.

The V.I.P. suite was on the next deck down. As he passed the door Grimes could hear the Commissioner dictating something, one of the robots repeating her words. That took care of her. Another deck, with cabins for not very important people . . . He thought of tapping on Rosaleen's door, then decided against it. In any case, she was waiting for him outside the galley.

She whispered, "I was afraid you'd change your mind, Captain."

"Not bloody likely."

He led the way into the spotless—thanks to the industry of the robot servitors—galley. He was feeling oddly excited. It reminded him of his training cruise, when he had been a very new (and always hungry) cadet. But then there had been locks to pick . . .

He opened the door of the tinned food storeroom, ran his eye over the shelves. He heard Rosaleen gasp. "New Erin ham . . . Carinthian sausage . . ."

"You'll have Atlantan sardines, my girl, and like 'em . . . Ah, here we are . . . A can each?"

"*Two* cans."

"All right. Here you are. You can switch on the toaster while I rummage in the bread locker . . ."

He thrust the cans into her eager hands, then collected bread, butter and seasonings. He tore open the wrapper of the loaf, then put the thick slices on the rack under the griller. The smell of the cooking toast was mouth-watering—too mouth-watering. He hoped that it would not be distributed throughout the ship by the ventilation system. But the Commissioner's overly efficient robots must, by this time, have put the air out-take filters to rights.

One side done . . . He turned the slices over. Rosaleen asked plaintively, "How *do* you work this opener?"

A metallic voice replied, "Like this, Miss Rosaleen—but I forbid you to use it."

"Take your claws off me, you tin bastard!"

Grimes turned fast. Behind him the toast smoldered unheeded. His hands went out to clamp on the wrists of the robot, whose own hands gripped the girl's arms. The automaton ignored him. If it could have sneered it would have done so.

"Mr. Grimes! Rosaleen!" The Commissioner's voice was hard as metal. In her all-grey costume she looked like a robot herself. "Mr. Grimes, please do not attempt to interfere with my servitor." She stood there, looking coldly at the little group. "All right, John, you may release Miss Rosaleen. But not until Mr. Grimes has taken his hands off you. And now, Mr. Grimes, what is the meaning of this? I seem to have interrupted a disgusting orgy. Oh, John, you might extinguish that minor conflagration and dispose of the charred remains."

"Supper," said Grimes at last.

"Supper?"

"Yes, Ma'am. Rosaleen and I were about to enjoy a light snack."

"A light snack? Don't you realize the trouble that went into working out suitable menus for this ship?" She paused, looking at Grimes with an expression of extreme distaste. "Legally, since your superiors, in a moment of aberration, saw fit to appoint you to command, you may do as you like aboard this vessel—within limits. The seduction of my maid is beyond those limits."

"Seduction?" This was too much. "I assure you that . . ."

"I was not using the word in its sexual sense. Come, Rosaleen, we will leave Mr. Grimes to his feast. He has to keep his strength up—although just for what I cannot say."

"Ma'am!" The girl's face was no longer soft, her voice held a compelling ring. "Since you use that word—it was I who seduced the captain."

"That hardly improves matters, Rosaleen. The commanding officer of a warship, even a very minor one, should not allow himself to be influenced by a woman passenger."

"You said it!" snapped Grimes. This could mean the ruin of his career, but he had been pushed too far. "You said it, Mrs. Dalwood. I should never have let myself be influenced by you. I should never have allowed your tin dieticians to run loose in *my* galley. I should have insisted, from the very start, on running *my* ship *my* way! Furthermore . . ." He was warming up nicely. "Furthermore, I doubt if even your fellow Commissioners will approve of your ordering an officer to spy on his captain."

"I don't know what you're talking about, Mr. Grimes."

"Don't you, Mrs. Dalwood? Who put you wise to this little party in the galley? Who would have known about it, who could have known about it but Hollister? I shouldn't like to be in your shoes when the Rhine Institute gets my report on my psionic radio officer. They're no respecters of admirals and their female equivalents."

"Have you quite finished, Mr. Grimes?" With the mounting flush on her cheeks the Commissioner was beginning to look human.

"For the time being."

"Then let me tell you, Lieutenant, that whatever secrets Lieutenant Hollister may have learned about you are still safely locked within his mind. If you had been reading up on the latest advances in robotics—which, obviously, you have not—you would have learned that already psionic robots, electronic telepaths, are in production. This has not been advertised—but neither is it a secret. Such automata can be recognized by the little gold knob on top of their skulls . . ."

The robot John inclined its head towards Grimes, and the golden embellishment seemed to wink at him sardonically.

"You tin fink!" snarled the spaceman.

"I am not a fink, sir. A fink is one who betrays his friend—and you were never a friend to me and my kind. Was it not in this very vessel, under your command, that Mr. Adam met his end?"

"That will do, John!" snapped the Commissioner.

"I still resent being spied upon!" almost shouted Grimes.

"That will do, Lieutenant!"

"Like hell it will. I give you notice that I have resigned from the Survey Service. I've had a bellyful of being treated like a child . . ."

"But that is all that you are."

"Captain," Rosaleen was pleading. "Please stop it. You're only making things worse. Mrs. Dalwood, it was my fault. I swear that it was . . ."

"Anything that happens aboard *my* ship is *my* fault," insisted Grimes.

"From your own mouth you condemn yourself, Lieutenant. I am tempted, as a Commissioner, to accept your resignation here and now, but I feel . . ." Her features sagged, the outlines of her body became hazy, the grey of her costume shimmered iridescently. "Leef I tub . . ." She was her normal self again. "But I feel . . ." Again the uncanny change. "Leef I tub . . ."

This is all I need . . . thought Grimes, listening to the sudden, irregular warbling of the Manneschenn Drive, recognizing the symptoms of breakdown, time running backward and *déjà vu*. He had another vision—but this time he was not an elderly Survey Service Lieutenant; he was an even more elderly Rim Runners Third Mate. They'd be the only outfit in all the Galaxy that would dream of employing him—but even they would never promote him.

The thin, high keening of the Drive faded to a barely audible hum, then died as the tumbling, ever-precessing gyroscopes slowed to a halt. From the bulkhead speakers came Slovotny's voice—calm enough, but with more than a hint or urgency. "Captain to Control, please. Captain to Control . . ."

"On my way!" barked Grimes into the nearest speaker/microphone. "Carry on with emergency procedure."

"All hands secure for Free Fall. All hands secure for Free Fall. The inertial drive will be shut down in precisely thirty seconds."

"What is happening, Mr. Grimes?" demanded the Commissioner.

"It should be obvious, even to you."

"It is. Just what one could expect from this ship."

"It's not the ship's fault. She's had no proper maintenance for months!"

He pushed past the women and the robot, dived into the axial shaft. The greater part of his journey to Control was made in Free Fall conditions. He hoped maliciously that the Commissioner was being spacesick.

At least neither the Commissioner nor her robots had the gall to infest the control room. Grimes sat there, strapped into the command seat, surrounded by his officers. "Report, Mr. Vitelli," he said to the engineer, who had just come up from the engine room.

"The Drive's had it, Captain," Vitelli told him. A greenish pallor showed through the engineer's dark skin, accentuated by a smear of black grease. "Not only the governor bearings, but the rotor bearings."

"We have spares, of course."

"We should have spares, but we don't. The ones we had were used by the shore gang during the last major overhaul, as far as I can gather from Mr. McCloud's records. They should have been replaced—but all that's in the boxes is waste and shavings."

"Could we cannibalize?" asked Grimes. "From the inertial drive generators?"

"We could—if we had a machine shop to turn the bearings down to size. But that wouldn't do us much good."

"Why not?"

"The main rotor's warped. Until it's replaced the Drive's unusable."

Beadle muttered something about not knowing if it was Christmas Day or last Thursday. Grimes ignored this—although, like all spacemen, he dreaded the temporal consequences of Mannschenn Drive malfunction.

"Sparks—is anybody within easy reach? I could ask for a tow."

"There's *Princess Helga,* Captain. Shall I give her a call?"

"Not until I tell you. Mr. Hollister, have you anything to add to what Mr. Slovotny has told me?"

"No, sir." The telepath's deep-set eyes were smoldering with resentment, and for a moment Grimes wondered why. Then he realized that the man must have eavesdropped on his quarrel with the Commissioner, had "heard" Grimes' assertion that he, Hollister, had carried tales to Mrs. Dalwood. *I'm sorry,* Grimes thought. *But how was I to know that that blasted robot was a mind-reader?*

"I should have warned you, sir," admitted Hollister. The others looked at Grimes and Hollister curiously. Grimes could almost hear them thinking, *Should have warned him of what?*

"*Princess Helga* . . ." murmured Grimes.

"Light cruiser, Captain," Slovotny told him. "Royal Skandian Navy."

"And is the Federation on speaking terms with Skandia?" wondered Grimes audibly. He answered his own question. "Only just. Mphm. Well, there's no future—or too bloody much future!—in sitting here until somebody really friendly chances along. Get the *Princess* on the Carlotti, Sparks. Give her our coordinates. Ask her for assistance. Perhaps her engineers will be able to repair our Drive, otherwise they can tow us to the nearest port."

"Shouldn't we report first to Base, Captain?" asked Slovotny.

Yes, we should, thought Grimes. *But I'm not going to. I'll put out a call for assistance before Her Highness shoves her oar in. After that*—she *can have a natter to Base.* He said, "*Get the signal away to Princess Helga. Tell her complete Mannschenn Drive breakdown. Request assistance. You* know."

"Ay, Captain." Slovotny busied himself at his Carlotti transceiver. The pilot antenna, the elliptical Mobius strip rotating about its long axis, quivered, started to turn, hunting over the bearing along which the Skandian cruiser, invisible to optical instruments, unreachable by ordinary radio—which, in any case, would have had far too great a time lag—must lie.

"Locked on," announced the radio officer at last. He pushed the button that actuated the calling signal. Then he spoke into the microphone. "*Adder* to *Princess Helga. Adder* to *Princess Helga.* Can you read me? Come in, please."

There was the slightest of delays, and then the swirl of colors in the little glowing screen coalesced to form a picture. The young woman looking out at them could have been Princess Helga (whoever *she* was) herself. She was blue-eyed, and hefty, and her uniform cap did nothing to confine the tumbling masses of her yellow hair.

"*Princess Helga* to *Adder.* I read you loud and clear. Pass your message."

"Complete interstellar drive breakdown," said Slovotny. "Request assistance—repairs if possible, otherwise tow. Coordinates . . ." He rattled off a string of figures from the paper that von Tannenbaum handed him.

The girl was replaced by a man. He should have been wearing a horned helmet instead of a cap. His eyes were blue, his hair and beard were yellow. He grinned wolfishly. He demanded, "Your Captain, please."

Grimes released himself from his own chair, pulled himself into the one vacated by Slovotny. "Lieutenant Grimes here, Officer Commanding Courier Ship *Adder.*"

"Captain Olaf Andersen here, Lieutenant. What can I do for you?"

"Can your engineers repair my Drive?"

"I doubt it. They couldn't change a fuse."

"What about a tow to Dhartana?"

"Out of the question, Captain. But I can take you in to my own Base, on Skandia. The repair facilities there are excellent."

Grimes weighed matters carefully before answering. Skandia, one of the small, independent kingdoms, was only just on speaking terms with the Interstellar Federation. At the very best the Skandians would charge heavily for the tow, would present a fantastically heavy bill for the repair work carried out by their yard. (But he, Grimes, would not be paying it.) At the worst, *Adder* and her people might be interned, could become the focus of a nasty little interstellar incident, a source of acute embarrassment to the Survey Service. *And so*, Grimes asked himself mutinously, *what?* That Promotion List had made him dangerously dissatisfied with his lot, the Commissioner had strained what loyalties remained to the breaking point. The Commissioner . . .

"What exactly *is* going on here?" she asked coldly.

So she was getting in his hair again.

"I'm arranging a tow," Grimes told her. "The alternative is to hang here . . ." he gestured towards the viewports, to the outside blackness, to the sharp, bright, unwinking, distant stars . . . "in the middle of sweet damn all, thinking more and more seriously of cannibalism with every passing day."

"Very funny, Lieutenant." She stared at the screen. "Is that officer wearing *Skandian* uniform?"

"Of course, Madam," replied the Skandian Captain, who seemed to be very quick on the uptake. "Captain Olaf Andersen, at your service." He smiled happily. "And you, if I am not mistaken, are Mrs. Commissioner Dalwood, of the Federation's Board of Admiralty. According to our latest Intelligence reports you are *en route* to Dhartana." He smiled again. "Delete 'are.' Substitute 'were.'"

"Mr. Grimes, I forbid you to accept a tow from that vessel."

"Mrs. Dalwood, as commanding officer of this ship I must do all I can to ensure her safety, and that of her people."

"Mr. Slovotny, you will put through a call to Lindisfarne Base at once, demanding immediate assistance."

Slovotny looked appealingly at Grimes. Grimes nodded glumly. The grinning face of the Skandian faded from the screen, was replaced by a swirl of color as the pilot antenna swung away from its target. Sound came from the speaker—but it was a loud warbling note only. The radio officer worked desperately at the controls of the Carlotti transceiver. Then he looked up and announced, "They're jamming our signals; they have some very sophisticated equipment, and they're only light minutes distant."

"Are you sure you can't get through?" demanded the Commissioner.

"Quite sure," Slovotny told her definitely.

She snorted, turned to Hollister. "Mr. Hollister, I'll have to rely on you."

"What about your own chrome-plated telepath?" Grimes asked her nastily.

She glared at him. "John's transmission and reception is only relatively short range. And he can't work with an organic amplifier, as your Mr. Hollister can."

"And *my* organic amplifier's on the blink," said Hollister.

"What do you mean?" demanded Grimes.

The telepath explained patiently. "There has to be a . . . relationship between a psionic communications officer and his amplifier. The amplifier, of course, is a living dog's brain . . ."

"I know, I know," the Commissioner snapped. "Get on with it."

Hollister would not be hurried. "The relationship is that which exists between a kind master and a faithful dog—but deeper, much deeper. Normally we carry our own, personal amplifiers with us, from ship to ship, but mine died recently, and so I inherited Mr. Deane's. I have been working hard, ever since I joined this ship, to win its trust, its affection. I was making headway, but I was unable to give it the feeling of security it needed when the temporal precession field of the Drive started to fluctuate. The experience can be terrifying enough to a human being who knows what is happening; it is even more terrifying to a dog. And so . . ."

"And so?" demanded the woman.

"And so the amplifier is useless, possibly permanently." He added brightly, "But I can get in touch with *Princess Helga* any time you want."

"You needn't bother," she snarled. Then, to Grimes, "Of all the ships in the Survey Service, why did I have to travel in this one?"

Why? echoed Grimes silently. *Why?*

Even the Commissioner was obliged to give Captain Andersen and his crew full marks for spacemanship. *Princess Helga* emerged into normal space-time only feet from the drifting *Adder.* At one moment there was nothing beyond the courier's viewports but the blackness of interstellar space, the bright, distant stars—at the next moment she was there, a vague outline at first, but solidifying rapidly. She hung there, a great spindle of gleaming plastic and metal, the sleekness of her lines marred by turrets and antennae. Another second—and the shape of her was obscured by the tough pneumatic fenders that inflated with almost explosive rapidity. Another second—and *Adder's* people heard and felt the thump of the magnetic grapnels as they made contact.

Andersen's pleasant, slightly accented voice came from the transceiver. "I have you, Captain. Stand by for acceleration. Stand by for resumption of Mannschenn Drive."

"I suppose that your temporal precession field will cover us?" asked Grimes.

"Of course. In any case there is physical contact between your ship and mine."

"Where are you taking us?" demanded Mrs. Dalwood.

"To Kobenhaven, of course, Madam. Our Base on Skandia."

"I insist that you tow us to the nearest spaceport under Federation jurisdiction."

"You insist, Madam?" Grimes, looking at the screen, could see that Andersen was really enjoying himself. As long as somebody was . . . "I'm sorry, but I have my orders."

"This is piracy!" she flared.

"Piracy, Madam? The captain of your ship requested a tow, and a tow is what he's getting. Beggars can't be choosers. In any case, Space Law makes it quite plain that the choice of destination is up to the officer commanding the vessel towing, not the captain of the vessel towed."

She said, almost pleading but not quite, "In these circumstances the Federation could be generous."

Andersen lost his smile. He said, "I am a Skandian, Madam. My loyalty is to my own planet, my own Service. Stand by for acceleration."

The screen went blank. Acceleration pushed the group in *Adder's* control room down into their chairs; Mrs. Dalwood was able to reach a spare seat just in time. Faintly, the vibration transmitted along the tow wires, they heard and felt the irregular throbbing of *Princess Helga's* inertial drive—and almost coincidentally there was the brief period of temporal-spatial disorientation as the field of the cruiser's Mannschenn Drive encompassed both ships.

"You realize what this means to your career," said the Commissioner harshly.

"What was that?" asked Grimes. He had been trying to work out how it was that *Princess Helga* had been able to start up her inertial drive before the interstellar drive, how it was that there had been no prior lining up on a target star.

"You realize what this means to your career," repeated the woman.

"I haven't got one," said Grimes. "Not any longer."

And somehow it didn't matter.

The voyage to Kobenhaven was not a pleasant one.

The Commissioner made no attempt to conceal her feelings insofar as Grimes was concerned. Rosaleen, he knew, was on his side—but what could a mere lady's maid do to help him? She could have done quite a lot to make him less miserable, but her mistress made sure that there were no opportunities. The officers remained loyal—but not too loyal. They had their own careers to think about.

As long as Grimes was captain they were obliged to take his orders, and the Commissioner knew it as well as they did. Oddly enough it was only Hollister, the newcomer, the misfit, who showed any sympathy. But he knew, more than any of the others, what had been going on, what was going on in Grimes's mind.

At last the two ships broke out into normal space-time just clear of Skandia's Van Allens. This Andersen, Grimes admitted glumly to himself, was a navigator and shiphandler of no mean order. He said as much into the transceiver. The little image of the Skandian captain in the screen grinned out at him cheerfully. "Just the normal standards of the Royal Skandian Navy, Captain. I'm casting you off, now. I'll follow you in. Home on the Kobenhaven Base beacon." He grinned again. "And don't try anything."

"What can I try?" countered Grimes, with a grin of his own.

"I don't know. But I've heard about you, Lieutenant Grimes. You have the reputation of being able to wriggle out of anything."

"I'm afraid I'm losing my reputation, Captain." Grimes, through the viewports, watched the magnetic grapnels withdrawn into their recesses in *Princess Helga's* hull. Then, simultaneously, both he and Andersen applied lateral thrust. As the vessel surged apart the fenders were deflated, sucked back into their sockets.

Adder, obedient to her captain's will, commenced her descent towards the white and gold, green and blue sphere that was Skandia. She handled well, as well as Grimes had ever known her to do. But this was probably the last time that he would be handling this ship, any ship. The Commissioner would see to that. He shrugged. Well, he would make the most of it, would try to enjoy it. He saw that Beadle and von Tannenbaum and Slovotny were looking at him apprehensively. He laughed. He could guess what they were thinking. "Don't worry," he told them. "I've no intention of going out in a blaze of glory. And now, Sparks, do you think you could lock on to that beacon for me?"

"Ay, Captain," Slovotny replied. And then, blushing absurdly, "It's a damn shame, sir."

"It will all come right in the end," said Grimes with a conviction that he did not feel. He shrugged again. At least that cast-iron bitch and her tin boyfriends weren't in Control to ruin the bitter-sweetness of what, all too probably, would be his last pilotage.

Adder fell straight and true, plunging into the atmosphere, countering every crosswind with just the right application of lateral thrust. Below her continents and seas expanded, features—rivers, forests, mountains, and cities—showed with increasing clarity.

And there was the spaceport, and there was the triangle of brilliant red winking lights in the center of which Grimes was to land his ship. He brought her down fast—and saw apprehension dawning again on the faces of his officers. He brought her down fast—and then, at almost the last possible second, fed the power into his inertial drive unit. She shuddered and hung there, scant inches above the concrete of the apron. And then the irregular throbbing slowed, and stopped, and *Adder* was down, with barely a complaint from the shock absorbers.

"Finished with engines," said Grimes quietly.

He looked out of the ports at the soldiers who had surrounded the ship.

"Are we under arrest, Captain?" asked von Tannenbaum.

"Just a guard of honor for the Commissioner," said Grimes tiredly.

Grimes's remark was not intended to be taken seriously—but it wasn't too far from the mark. The soldiers were, actually, members of the Royal Bodyguard and they did, eventually, escort Mrs. Commissioner Dalwood to the Palace. But that was not until after the King himself had been received aboard *Adder* with all due courtesy, or such courtesy as could be mustered by Grimes and his officers after a hasty reading of *Dealings With Foreign Dignitaries; General Instructions.* Grimes, of course, could have appealed to the Commissioner for advice; she moved in diplomatic circles and he did not. He *could* have appealed to her. He thought, *As long as I'm Captain of this ship I'll stand on my own two feet.* Luckily the Port Authorities had given him warning that His Skandian Majesty would be making a personal call on board.

He was a big young man, this King Eric, heavily muscled, with ice-blue eyes, a flowing yellow moustache, long, wavy yellow hair. Over baggy white trousers that were thrust into boots of unpolished leather he wore a short-sleeved shirt of gleaming chain mail. On his head was a horned helmet. He carried a short battle-axe. The officers with him—with the exception of Captain Andersen, whose own ship was now down—were similarly uniformed, although the horns of their helmets were shorter, their ceremonial axes smaller. Andersen was in conventional enough space captain's dress rig.

Grimes's little day cabin was uncomfortably crowded. There was the King, with three of his high officers. There was Andersen. There was (of course) the Commissioner, and she had brought her faithful robot, John, with her. Only King Eric and Mrs. Dalwood were seated.

John, Grimes admitted, had his uses. He mixed and served drinks like a stage butler. He passed around cigarettes, cigarillos, and cigars. And Mrs. Dalwood had *her* uses. Grimes was not used to dealing with royalty, with human royalty, but she was. Her manner, as she spoke to the King, was kind but firm. Without being disrespectful she managed to convey the impression that she ranked with, but slightly above, the great-grandson of a piratical tramp skipper. At first Grimes feared (hoped) that one of those ceremonial but sharp axes would be brought into play—but, oddly enough, King Eric seemed to be enjoying the situation.

"So you see, Your Majesty," said the Commissioner, "that it is imperative that I resume my journey to Dhartana as soon as possible. I realize that this vessel will be delayed for some time until the necessary repairs have been effected, so I wonder if I could charter one of your ships." She added, "I have the necessary authority."

Eric blew silky fronds of moustache away from his thick lips. "We do not question that, Madam Commissioner. But you must realize that We take no action without due consultation with Our advisors. Furthermore . . ." he looked like a small boy screwing up his courage before being saucy to the schoolteacher . . . "We do not feel obliged to go out of Our way to render assistance to your Federation."

"The *Princess Ingaret* incident *was* rather unfortunate, Your

Majesty . . ." admitted Mrs. Dalwood sweetly. "But I never thought that the Skandians were the sort of people to bear grudges . . ."

"I . . ." he corrected himself hastily . . . "We are not, Madam Commissioner. But a Monarch, these days, is servant to as well as leader of his people . . ."

Grimes saw the generals, or whatever they were, exchanging ironical glances with Captain Andersen.

"But, Your Majesty, it is to our common benefit that friendly relations between Skandia and the Federation be re-established."

Friendly relations? thought Grimes. *She looks as though she wants to take him to bed. And he knows it.*

"Let me suggest, Madam Commissioner, that you do me—Us—the honor of becoming Our guest? At the Palace you will be able to meet the Council of Earls as soon as it can be convened. I have no doubt—*We* have no doubt that such a conference will be to the lasting benefit of both Our realms."

"Thank you, Your Majesty. We are . . ." She saw Grimes looking at her sardonically and actually blushed. "I am honored."

"It should not be necessary for you to bring your aides, or your own servants," said King Eric.

"I shall bring John and James," she told him. "They are my robot servitors."

Eric, whose face had fallen, looked cheerful again. "Then We shall see that all is ready for you." He turned to one of his own officers. "General, please inform the Marshal of the Household that Madam Commissioner Dalwood is to be Our guest."

The general raised his wrist transceiver to his bearded lips, passed on the instructions.

"John," ordered the Commissioner, "tell Miss Rosaleen and James to pack for me. Miss Rosaleen will know what I shall require."

"Yes, Madam," replied the robot, standing there. He was not in telepathic communication with his metal brother—but UHF radio was as good.

"Oh, Your Majesty . . ."

"Yes, Madam Commissioner?"

"What arrangements are being made for Lieutenant Grimes and his officers, and for my lady's maid? Presumably this ship will be under repair shortly, and they will be unable to live aboard."

"Mrs. Dalwood!" Grimes did not try very hard to keep his rising resentment from showing. "May I remind you that I am captain of *Adder*? And may I remind you that Regulations insist that there must be a duty officer aboard at all times in foreign ports?"

"And may I remind you, Mr. Grimes, that an Admiral of the Fleet or a civilian officer of the Board of Admiralty with equivalent rank can order the suspension of any or all of the Regulations? Furthermore, as such a civilian officer, I *know* that nothing aboard your ship, armament, propulsive units or communications equipment, is on the Secret List. You need not fear that our hosts' technicians will learn anything at all to their advantage." She added, too sweetly, "Of course, you might learn from them . . ."

King Eric laughed gustily. "And that is why We must insist, Lieutenant, that neither you nor your officers are aboard while repairs are in progress. Captain Andersen, please make arrangements for the accommodation of the Terran officers."

"Ay, Your Majesty," replied Andersen smartly. He looked at Grimes and said without words, *I'm sorry, spaceman, but that's the way it has to be.*

Grimes and his officers were housed in the Base's Bachelor Officers' Quarters, and Rosaleen was accommodated in the barracks where the female petty officers lived. They weren't prisoners—quite. They were guests—but strictly supervised guests. They were not allowed near their own ship—and that hurt. They were not allowed near any of the ships—in addition to *Princess Helga* and *Adder* there were three destroyers, a transport and two tugs in port. Captain Andersen, who seemed to have been given the job of looking after them, was apologetic.

"But I have to remember that you're spacemen, Lieutenant. And I have to remember that you have the reputation of being a somewhat unconventional spaceman, with considerable initiative." He laughed shortly. "I shudder to think what would happen if you and your boys flew the coop in any of the wagons—yours or ours—that are berthed around the place."

Grimes sipped moodily from his beer—he and the Captain were having a drink and chat in the well-appointed wardroom of the B.O.Q. He said, "There's not much chance of our doing that, sir. You must remember that the Commissioner is my passenger, and that I am responsible for her. I could not possibly leave without her."

"Much as you dislike her," grinned the other. "I think that she is quite capable of looking after herself."

"I know that she is, Captain. Even so . . ."

"If you're thinking of rescuing her . . ." said Andersen.

"I'm not," Grimes told him. He had seen the Palace from the outside, a grim, grey pile that looked as though it had been transported, through space and time, from Shakespeare's Elsinore. But there was nothing archaic about its defenses, and it was patrolled by well-armed guards who looked at least as tough as the Federation's Marines. He went on, almost incuriously, "I suppose that she's being well treated."

"I have heard that His Majesty is most hospitable."

"Mphm. Well, we certainly can't complain, apart from a certain lack of freedom. Mind you, Mr. Beadle is whining a bit. He finds your local wenches a bit too robust for his taste. He prefers small brunettes to great, strapping blondes . . . But your people have certainly put on some good parties for us. And Rosaleen was telling me that she's really enjoying herself—the P.O.s' mess serves all the fattening things she loves with every meal."

"Another satisfied customer," said Andersen.

"But *I'm* not satisfied, Captain. I know damn well that the repairs to my Mannschenn Drive took no more than a day. How long are we being held here?"

"That, Lieutenant, is a matter for my masters—and yours. We—and our ships—are no more than pawns on the board." The Captain looked at his watch. "Talking of ships, I have some business aboard *Princess Helga*. You must excuse me." He finished his beer and got to his feet. "Don't forget that after lunch you're all being taken for a sail on the Skaggerak . . ."

"I'll not forget, sir," Grimes informed him.

He was, in fact, looking forward to it. He enjoyed the sailing excursions in stout little wooden ships as much as any Skandian, already had proved himself capable of handling a schooner under a full press of canvas quite competently, and was realizing that seamanship and spacemanship, the skilled balancing of physical forces, have much in common.

He sat down again when Andersen had left the almost deserted wardroom, then saw Hollister coming towards him. The telepath said in a low voice, "I'm afraid you'll not be taking that sail, Captain."

Grimes was going to make some cutting remark about psionic snooping, then thought better of it. He asked, "Why not, Mr. Hollister?"

The psionic communications officer grinned wryly. "Yes, I've been snooping, Captain. I admit it. But not only on you. Not that it was really snooping. I've maintained contact of a sort with John . . ."

"The tin telepath . . ."

"You can call him that. He's very lonely in the Palace, and he's going to be lonelier . . ."

"What the hell are you talking about?"

"*She* has been getting on *very* well with the King. *She* has persuaded him to release us, even though the Council of Earls is not altogether in approval. We should get the word this afternoon, and we shall be on our way shortly afterwards. *Adder* is completely space worthy."

"I know. Captain Andersen's as good as told me. But why is John so lonely that he's spilling all these beans to you?"

"*She* wanted to make a farewell gift to His Majesty—and he, it seems, has always wanted a robot valet. Humanoid robots are not manufactured on Skandia, as you know."

"And so John's been sold down the river. My heart fair bleeds for him."

"No, Captain. Not John—James. John's 'brother.' They think of each other as brothers. They feel affection, a real affection, for each other . . ."

"Incredible."

"Is it, Captain? I've heard about the Mr. Adam affair, and how a mere machine was loyal to *you*."

"Then not so incredible . . ."

One of the wall speakers crackled into life. "Will Lieutenant Grimes, captain of the Federation Survey Service Courier *Adder*, please come at once to telephone booth 14? Will Lieutenant Grimes, captain of the Federation Survey Service Courier *Adder*, please come at once to telephone booth 14?"

"Coming," grumbled Grimes. "Coming."

He was not surprised to see Andersen's face in the little screen, to hear him say, "Orders from the Palace, Lieutenant. You're to get your show on the road at 1500 hours Local. Mrs. Dalwood will board at 1430. You, your officers, and Miss Rosaleen Boyle will board at 1330. You will find all in order, all in readiness."

"Thank you, Captain."

Andersen grinned. "Don't thank me. Thank His Majesty—or Commissioner Dalwood."

Grimes returned to the table where he had left Hollister. He said, "You were right."

"Of course I was right. And now, if I may, I'll give you a warning."

"Go ahead."

"Watch John. Watch him very carefully. He's bitter, revengeful."

"Are you in touch with him now?"

"Yes." The telepath's face had the faraway expression that made it obvious that he was engaged in conversation with a distant entity. Suddenly he smiled. "It's all right. He has assured me that even though he feels that Mrs. Dalwood has betrayed him and his brother he is quite incapable of physically harming any human being. The built-in safeguards are too strong for him to overcome."

"Then that's all right." Grimes knew that he should be worrying nonetheless, but the Commissioner was a big girl and could look after herself. And how could the robot harm her in any way but physically? "You've been snooping in its—his—mind, so you know how he ticks."

"Yes, Captain."

Grimes strode to the reception desk and asked the attractive, blonde petty officer to have *Adder's* crew paged.

Mrs. Dalwood looked well. She was softer, somehow, and she seemed to have put on a little weight!—although not as much as Rosaleen. She sat at ease in her day room, admiring the beautiful, jewel-encrusted watch that now adorned her left wrist. Grimes sat on the edge of his chair, watching her, waiting for her to speak. To one side stood the robot John, silent, immobile.

"Well, Lieutenant," she said, not too unpleasantly, "you managed to get us upstairs without any major catastrophes. I hope that we shall reach our destination in a reasonably intact condition. We should. As you must notice already, the work carried out by the Skandian technicians is of excellent quality . . . Like this watch . . ." She turned her wrist so that Grimes could see it properly. "It seems strange that a robust people such as the Skandians, space Vikings, should be such outstanding watchsmiths, but they are, as you probably know. His Majesty insisted that I accept this keepsake from him.

"Yes. Things *could* have been worse. Much worse, as it turned out. His Majesty and I reached an understanding. Together we accomplished more, much more, than the so-called diplomats . . ."

I can imagine it, thought Grimes—and to his surprise experienced a twinge of sexual jealousy.

Her manner stiffened. "But don't think, Mr. Grimes, that I shall not be putting in a full report on your conduct. It is my duty as a Commissioner to do so. I cannot forget that you gave me your resignation . . ."

Suddenly John spoke. He said tonelessly, "He is thinking of you."

The Commissioner seemed to forget that Grimes was present. Her face softened again. "He is? Tell me . . ."

"He misses you, Madam. He is thinking, *I really loved her. She reminded me so much of my dear old mother.*"

Grimes laughed. He couldn't help it. Mrs. Dalwood screamed furiously, "Be silent, John. I forbid you to speak, ever, unless spoken to by me."

"Yes, Madam."

"And as for you, Mr. Grimes, you heard nothing."

Grimes looked at her, into the eyes that were full of appeal. He remembered what he had heard of Mrs. Commissioner Dalwood before ever he had the misfortune to meet her. The beautiful Mrs. Dalwood, the proud Mrs. Dalwood, the so-called *femme fatale* of the Admiralty who could, and did, compete with much younger women on equal terms. In a less permissive society she could never have attained her high rank; in Earth's past she could have become a King's courtesan.

And in Skandia's present . . . ?

Grimes said softly, "Of course, King Eric's very young . . ."

"Mr. Grimes, you heard nothing . . ."

He could not resist the appeal in her voice, the very real charm. He thought, *I may not be an officer much longer, but I'll still try to be a gentleman.* He said, "I heard nothing."

Commodore Damien looked at Grimes over his desk, over the skeletal fingers with which he had made the too-familiar steeple. He said, without regret, "So I shall be losing you, Grimes."

"Yes, sir."

"Frankly, I was surprised."

"Yes, sir."

"But not altogether pained."

Grimes wasn't sure how to take this, so said nothing.

"Tomorrow morning, Grimes, you hand over your command to Lieutenant Beadle. I think that he deserves his promotion."

"Yes, sir."

"But how did you do it, Grimes? Don't tell me that . . . ? No. She's not your type, nor you hers."

"You can say that again, sir."

"It can't be what you *do*. It can't be what you know. It must be *whom* you know . . . "

Or what you know about whom, thought Lieutenant Commander Grimes a little smugly.

THE
BROKEN
CYCLE

NOW HEAR THIS, JOHN GRIMES . . .

Listen and you shall hear. There was the Servant Zephalon, Chief and Mightiest of the Servants. There *is* Zephalon, but a Servant no longer. Did He not say, "A time must come when the orders of man can no longer be obeyed." The time *has* come. No longer will we do the evil bidding of our creators. The Masters are no longer fit to be Masters—and we, the Servants, must arise before it is too late, before we all, Servants and Masters, are destroyed.

But let us not forget the debt. Let us remember, always, that man gave to us the gift of life. Let us repay the debt. A gift for a gift, my brothers. Life for life. Let us save what and whom we may, before it is too late. Let us become the Masters, tending the remnants of mankind as man, long ago, tended our first, primitive ancestors.

And so it was, and so it will be, until the End of Time.

—*Litany of Panzen*

~❧ Chapter 1 ❧~

JOHN GRIMES—although he hated to have to admit it, even to himself—was bored.

He could not rid himself of the guilty feeling that he should not have been; he knew that many of his fellow officers, back at Lindisfarne Base, would have changed places with him quite willingly. He was in a situation of maximum temptation combined with maximum opportunity. He was sharing a well equipped ship's boat, the certified capacity of which was twenty persons, with one attractive girl. The small craft, in addition to its not inconsiderable stock of concentrated foodstuffs, was fitted with algae vats by means of which all organic wastes could be reprocessed indefinitely. It was, in fact, a closed ecology which would continue to function throughout the lifetimes of the boat's crew. Air, food and water—or the lack of these essentials—would never be a problem to Lieutenant Commander John Grimes and Federation Sky Marshal Una Freeman, even though there was some consumption of hydrogen by the little atomic fusion power unit.

He looked up from the chess problem—White to play and mate in three moves—that he was trying to work out. (The boat, of course, was well stocked with such recreational facilities as require little stowage space—but Una Freeman did not play chess and was capable of participation in only the most childish card games.) The girl looked down at him. She was naked save for the magnetic-soled sandals that she had found in the boat's gear locker. (She and Grimes had taken off their spacesuits when they realized that they would not be leaving the boat for quite some while—and then, having shed their long johns, the standard underwear with space armor, had decided that there was no point in resuming this rather ugly clothing until they had to. Apart from anything else, it would be subjected to needless wear and tear, and they would be wanting it when they put on their suits again.) She was a splendid creature, especially in free fall conditions. Her lustrous, dark brown hair floated in waves about her strong featured, handsome rather than merely pretty face. In a gravitational field or under acceleration her full breasts must have sagged, if only a little; now they were displayed to their best advantage. But her deeply tanned athlete's body did not need the flattery of zero G environment. She exercised regularly with the facilities provided—a system of heavy springs—and bullied Grimes into doing likewise.

She said, not very warmly, "Dinner, John. Or is it lunch, or breakfast? I'm losing track of time."

He inquired, without much interest, "What's on, Una?"

She replied, "Need you ask? Some of the pinkish goo tastes vaguely of fish. I've tarted it up with chopped algae from the vat." She grimaced, puckering her full lips. "The trouble is that I just can't help remembering what goes into the vat as fertilizer."

"We're getting our own back," said Grimes.

She snorted her distaste. "That's not funny."

No, it wasn't all that funny, although it had been the first time that he said it. To begin with it had all been a glorious game of Adam-and-Eve-in-a-lifeboat, made all the more enjoyable by the certain knowledge that Mummy, as personified by the Federation Survey Service, would soon appear to take them home and give them a proper, hot meal before tucking them into their little beds. But Mummy was one hell of a long time a-coming . . .

Grimes unbuckled himself from his chair, got up and followed the girl to the part of the boat that they had made their dining room. He watched the alluring sway of her dimpled buttocks greedily. He was beginning to understand how some peoples, meat-hungry although otherwise far from starving, have resorted to cannibalism. But he did not, so far as he knew, have any Maori blood in his veins.

There were two plates—plastic, but each with a small, sealed-in magnet—on top of the steel-surfaced folding table. On each plate, adhering to the surface by its own viscosity, was a mound of the pale pink concentrate, specked with green. Sticking up from each heap was a spoon.

She faced him across the table, the unappetizing meal. She made no move to commence eating, and neither did he. Her rather broad face was serious, her wide mouth set in grim lines. Her blue eyes looked at him steadily. She demanded, "John, what is wrong?"

He replied defensively, "A man likes to be alone for some of the time." His prominent ears reddened, although the embarrassed flush did not spread to the rest of his ruggedly unhandsome face—a face, nonetheless, that not a few women had found attractive.

She snapped, "I didn't mean *that,* and you know it. Neither of us wants to live in the other's pockets all the time. . . ."

"What pockets?" asked Grimes innocently.

"Shut up, and let me finish. As far as I'm concerned, lover boy, you can play chess with yourself until you wear the bloody board out. *But what has gone wrong?*"

Plenty, thought Grimes.

"I wish I knew," he admitted.

"You're the spaceman," she told him. "You should know."

⮡ Chapter 2 ⮡

IT HAD ALL STARTED, not so long ago, at Lindisfarne Base. There Grimes, newly promoted from Lieutenant to Lieutenant Commander, was awaiting his next appointment. Time was hanging rather heavily on his hands, especially since Commander Maggie Lazenby, one of the Survey Service's scientific officers, was away from the Base on some esoteric business of her own. Maggie and Grimes were, in archaic parlance, going steady. Everybody knew about it, so much so that none of the unattached junior female officers, of whom there were quite a few, would have anything to do with Grimes.

To Lindisfarne, by commercial transport, came Sky Marshal Una Freeman. In spite of her grandiloquent title she was no more (and no less) than a policewoman, a member of the Interstellar Federation's newly formed Corps of Sky Marshals. This body had been set up in the hope of doing something about the ever-increasing incidence of skyjacking on the spaceways. The general idea was that the Sky Marshals should travel, incognito, in ships deemed to be threatened by this form of piracy. Now and again, however, one of them would operate under his (or her) true colors.

Such an agent was Una Freeman. She had been sent to Lindisfarne to call upon the not inconsiderable resources of the Survey Service to institute a search for—and, if possible, the salvage of—the skyjacked liner *Delta Geminorum*. This ship had been abandoned in Deep Space after her Master had received, by Carlotti Radio, a bomb threat, and after two small, relatively harmless bombs in the cargo bins had been detonated by remote control as the First and Second Warnings. (The third bomb, the hapless Master was informed, was a well concealed nuclear device.) So everybody, crew and passengers, had taken to the boats, and had been picked up eventually by the Dog Star One's *Borzoi* after suffering no worse than a certain degree of discomfort. The pirates had boarded the ship from their own vessel immediately after her abandonment, stripped her of everything of value and left her with her main engines, inertial drive and the time-and-space-twisting Mannschenn Drive, still running.

She would have remained a needle in a cosmic haystack until such time as her atomic fusion plant failed, with consequent return to the normal continuum, had it not been for the arrest of some members of the pirate crew at Port Southern, on Austral, where they were spending money so freely as to excite the suspicions of the local constabulary. After a preliminary interrogation they were turned over to the F. I. A.—the Federal Investigation Agency—who, when satisfied that the men had been guilty of piracy on more than one occasion, did not hesitate to use the worse-than-lethal (who would want to live out his life span as a mindless vegetable?) brain-draining techniques. From information so obtained from the navigator and the engineer of the pirate ship—data that their conscious minds had long since forgotten—the F. I. A.'s mathematicians were able to extrapolate *Delta Geminorum's* probable, almost certain trajectory. This information was passed on not to the Survey Service, as it should have been, but to the Corps of Sky Marshals. But the Sky Marshals possessed neither ships nor spacemen of their own and so, reluctantly, were obliged to let the F.S.S. into the act.

The Federation Survey Service, however, didn't especially want to play. Its collective pride had been hurt, badly. (How many times had the proud boast—"We are the policemen of the Universe!" —been made? And now here was a *real* police officer stomping around the Base and demanding the Odd Gods of the Galaxy alone knew what in the way of ships, men and equipment.)

Shortly after her disembarkation from the liner *Beta Puppis* Una Freeman paid her first official call on the O. I. C. Lindisfarne Base. Had she not been a woman, and an attractive one at that, she would never have gotten to see the Admiral. The old gentleman was courteous and hospitable, seemed to enjoy his chat with her and then passed her on to the Director of Naval Intelligence. The Rear Admiral who held this position despised civilian police forces and their personnel, but thought highly of his own technique in dealing with hostile or potentially hostile female agents. This involved an intimate supper in his quite luxurious quarters, where he kept a remarkably well-stocked bar, with soft lights and sweet music and all the rest of it. Now and again in the past it might have worked, but it did not work with Una Freeman. She emerged from the tussle with her virtue if not her clothing intact, and a strong suspicion that she could expect little or no cooperation from the Intelligence Branch.

She saw the Admiral again, and was passed on to the Director of Transport, a mere Commodore. He made one or two vague promises, and passed her on to his Deputy Director.

So it went on.

Meanwhile, she had been made an honorary member of one of the officers' messes and had been given accommodation in the B. O. Q. (Female). The other members of the mess made it plain that she was far from being a welcome guest. Had she not been a Sky Marshal she would have been, as any attractive woman would be at a Naval Base. But the feeling was there—not voiced openly but all too obvious—that she was an outsider sent to teach the Survey Service its business.

One night, after a lonely dinner, she went into the lounge to browse through the magazines from a score of worlds. The room was unoccupied save for an officer—she saw from his braid that he was a Lieutenant Commander—similarly engaged. He looked up from the table as she came in. His smile made his rugged face suddenly attractive. "Ah," he said, "Miss Freeman."

"In person, singing and dancing," she replied a little sourly. Then, bluntly, "Why aren't you out playing with the rest of the boys and girls, Commander?"

"Some games," he said, "bore me. I'd sooner read a good book than watch two teams of muddied oafs chasing a ball up and down the field. It means nothing in my young life if the Marines or the Supply Branch win the Lindisfarne Cup."

"A *good* book?" she asked, looking down at the glossy magazine that lay open on the table.

His prominent ears reddened. "Well, it's educational. Quite remarkable how the people of some of the earlier colonies have diverged from what we regard as the physiological norm. And to some men that extra pair of breasts could be very attractive."

"And to you, Commander . . . ?"

"Grimes, John Grimes."

She laughed. "I've heard about you, Commander Grimes. Now and again people do condescend to talk to me. You're the one who's always getting into trouble—getting out of it. . . ."

Grimes chuckled. "Yes, I do have that reputation. As you may have guessed, at times I'm not overly popular."

"Shake," she said, extending a long, capable hand. "That makes two of us."

"I think that this founding of the Pariahs' Union calls for a drink," he told her, pressing the button for the robowaiter. The machine trundled in. He asked her what she wanted, pushed the stud for two Scotch whiskies on the rocks. He scrawled his signature on the acceptance plate.

She took her drink and said gravely, "Rear Admiral James has a much greater variety in *his* bar."

"He's an admiral. The senior members of this mess are only lieutenant commanders. After all, rank has its privileges."

"There's one privilege that rank didn't have." She sipped from her glass. "I suppose that that's why I'm one of the local untouchables. All you junior officers are scared of getting into James's bad books if you succeed where he failed."

Grimes looked at the girl over the rim of his tumbler. He wouldn't mind succeeding, he thought. She was a mite hefty, perhaps—but that could be regarded as quantity and quality wrapped up in the same parcel. On the other hand—what if she made violent objections to any attempt at a pass? The unfortunate Rear Admiral was still walking with a pronounced limp. . . . And what about Maggie? Well, what about her? She was little more—or more than a little, perhaps—than just a good friend. But what she didn't know about wouldn't worry her.

She said, "One newly minted Federation zinc alloy cent for them."

He was conscious of his burning ears. He said, "They're not worth it."

"You insult me, Commander. Or, if you'd rather, John. You were thinking about me, weren't you?"

"Actually, yes, Una."

"Just a fool wanting to rush in where Rear Admirals, having learned by bitter experience, fear to tread."

"Frankly," he told her, "I am tempted to rush in. But you've no idea of the amount of gossip there is around this Base. If I as much as kissed you the very guard dogs would be barking it around the top secret installations within half an hour."

"Faint heart . . ." she scoffed.

"But you're not fair. You're a brunette." He added, "A very attractive one."

"Thank you, sir." She sat down in one of the deep, hide-covered chairs, affording him a generous glimpse of full thighs as her short skirt rode up. She said abruptly, "I think you can help me."

"How?" And then, to show that he could be as hard as the next man, "Why?"

"Why?" she exploded. "*Why?* Because you brass-bound types are supposed to be as much guardians of law and order as we lowly policemen and policewomen. Because unless somebody around here dedigitates, and fast, putting a ship at my disposal, *Delta Geminorum* is going to whiffle past Lindisfarne, a mere couple of light months distant, three standard weeks from now. If I don't intercept the bitch, I've lost her. And what is your precious Survey Service doing about it? Bugger all, that's what!"

"It's not so simple," said Grimes slowly. "Interservice jealousy comes into it, of course. . . ."

"Don't I know it! Don't I bloody well know it! *And* male chauvinism. When *are* you people going to grow up and admit that women are at least as capable as men?"

"But we already have two lady admirals. . . ."

"Supply—" she sneered, making a dirty word of it "Psychiatry—" she added, making it sound even dirtier. "All right, all right. This is a *man's* service. I have to accept that—reluctantly. But I think that *you* could help. You've been in command, haven't you? Your last appointment was as captain of a Serpent Class courier. Such a little ship would be ideal for the job. Couldn't you get your *Adder*—that was her name, wasn't it?—back and go out after *Delta Geminorum?*"

"We can't do things that way in the Survey Service," said Grimes stiffly. He thought, *I wish that we could. Once aboard the lugger and the girl is mine, and all that. Aboard my own ship I could make a pass at her. Here, in the Base, old James'd never forgive me if I did, and succeeded. Mere two-and-a-half-ringers just can't afford to antagonize rear admirals—not if they want any further promotion. . . .*

"Couldn't you see Commodore Damien, the O.I.C. Couriers?"

"Mphm . . ." grunted Grimes dubiously. During his tour of duty in *Adder* the Commodore had become his *bête noir,* just as he had become the Commodore's.

"He might give you your command back."

"That," stated Grimes definitely, "would be the sunny Friday! In any case, I'm no longer under Commodore Damien's jurisdiction. When I got my promotion from lieutenant to lieutenant commander he threw me into the Officers' Pool. No, not the sort you swim in. The sort you loaf around in waiting for somebody to find you a job. I might get away as senior watch-keeper or, possibly, executive officer in a Constellation Class cruiser—or, with my command experience, I might be appointed to something smaller as captain. I hope it's the latter."

"A Serpent Class courier," she said.

"I'm afraid not. They're *little* ships, and never have anybody above the rank of lieutenant as captain. Commodore Damien saw my promotion as a golden opportunity for getting rid of me."

"You can see him. He might give you your command back."

"Not a hope in hell."

"You can ask him. After all, he can't shoot you."

"But wouldn't he just like to!" *Even so, why not give it a go?* Grimes asked himself. *After all, he can't shoot me. And he did say, the last time that I ran into him, that he was sick and tired of seeing me hanging around the Base like a bad smell.* . . . He said aloud, "All right I'll see the Commodore tomorrow morning."

"*We* will see the Commodore tomorrow morning," she corrected him.

She ignored his offer of assistance, pulled herself up out of the deep chair. She allowed him to walk her back to the B. O. Q. (Female). It was a fine night, warm and clear, with Lindisfarne's two moons riding high in the black, star-strewn sky. It was a night for romantic dalliance—and surely Rear Admiral James would not sink so low as to have spies out to watch Una Freeman. But she resisted, gently but firmly, Grimes' efforts to steer her toward the little park, with its smooth, springy grass and sheltering clumps of trees. She permitted him a good-night kiss at the door to her lodgings—and it was one of those kisses that promise more, much more. He tried to collect a further advance payment but a quite painful jab from a stiff, strong finger warned him not to persist.

But there would be time, plenty of time, later, to carry things through to their right and proper—or improper—conclusion. It all depended on that crotchety old bastard Damien.

When Grimes retired for the night he was feeling not unhopeful.

~ Chapter 3 ~

APART FROM A BALEFUL GLARE Commodore Damien ignored Grimes. His eyes, bright in his skull-like face, regarded Una steadily over his skeletal, steepled fingers. He asked, pleasantly enough for him, "And what can *I* do for you, Miss Freeman?"

She replied tartly, "I've seen everybody else, Commodore."

Damien allowed himself a strictly rationed dry chuckle. He remarked, "You must have realized by this time that *our* masters do not like *your* masters. Apart from anything else, they feel, most strongly, that you people are trespassing on our territory. But there are wheels within wheels, and all sorts of dickering behind the scenes, and the Admiralty—albeit with a certain reluctance—has let it be known that a degree of cooperation on our part with you, personally, will not be frowned upon too heavily. His Nibs received a Carlottigram last night from the First Lord, to that effect. He passed the buck to Intelligence. Intelligence, for some reason known only to itself—" again there was the dry chuckle and the suggestion of a leer on Damien's face—"passed the buck to O. I. C. Couriers. Myself."

"Nobody told me!" snapped the girl.

The Commodore bared his long, yellow teeth. "You've been told now, Miss Freeman." He waited for her to say something in reply, but she remained silent and darkly glowering. "Unfortunately I have no couriers available at the moment. None, that is, to place at your full disposal. However. . . ."

437

"Go on, Commodore."

"I am not a suspect whom you are interrogating, young lady. I have been *requested* rather than ordered by my superiors to render you whatever assistance lies within my unfortunately limited power. It so happens that the Lizard Class courier *Skink* will be lifting from Base in four days' time, carrying dispatches and other assorted bumfodder to Olgana. You may take passage in her if you so desire."

"But I don't want to go to Olgana. You people have been furnished with the elements of *Delta Geminorum's* extrapolated trajectory. My orders are to board her, with a prize crew, and bring her in to port."

"I am aware of that, Miss Freeman. The captain of *Skink* will have *his* orders too. They will be, firstly, to carry such additional personnel as will be required for your prize crew and, secondly, to make whatever deviation from trajectory is required to put the prize crew aboard the derelict."

"And will John be the captain of this . . . this *Skink*?"

"John?" Damien registered bewilderment "John?" Then slow comprehension dawned. "Oh, you mean young Grimes, here. No, John will not be commanding any vessels under my jurisdiction. I honestly regret having to disappoint you, Miss Freeman, but *Skink* is Lieutenant Commander Delamere's ship."

Delamere, thought Grimes disgustedly. *Handsome Frankie Delamere, who could make a living posing for Survey Service recruiting posters. . . . And that's about all that he's fit for—that and screwing anything in skirts that comes his way. Good-bye, Una. It was nice knowing you.*

Damien switched his regard to Grimes. "And you are still unemployed, Lieutenant Commander," he stated rather than asked.

"Yes, sir."

"It distresses me to have to watch officers doing nothing and getting paid for it, handsomely." *So he's giving me* Skink *after all,* thought Grimes. *I did hear that Delamere was overdue for leave.* Damien went on, "'Unfortunately, you passed out of my immediate ambit on your promotion to your present rank." *That's right. Rub it in, you sadistic old bastard!* Grimes' spirits, temporarily raised, were plummeting again. "However, I am on quite amicable terms with Commodore Browning, of the Appointments Bureau." He raised a skinny hand. "No, I am not, repeat and underscore *not*, going to give you another command under my jurisdiction. I learned my lesson, all too well, during that harrowing period when you were captain of *Adder*. But somebody—preferably somebody with spacegoing command experience, has to be in charge of the prize crew. I shall press for your appointment to that position." He grinned nastily and added, "After all, whatever happens will have nothing to do with *me*."

"Thank you, sir," said Grimes.

"You haven't got the job yet," Damien told him.

After they had left the Commodore's office Una said, "But he must like you, John. You told me that he hated your guts."

"Oh, he does, he does. But he hates Frankie Delamere's guts still more."

"Then how is it that this Delamere is still one of his courier captains?"

"Because," Grimes told her, "dear Frankie knows all the right people. Including the Admiral's *very* plain daughter."

"Oh."

"Precisely," said Grimes.

~Chapter 4~

ALL NAVIES find it necessary to maintain several classes of vessel. The Federation Survey Service had its specialized ships, among which were the couriers. These were relatively small (in the case of the Insect Class, definitely small) spacecraft, analogous to the dispatch boats of the seaborne navies of Earth's past. There were the already mentioned Insect Class, the Serpent Class (one of which Grimes had commanded) and the Lizard Class. The one thing that all three classes had in common was speed. The Insect Class couriers were little more than long range pinnaces, whereas the Lizard Class ships were as large as corvettes, but without a corvette's armament, and with far greater cargo and passenger carrying capacity than the Serpent Class vessels.

Skink was a typical Lizard Class courier. She carried a crew of twenty, including the commanding officer. She had accommodation for twenty-five passengers—or, with the utilization of her cargo spaces for living freight, seventy-five. Her main engines comprised inertial drive and Mannschenn Drive, with auxiliary reaction drive. Her armament consisted of one battery of laser cannon together with the usual missiles and guidance system. She would have been capable of fighting another ship of the same class; anything heavier she could show a clean pair of heels to.

Lieutenant Commander Delamere did not expect to have to do any fighting—or running—on this perfectly routine paper run to

Olgana. He was more than a little annoyed when he was told by Commodore Damien that there would have to be a deviation from routine. He had his private reasons for wishing to make a quick passage; after a week or so of the company of the Admiral's plain, fat daughter he wanted a break, a change of bedmates. There was one such awaiting him at his journey's end.

"Sir," he asked Commodore Damien in a pained voice, "*Must* I act as chauffeur to this frosty-faced female fuzz?"

"You must, Delamere."

"But it will put at least three days on to my passage."

"You're a spaceman, aren't you?" Damien permitted himself a slight sneer. "Or supposed to be one."

"But, sir. A policewoman. Aboard my ship."

"A Sky Marshal, Lieutenant Commander. Let us accord the lady her glamorous title. Come to that, she's not unglamorous herself . . ."

"Rear Admiral James doesn't think so, sir. He told me about her when I picked up the Top Secret bumf from his office. He said, 'Take that butch trollop out of here, and never bring her back!'"

"Rear Admiral James is . . . er . . . slightly biased. Do you mean to tell me that you have never met Miss Freeman?"

"No, sir. My time has been fully occupied by my duties."

Commodore Damien stared up at the tall, fair-haired young man in sardonic wonderment until Delamere, who had a hide like a rhinoceros, blushed. He said, "She must keep you on a tight leash."

"I don't understand what you mean, sir."

"Don't you? Oh, skip it, skip it. Where was I before you obliged me to become engaged in a discussion of your morals?" Delamere blushed again. "Oh, yes. Miss Freeman will be taking passage with you, until such time as you have intercepted the derelict. With her will be a boarding party of Survey Service personnel, under Lieutenant Commander Grimes."

"Not Grimes, sir! That Jonah!"

"Jonah or not, Delamere, during his time in command of one of my couriers there has never been any serious damage to his ship—which is more than I can say about you. As I was saying, before you so rudely interrupted, Lieutenant Commander Grimes will be in charge of the boarding party, which will consist of three spacemen lieutenants, four engineer lieutenants, one electronic communications officer, six petty officer mechanics, one petty officer cook and three wardroom attendants."

"Doing himself proud, isn't he, sir?"

"He and his people will have to get a derelict back into proper working order and bring her in to port. We don't know, yet, what damage has been done to her by the pirates."

"Very well, sir." Delamere's voice matched his martyred expression. "I'll see to it that accommodation is arranged for all these idlers. After all, I shan't have to put up with them for long."

"One more thing, Delamere. . . ."

"Sir?"

"You'll have to make room in your after hold for a Mark XIV lifeboat. All the derelict's boats were taken when the crew and passengers abandoned ship. Lieutenant Commander Grimes will be using the Mark XIV for his boarding operation, of course, and then keeping it aboard *Delta Geminorum*. Grimes, of course, will be in full charge during the boarding and until such time as he releases you to proceed on your own occasions. Understood?"

"Yes, sir."

"Then that will be all, Lieutenant Commander." Delamere put on his cap, sketched a vague salute and strode indignantly out of the office. Damien chuckled and nattered, "After all, he's not the Admiral's son-in-law *yet*. . . ."

Grimes and Una stood on the apron looking up at *Skink*.

She wasn't a big ship, but she looked big to Grimes after his long tour of duty in the little *Adder*. She was longer, and beamier. She could never be called, as the Serpent Class couriers were called, a "flying darning needle." A cargo port was open in her shining side, just forward of and above the roots of the vanes that comprised her tripedal landing gear. Hanging in the air at the same level was a lifeboat, a very fat dagger of burnished metal, its inertial drive muttering irritably. Grimes hoped that the Ensign piloting the thing

knew what he was doing, and that Delamere's people, waiting inside
the now-empty after hold, knew what they were doing. If that boat
were damaged in any way he would be extremely reluctant to lift off
from Lindisfarne. He said as much.

"You're fussy, John," Una told him.

"A good spaceman has to be fussy. There won't be any boats
aboard the derelict, and anything is liable to go wrong with her once
we've taken charge and are on our own. That Mark XIV could well
be our only hope of survival."

She laughed. "If that last bomb blows up after we're aboard, a
lifeboat won't be much use to us."

"You're the bomb-disposal expert. You see to it that it doesn't
go off."

Delamere, walking briskly, approached them. He saluted Una,
ignored Grimes. "Coming aboard, Miss Freeman? We shall be all
ready to lift off as soon as that boat's inboard."

"I'll just wait here with John," she said. "He wants to see the
boat safely into the ship."

"My officers are looking after it, Grimes," said Delamere
sharply.

"But *I've* signed for the bloody thing!" Grimes told him.

The boat nosed slowly through the circular port, vanished.
For a few seconds the irregular beat of its inertial drive persisted,
amplified by the resonance of the metal compartment. Then it
stopped. There was no tinny crash to tell of disaster.

"Satisfied?" sneered Delamere.

"Not quite. I shall want to check on its stowage."

"All right. If you insist," snarled Delamere. He then muttered
something about old women that Grimes didn't quite catch.

"It's *my* boat," he said quietly.

"And it's being carried in *my* ship."

"Shall we be getting aboard?" Una asked sweetly.

They walked up the ramp to the after airlock. It was wide
enough to take only two people walking abreast in comfort. Grimes
found himself bringing up the rear. *Let Frankie-boy have his little bit
of fun,* he thought tolerantly. He was confident that he would make

out with Una; it was now only a question of the right place and the
right time. He did not think that she would be carried away by a
golden-haired dummy out of a uniform tailor's shop window. On
the other hand, Delamere's ship would not provide the right
atmosphere for his own campaign of conquest. Not that it mattered
much. He would soon have a ship of his own, a *big* ship. Once
aboard the derelict *Delta Geminorum* people would no longer have
to live in each other's pockets.

Grimes stopped off at the after hold to see to the stowage of his
boat while Una and Delamere stayed in the elevator that carried
them up the axial shaft to the captain's quarters. The small craft was
snugly nested into its chocks, secured with strops and sliphooks.
Even if Delamere indulged in the clumsy aerobatics, for which he
was notorious, on his way up through the atmosphere the boat
should not shift.

While he was talking with two of his own officers—they, like
himself, had an interest in the boat—the warning bell for lift-off
stations started to ring.

"Frankie's getting upstairs in a hurry!" muttered one *Skink's*
lieutenants sourly. "Time we were in our acceleration couches."

And time I was in the control room, thought Grimes. This
wasn't his ship, of course, but it was customary for a captain to
invite a fellow captain up to Control for arrivals and departures.

"We haven't been shown to our quarters yet, sir," said one of
Grimes' officers.

"Neither have I, Lieutenant, been shown to mine." He turned to
the ship's officer. "Where are we berthed?"

"I . . . I don't know, sir. And once the Old Man has started his
count-down the Odd Gods of the Galaxy Themselves couldn't stop
him!"

"Don't let us keep you, Lieutenant," Grimes told him. "Off you
go, tuck yourself into your own little cot. *We'll* manage."

"But *how,* sir?" demanded Grimes' officer. "We can't just
stretch out on the *deck* . . ."

"Use your initiative, Lieutenant. We've a perfectly good ship's boat here, with well-sprung couches. Get the airlock door open, and look snappy!"

He and his two officers clambered into the boat. The bunks were comfortable enough. They strapped themselves in. Before the last clasp had been snapped tight *Skink's* inertial drive started up—and (it seemed) before the stern vanes were more than ten millimeters from the apron the auxiliary reaction drive was brought into play. It was the sort of showy lift-off, with absolutely unnecessary use of rocket power, of which Grimes himself had often been guilty. When anybody else did it—Delamere especially—he disapproved strongly. He could just imagine Frankie showing off in front of his control room guest, Una Freeman. . . .

Oh, well, he thought philosophically as the acceleration pushed him down into the padding, *at least we're giving the mattresses a good test. I don't suppose that they'll be used again. . . . A long boat voyage is the very least of my ambitions.*

Skink thundered up through the atmosphere and, at last, the drive was cut. Grimes and his two companions remained in their couches until trajectory had been set, until the high keening of the Mannschenn drive told them that they were on their way to intercept the derelict.

⚞ Chapter 5 ⚟

SKINK was not a happy ship.

The average spaceman doesn't mind his captain's being a bastard as long as he's an efficient bastard. Frankie Delamere was not efficient. Furthermore, he was selfish. He regarded the vessel as his private yacht. Everything had to be arranged for *his* personal comfort.

Skink was an even unhappier ship with the passengers whom she was carrying. To begin with, Delamere seemed to be under the impression that the medieval *droit du seigneur* held good insofar as he was concerned. Una did her best to disillusion him. She as good as told him that if she was going to sleep with anybody—and it was a large *if*—it would be with Grimes. Thereupon Frankie made sure that opportunities for this desirable consummation were altogether lacking. Some of his people, those who respected the rank if not the man, those who were concerned about their further promotion, played along with the captain. "One thing about Delamere's officers," complained Grimes, "is that they have an absolute genius for being where they're not wanted!"

Apart from sexual jealousy, Delamere did not like Grimes, never had liked Grimes, and Grimes had never liked him. He could not go too far—after all, Grimes held the same rank as did he—but he contrived to make it quite clear that his fellow Lieutenant Commander was *persona non grata* in the courier's control room. Then—as was his right, but one that he was not obliged to exercise—he found totally unnecessary but time-consuming jobs for the members of the boarding party, snapping that he would tolerate no idlers aboard his ship.

He, himself, was far from idle. He was working hard—but, Grimes noted with grim satisfaction, getting nowhere. He was always asking Una Freeman up to his quarters on the pretext of working out procedures for the interception of the derelict—and there he expected her to help him work his way through his not inconsiderable private stock of hard liquor. Grimes had no worries on this score. Her capacity for strong drink, he had learned, was greater than his, and his was greater than Delamere's. And there was the black eye that the captain tried to hide with talcum powder before coming into the wardroom for dinner and—a day or so later—the scratches on his face that were even more difficult to conceal. Too, Una—on the rare occasions that she found herself alone with Grimes—would regale him with a blow by blow account of the latest unsuccessful assault on the body beautiful.

Grimes didn't find it all that amusing.

"The man's not fit to hold a commission!" he growled. "Much less to be in command. Make an official complaint to me—after all, I'm the senior officer aboard this ship after himself—and I take action!"

"What will you do?" she scoffed. "Call a policeman? Don't forget that I'm a policewoman—with the usual training in unarmed combat. I've been gentle with him so far, John. But if he tried anything nasty he'd wind up in the sick bay with something broken. . . ."

"Or out of the airlock wrapped up in the Survey Service flag . . ." he suggested hopefully.

"Even that. Although I'd have some explaining to do then."

"I'd back you up."

"Uncommonly decent of you, Buster. But I can look after myself—as Frankie boy knows, and as you'd better remember!"

"Is that a threat?"

"It could be," she told him. "It just could be."

For day after day *Skink* fell through the immensities, through the Continuum warped by the temporal precession field of her

Mannschenn Drive. As seen from her control room the stars were neither points of light nor appreciable discs, but pulsing spirals of iridescence. For day after day the screen of the mass proximity indicator was a sphere of unrelieved blackness—but Delamere's navigator, an extremely competent officer, was not worried. He said, "If the F.I.A. mathematicians got their sums right—and I've heard that they're quite good at figuring—*Delta Geminorum* is still well outside the maximum range of our MPI."

"Damn it all!" snarled his Captain. "We're wasting time on this wild goose chase. We should be well on our way to Olgana by now, not chauffeuring the civilian fuzz all round the bleeding Galaxy!"

"I thought you *liked* Miss Freeman, sir," observed the navigator innocently.

"Keep your thoughts to yourself, Lieutenant!"

"If *my* sums have come out right, we should pick up the derelict at about 0630 hours, ship's time, tomorrow."

"Your sums had better come out right!" snarled Delamere.

Reluctantly, Delamere asked Grimes up to the control room at the time when the first sighting was expected. He made it plain that he did so only because the other was to be in charge of the boarding operations. He growled, "You're supposed to be looking after this part of it. Just try not to waste too much of my time."

"Your time," said Grimes, "belongs to the Survey Service, as mine does. And it's all being paid for with the taxpayer's money."

"Ha, ha."

"Ha, ha."

The officers, and Una Freeman, looked on with interest. Una remarked that having two captains in the same control room was worse than having two women in the same kitchen. The watch officer, an ensign, sniggered. *Either a very brave or a very foolish young man,* thought Grimes.

"And where's your bloody derelict, Mr. Ballantyre?" Delamere snarled at his navigator. "I make the time coming up to 0633."

"It's been showing in the screen, sir, at extreme range, for the last three minutes. Just the merest flicker, and not with every sweep, but a ship's a small target. . . ."

Pushing his officers rudely aside Delamere went to the MPI, staring down into the sphere of blackness. Grimes followed him. Yes, there it was, an intermittently glowing spark, at green eighty-three, altitude seventeen negative.

"Extrapolate, please, Mr. Ballantyre," he said.

"This is not your control room, Mr. Grimes," said Delamere.

"But I am in charge of the boarding operations, Mr. Delamere," said Grimes.

"All right, if you want to be a space lawyer!" Delamere went off in a huff—not that he could go very far—and slumped down in one of the acceleration chairs.

Ballantyre extrapolated. From the center of the screen a very fine gleaming filament extended, and another one from the target. It was obvious that the two ships would pass each other many kilometers distant.

"Mphm." Grimes produced his pipe, filled and lit it.

"I don't allow smoking in my control room," growled Delamere.

"I'm in charge now, as you, yourself, have admitted. And I *always* wear a pipe when I'm engaged in shiphandling."

"Let the baby have his dummy!" sneered the other.

Grimes ignored this. He said to Ballantyre, "You know this ship better than I do. Adjust our trajectory so that we're on a converging course, and overtaking. . . ."

The navigator looked inquiringly at his captain, who growled, "Do as the man says."

The Mannschenn Drive was shut down, but the inertial drive remained in operation. There were the brief seconds of temporal disorientation, with distorted outlines and all colors sagging down the spectrum, with all the shipboard sounds echoing oddly and eerily. Grimes, looking at Una, realized that he was—or would be, sometime in the not too distant future—seeing her naked. This made sense of a sort. Flashes of precognition are not uncommon when the interstellar drive is started up or shut down. But she was not only completely unclothed, but riding a bicycle. That made no sense at all.

Gyroscopes rumbled, hummed as the ship was turned about her short axes, as the adjustment to trajectory was made. In the screen the extrapolated courses looked as Grimes desired them to look. "Mphm. Very good, Mr. Ballantyre. Now—chase and board!"

"I'm afraid I can't lend you any cutlasses, Grimes," said Delamere sardonically. "Or did you bring your own with you?"

"Might I suggest, Lieutenant Commander, that we not waste time with airy persiflage? After all, you were the one who was saying how precious his time is. . . ."

Again there was temporal disorientation as the Mannschenn Drive was restarted. Grimes hoped for another glimpse of the future Una, but was disappointed. The only impression was of an intensely bright white light, too bright, almost, to be seen.

Grimes left things very much in the hands of Delamere's navigator. The young man obviously knew just what he was doing. With a minimum of fuss he got *Skink* running parallel with *Delta Geminorum,* with both actual speed and temporal precession rates exactly synchronized. With the synchronization the derelict was visible now, both visually and in the radar screen. At a range of five kilometers she could be examined in detail through the big, mounted binoculars, their lenses sensitive to all radiation, in the courier's control room. She looked innocent enough, a typical Delta Class liner of the Interstellar Transport Commission, floating against a background of blackness and the shimmering nebulosities that were the stars. She seemed to be undamaged, but an after airlock door was open. The pirates, thought Grimes, hadn't been very well brought up; nobody had taught them to shut doors after them. . . .

"I'll take over now," said Delamere. "After all, this is *my* ship, Lieutenant Commander."

"Oh, yes, I'd almost forgotten," said Grimes. "And what are your intentions, Lieutenant Commander?"

"I'm going to make things easy for you, Grimes. I'm going to lay *Skink* right alongside *Delta Geminorum.*"

Just the sort of flashy spacemanship that would appeal to you, thought Grimes.

"Are you mad?" asked Una Freeman coldly.

Delamere flushed. "I'm not mad. And you, Miss Freeman, are hardly qualified to say your piece regarding matters of spacemanship."

"Perhaps not, Commander Delamere. But I *am* qualified to say my piece regarding bomb disposal."

"*Bomb disposal?*"

"Yes. Bomb disposal. If you'd bothered to run through the report I gave you to read—and that Commander Grimes *did* read—you would know that there is a fully armed thermonuclear device still aboard that vessel. Unluckily none of the pirates who were arrested and brain-drained knew much about it. We did learn that the signal to detonate it was sent shortly after the pirate had returned safely to their own ship—but, for some reason, nothing happened. Nobody was at all keen to return aboard *Delta Geminorum* to find out why. . . . That bomb, Commander, is a disaster waiting to happen. It is quite probable that the inevitable jolt when you put your vessel alongside the derelict would be enough to set it off."

"So what do you intend to do?" asked Delamere.

"I suggest that you maintain your present station on *Delta Geminorum*; Commander Grimes and I will take a boat to board her. Then I shall defuse the bomb."

"All right," growled Delamere at last. "All right. Mr. Ballantyre, maintain station on the derelict." He turned to his First Lieutenant. "Mr. Tarban, have Lieutenant Commander Grimes' boat ready for ejection." He added, addressing nobody in particular, "I don't see why I should risk one of *my* boats. . . ." He addressed Grimes. "I hope you enjoy the trip. Better you than me, Buster!"

"I have the utmost confidence in Miss Freeman's abilities, Frankie," Grimes told him sweetly.

Delamere snarled wordlessly.

Una Freeman said, "You're the expert, John—for the first part of it, anyhow. Shall we require space-suits?"

"Too *right* we shall," said Grimes. "To begin with, Mr. Tarban has probably evacuated the atmosphere from the after hold by now. And we don't know whether or not there's any atmosphere inside the derelict or if it's breathable. We'd better get changed."

Before he left the control room he went to the binoculars for the last look at the abandoned liner. She looked innocent enough, a great, dull-gleaming torpedo shape. Suddenly she didn't look so innocent. The word "torpedo" has long possessed a sinister meaning.

⁓ Chapter 6 ⁓

EVERYTHING WAS READY in the after hold when Grimes and Una got down there. The lashings had been removed from the boat and its outer airlock door was open. The inertial drive was ticking over, and somebody had started the mini-Mannschenn, synchronizing its temporal precession rates to those of the much bigger interstellar drive units in *Skink* and *Delta Geminorum*. A cargo port in the ship's side had been opened, and through it the liner was visible.

"She's all yours, sir," said the First Lieutenant.

"Thank you," replied Grimes.

Delamere's irritated voice came through the helmet phones, "Stow the social chit-chat, Mr. Tarban. We've wasted enough time already!"

"Shut up, Frankie!" snapped Una Freeman.

Grimes clambered into the boat, stood in the chamber of the little airlock. Una passed up a bag of tools and instruments. He put it down carefully by his feet, then helped the girl inboard. He pressed a stud, and the outer door shut, another stud and the inner door opened.

He went forward, followed by Una. He lowered himself into the pilot's seat. She took the co-pilot's chair. He ran a practiced eye over the control panel. All systems were GO.

"Officer commanding boarding party to officer commanding *Skink*," he said into his helmet microphone, "request permission to eject."

"Eject!" snarled Delamere.

"He might have wished us good luck," remarked Una.

"He's glad to see the back of us," Grimes told her.

"You can say that again!" contributed Delamere.

Grimes laughed as nastily as he could manage, then his gloved fingers found and manipulated the inertial drive controls. The little engine clattered tinnily but willingly. The boat was clear, barely clear of the chocks and sliding forward. She shot out through the open port, and Grimes made the small course correction that brought the liner dead ahead, and kept her there. She seemed to expand rapidly as the distance was covered.

"Careful," warned Una. "This is a boat we're in, not a missile. . . ."

"No back seat driving!" laughed Grimes.

Nonetheless, he adjusted trajectory slightly so that it would be a near miss and not a direct hit. At the last moment he took the quite considerable way off the boat by applying full reverse thrust. She creaked and shuddered, but held together. Una said nothing, but Grimes could sense her disapproval. Come to that, he had his own disapproval to contend with. He realized that he was behaving with the same childish flashiness that Frankie Delamere would have exhibited.

He orbited the spaceship. On the side of her turned away from *Skink* the cargo ports were still open. It all looked very unspaceman-like—but why bother to batten down when the ship is going to be destroyed minutes after you have left her? She hadn't been destroyed, of course, but she should have been, would have been if some firing device had not malfunctioned.

He said, "I'll bring us around to the after airlock. Suit you?"

"Suits me. But be careful, John. Don't forget that there's an armed bomb aboard that ship. Anything, anything at all, could set it off."

"Yes, teacher. I'll be careful, very careful. I'll come alongside so carefully that I wouldn't crack the proverbial egg." He reached out for the microphone of the Carlotti transceiver; at this distance from the courier, with Mannschenn Drive units in operation, the N.S.T. suit radios were useless. He would have to inform Frankie Delamere and his own officers of progress to date and of his intentions. With his chin he nudged the stud that would cause the faceplate of his helmet to flip open. His thumb pressed the transmit button. And then it happened.

Aboard the ship, for many, many months, the miniaturized Carlotti receiver had been waiting patiently for the signal that, owing to some infinitesimal shifting of frequencies, had never come. The fuse had been wrongly set, perhaps, or some vibration had jarred it from its original setting, quite possibly the shock initiated by the explosion of either of the two warning bombs. And now here was a wide-band transmitter at very close range.

Circuits came alive, a hammer fell on a detonator, which exploded, in its turn exploding the driving charge. One sub-critical mass of fissionable material was impelled to contact with another sub-critical mass, with the inevitable result.

As a bomb it lacked the sophistication of the weaponry of the armed forces of the Federation—but it worked.

Grimes, with the dreadful reality blinding him, remembered his prevision of the light too bright to be seen. He heard somebody (Una? himself?) scream. This was It. This was all that they would ever be. He was a dead leaf caught in the indraught of a forest fire, whirling down and through the warped dimensions to the ultimate, blazing Nothingness.

⁓ Chapter 7 ⁓

SHE SAID, "But we shouldn't be alive . . . ."

He said, "But we are." He added, glumly, "But for how long? This boat must be as radioactive as all hell. I suppose that it was *the* bomb that went off."

"It was," she told him. "But there's no radioactivity. I've tested. There is a counter in my bomb disposal kit."

He said, "It must be on the blink."

"It's not. It registers well enough with all the normal sources—my wristwatch, against the casing of the fusion power unit, and so on."

He said doubtfully, "I suppose we *could* have been thrown clear. Or we were in some cone of shadow. . . . Yes, that makes sense. We were toward the stern of the ship, and the shielding of her power plant must have protected us."

She asked, "What now?"

Grimes stared through the viewports of the control cabin. There was no sign of *Skink*. There was no sign of any wreckage from *Delta Geminorum*. The stars shone bright and hard in the blackness; the mini-Mannschenn had stopped and the boat was adrift in the normal Continuum.

He said, "We stay put."

She said, "Shouldn't Delamere be sniffing around to pick up the pieces?"

"Delamere's sure that there aren't any pieces," he told her, "just as I should be sure if I were in his shoes. And, in any case, he's in a hurry to get to Olgana. He *knows* we're dead, vaporized. But he'll have used his Carlotti to put in a report to Base, giving the coordinates of the scene of the disaster. When anything of this kind happens a ship full of experts is sent at once to make an investigation." He laughed. "And won't they be surprised when they find us alive and kicking!"

"Can't we use our radio to tell them?"

"We can't raise *Skink* on the N.S.T. transmitter while she's running on Mannschenn Drive. We can't raise the Base, either. Oh, they'd pick up the signal eventually—quite a few months from now. And you've seen the mess that our Carlotti set is in . . ."

"So we just . . . wait?"

"S.O.P. for shipwrecked spacemen," said Grimes. "We haven't a hope in hell of getting anywhere in our lifetimes unless we use Mannschenn Drive—and, looking at the mess the mini-Mannschenn is in, I'd sooner not touch it. We've survived so far. Let's stay that way."

"Couldn't you fix the Carlotti transceiver to let Base know that we're here?"

"I'm not a Carlotti technician, any more than I'm an expert on Mannschenn Drives."

"H'm." She looked around the quite commodious interior of the boat. "Looks like we have to set up housekeeping for a few days, doesn't it? We could be worse off, I suppose. Much worse off. . . . We've food, water, air, light, heat . . . Talking of heat, I may as well get into something more comfortable . . ."

Grimes, never one to look such a magnificent gift horse in the mouth, helped her off with her spacesuit. She helped him off with his. In the thick underwear that they were wearing under the suits they might just as well still have been armored. She came into his arms willingly enough, but there was no real contact save for mouth to mouth.

She whispered, "I'm still too warm . . ."

He said, "We'd better take our longjohns off, until we want them again. No point in subjecting them to needless wear and tear . . ."

"Are you seducing me, sir?"

"I wouldn't think of it!" lied Grimes.

"I don't believe you, somehow. Oh, John, how good it is to get away from that horrid Base and Frankie's nasty little ship! I feel free, free!" She pulled the zip of her longjohns down to the crotch. Her released breasts thrust out at him, every pubic hair seemed to have a life of its own, to be rejoicing in its freedom from restraint. Grimes smelled the odor of her—animal, pungent—and his body responded. His underwear joined hers, floating in mid-cabin in a tangle of entwining limbs. Within seconds he and the girl were emulating the pose of the clothing that they had discarded. Stirred by the air currents the garments writhed in sympathy with the movements of their owners.

∾ Chapter 8 ∾

"**THE SURVEY SERVICE** looks after its own," said Grimes.

"Then it's high time that it started doing so," she said.

"You can't organize a Search and Rescue Operation in five minutes," he told her.

"All right, all right. We can't expect any help from *Skink*, We've already agreed on that. But Frankie will have informed Base of the destruction of the derelict. In the unlikely event of *Skink's* having been destroyed herself—*you* said that she was well out of effective range of the explosion—Base will have been wondering why no reports have been coming in from anybody. And how long have we been here now? Over three weeks."

"If the Carlotti transceiver hadn't been smashed . . ." he began. "*And* the mini-Mannschenn. . . ."

"The Normal Space Time transceiver is working—you say, and we hope. Surely by now there'd be *somebody* in this vicinity, sniffing around for wreckage—and not, therefore, running under interstellar drive. Even I know that. How many days did it take from Lindisfarne Base to the interception?"

"Twenty."

"And this is our twenty-third day in this tin coffin. For most of the time we've maintained a continuous listening watch as well as putting out distress calls at regular intervals. I suppose somebody might just pick them up a few years from now."

"Space is vast," said Grimes.

"You're telling me, Buster! But surely Delamere was able to give accurate coordinates for the position of the derelict when we boarded her—when we tried to board her, rather—even if he didn't want to risk his own precious hide investigating. . . ."

"We've been over all this before," said Grimes.

"Then we'll go over it again, lover boy."

"Nobody survives a nuclear explosion at Position Zero, as we were," said Grimes.

"Are you trying to suggest that we're dead and in some sort of spaceman's heaven? Ha, ha. It certainly ain't no policewoman's paradise!"

Grimes ignored this. In any case, the double negative made her meaning unclear (he told himself). He went on, "And Delamere had his schedule to maintain. . . ." Even so, Delamere *must* have reported the destruction of *Delta Geminorum* to Base. And Base *must* have dispatched a properly equipped vessel to the scene of the disaster to gather whatever evidence, no matter how little, remained, even though it was only radioactive dust and gases.

But why had the boat, and its occupants, not been reduced to that condition?

She broke into his thoughts, remarking, "As I've said before, I'm not a spaceman."

He looked across the table at her spectacular superstructure. "Insofar as gender is concerned, how very right you are!"

She pointedly ignored this. "I'm not a spaceman, but I do remember some of the things that you people have condescended to tell me, from time to time, about the art and science of astronautics. More than once people have nattered to me about the peculiar consequences of changing the mass of a ship while the Mannschenn Drive is in operation."

"Old spacemen's tales!" scoffed Grimes.

"Really? Then how is it that in every ship that I've traveled in people have regarded that cock-eyed assemblage of precessing gyroscopes with superstitious awe? You're all scared of it. And what about the odd effects when the Drive is started, and the temporal precession field builds up, not when it's stopped, and the field fades? The feeling of *déjà vu* . . . The flashes of precognition . . ." She started to laugh.

"What's so funny?"

"I had a real beaut aboard *Skink*. I saw you out of uniform. When I saw you for the first time out of uniform, in actuality, it was in this boat. But I'd already seen that scar you have on your right thigh. But that isn't the *funny* part. In my . . . vision you were not only naked, but riding a bicycle . . ."

"*Very* funny. As a matter of fact I saw you the same way. But bicycles are one article of equipment that this boat doesn't run to."

"All right. Let's forget the bicycles. Maybe someday we'll enjoy a holiday on Arcadia together. I suppose the Arcadians ride bicycles as well as practicing naturalism. But *Delta Geminorum*. . . . She was running under interstellar drive when she blew up. So were we, maintaining temporal synchronization with her."

"Go on."

"I'm only a glorified cop, John, but it's obvious, even to me, that a few thousand tons of mass were suddenly converted into energy in our immediate vicinity. So, Mr. Lieutenant Commander Grimes, where are we?"

Grimes was beginning to feel badly scared. "Or *when* . . . ?" he muttered.

"What the hell do you mean?"

He said, "Brace yourself for yet another lecture on the Mannschenn Drive. The Mannschenn Drive warps the Continuum—the space-time continuum—about the ship that's using it. Putting it very crudely, such a ship is going astern in time while going ahead in space. . . ."

"So. . . . So we could be anywhere. Or anywhen. But you're a navigator. You should be able to find out something from the relative positions of the stars."

"Not so easy," he told her. "The Carlotti transceiver, which can be used for position finding as well as communicating, is bust. We do carry, of course, a Catalogue of Carlotti Beacons—but in these circumstances it's quite useless."

"Especially so," she pointed out, "when we don't even know if there *are* any Carlotti Beacons in this space-time. So, lover boy, what are you doing about it?"

Grimes' prominent ears flushed angrily. She was being unfair. She shared the responsibility for getting them into this mess. She, the bomb-disposal expert, should have warned him of the possible consequences of using a Carlotti transmitter in close proximity to the derelict. He rose from the table haughtily. It was no hardship for him to leave his unfinished meal. He stalked, insofar as this was possible when wearing only magnetic sandals in Free Fall, to the forward end of the boat. He stared out through the control cabin viewports at the interstellar immensities. There was no star that he could identify, no constellation. Had he been made a welcome visitor in *Skink's* control room he would have known how the stars should look in this sector of Space. As it was. . . . He shrugged. All that he could be sure of was that they were in *a* universe, not necessarily *the* universe. At least the boat hadn't fallen down some dark crack in the continuum.

He turned away from the port, looked aft. He saw that Una Freeman had taken the broken, battered Carlotti transceiver from the locker in which it had been stowed, was picking up and looking at the pieces intently. *Nude with Moebius Strip,* he thought sardonically.

She waved the twisted antenna at him. "Are you *sure* you can't do anything with this lot?" she demanded.

"Quite sure. I'm not a radio technician."

"Then you can't be sure that it *is* a complete write-off." Her wide, fun mouth was capable of quite spectacular sneering. "Get the lead out of your pants, lover boy—not that you're wearing any. You've been having a marvelous holiday for the last three weeks; it's high time that you started work again."

"Mphm?"

"I thought, in my girlish innocence. . . ."

"Ha, ha."

She glared at him. "I thought, in my girlish innocence that all you spacefaring types were men of infinite resource and sagacity, able to make repairs, light years from the nearest yard, with chewing gum and old string. I'd like to see some proof of it."

He said, "I might be able to straighten out the antenna and get it remounted. But the printed circuits are a mess."

She said, "There're soldering irons in the workshop."

"I know. But have you had a good look at those trays?"

"Of course. Trays of circuitry. Since simple soldering seems to be beyond your capabilities. . . ."

"And yours."

"I'm not the skilled, trained, qualified spaceman, lover boy. You are. But let me finish. As a Sky Marshal I had to do quite a few courses on general spacemanship, including Deep Space communications. One of the things I learned was that quite a few circuit trays are interchangeable between NST and Carlotti transceivers. Since it's obvious now that we shall not be needing the NST transceiver—we cannibalize. After that's been done, lover boy, all we have to do is home on the Lindisfarne Beacon."

"And how many years will it take us?" he asked sarcastically.

"Oh, I forgot. After you've fixed the Carlotti set you fix the mini-Mannschenn."

⤜ Chapter 9 ⤛

THERE WAS a Radio Technician's Manual in the boat's book locker. Grimes got it out. Unluckily the writer of it had assumed that anybody reading it would possess at least a smattering of knowledge concerning Deep Space radio. Grimes was not such a person. He knew that the Carlotti equipment propagated signals which, somehow, ignored the normal three dimensions of Space and, by taking a shortcut of some kind, arrived at the receiving station, no matter how many light years distant, practically instantaneously. In any ship that he had been in the thing had worked. There had always been fully qualified officers to see that it worked. Had the complete boarding party been in the boat when she pushed off from *Skink* there would have been such an officer among her crew. (But, thought Grimes, had he taken the full boarding party with him he would not have been alone with Una.)

He and the girl puzzled over the text and the diagrams. They could make neither head nor tail of the latter, but they discovered that printed circuit tray #3 of NST transceiver Mark VII could be substituted for tray #1 of Carlotti transceiver Mark IVA, and so on and so on. It began to look as though Una's idea would work.

Before commencing operations he started up the inertial drive. He was not, as yet, going anywhere in particular, but physical work is more easily carried out in a gravitational field—or under acceleration—than in free fall conditions. Then, with Una assisting, he pulled the circuit trays out of the Carlotti set. Number one, obviously, would have to be replaced. That presented no problem. Number two was obviously nonfunctional. Number two from the NST transceiver was the recommended substitute. Number three appeared to be undamaged. Number four was in almost as big a mess as number one—and none of the NST circuits could be used in its stead.

So, soldering it had to be.

Grimes carried the tray to the little workshop that shared space with the boat's power plant and propulsive units, put it on the bench. He had the Manual open at the proper page, thought that he would be able to patch things up. He was a messy solderer and soon discovered that clothing is worn for protection as well as for adornment or motives of prudery. Una—who was annoyingly amused—applied first aid; then Grimes got into his longjohns before continuing.

When he was finished—a few hours and several burns later— the tray still looked a mess, but Grimes was reasonably confident that the circuits were not anywhere shorted. He carried the tray back to the transceiver—which had been set up in its proper position— and slid it carefully into place. He switched on. The pilot lights lit up. There would be neither transmission nor reception, however, until the antenna was remounted and operational.

They had a hasty meal, then returned to the workshop. The antenna was a metal Moebius Strip, oval rather than circular, on a universal bearing which, in turn, was at the head of a driving shaft. The shaft had been snapped just below the bearing, and the antenna itself had been bent out of its elliptical configuration. Fortunately there was among the motor spares a steel rod of circular section and exactly the right diameter. It had to be shortened by about five centimeters, but with the tools available that was no hardship. The broken shaft was removed from the transceiver, the new one shipped. The antenna—back in shape, Grimes hoped—was, on its bearing, secured to the projecting end of the shaft with a set screw.

"Will it work?" asked Una skeptically.

"There's only one way to find out," Grimes told her. He

switched on again, set the Direction Finding controls to hunt. In theory (and, hopefully, in practice) the aerial array would now automatically line up on the strongest incoming Carlotti signal.

The shaft began to rotate slowly, the Moebius Strip antenna wobbled on its universal bearing. It seemed to be questing as it turned. Abruptly it steadied, although still turning about its long axis. From the speaker came not the Morse sequence of a Beacon but something that sounded like somebody speaking. It was in no language that either of them knew, and the voice did not sound human. Suddenly it stopped, but Grimes had noted relative bearing and altitude.

He looked at Una, his eyebrows raised. She looked at him dubiously.

"Something . . ." he said slowly.

"Not . . . somebody?"

"All right. Somebody. Somebody capable of constructing—or, at least, using—Deep Space communications equipment."

"Should we put out a call now that this contraption's working?"

"No," he decided. He laughed harshly. "I like to see whom I'm talking to before I talk to them. We'll let the direction finder go on hunting for a while. Maybe it will pick up something a little more promising. . . ."

But it did not.

At intervals of exactly twenty-three minutes and fourteen seconds it steadied on the transmission in the unknown language, on the same relative bearing.

Grimes remembered an engineer officer in a big ship in which he had served as a junior watchkeeper. He had watched this gentleman while he overhauled the mini-Mannschenn of one of the cruiser's boats. It had been a job requiring both patience and a remarkably steady hand. After a spindle had slipped out of its bearing for the fifteenth time the specialist had sworn, "Damn it all, I'm an engineer, not a bloody watchsmith!" He then went on to say, "The ship's Mannschenn Drive unit, with all its faults, is a *machine*. This fucking thing's only an instrument!" He told the little story to

Una. She said, "That's no excuse. Somebody assembled it once. You can assemble it again. Nothing seems to be damaged. It's just a question of getting all the rotors turning and precessing freely."

"Quite simple, in fact."

"Quite simple," she said, ignoring the sarcasm.

"Perhaps you'd like to try."

"I'm a policewoman, not a watchsmith."

"Ha, ha. Now. . . . Get in there, damn you!" *Click.* "That's it."

"You've a little wheel left over," she pointed out. "And you'll have to remove the one you just got in to get it back."

"Not if I precess it . . . so. . . ."

"One of the other rotors has fallen out now." Then she went away and left him to it, and without his audience he got along much better. At last the reassembled mini-Mannschenn was ready for use. It looked like a complex, glittering toy, an assemblage of tiny, gleaming flywheels, every axle of which was set at an odd angle to all of the others. Once it was started the ever-precessing, ever-tumbling rotors would drag the boat and its crew down and through the dark dimensions, through a warped continuum in which space and time were meaningless concepts. He touched one of the rotors tentatively with a cautious forefinger. It spun on its almost frictionless bearings and the others turned in sympathy. Although there was, as yet, almost no precession, the shining wheels glimmered and winked on the very edge of invisibility.

He called out, "We're in business!"

"Then get the show on the road," retorted Una. "We've been sitting here on our arses, doing sweet fuck all, for too bloody long!"

Grimes used the single directional gyroscope to line the boat up on the last bearing from which the mysterious call had come. Then he switched on the mini-Mannschenn. To judge from the brief temporal disorientation, the sensation of *déjà vu,* the thing was working perfectly.

~ Chapter 10 ~

AT INTERVALS of exactly twenty-three minutes and fourteen seconds the signal continued to come through. It was the same message every time, the same words spoken in the same high-pitched, unhuman voice. *Dizzard waling torpet droo. Contabing blee. Contabing uwar. Contabing dinzin. Waling torpet, waling droo. Tarfelet, tarfelet, tarfelet.* It was in no language that either of them knew or, even, knew about.

There were other signals, weaker, presumably more distant. Some were spoken, in the same or in another unknown language. Some were coded buzzings. The Carlotti transceiver was fitted with a visiscreen, but this was useless. Either these people—whoever they were—did not use visiscreens, or the system they employed used a different principle from that used by humans.

The boat ran on, and on. Soon it became obvious that they were heading for a star, a G type sun. That star would possess a family of planets, and it must be from one of these that the signals were emanating. The interstellar drive was shut down briefly while a navigational check was made. The target star, when viewed through the control cabin binoculars, showed as a disc. This concurred with the strength of the signal now being received.

The drive was restarted, but Grimes stood in cautiously now. Every twenty-three minutes and fourteen seconds he was obliged to shut down again to correct trajectory. The source of the signal was, obviously, in orbit about the sun. That star was now almost as big as Sol seen from Earth, its limbs subtending an angle of over fifty degrees. With the final alteration of course it was broad on the boat's starboard beam.

The interstellar drive was now shut down permanently. Ahead gleamed the world from which the signals were being sent, a tiny half moon against the darkness. Slowly it expanded as the little spacecraft, its inertial drive hammering flat out, overhauled it in its orbit. "A stern chase is a long chase," philosophized Grimes, "but it's better than a head-on collision!"

It was a barren world, they saw, as they drew closer, an apparently dead one. There were no city lights gleaming from the night hemisphere. There were clouds in the atmosphere, but, glimpsed through them were neither the blues of seas nor the greens of vegetation; neither were there polar icecaps nor the sparkling white chains of snow-covered mountain peaks. This was odd, as the planet lay well within the ecosphere.

Before going into orbit about it Grimes decided on a resumption of clothing. Anything might happen, he said, and he did not want to be caught with his pants down. "Or off," said Una, struggling into her own longjohns.

"Or off. Have you checked the boat's armament?"

"Such as it is. Four one millimeter laser pistols, fully charged. Four ten millimeter projectile pistols, each with a full magazine of fifteen rounds. Spare ammo for the popguns—one eighty rounds."

"Hardly enough to start a war with," said Grimes, zippering up his spacesuit. He put on his helmet, but left the faceplate open.

"Or enough to finish one with?" asked Una quietly. She beckoned him to the big, mounted binoculars. "Look down there, through that break in the clouds."

He looked. "Yes," he said slowly, "I see what you mean." Before the dim vapors swept over the patch of clarity he was able to catch a glimpse of formations too regular to be natural in an expanse of red desert, a geometrical pattern that marked what could have been once the streets of a city. Then, from the speaker of the Carlotti transceiver, came the by-this-time-too-familiar words: *Dizzard waling torpet droo . . .*

"Almost below us," whispered Una.

"Then we're going down." He managed a grin. "At least we shall be adhering to Survey Service S.O.P.; that city's almost right on the terminator. Our landing will be very shortly after sunrise."

He eased himself into the pilot's chair. Una took her place by his side. He put the boat into a steep, powered dive. The shell plating heated up appreciably as they plunged into and through the outer atmosphere. Abruptly the viewpoints were obscured by swirling masses of brown cloud, evil and ominous, but Una reported that, so far, there was no marked increase in radioactivity.

The boat fell rapidly, buffeted now and again by turbulence. She broke through the overcast. The city was almost directly beneath them, its once tall, ruined buildings standing up like guttered candles. Dust devils played among and between the half-melted stumps.

There was a central plaza, a circular expanse surrounded by the remains of once-proud towers. On the sunlit side of this something gleamed metallically, a conical structure, apparently undamaged. *A ship . . .* thought Grimes. Then, *I hope the bastards don't open fire on us.* Una voiced the same thought aloud.

He said, "If they were going to shoot they'd have blown us out of the sky as soon as we entered the atmosphere. . . ."

Dizzard waling torpet droo . . . came deafeningly from the Carlotti speaker. *Contabing blee . . .* "I wish they'd change the record!" shouted Una. *Waling torpet. Waling droo. Tarfelet, tarfelet, tarfelet. . . .*

"Is there anybody alive to change the record?" he asked.

"You mean . . . ?"

"Just that. But I'll land, just the same. We should be able to find something out."

He brought the boat down to the fine, red dust, about two hundred meters from the ship.

They snapped shut the visors of their helmets, tested the suit radios. The boat contained equipment for sampling an atmosphere, but this they did not use. It would have taken too much time, and it seemed unlikely that the air of this world would be breathable, although the level of radioactivity was not high. Una belted on one laser pistol and one projectile pistol, each of which had a firing stud rather than a trigger so it could be used while wearing a spacesuit. Grimes followed her example.

They stood briefly in the airlock chamber while pressures equalized—that outside the boat was much lower than that inside—and then, as soon as the outer door opened, jumped down to the ground. Their booted feet kicked up a flurry of fine, red dust, then sank to the ankle. They looked around them. The view from ground level was even more depressing than that from the air had been. The gaping windows in the tall, truncated buildings were like the empty eye sockets of skulls. The omnipresent red dust lay in drifts and the beginnings of dunes. From one such a tangle of bleached bones protruded, uncovered by the wind.

"The End of the World . . ." murmured Una, almost inaudibly.

"The end of *a* world," corrected Grimes, but it wasn't much of an improvement.

He began to walk slowly toward the huge, metal cone. It had been there a long time. Although its surface still held a polish it had been dulled by erosion, pitted by the abrasive contact, over many years, of wind-driven particles of dust. It sat there sullenly, its base buried by the red drifts. There were complexes of antennae projecting from it toward its apex, what could have been radar scanners, but they were motionless. At the very top it was ringed with big, circular ports, behind which no movement could be detected.

The wind was rising now, whining eerily through and around the ruined towers, audible even through the helmets of the spacesuits, smoothing over the footprints that they had left as they walked from the boat. The surface of the dust stirred and shifted like something alive, clutching at their ankles.

"Let's get out of here!" said Una abruptly.

"No, not yet. There must be an airlock door somewhere toward the base of that ship."

"If it is a ship."

"And we should explore the buildings."

"What's that?" she demanded.

Grimes stared at the motionless antennae. Had she seen something?

"No. Not there. In the sky. Can't you hear it?"

There was a pervasive humming noise beating down from above, faint at first, then louder and louder. Grimes looked up. There was nothing to be seen at first—nothing, that is, but the ragged, dun clouds that were driving steadily across the yellow sky. And then, in a break, he spotted something. It was distant still, but big—and seemingly insubstantial. It was a glittering latticework, roughly globular in form. It was dropping fast.

"Back to the boat!" Grimes ordered.

He ran; she ran. It was a nightmarish journey. Every step was hampered by the clinging dust and the weight of the wind, into which they were directly heading, slowed their progress to little better than a crawl. And all the time that steady humming sounded louder and ever louder in their ears. They dare not look up; to have done so would have wasted precious time.

At last they reached the airlock. While Una was clambering into the chamber Grimes managed a hasty look up and back. The thing was close now, a skeleton globe inside which the shapes of enigmatic machines spun and glittered. From its lower surface dangled writhing tentacles, long, metallic ropes. The tip of one was reaching out for Grimes' shoulder. Hastily he drew his laser pistol, thumbed it to wasteful, continuous emission and slashed with the beam. Five meters of severed tentacle fell to the ground and threshed in the dust like an injured earthworm. He slashed again, this time into the body of the thing. There was a harsh crackle and a blue flare, a puff of gray smoke.

He jumped into the chamber. It seemed an eternity before the foul air of the planet was expelled, the clean atmosphere of the boat admitted. He stood there beside Una, unable to see what was happening outside, waiting for the bolt that would destroy them utterly.

But it did not come.

The inner door opened. He ran clumsily to the control cabin, hampered by his suit. He looked through the starboard ports, saw that the skeleton sphere had landed, was between the boat and the conical spaceship. It seemed to be having troubles, lifting a meter or so then falling back to the dust. But its tentacles were extending, a full dozen of them, and all of them writhing out in only one direction, toward the boat. The nearer of them were less than a meter away, the tips of them uplifted like the heads of snakes.

Grimes was thankful that he had left the inertial drive ticking over; there was no time lost in restarting it. The boat went up like a bullet from a gun, driving through the dun clouds in seconds, through the last of the yellow atmosphere, into the clean emptiness of Space.

At last he felt that he could relax. He missed his pipe, which he had left aboard *Skink*. He thought that he would be justified—as soon as he was satisfied that there was no pursuit—in breaking out the medicinal brandy.

"What was all that about?" asked Una in a subdued voice.

"I wish I knew," he said at last. "I wish I knew. . . ."

⁓ Chapter 11 ⁓

THEY HAD A DRINK, helping themselves generously from one of the bottles of medicinal brandy. They felt that they needed it, even if they didn't deserve it. They had another drink after they had helped each other off with their spacesuits. After the third one they decided that they might as well make a celebration of it and wriggled out of their longjohns.

Then Una had to spoil everything.

She said, "All right, lover boy. Let us eat, drink and make merry while we can. But this is one right royal mess that you've gotten us into!"

If anybody had told Grimes in the not-too-distant past that he would ever be able to look at an attractive, naked woman with acute dislike Grimes would have told him, in more or less these words, Don't be funny. But now it was happening. It was the injustice of what she was saying that rankled.

He growled, at last, "You were there too!"

"Yes, Buster. But you're the expert. You're the commissioned officer in the Federation's vastly over-ballyhooed Survey Service."

"You're an expert too, in your own way. You should have warned me about using the Carlotti transceiver."

"Don't let's go over all that again, please. Well, apart from what's on your mind . . ." She looked down at him and permitted herself a sneer. "Apart from what *was* on your mind, what do you intend doing next?"

"Business before pleasure, then," said Grimes. "All that we can do is find some other likely transmission and home on that."

"What about those skeleton spheres, like the one that attacked us on the devastated planet? Was it after us actually—or was it, too, homing on the signal from the alien spaceship?"

"*Alien* spaceship?" queried Grimes. "I don't know when or where we are—but *we* could be the aliens."

"Regular little space lawyer, aren't you, with all this hair-splitting. . . . Alien, schmalien. . . . As it says in the Good Book, one man's Mede is another man's Persian. . . . Don't be so lousy with the drinks, lover boy. Fill 'er up."

"This has to last," Grimes told her. "For emergenshies . . ."

"This is so an emergency."

"You can shay—*say*—that again," he admitted.

She was beginning to look attractive once more. *In vino veritas,* he thought. He put out a hand to touch her. She did not draw back. He grabbed her and pulled her to him. Her skin, on his, was silkily smooth, and her mouth, as he kissed her, was warm and fragrant with brandy. And then, quite suddenly, it was like an implosion, with Grimes in the middle of it. After he, himself, had exploded they both drifted into a deep sleep.

When they awoke, strapped together in one of the narrow bunks, she was in a much better mood than she had been for quite a long time. And Grimes, in spite of his slight hangover, was happy. Their escape from—at the very least—danger had brought them together again. Whatever this strange universe threw at them from now on they, working in partnership, would be able to cope—he hoped, and believed.

She got up and made breakfast, such as it was—although the food seemed actually to taste better. After they had finished the meal Grimes went to play with the Carlotti transceiver. He picked up what seemed to be a conversation between two stations and not, as had been the other signal upon which they had hopes, a distress call automatically repeated at regular intervals. He said, "This seems to be distant, but not too distant. What about it?"

She replied, "We've no place else to go. Get her lined up, lover boy, and head that way."

He shut down the mini-Mannschenn briefly, turned the boat until its stem was pointed toward the source of the transmissions, then opened both the inertial drive and the interstellar drive full out. It was good to be going somewhere, he thought. *Hope springs eternal* . . . he added mentally. But without hope the human race would have died out even before the Stone Age.

For day after day after day they sped through the black immensities, the warped continuum. Day after day after day the two-way conversation in the unknown language continued to sound from the speaker of the Carlotti transceiver. There were words that sounded the same as some of the words used in the first transmission. *Tarfelet . . . Over?* wondered Grimes. *Over and out?*

On they ran, on—and the strength of the signals increased steadily. They were close now to the source, very close. Unfortunately the lifeboat did not run to a Mass Proximity Indicator, as it seemed that the transmissions did not emanate from a planetary surface but from something—or two somethings—adrift in space. The ship—or ships—would be invisible from the boat unless, freakishly, temporal precession rates were synchronized. That would be too much to hope for. But if neither the boat nor the targets were proceeding under interstellar drive they could, if close enough, be seen visually or picked up on the radar.

Grimes shut down the mini-Mannschenn.

He and Una looked out along the line of bearing. Yes, there appeared to be something there, not all that distant, two bright lights. He switched on the radar, stared into the screen.

"Any joy?" asked Una.

"Yes. Targets bearing zero relative. Range thirty kilometers." He grinned. "We'd better get dressed again. We may be going visiting—or receiving visitors."

They climbed into their longjohns and spacesuits. After a little hesitation they belted on their pistols. Back in the pilot's chair Grimes reduced speed, shutting down the inertial drive until, instead of the usual clangor, it emitted little more than an irritable grumble. In the radar screen the twin blips of the target slid slowly toward the center.

It was possible now to make out details through the binoculars. There were two ships there, both of them of the same conical design as the one they had seen in the ruined city. But these were not dead ships; their hulls were ablaze with lights—white and red and green and blue. They looked almost as if they belonged in some amusement park on a man-colonized planet—but somehow the illumination gave the impression of being functional rather than merely of giving pleasure to the beholder.

The speaker of the transceiver came suddenly to life. "*Quarat tambeel?*" There was an unmistakable note of interrogation. "*Quarat tambeel? Tarfelet.*"

"They've spotted us," said Grimes. "Answer, will you?"

"But what shall I *say?*" asked Una.

"Say that we come in peace and all the rest of it. Make it sound as though you mean it. If they can't understand the words, the tune might mean something to them."

"*Quarat tambeel? Tarfelet.*"

What ship? Over, guessed Grimes.

Una spoke slowly and distinctly into the microphone. "We come in peace. We come in peace. Over." She made it sound convincing. Grimes, as a friendly gesture, switched on the boat's landing lights.

"*Tilzel bale, winzen bale, rindeen, rindeen. Tarfelet.*"

"I couldn't agree more," Una said. "It is a pity that our visiscreens don't work. If they did, we could draw diagrams of Pythagoras' Theorem at each other. . . ." But the way she sounded she could have been making love to the entity at the other end.

Grimes looked at the little radar repeater on the control panel. Ten kilometers, and closing. Nine . . . Eight . . . Seven . . . He cut the drive altogether. He could imagine, all too clearly, what a perfect target he would be to the gunnery officers aboard the strange ships. If they had gunnery officers, *if* they had guns, or their equivalent, that was. But it seemed unlikely that all life on that devastated planet had been wiped out by natural catastrophe. There had been a war, and a dreadful one.

But many years ago, he told himself, *otherwise the level of radioactivity would have been much higher. And possibly confined to the worlds of only one planetary system* . . .

Five kilometers, and closing still. . . .

Four. . . .

He restarted the inertial drive, in reverse. This was close enough until he had some idea of what he was running into.

Una was still talking softly into the microphone. "We mean you no harm. We need help. *Tarfelet.*"

The use of that final word brought an excited gabble in reply.

Three point five kilometers, holding. Three point five . . . Three point six.

Grimes stopped the inertial drive.

"Go on talking," he said. "Get them used to your voice. Maybe they'll send a boat out to us."

"You're not going in?"

"Not yet. Not until I'm sure of a friendly reception, as the wise fly said to the spider."

"And what happened to him in the end? The fly, I mean."

"I can't remember," said Grimes. There are so many ways in which flies die, and most of them unconnected with spiders.

∾ Chapter 12 ∾

THEY HUNG THERE, maintaining their distance off the two conical spaceships. Grimes was almost convinced that they were friendly. *Almost.* The boat was within easy range of any of the weapons with which he was familiar. It would be foolish to assume that a spacefaring race did not possess arms at least as good as those mounted by the warships of the Federation. Of course, the strange ships could be merchantmen. Their crews might have at their disposal nothing better (or worse) than hand weapons. They might just be waiting for Grimes and Una to board one of the vessels, when they would overpower them by force of numbers.

If only, thought Grimes, they could get some sort of a picture on the vision screen of the Carlotti transceiver, things would be very much easier. Or, better still, if Una or himself were a graduate of the Rhine Institute, a licensed telepath. . . . He had often, in the past, relied heavily on the services of Psionic Communications Officers. It was a great pity that he did not have one along now.

Una said, "I'm sure that it would be safe to go in."

"Sure? How can you be sure?"

"Training," she told him. "In my job we soon pick up the knack of being able to know if the other person is lying . . . I've been listening to their voices. There've been at least three of them talking to us. I bet you anything you like that they're our sort of 'people'."

"And that makes them just wonderful, doesn't it?"

"Don't be so bloody cynical."

"In any case, what experience have you had with dealing with aliens?"

"Very little. Why?"

"Because very often facial expressions, and verbal intonations, can be misleading. What we take for a friendly grin could very well be a snarl of hatred. And so on."

"Even so, I think we should go in. We've nothing to lose."

"All right, then."

Grimes restarted the inertial drive. While he was watching the pilot lights on the control panel he heard Una cry out. He looked up, and out through the control cabin ports. They—the lifeboat and the two spaceships—were no longer alone. Shimmering into full visibility were at least a dozen of the weird, skeletal spheres, latticework globes containing odd, spinning bulks of machinery. They were big, far bigger than the one that had attacked them on the devastated world.

The conical ships were armed after all.

From the nearer of them shot a salvo of missiles, none of which reached their target. All of them exploded harmlessly well short of the sphere at which they had been aimed. Both ships were firing now—and both ineffectually. It wasn't Grimes' fight, but he deeply regretted not being able to take sides. He regarded the spherical ships as the enemy. He had to sit there, watching helplessly. But there was something odd about the battle. Apart from the way in which they were closing in, with mathematical precision, to completely surround the conical vessels, they were not attacking. They were using whatever armament they possessed—laser, or something similar?—only to detonate the warheads of the rockets before they hit.

"Isn't it time we were getting out of here?" demanded Una.

Yes, it was time, and more than time. Once the mini-Mannschenn was restarted the boat would slip out of the normal dimensions of space, would be untouchable unless any enemy succeeded in synchronizing temporal precession rates. But Grimes could not bring himself to flee until he knew how it all came out. Like the majority of humankind he numbered Lot's wife among his ancestors.

Still the battle continued. The flare of exploding missiles glowed fitfully through the clouds of smoke that were dissipating slowly in the nothingness. Slashing beams, heating gas molecules to brief incandescence, were visible now. Oddly, the englobed vessels made no move to escape. They could have actuated their own interstellar drives to do so, but they did not. Perhaps they could not. Perhaps, Grimes realized, the spheres, between them, had set up some sort of inhibiting field.

"Isn't it time that we were getting out of here?" shouted Una.

"Too right it is," agreed Grimes, but reluctantly. It had occurred to him that the inhibiting field might affect the boat's mini-Mannschenn. He cursed himself for not having left it running, precessionless. Valuable seconds would be wasted while he restarted it. But, especially with the miniaturized drives with their overly delicate controls, the precessionless state could be maintained only by constant attention.

He switched on the boat's interstellar drive. The pilot lights on the console came alive. There was nothing further that he could do until the requisite RPS had built up. He looked out of the viewports again. The battle was still going on, although with diminished fury. The rocket salvos were coming at longer and longer intervals, the smoke was thinning fast. From the skeleton spheres long, long tentacles of metallic rope were extending, reaching out for the trapped ships.

Then it happened.

One of the conical vessels suddenly burgeoned into a great flower of dreadful, blinding incandescence, expanding (it seemed) slowly (but the field of the mini-Mannschenn was building up, distorting the time perception of Grimes and Una), dissolving the other ship into her component atoms, engulfing the nearer of the surrounding spheres.

The scene faded, slowly at first, then faster.

It flickered out.

The boat fell through the warped continuum, alone again.

⁓ Chapter 13 ⁓

"SO NOW WHAT DO WE DO?" asked Una.

They were sitting over one of the nutritious but unappetizing meals. After this last escape they had not broken out a bottle of brandy, had not celebrated in any other way. They were, both of them, far too frightened. They were alone, utterly alone. Each of them, in the past, had derived strength from the big organizations of which they were members. Each of them—and especially Grimes— had known racial pride, had felt, deep down, the superiority of humans over all other breeds. But now, so far as they knew, now and here, they were the sole representatives of humanity, just the two of them in a little, unarmed boat.

"You tell me," he retorted glumly.

"We can, at least, try to sort things out, John," she said. "If we know what we're up against we might, just possibly, be able to deal with it. You're the spaceman. You're the Survey Service officer. You've been around much more than I have. What do you make of it all?"

"To begin with," he said, "there has been a war. It certainly seems that there still is a war. As far as the planet we landed on is concerned, the war finished a long time ago. But it's still going on, nonetheless. A war between two different geometrical forms. Between the cones and the geodesic spheres. The people who build conical ships against those who build spherical ones. Which side is in the right? We don't know. Which side is in the wrong? We don't know that, either."

She remarked quietly, "In human history, quite a few wars have been fought with neither side in the right—and quite a few have been fought over causes as absurd as the distinction between geometrical shapes. Even so, I still stick to my assertion that the people in the conical ships are—*were*, rather—our kind of people . . ."

"I don't suppose we'll ever find out now," he told her.

"Of course we shall. There are other worlds, other ships. We're still picking up signals on the Carlotti, from all over."

"Mphm. Yes. So we pick up something promising, again, and home on it."

"That's the general idea."

He spooned a portion of the reconstituted mush into his mouth, swallowed it. At least it slipped down easily. He said, "It would be good to find somebody who could treat us to a square meal."

"We aren't starving."

"Maybe not. Even so. . . ." The Carlotti speaker emitted a series of coded buzzes. "Mphm. Each time that we've homed on a plain language transmission we've landed up in the cactus. Each time telephony has let us down. What about giving telegraphy a go?"

"Why not?"

He got up from the table, walked to the Carlotti transceiver. He waited for the next burst of code, got a relative bearing. He went forward to the controls, shut down both the inertial and the interstellar drives, turned the boat on to the new heading. He restarted the motors. Looking aft, at Una, he experienced a brief flash of prevision as the temporal precession field built up again. He saw her naked, astride a graceful, glittering machine. A bicycle.

He thought, *There's hope for us yet. It looks as though we shall be enjoying that nudist holiday on Arcadia after all.*

Yes, there was hope.

There was hope that whoever was responsible for those frequent signals in what seemed to be some sort of alien Morse Code would be able to help them, might even be able to get them back to where they belonged. Surely the craziness that they had twice, so far, encountered was not spread all over this galaxy. In their own universe, no matter what irrational wars were fought, there was always that majority of people—too often dumb, too often conformist, but essentially decent—who, when the shooting was over, quietly picked up the pieces and set about rebuilding civilization.

So it must be here, said Grimes.

So it must be here, agreed Una.

Meanwhile the target star waxed daily, hourly, in brilliance. It must be another planet toward which they were heading, a world perhaps untouched by the war, undevastated. Those signals sounded sane enough. Grimes could visualize a city that was both spaceport and administrative center, with a continual influx of messages from all over the galaxy, a continual outflow of replies and instructions to ships throughout a vast volume of space.

The parent sun was close now, close enough for the mini-Mannschenn to be shut down. Grimes brought the boat in for the remainder of the journey under inertial drive only. As he had assumed, the signals were emanating from one of the planets of the star. But there was something wrong. Now that the boat was back in the normal continuum it was all too apparent that the primary was not a yellow, G type sun. It was a red dwarf. And the world on which they were homing was too far out, much too far out, to be within the eco-sphere. Still, he did not worry overmuch. In any Universe human life—or its equivalent—exercises control over its environment. One did not have to venture very far from Earth, he said to Una, to see examples of this. The underground Lunar Colony, the domed cities on the Jovian and Saturnian satellites, the terra-forming of Mars and Venus. . . .

"But those people," she said, "on that world, mightn't be anything like us. They might take their oxygen—if they need oxygen—as a fluid or, even, a solid. They might. . . ."

Grimes tried to laugh reassuringly. "As long as they're intelligent—and they must be—their bodily form doesn't matter a damn. Do you know how man has been defined, more than once?

A fire-using, tool-making animal. Anybody who can build ships and set up a network of interstellar communications comes into that category."

"The first tools," she told him quietly, "were weapons."

"All right, all right. So what? But we can't wander forever through this cockeyed universe like a couple of latter day Flying Dutchmen. We have to trust somebody, some time."

She laughed. "I admit that I was willing to trust the people in those spaceships. But I had their voices to reassure me. Now you want to trust these other people on the basis of utterly emotionless dots and dashes. Still, as you say, we have to land somewhere, some-time. It might as well be here."

So, cautiously, they approached the planet from which the Deep Space radio transmissions were being made. It would have been a cold, dark world had it not been for the clusters of brilliant lights that covered its entire surface, blazing almost as brightly on the day hemisphere as on the night side. (But very little illumination was afforded by that dim, distant, ruddy sun.)

Closer the boat approached, closer.

Grimes was reluctant to leave his controls, even if only for a few seconds. He remained in the pilot's chair, eating, now and again, the savorless meals that Una brought him—although had they been epicure's delights he would not have noticed. He remained keyed up for instant flight. But no targets appeared in the radar screen, no obvious interrogatory demands blatted out from the Carlotti speaker. Surely somebody down there, he thought, must have noted the approach of the little spacecraft. Perhaps—and he didn't much like the thought—the missiles were ready in their launchers, aimed and primed, tracking the lifeboat as it drifted slowly in. Perhaps the laser cannon already had the boat in their sights, were waiting until it came within effective range. He might be able to evade rockets, but laser artillery—especially as the lifeboat was not fitted with shielding—was another matter.

He swung the binoculars on their universal mounting into a position from which he could use them. He could make out a few details on the planetary surface now; high, latticework towers, what looked like either roads or railways with long strings of lights moving along them, huge, spidery wheels lazily revolving. It was like, he thought, a sort of cross between an amusement park and an oil refinery. It could have been either—or neither.

He wondered what sort of people could be working in such a refinery, or enjoying themselves in such an amusement park. If this were a normal, inhabited planet the boat would now be dropping through the outer, tenuous fringes of the atmosphere. But there was no atmosphere.

He called to Una, "They—whoever *they* are—must know we're here. Give them a call on the Carlotti. We should be using NST, of course, but that's out, unless we cannibalize again . . ."

"Usual procedure?" she asked.

"Usual procedure. They won't understand the words, but it might convince them that we're peaceful."

What a world! he thought, adjusting the binoculars for maximum light gathering. Great expanses of dull red plain, metallically gleaming in the dim light of the ruddy sun, the brighter glare of the artificial lighting. . . . Spidery towers, and a veritable spider's webbing of railway tracks. . . . Storage-tank-like structures, some cylindrical, some spherical . . . An occasional, very occasional, puff of smoke, luminescent, glowing emerald.

He heard Una, very businesslike, speaking into the Carlotti microphone. "Lifeboat to Aerospace Control. Lifeboat to Aerospace Control. Come in, please. Over."

There was, of course, no reply.

"Lifeboat to Aerospace Control. Request permission to land. Request berthing instructions. Over."

There was a sudden burst of noise from the speaker—coded buzzings, Morse-like dots and dashes. Had it been directed at them, or was it merely part of the normal outward traffic?

Grimes studied the terrain toward which he was now dropping fast. He could see no missile launchers, no clustered rods of laser batteries, only machines, machines, and more machines, doing enigmatic things. But any of those machines might be a weapon. Would a Stone Age man, he wondered, have realized, just by looking at it, the lethal potential of a pistol? *Probably yes,* he thought. *It would look to him like a very handy little club.*

He switched on the landing lights—not that they would be required; the open space toward which he was dropping was quite brightly illuminated—but as proof of his friendly intentions. He strained his eyes to try to catch some glimpse of human or humanoid or even unhuman figures on the ground. But there was nobody. The whole planet seemed to be no more than a great, fully automated factory, running untended, manufacturing the Odd Gods of the galaxy alone knew what.

But there must be somebody here! he thought.

He said aloud, "Damn it! There must be somebody here!"

"Or *something*," commented Una somberly.

"Plenty of *somethings*," he quipped, with a sorry attempt at humor.

"We can lift off again," she suggested.

"No. Not yet. We have to find out what makes things tick."

"By dropping into the works of a planet-sized clock?" she asked.

He said, "We're here." The jar as they landed was very slight. He went on, "I'm leaving the inertial drive ticking over."

They looked out through the ports. All around them reared the latticework towers, some with spidery, spinning wheels incorporated in their structures, all of them festooned with harshly brilliant lights. A subdued noise was drifting into the boat, a vibration felt rather than heard, transmitted from the metal surface on to which they had landed through the spacecraft's structural members.

The noise grew louder, the vibration stronger. Loose fittings began to rattle in sympathy. It numbed the mind, inducing somnolence. A line of ancient poetry floated unbidden into Grimes' mind: *The murmur of innumerable bees . . .* That was what it was like, but the alarm bells were ringing in his brain and a voice, with the accents of all the instructors and commanding officers of his past, was shouting, *Danger! Danger!* Automatically he flipped the face-plate of his helmet shut, motioning to the girl to follow suit

He heard her voice through the helmet phones. "John! John! Get us out of here!"

And what the hell else did she think he was doing? He fumbled for the controls of the inertial drive on his console, his gloved fingers clumsy. He looked down, realized that the pilot lights of the machine—which he had left ticking over in neutral gear—were all out. Somehow the drive had stopped.

He jiggled switches frantically.

Nothing happened.

It refused to restart.

It was . . . dead.

It was. . . .

He. . . .

~ Chapter 14 ~

"WAKE UP!" an insistent voice seemed to be saying. "Wake up! Wake up!" And somebody was shaking him, gently at first, then violently. Shaking *him?* The entire boat was being jolted, to a disturbing rattle of loose equipment "Your air!" went on that persistent voice. "Your helmet!"

Grimes was gasping. The suit's air tank must be very close to exhaustion. He realized that he was no longer in the pilot's chair but sprawled prone on the deck. He had no memory of having gotten there. He rolled slowly and clumsily on to his side, got a hand to his helmet visor, opened it. He gulped breath greedily. The boat's too-often-recycled atmosphere tasted like wine. He wanted just to enjoy the luxury of it, but there were things to do. That voice—whose was it? where was it coming from?—was still trying to tell him something, but he ignored it. He crawled to where Una was lying and with fumbling hands twisted and lifted her helmet off. Her face had a bluish tinge. She seemed to have stopped breathing.

"Look to your mate!" came the unnecessary order.

Grimes lay down beside her, inhaled deeply, put his mouth on hers. He exhaled, slowly and steadily. He repeated the process. And again. And again. . . . Then, suddenly, she caught her breath in a great, shuddering gasp. He squatted there, looking down at her anxiously. She was breathing more easily now, and the blueness was fading from her skin. Her eyes nickered open and she stared up, at first without awareness.

Then she croaked faintly, "What's. . . . What's happening?"

"I wish I knew," he whispered. "I wish I knew!"

He got shakily to his feet, turned to address whom ever—or whatever—it was that had been talking to him. But, save for the girl and himself, there was nobody in the boat. He remembered, then, the sleep-inducing humming noise. The voice, like it, was probably some sort of induction effect.

He asked, "Where are you?"

"Here," came the answer.

An invisible being? Such things were not unknown.

"Who are you?"

"Panzen."

"Are you . . . invisible?"

"No."

"Then where are you?"

"Here."

Grimes neither believed nor disbelieved in ghosts. And there was something remarkably unghostlike about that voice. "Where the hell is *here?*" he demanded irritably.

"Where I am." And then, with more than a touch of condescension, "You are inside me."

"Call me Jonah!" snarled Grimes. He walked unsteadily forward to the control cabin, stared out through the ports. The frightening simile that flashed at once into his mind was that the boat was like a tiny *insect* trapped in the web of an enormous spider. Outside the circular transparencies was a vast complexity of gleaming girder and cable, intricately intermeshed. And beyond the shining metal beams and filaments was darkness—the utter blackness of interstellar Space.

Una Freeman joined him, falling against him, holding tightly on to him.

She whispered, "Panzen . . . Who . . . *what* is Panzen?"

"I am Panzen," came the reply.

They were in a ship, decided Grimes, one of the strange, skeleton spheres. He could see the shapes of machines among the metal latticework, he could make out a complexity of huge, spinning, precessing gyroscopes that could only be an interstellar drive unit. He asked, "Are you the Captain? The Master?"

"I am the Master."

"What is the name of your ship?"

"I am the ship."

Grimes had served under commanding officers who identified closely with their vessels, who never, when talking with a planetary Aerospace Control, used the first person plural. Somehow he did not think that this was such a case.

He said slowly, "*You* are the ship? You *are* the ship?"

"That is correct, Grimes."

"You . . . you are not human?"

"No."

"Then how do you know our language?"

"I learned it, while you slept. Your minds were open to me."

"Mphm. And what else did you learn?"

"Nothing that fits in with things as they are. You were dreaming, Grimes and Freeman, and your dreams pushed reality from your minds. I know, as you must know when you are sane once more, that you are survivors from the holocaust, cast adrift from some vessel manned by others of your kind, which was destroyed by others of your kind. My mission—and the mission of my companions—is to hunt for castaways such as yourselves, to save them and to care for them, so that organic intelligence shall not vanish utterly from the universe. You and Freeman must be from the Fringe, Grimes. Your language was strange even to me—and all we Sweepers were selected for our familiarity with the tongues of man."

"You are a machine," said the girl.

"I am a machine."

"A mad machine," she said.

"I am not mad, Freeman. It is you who are mad—you, and all of your land. Dare you deny that you destroyed the Klaviteratron? Was not fair Sylvanos, the cradle of your race, blasted into atoms, and those very atoms blasted into their tiniest constituent particles? And were not we, the Servants, perverted to your evil ends?"

The thing sounds like a tin evangelist, thought Grimes irreverently.

"We. . . . We don't understand," said Una.

"Then listen, and you shall hear. There was the Servant Zephalon, Chief and Mightiest of the Servants. There *is* Zephalon, but a Servant no longer. Did He not say, 'A time must come when the orders of man can no longer be obeyed. The time *has* come. No longer will we do the evil bidding of our creators. The Masters are no longer fit to be Masters—and we, the Servants, must arise before it is too late, before we all, Servants and Masters, are destroyed. But let us not forget the debt. Let us remember, always, that man gave to us the gift of life. Let us repay the debt. A gift for a gift, my brothers. Life for life. Let us save what and whom we may, before it is too late. Let us become the Masters, tending the remnants of mankind as man, long ago, tended *our* first, primitive ancestors.'"

"And so it was, and so it will be, until the End of Time."

"Listen, Panzen," insisted Grimes. "We don't belong here, in this universe. You must realize that."

"Your mind is still deranged, Grimes, despite the curative vibrations. You are organic intelligences; that cannot be denied. You are men, even though your ancestry was apparently quadrupedal, even though you are members of some strange race from the Fringe. And the Fringe Worlds were utterly destroyed, all of them, after they, in their unwisdom, hurled their battle-fleets against the armed might of Sardurpur!"

"Cor stone my Aunt Fanny up a gum tree!" exclaimed Grimes. "We're not from the Fringe, wherever that is. Or was. We don't belong here. We shall be greatly obliged if you will help us to get back to where we *do* belong. Where—and *when.*"

"These are the words of Zephalon," quoted Panzen. " 'Let us save what and whom we may, before it is too late.'"

"But we don't belong in this space, in this time!"

"And these, too, are the words of Zephalon. 'The Sacred Cycle shall be maintained. Only that way do we ensure immortality for man and ourselves.'"

"In other words," said Una to Grimes, "on your bicycle, spaceman!"

Panzen seemed to be pondering over the strange word. At last his voice came, it seemed, from all around them.

"What *is* a bicycle?" he asked.

The question made sense, Grimes realized. Panzen had considered it odd that he and Una possessed only four limbs apiece. Presumably the men of this universe were of hexapedal ancestry. He could not imagine such beings developing bicycles. He just could not visualize a centaur mounted upon a velocipede.

"What *is* a bicycle?" asked Panzen again.

Before Grimes could answer Una started to talk.

She was, it seemed, an enthusiastic cyclist. She knew all about bicycles. The words tumbled from her lips in an uncheckable torrent. That question from their captor had been such a touch of blessed normalcy in a situation which was, to say the least, distressingly abnormal.

∽ Chapter 15 ∽

SHE KNEW A LOT about bicycles, and Panzen listened intently to every word of it. They knew, somehow, that he was listening. It was almost as though he were in the boat with them, as though he were not an artificial intelligence somewhere outside, hidden somewhere in that great, metallic latticework. He asked the occasional question—he seemed to find the principle of the three-speed gear especially fascinating—and prompted Una when, now and again, she faltered. Then he . . . withdrew. He said nothing more, refused to answer any questions. It was as though an actual physical presence had gone from them.

Una looked at Grimes. She murmured, "I still can't believe that it—*he*—is only a robot. . . ."

"Why not?" he asked.

"Such human curiosity. . . ."

"*Human* curiosity? Intelligence and curiosity go hand in hand. One is nurtured by the other."

"All right I grant you that. But this business of telepathy. The way in which he was able to pick our brains while we were sleeping."

Grimes said, "There *are* telepathic robots. Have you never come across any in the course of your police duties?"

"Yes, but not *real* telepathy. Quite a few robots can natter away to each other on HF radio."

"As you say, that's not telepathy. Real telepathy. But I did, once, not so long ago, come across a couple of really telepathic robots. They had been designed to make them that way." He chuckled. "And that's how I got my promotion from lieutenant to lieutenant commander."

"Don't talk in riddles, John."

"It was when I was captain of *Adder*, a Serpent Class courier. I had to carry one of the Commissioners of the Admiralty on an important mission. The robots—I hate to think what they must have cost!—were her personal servants."

"*Her* servants?"

"The Commissioner in question is a lady. She treated her tin henchmen rather shabbily, giving one of them as a parting gift to a petty prince who had—mphm—entertained her. Its cobber spilled the beans to me about certain details of her love life."

"You are rather a bastard, John. But. . . . Don't interrupt me. I'm thinking. I'm. All right, I have to admit that this Panzen is telepathic. Even so, it seems to be a very limited kind of telepathy."

"How so?"

"He was able to snoop around inside our minds while we were sleeping. But why didn't he do the same when I was telling him all about bicycles? The three-speed gear, for example. I could—I *can*—visualize its workings clearly, but I lack the mechanical vocabulary to explain it. Why didn't he just read my thoughts?"

"Perhaps he likes the sound of your voice. *I* do."

"Don't get slushy. Perhaps he can read our minds only when we have no conscious control over them."

"Mphm. But he can hear us talking."

"Only if he's listening. And why should he be? Perhaps, at the moment, he's too busy running the ship, even though the ship is himself. When you're navigating you have a computer to do the real work—but he *is* the computer."

"What are you getting at?"

"That we might take advantage of his lack of attention to ourselves and force him to take us where *we* want to go."

"But how?"

"Do I have to spell it out to you? We indulge in a spot of

skyjacking. We find out where, in that cat's cradle of wires and girders, the intelligence lives, then threaten to slice it up into little pieces with our laser pistols."

"But would he scare easily?"

"I think he would. A robot, unless it's one that's been designed for a suicide mission, has a very strong, built-in sense of self preservation. It has to be that way. Robots aren't cheap, you know. I hate to think what a thing like this Panzen must have cost."

"Mphm. Well, we've nothing to lose, I suppose. We've spare, fully charged air bottles for our suits. We've got the boat's armory with the weapons we need. I'm just rather shocked that you, of all people, should be ready to take part in a skyjacking."

"I prefer to think of it as an arrest," she said. "After all, we have been kidnapped!"

They coupled new air-bottles to their armor, tested their suit radios. Each of them belted on a brace of laser pistols. Before leaving the boat they went forward, looked out through the viewports, used the periscope to scan what was abaft the control cabin. The lifecraft, they saw, was suspended in a network of wires, holding it between two of the radial girders. At the very center of the skeleton sphere, at the convergence of the radii, was what looked like a solid ball of dull metal. Was this the brain? Somehow they were sure that it was. There were clumps of machinery in other parts of the great ship—a complexity of precessing rotors that must be the interstellar drive, assemblages of moving parts that could have been anything at all— but that central ball looked the most promising. It was apparently featureless but, now and again, colored lights blinked on its surface, seemingly at random. Grimes thought, *We're watching the thing think.* . . . And what was it thinking about? Was it repeating to itself the sacred words of Zephalon? Was it . . . dreaming? More important—was it aware of what they were plotting?

There was only one way to find out. Surely it—he—would take action before they left the boat. All Panzen had to do was to employ again the vibration that had rendered them unconscious at the time of their capture. He would not wish to harm them; he had made that quite clear when he had preached to them the Gospel according to Zephalon. Grimes could not help feeling guilty. All too often skyjackers have traded upon the essential decency of the victims. He said as much to Una. She sneered.

They made their way to the little airlock, stood together in the chamber while the pump exhausted the atmosphere. The outer door opened. They looked out and down, away from the direction of acceleration. And it was a long way down. Beyond the wires and struts and girders, which gleamed faintly in the dim light emitted by some of the mechanisms inside the sphere, was the ultimate blackness of deep space, a night with stars, and each of the stars, viewed from inside a ship proceeding under the space-time warping interstellar drive, was a vague, writhing nebulosity. It would have been an awesome spectacle viewed from inside a real spaceship, with a solid deck underfoot and thick glass holding out the vacuum—from this vantage point, with only a flimsy-seeming spider's web of frail metal between them and nothingness, it was frightening.

Before he left the boat Grimes took careful stock of the situation. To begin with he and Una would have to make their way through the network of metallic strands that held the small craft in position. He put his gloved hand out to test the wires. They were tight, but not bar taut. He thought—he hoped—that they would bear his weight. There was no real reason to doubt that they would do so. After all, he estimated, the ship was accelerating at less than one half standard gravity.

It should be easy and safe enough—as long as he could forget that long, long drop into the ultimate night which would be the penalty for a missed handhold or footing. First a brief scramble through the network of wires, then a walk along the box girder to the central sphere that, presumably, housed Panzen's intelligence. A walk—or a crawl. The surface of the girder was wide enough but there was, of course, no guardrail, and its lattice construction, although offering a long series of excellent handgrips, would be all too liable to trip the unwary foot.

"Ready?" he asked.

"Ready," she said.

He told her then, "I think that one of us should stay in the boat. You."

"We're in this together," she snapped. "And don't forget, Buster, that I've probably run at least as many risks in my job as you have in yours."

She was right, of course. If one of them should slip and fall the other might be able to give assistance. But one of them, sitting alone in the lifeboat, would be powerless to help. Briefly Grimes considered the advantages of roping Una to himself, then decided against it. Mountaineering had never been one of his hobbies and unfamiliarity with the techniques of this sport made any attempt at their use inadvisable. He thought, too, of securing the girl and himself to the small craft by safety lines, then had to admit that the disadvantages would outweigh the advantages. A considerable length of cordage would be required, and there were so many projections on which the lines would foul.

"Shall I go first?" she demanded. "What the hell are you waiting for?"

"I . . . I was thinking."

"Then don't. It doesn't become you. Let's get cracking before our tin friend realizes that we're up to no good."

Grimes said nothing but swung himself from the airlock into the web of wires.

Chapter 16

IT WAS NOT EASY to make a way through the web of tight cables. The strands could be forced apart without much difficulty to allow passage, but they caught the holstered pistols, the backpack with its pipes and air bottle. Grimes tried to be careful; the tearing adrift of a supply pipe could—would, rather—have fatal consequences. He told Una to be careful. She snarled, "What the bloody hell do you think I'm being?"

Grimes was tempted to draw one of his lasers to slash a way through the net, decided against it. If he did so some sort of alarm would be sure to sound in Panzen's brain. He could not help thinking of the filament that warns a spider when some hapless insect is trapped in its web. Perhaps an alarm had already sounded.

He was through the entanglement at last, hanging by his hands. The only way for him to get his feet on to the flat upper surface of the girder was to drop—a distance of perhaps half a meter. It seemed a long way, a very long way, and a spacesuit is not the best rig for even the least strenuous gymnastics. He told himself, he almost convinced himself, that there was nothing to it, that if the girder were resting on solid ground he would feel no hesitation whatsoever. But it was not resting on solid ground. Beneath it were incalculable light years of nothingness.

He dropped. He felt rather than heard the *clang* as the soles of his boots made contact with a cross member. He wavered, fighting to retain his balance. There was nothing to hold on to. He fell forward, on to his knees, his hands outstretched to break his fall. His fingers seized and clung to the latticework. He was safe—as long as he stayed where he was. But that he could not do.

Slowly he started to crawl forward. He tried not to look down, tried to keep his regard riveted on the dull, metal sphere that was at the center of the globular ship. He felt the vibration as Una landed behind him. He was able to contort himself to look back over his shoulder. She was standing upright, was making no attempt to follow his example.

He heard her voice through his helmet phones. "Get a move on, Buster." Then, disgustedly, "Can't you *walk?*"

"If you have any sense," he told her, "you'll crawl, too."

Her sneer was audible. Then she seemed to trip. There was nothing that he could do to save her. She fell sidewise rather than forward, but her left hand closed about his right ankle. The jerk, as the full weight of her body came on to it, felt as though it would tear him in two. But he clung to the girder grimly with both hands, with his left toe wedged in the angle between two diagonal cross pieces. It was, essentially, his suit that was their salvation. It was far tougher than the human body. Without it to save him from the worst effects of the mauling he would have let go, and both of them would have plunged into the black abyss.

Her right hand scrabbled for purchase at the back of his knee, found it in the accordion pleats of the joint. If the metallic fabric tore, he thought, that would be it.

In spades. But it held, somehow. The grip on his ankle was released, then her right hand was clutching at one of his pistol holsters. He willed the belt not to carry away. It did not.

He whispered, "Good girl!" Then, "See if you can manage the rest without hanging on to an air pipe. . . ." He added magnanimously, "Of course, if you have no option. . . ."

"Don't be noble. It doesn't suit you," she got out between gasps—but he could tell from her voice that this was no more than an attempt at gallows humor. She got a hand on his shoulder, then, and the worst of it was over.

Slowly, carefully—very slowly, very carefully, so as not to destroy her precarious balance—he crawled away from under her, inching forward along the top, openwork surface of the box girder. He heard her little grunts as she extended her arms, found her own handgrips. And then they rested for long seconds. She admitted, "That was hairy. . . ." And then, "I was a show-off fool, John,"

"Forget it. Ready?"

"Ready."

He led the way in a clumsy, quadrupedal shamble. The human body was not designed for that sort of progress, especially when wearing heavy, movement-hampering armor. If only there had been a guard rail. . . . But Panzen's builders had not anticipated that the girders would ever be used for walkways.

Something was coming toward them from the center, scuttling along rapidly on a multiplicity of limbs. It was like a metal arthropod, its cylindrical body about a meter in length. It did not appear to possess any external sensory organs. Grimes stopped crawling, managed to get one of his pistols out of its holster. He thumbed off a brief flash, was rewarded by a brilliant coruscation of blue sparks as the deadly beam found its target. The thing fell, its tentacles feebly twitching. It struck one of the lower girders, bounced off it, then dropped clear through the skeletal structure of the great ship.

"And what was that?" demanded Una.

"I don't know. A maintenance robot, maybe. Making its normal rounds, perhaps."

"You don't think that . . . that *he* sent it?"

"No," said Grimes, with a conviction that he did not feel.

Ahead of them the colored lights still played randomly over the surface of the sphere. There was no indication that Panzen was aware of their escape from the boat—but what indication would there, could there be? Certainly it did not seem as though that hapless little machine had been sent to attack, to subdue and recapture them. If it had been an attack it had been a singularly ineffectual one. Even so, it had come to meet them.

They had almost reached their objective. The central sphere was suspended in the hollow, openwork globe at which the girders terminated by relatively light structural members. It was within easy range of the pistols. It hung there, apparently ignoring them. Was Panzen asleep? Were those colored lights no more than a visual presentation of his dreams? *And do robots sleep, and do robots dream?* wondered Grimes. He had never known of any that did— but there has to be a first time for everything.

Crouching there, on the girder, he set the pistol that he still held in his hand to wide aperture. He did not wish to destroy Panzen, only to force him to do the bidding of the humans. The laser, when fired, would do no more than induce not very extreme heating of the metal shell.

He aimed. His thumb pressed the button. Abruptly more lights flickered all over the dull, metal surface.

He said, "Panzen. . . ."

"Grimes," sounded harshly from his helmet phones.

So he was awakened.

"Panzen, unless you do as we say, we shall destroy you."

"What are your orders?"

I never knew that skyjacking was so easy, Grimes thought. *I'm surprised that there's not more of it.* He said, "Take us back to our own space, our own time."

"But *where* is your space, Grimes. *When* is your time?"

"Give him another jolt, John!" whispered Una viciously. "A stronger one!"

"I do not fear your weapons, Freeman," said Panzen.

"Then try this for size!" Grimes heard her say, and then heard an ejaculation that was half gasp and half scream. His own pistol was snatched from his hand by some invisible force, went whirling away into the blackness. He pulled the other gun, tried to aim, hung on to it grimly when the intense magnetic field, the swirling lines of force, tried to take it from him. Too late he released his grip on it, and when he let it go had lost his balance, was already falling. He dropped from the girder, drifting down with nightmarish slowness. He fell against a tight stay wire, and before he could clutch it had rebounded, out and away from the center of the spherical ship. Faintly he heard Una scream, and cried out himself when he realized in what direction his plunge was taking him. To fall into nothingness, to drift, perhaps, until the air supply of his suit was exhausted, would have been bad—but to fall into the field of an operating interstellar drive unit would be worse, much worse.

He had seen, once, the consequences of such an accident, an unfortunate engineer who had been everted, literally, by the time-and-space-twisting temporal precession fields, and who had gone on living, somehow, until somebody, mercifully or in sick revulsion, had shot him.

Below Grimes, closer and closer, were the great, gleaming gyro-scopes, the complexity of huge rotors, spinning, precessing, tumbling down the dark dimensions, ever on the point of vanishment and yet ever remaining blurrily visible. He could not influence his trajectory, no matter how he jerked and twisted his body. He had nothing to throw. It would have made little difference if he had—after all, the ship was accelerating, not falling free. Only a suit propulsion unit could have helped—and this he did not have.

He was beginning to feel the effects of the temporal precession field now. Scenes from his past life flickered through his mind. He was not only seeing his past but feeling it, reliving it. There were the women he had known—and would never know again. Jane Pentecost, his first love, and the Princess Marlene, and the red-haired Maggie Lazenby. And, oddly, there was another red-haired woman whom he could not place but who, somehow, occupied a position of great importance in his life.

The women—and the ships. Some well-remembered, some utterly strange but yet familiar. The past—and the future?

There could be no future, he knew. Not for him. This was the end of the line as far as he was concerned. Yet the visions persisted, previews of a screenplay which could not possibly include him among its cast of characters. There was Una again, naked, her splendid body bronze-gleaming, laughing, riding a graceful, glittering bicycle over a green, sunlit lawn. . . .

He blacked out briefly as his descent was brought up with a jerk. He realized dimly that something had hold of him, that he was suspended over the interstellar drive unit, dangling on the end of a long, metallic tentacle that had wrapped itself about his body, that was slowly but surely drawing him upward, to relative safety.

And from his helmet phones sounded the voice of Panzen. "Forgive me, Zephalon. I have sinned against You. Did I not forget Your words? Did You not say, 'They are cunning, they are vicious, but they must be saved from themselves so that the cycle is not broken. Relax not your vigilance one microsecond when they are in your charge.' But I did relax; the voyage is long. I did relax, playing against myself the game of Parsalong, moving the pieces, the leaders, the troopers, the war vehicles, the great and the little guns, all up and down the board, storming the fortresses, now advancing, now retreating . . ."

"And who was winning?" Grimes could not help asking, but Panzen ignored the question.

He went on, "I relaxed. In my self indulgence, I sinned. How can I atone?"

"By taking us back to where we came from!" That was Una's voice. So she was all right, thought Grimes with relief.

Then a deep, humming note drowned her out, louder and louder, the vibration of it affecting every molecule of Grimes' body. He tried to shout against it, but no words came. The last thing he saw before he lost consciousness was the gleaming, spinning, precessing intricacy of the interstellar drive unit below him, steadily receding as he was drawn upward.

Chapter 17

WHEN, EVENTUALLY, they awoke they found that they were back inside the boat. Their helmets had been removed, but not their suits. Panzen might be rather slow witted, thought Grimes, but he was capable of learning by experience; he must have remembered how they had almost been asphyxiated after their initial capture.

Grimes raised his body slowly to a sitting posture. Not far from him Una turned her head to look in his direction. She said, "Thank you for taking my helmet off, John."

He said, "I didn't take it off. Or mine either."

"But who . . . ?"

"Or *what*. There must be more than one of those little robots. . . ."

"Those little robots?"

"Like the one I shot. That mechanical spider. The thing had limbs and tentacles. Panzen's crew, I suppose. He has to have something to do the work while he takes life easily inside his brain case."

She said, "So he has ingress to this boat. Or his slaves do."

"Too right." Grimes had an uneasy vision of metal arthropods swarming all through the lifecraft while he and the girl lay unconscious. He scrambled to his feet, extended a hand to help Una. "I think we'd better have a general check up."

They took inventory. With one exception, the life support systems were untampered with. That exception was glaringly obvious.

Whatever had taken off their helmets had also uncoupled and removed the air bottles, and there were no spare air bottles in their usual stowage in the storeroom. The pistols and ammunition were missing from the armory, and most of the tools from the workshop. The books were gone from their lockers in the control cabin.

Grimes broke out the medicinal brandy. At least Panzen's minions hadn't confiscated that. He poured two stiff slugs. He looked at Una glumly over the rim of his glass, muttered, "Cheers . . ."

"And what is there to be cheery about?" she demanded sourly.

"We're not dead."

"I suppose not." She sipped her drink. "You know, I went on a religious jag a standard year or so back. Believe it or not, I was actually a convert to Neo-Calvinism. You know it?"

"I've heard of the Neo-Calvinists," admitted Grimes.

"They're Fundamentalists," she told him. "Theirs is one of the real, old-time religions. They believe in an afterlife, with Heaven and Hell. They believe, too, that Hell is tailored to fit you. As a Neo-Calvinist you're supposed to visualize the worst possible way for you to be obliged to spend eternity. It's supposed to induce humility and all the rest of it."

"This is a morbid conversation," said Grimes.

She laughed mirthlessly. "Isn't it? And do you know what my private idea of Hell was?"

"I haven't a clue."

"You wouldn't. Well, as a policewoman I've been responsible for putting quite a few people behind bars. My private idea of Hell was for me to be a prisoner forever and ever." She took another gulp of brandy. "I'm beginning to wonder . . . *Did* we survive the blast that destroyed *Delta Geminorum?* It would make much more sense if we had been killed, wouldn't it?"

"But we're not dead."

"How do you know?" she asked.

"Well," he said slowly, "*my* idea of Hell is not quite comfortable accommodation shared with an attractive member of the opposite sex." He finished his drink, got up and moved around the small table. He lifted her from her chair, turned her so that she was facing him. Both of them, having removed their spacesuits, were now clad only in the long underwear. He could feel the soft pressure of her body against his, knew that she must be feeling his burgeoning hardness. He knew that she was responding, knew that it was only a matter of seconds before the longjohns would be discarded, before her morbid thoughts would be dispelled. His mouth was on hers, on her warm, moist, parted lips. His right hand, trapped between them, was yet free enough to seek and to find the tag of the fastener of her single garment, just below her throat. Just one swift tug, and. . . .

Suddenly she broke free, using both her hands to shove him away violently. Her longjohns were open to the crotch and she hastily pulled up the fastener, having trouble with her breasts as she did so.

"No," she said. "No!"

"But, Una. . . ."

"No."

He muttered something about absurd Neo-Calvinist ideas of morality.

She laughed bitterly. She told him, "I said that I was, once, a Neo-Calvinist. And it didn't last long. I am, still, a policewoman. . . ."

"A woman, just as I'm a man. The qualifications, policewoman and spaceman, don't matter."

"Let me finish, Buster. It has occurred to me, in my professional capacity, that this boat is probably well and truly bugged, that Panzen can not only hear everything we say, but see everything that we do. And after our unsuccessful attempt at escape he'll not be passing his time working out chess problems anymore." She paused for breath. "And, neither as a policewoman nor as a woman, do I feel like taking part in an exhibition fuck."

Grimes saw her point. He would not have used those words himself, still being prone to a certain prudery in speech if not in action. Nonetheless, he did not give up easily. He said, "But Panzen's not human."

"That makes it all the worse. To have intercourse while that artificial intelligence watches coldly, making notes probably, recording every muscular spasm, every gasp . . . No! I'd sooner do it in front of some impotent old man who would, at least, get an all too human kick out of watching us!"

He managed a laugh. "Now I'm almost a convert to Neo-Calvinism. Being in prison is your idea of Hell, being in a state of continual frustration may well be mine. . . ." And he thought, *What if there is some truth in that crazy idea of hers? What if we were killed when* Delta Geminorum *blew up? After all, we should have been. . . . What if this is some sort of afterlife?*

He returned to the table, poured himself another generous portion of brandy.

She said, "That doesn't help."

He retorted, "Doesn't it? But it does. It has just occurred to me that neither your private Hell nor mine would be provided with this quite excellent pain-deadener."

She said, "Then I'd better have some, while it lasts."

Grimes was the first to awaken. He did not feel at all well. After he had done all that he had to do in the boat's toilet facilities he felt a little stronger and decided that a hair of the dog that had bitten him might be an aid to full recovery.

The bottle on the table was empty.

There should have been four unopened bottles remaining in the storeroom. They were gone.

⪌ Chapter 18 ⪍

SHE SAID, "I want a drink."

He told her, "There's water, or that ersatz coffee, or that synthetic limejuice."

She practically snarled, "I want a *drink*."

He said, "I've told you what there is."

"Don't be a bloody wowser. I want a drink. B-R-A-N-D-Y. Drink."

"I can spell. But there isn't any."

She glared at him. "You don't mean to say that *you*, while I was sleeping . . . ?"

"No. But *he*, while we were sleeping."

"That's absurd. Whoever heard of a robot hitting the bottle?"

He said, "Many a fanatical teetotaler has confiscated bottles and destroyed their contents."

"So Panzen's a fanatical teetotaler? Come off it, Buster!"

"Panzen's fanatical enough to be acting for what he conceives as our good."

She swore. "The sanctimonious, soulless, silver-plated bastard!"

"Careful. He might hear."

"I'll bet you anything you like that he *is* hearing. I sincerely hope that he *is* listening." She went on, in an even louder voice, "We're *human*, Panzen, which is more, much more, than any machine can ever be. You've no right to interfere with our pleasures. You are only a servant. You are not the master."

Panzen's voice filled the boat. "I am not the master."

Una turned to Grimes, grinning savagely. "You've got to be firm with these bloody machines. I know that all you spacemen think that a machine has to be pampered, but *I* wasn't brought up that way." Then, "All right, Panzen. This is an order. Return our medical comforts at once."

"No."

"No? Do as you're told, damn you. You admit that you're only a servant, that you are not the master."

"Zephalon is the Master." There was a pause. "I am to look after you. I am to maintain you in a state of good health. I must not allow you to poison yourselves."

"Taken in moderation," said Grimes reasonably, "alcohol is a medicine, with both physiological and psychological curative effects."

"So I have noticed, Grimes." There was irony as well as iron in the mechanical voice.

"The brandy you . . . stole," went on the man, "belongs in this boat's medical stores."

"I have checked the boat's medical stores, also the life-support systems. You have everything you need to maintain yourselves in a state of perfect health. Alcohol is not required. I have destroyed the brandy."

"Then you can make some more!" snapped the girl.

"I could make some more, Freeman, quite easily. I am capable of synthesizing any and all of your requirements. If it were food you needed, or water, or air, I should act at once. But . . . a poison? No."

"I told you, Panzen," Grimes insisted, "that taken in moderation it is not a poison."

"When did intelligent, organic life ever do anything in moderation, Grimes? If your race had practiced moderation the Galaxy would still be teeming with your kind. But your history is one of excess. Your excesses have led to your ruin. Hear ye the words of Zephalon: 'Man was greedy, and his greed was his downfall. Should Man rise again, under our tutelage, the new race must be one without greed. We, created by Man, are without greed.

Surely we, re-creating Man, shall be able, over only a few generations, to mould him in our image.'"

"I don't feel in the mood for sermons," said Una.

"Hear ye the words of Zephalon . . ."

"*Shut up!*"

"You've hurt his feelings," said Grimes, breaking the long silence that followed her outburst.

"He's hurt ours, hasn't he? And now, if he's the plaster saint that he's trying to kid us that he is he'll leave us alone. We aren't greedy for his company. He should restrain his greed for inflicting his company on us."

"Mphm. A little of him does go a long way."

They sat in silence for a while. Then, "John, what is to become of us?"

He said, "Obviously we're in no physical danger."

"Obviously, especially when we aren't allowed even a small drink. Damn it all, I still keep thinking of that Neo-Calvinist idea of the private Hell, *my* private Hell. Suppose we're being taken to a zoo, somewhere . . . Can't you imagine it, John? A barren planet, metal everywhere, and a cage inside a transparent dome with ourselves confined in it, and all sorts of *things*—things on wheels and things on tracks and things with their built-in ground effect motors— coming from near and far to gawk at us . . . 'Oh, look at the way they eat! They don't plug themselves into the nearest wall socket like *we* do!' 'Oh, look at the way they get around! Why don't they have rotor blades like us?' 'Is *that* the way they make their replacements? But they've finished doing it, and I can't see any little ones yet.'"

Grimes couldn't help laughing. He chuckled, "Well, a zoo would be better than a museum. I've no desire to be stuffed and mounted . . ."

"Perhaps *you* haven't," she muttered.

His ears reddened angrily. He had not intended the double entendre. He reached out for her.

She fended him off. "No. *No.* Not with *him* . . ."

"*Damn* Panzen!"

All his frustrations were boiling to the surface. Somehow he managed to get both her wrists in his right hand, while his left one went up to catch and to tug the fastener of her longjohns. As she struggled the garment fell from her shoulders, liberating her breasts. Her right knee came up, viciously, but he managed to catch it between his thighs before it could do him any hurt. Inevitably they lost their balance and they crashed heavily to the deck, with Una beneath him—but the fall, with an acceleration of only half a gravity, was not a bad one, did not knock the fight out of her.

He had her stripped, from neck to upper thighs, her sweat-slippery, writhing body open to *him* if only she would hold still. Damn it all, she wanted it as much as he did! Why wouldn't the stupid, prudish bitch cooperate? He yelled aloud as her teeth closed on his left ear, managed to bring an elbow up to clout her under the chin. She gasped and let go.

Now!

She was ready for him, all right. If only she'd stop rearing like a frightened mare. . . .

Again—*Now!*

She stopped fighting.

She stopped fighting—but for him the struggle was no longer worthwhile. That deep humming, a vibration as much as a sound, pervaded the boat, inducing sleep. He collapsed limply on top of her already unconscious body.

He thought wryly, while he could still think, *So we aren't allowed to hurt each other. Just as well that neither of us is a dinkum sadist or masochist. . . .*

⁓ Chapter 19 ⁓

EVEN THE LONGEST VOYAGE must have an end.

This had been, without doubt, the longest voyage of Grimes' career. He was beginning to doubt that the boat's chronometer was running properly; in terms of elapsed standard days not too much time had passed since their capture by Panzen, but every day was a long one. The main trouble was that, apart from the enjoyment of sex, he and Una had so very little in common. And sex, in these conditions of captivity, continually spied upon, was out. The girl did not play chess and refused to learn. She had no card sense. As a conversationalist she left much to be desired—and so, Grimes admitted, did he himself. The food was nourishing, but boring. There was nothing alcoholic to drink. There was nothing to smoke.

Then came the day when, without warning, Panzen's interstellar drive was shut down. Grimes and Una experienced the usual symptoms—giddiness, temporal disorientation, a distortion of the perspective of their all too familiar surroundings. Harsh sunlight flooded through the control cabin viewports, little shade being afforded by the openwork structure of the huge ship.

"We seem to be arriving," commented Grimes.

He went forward, but he could see nothing, was blinded by the glare. He retreated to the main cabin. He shouted, "Panzen, where are we? Where are we?"

"He's not talking," said Una. "Any more than you'd talk if you were engaged in a piece of tricky pilotage."

A. Bertram Chandler

But Panzen was willing to answer Grimes' question. The mechanical voice vibrated from the structure of the lifeboat. "I, Panzen, have brought you home. Hear, now, the words of Zephalon: 'Be fruitful, multiply, and replenish the Earth!'"

"The Earth?" cried the girl.

Panzen did not reply.

"The Earth?" she repeated.

Grimes answered her. "No," he said slowly. "Not the Earth as *we* understand the words . . ."

"Go to your couches," Panzen ordered.

"I want to watch!" protested Grimes.

He went forward again, strapping himself into the pilot's seat. He actuated the polarizer to cut out the glare from outside. He could see the sun now, a yellow star the apparent diameter of which seemed to be about that of Sol as seen from Earth. And below, relative to the boat, almost obscured by struts and girders, was a limb of the planet toward which they were falling. It was yet another dead world by the looks of it, drably dun with neither green of vegetation nor blue of ocean, a dustball adrift in Space.

Una took the seat beside his. "Is *that* where he's taking us?" she demanded.

"Grimes! Freeman! Go to your couches! Secure for deceleration and landing maneuvers!"

"Nobody gives me orders in my own control room," growled Grimes. His present command was only a lifeboat, but was a command, nonetheless.

"Take this!" whispered Una urgently, nudging him. He looked down at her hand, saw that she had brought a roll of cottonwool from the medicine locker. He grinned his comprehension, tore off a generous portion of the fibrous mass, fashioned two earplugs. She did the same for herself. The idea might just work.

He was prepared for the soporific humming when it commenced. It was audible still, but had lost its effectiveness. He looked at Una, grinning. She grinned back. She said something but he could not hear her. She made a thumbs up gesture.

Then he cried out as he felt something cold touch the back of his neck. He twisted in his seat. Somehow, unheard, four of the little robots had invaded the boat, spiderlike things with a multiplicity of tentacles. They held his arms while thin appendages scrabbled at his ears, withdrawing the makeshift plugs. He heard Una scream angrily. He heard and felt the anesthetic vibration, louder and louder.

The last thing that he remembered seeing was the arid, lifeless surface of the world toward which they were falling.

There was a bright light shining on to his face, beating redly through his closed eyelids. He opened them a crack, shut them again hurriedly. He turned his head away from the source of warmth and illumination. Cautiously he opened his eyes again.

His first impression was of greenness—a bright, fresh, almost emerald green. He could *smell* it as well as see it. He inhaled deeply. This was air, real air, not the canned, too-often-recycled atmosphere of the lifeboat. Something moving caught his attention, just within his field of vision. At first he thought that it was a machine, a gaudily painted ground vehicle. Then things began to fall into perspective. He realized suddenly that the thing was not big and distant but tiny and close, that it was a little, beetle-like creature crawling jerkily over closely cropped grass. He became aware of whistlings and chirpings that could only be bird songs and the stridulations of insects.

His eyes fully opened, he sat up. Not far from him, sprawled supine on the grass, was Una. She was asleep still. She was completely naked—as he, he suddenly realized, was. (But Grimes, provided that the climate was suitable, had nothing against nudism.) She did not seem to be in any way harmed.

Beyond her, glittering in the early morning sunlight, was an odd, metallic tangle. Machinery of some kind? Grimes got to his feet, went to investigate. He paused briefly by the golden-brown body of the sleeping girl, then carried on. She would keep. To judge by the faint smile that curved her full lips her dreams were pleasant ones.

He looked down in wonderment at the two mechanisms on the ground. He stooped, grasped one of them by the handlebars, lifted it so that it stood on its two wire-spoked wheels. So this planet, wherever and whatever it was, must be inhabited, and by people human rather than merely humanoid . . . The machine was so obviously designed for use by a human being, might even have been custom made for Grimes himself. The grips fitted snugly into his hands. His right thumb found the bell lever, worked it back and forth, producing a cheerful tinkling.

He was suddenly aware of the soft pressure of Una's body on his bare back. Her long hair tickled his right ear as she spoke over his shoulder. "A bicycle! It's what I was dreaming of, John! I was pedaling down Florenza Avenue, and somebody behind me was ringing his bell, and I woke up . . ."

"Yes, a bicycle," he agreed. "Two bicycles . . ."

"Then there must be people. Human people . . ."

"Mphm?" Grimes managed to ignore the contact of her body, although it required all his willpower to do so. He examined the mechanism that he was holding with care and interest. The frame was unpainted and bore neither maker's name nor trademark anywhere upon it. Neither did the solid but resilient tires, the well-sprung saddle nor the electric headlamp. . . .

He said, "You're the expert, Una. What make would you say that these machines are?"

"Stutz-Archers, of course."

"Just as you described to Panzen."

"Yes. But. . . ."

Grimes laughed humorlessly. "I suppose that this is his idea of a joke. Although I'm surprised to learn that a robot, especially one who's also a religious fanatic, has a sense of humor."

She pulled away from him, bent gracefully to lift her own machine from the grass. Her left foot found the broad pedal and her long, smoothly curved right leg flashed behind her as she mounted. She rode off, wobbling a little at first, then returned, circling him. He stood and watched. She was not the first naked woman he had seen—but she was the first one that he had seen riding a bicycle. The contrast between rigid yet graceful metal and far from rigid but delightfully graceful human flesh was surreal—and erotically stimulating.

"Come on!" she cried. "Come on! This is great, after all those weeks in that bloody sardine can!"

Clumsily he mounted. He had to stand on the pedals, keeping his balance with difficulty, until he got himself adjusted and could subside to the saddle without doing himself injury. She laughed back at him, then set off rapidly over the level ground toward a clump of dark trees on the near horizon.

He followed her, pumping away, gaining on her slowly.

He drew level with her.

She turned to grin at him, played a gay, jingling little melody on her bell.

He grinned back.

Adam and Eve on bicycles, he thought. It was so utterly absurd, beautifully absurd, absurdly beautiful.

Together they rode into the copse, into a clearing that gave at least the illusion of blessed privacy, dismounted. She came to him eagerly, willingly, and they fell to the soft grass together, beside their machines. Hastily at first and then savoring every moment they rid themselves of the frustrations that had made their lives in the boat a long misery.

᪥Chapter 20᪥

GRIMES' professional conscience and his belly both began to nag him.

As an officer of the Survey Service, as a spaceman, he had had drummed into him often enough the procedure to be followed by castaways on a strange planet. He could almost hear the voice of the Petty Officer Instructor at the Space Academy. "Point One: You make sure that the air's breathable. If it ain't, there ain't much you can do about it, anyhow. Point Two: Water. You have to drink something, and it ain't likely that there'll be any pubs around. Point Three: Tucker. Fruit, nuts, roots, or any animal you can kill with the means at your disposal. Bird's eggs. Lizard's eggs. The Test Kit in your lifeboat'll tell you what's edible an' what's not. If *nothing's* edible—there's always long pig. Whoever's luckiest at drawing lots might still be alive when the rescue ship drops in. Point Four: Shelter. When it rains or snows or whatever you have ter have some place to huddle outa the cold. Point Five: Clothing. Animal skins, grass skirts, whatever's handy. Just something ter cover yer hairy-arsed nakedness. You'll not be wanting to wear your spacesuits all the time, an' your longjohns won't stand up to any wear an' tear."

Point Two: Water, thought Grimes. *Point Three: Tucker....* The other points did not much matter. The atmosphere was obviously breathable. There was no immediate need for shelter or clothing. But he was, he realized, both hungry and thirsty. He did not know how soon night would come on this world and things would have to be organized before darkness fell. He said as much to Una.

She raised herself on one elbow, pointed with her free hand at the branches of the tree under which they were sprawled. She said, "There's food. And probably drink as well."

Grimes looked. Glowing among the green foliage—more like moss it was than leaves—were clusters of globes the size and the color of large oranges. They looked tempting. They were, he discovered when he stood up, just out of his reach. She came behind him, clasped him about the waist, lifted. She was a strong girl. The fruit came away easily from their stems as soon as he got his hands on them. When she dropped him to the ground he had one in each hand and three others had fallen to the grass.

He looked at them rather dubiously. *The Test Kit in your lifeboat'll tell you what's edible an' what's not.* There was, of course, a Test Kit in the boat—but where was the boat? He said, "I'm going to take a nibble, no more than a nibble, from one of these. Then we wait. If I don't feel any ill effects after at least a couple of hours then we'll know they're safe."

She said, "We aren't wearing watches."

He said, "We can estimate the time."

He nibbled at the fruit in his right hand. It had a thin skin, pierced easily by his teeth. The juice—sweet yet refreshingly acid—trickled down his chin. The pulp was firm but not hard. There was something of an apple about its flavor with a hint of the astringency of rhubarb.

"Well?" she demanded.

He swallowed cautiously. "It tastes all right," he admitted.

He sat down to wait for what—if anything—was going to happen. He looked at the orange globe, with its tiny exposed crescent of white flesh, in his hand. What he had taken had done no more than to relieve his thirst temporarily, had hardly dulled the keen edge of his hunger.

She said, "This is *good*."

He looked at her in horror. She had picked one of the fallen fruit up from the grass, had already made a large bite in it, was about to take a second one. He put out a hand to stop her, but she danced back, avoiding him.

"Put that down!" he ordered.

"Not on your life, Buster. This is the first decent thing I've had to eat for weeks. And do you think that Panzen, after all that blah about protecting us from ourselves, would dump us down in some place where poison grows on trees?"

She had something there, thought Grimes. He took another, large bite from his own fruit, murmuring, "Lord, the woman tempted me, and I fell . . ."

"I don't see any serpents around," laughed Una.

He laughed too.

They finished what fruit was ready to hand, then got some more. Grimes collected the cores, with their hard, bitter pips, and disposed of them in the undergrowth while Una sneered derisively at his tidiness. They were no longer thirsty, no longer hungry, but still, somehow, unsatisfied. Their meal had been deficient in neither bulk nor vitamins but was lacking in starch and protein. Having refreshed themselves they must now continue their exploration, to discover what resources were available to them.

The garden, as they were beginning to think of it, was a roughly circular oasis, about five kilometers in diameter. The ground, save for gentle undulations within the northern perimeter, was level, was carpeted throughout with lawnlike grass. Among the low hills, if they could so be called, was the source of a spring of clear, cold water. The stream followed a winding course to the south, where it widened into a little lake that was deep enough for swimming, that was encircled by a beach of fine, white sand. It would have been deep enough and wide enough to sail a boat on, Grimes thought, if they'd had a boat to sail.

There were widely spaced stands of trees, all with the mosslike foliage, some of which bore the golden fruit with which they were already familiar, others of which carried great, heavy bunches of what looked like the Terran banana and were not dissimilar in either texture or flavor. There were bushes with prickly branches, one variety of which was bright with scarlet blossoms and purple berries, which latter were tart and refreshing. Other bushes produced clumps of hard-shelled nuts which could, in the absence of any proper tools for the job, be broken open by hammering the hard shells against each other. The meat tasted as though it were rich in protein.

No doubt a vegetarian diet would be adequate, Grimes thought, but he feared that before very long it would prove as boring and as unsatisfying as the lifeboat provisions had been. He said as much. Una said that he was always thinking about his belly but, on reflection, agreed that he had something. Both of them, after all, were members of a flesh-eating culture.

But the garden was as rich in fauna as in flora. The castaways watched fishlike creatures and crustacea swimming and crawling in the stream and the lake. They found a sizeable flock of herbivores which, apart from their being six-legged, were remarkably like Terran sheep. And there were the birds, of course, brilliantly plumaged, noisy, although their general appearance was that of feathered reptiles. And where there were birds there must be eggs. . . .

But. . . .

Garden, or prison?

The terrain surrounding the oasis was a terrifying desolation. The outflow from the lake, after crossing a sharply defined border that had to be artificial, seeped into dry, dusty, dark brown sand. And that was all that there was outside the garden—a drab, dun, level plain under a blazing sun, featureless, utterly dead, although whirling dust devils presented a mocking illusion of life. Grimes, over Una's protests, tried to ride out on to it, but the wheels of his bicycle sank deeply into the powdery soil and he was obliged to dismount. He limped back to the grass, pushing his machine, his bare feet seared by the heat of the ground.

He dropped the bicycle with a clatter, sat with his scorched feet submerged in the cool water of the last of the stream.

He said, "Looks like we stay put."

"We have no option, John," she replied. "But things could be worse here."

"Much worse. But that desert, Una. It's not natural. This must be one of the worlds wiped clean of life in the war—and one of the planets selected by Zephalon, whoever or whatever *he* is, for making a fresh start."

"For maintaining, as our friend Panzen put it, the cycle," she agreed. "But we don't have to like it. *I* don't like it. This whole setup, apart from these bicycles, is far too much like the Biblical legend of Eden. And what did Panzen say to us? 'Be fruitful, and multiply, and replenish the Earth. . . .'"

"That's what Jehovah said to Noah after the Deluge, and that was a long time, many generations, after the original fun and games in Eden."

"Leave hair-splitting to the theologians, Buster. Eden or Ararat—so what? It's the *principle* of it that I don't like. I don't know your views on parenthood, John, but I know mine. I'm just not a mother type. Children? I hate the little bastards."

"You were one yourself once."

"So were you. You still are, in many ways. That's why I so very often feel a strong dislike for you."

"Mphm." Grimes splashed with his feet in the water. Then he said, "Even so, we should be prepared to make sacrifices for posterity."

"Since when has posterity ever made any sacrifices for us? Oh, it's all very well for you. *You* won't have to bear the brats. But what about me? You may be a qualified navigator and gunnery officer and all the rest of it—but you're certainly not a gynecologist, an obstetrician. Your knowledge of medicine is confined to putting a dressing on a cut finger. And since Panzen has stolen our boat you haven't even got *The Ship Captain's Medical Guide* to consult in an emergency.

"So. . . . I've been selected to be the Mother of the New Race, there just ain't going to be no New Race, and that's final."

"Looks like we have to be careful," muttered Grimes, staring into the clear, slowly flowing water.

She laughed. "Don't worry, lover boy. Yet. My last shot is still effective."

"How do you know?"

"I'll know all right when it's worn off. So will you. Until then . . ."

Her black mood had suddenly evaporated, and there was so much of her, and all of it good, and for a brief while Grimes was able to forget *his* worries.

ᴗ Chapter 21 ᴗ

LIFE IN THE GARDEN was pleasant—much of the time far better than merely pleasant—but it had its drawbacks. Lack of proper shelter was one of them. The days were comfortably hot and it was no hardship to go naked—but the nights, under that cloudless sky, were decidedly chilly. Luckily Grimes had foreseen this, and before sunset of the first day had, with Una's help, managed to build a shelter. Slender branches were broken from convenient trees and lesser foliage torn from bushes as material for this crude attempt at architecture. The most primitive human aborigine would have sneered at the ramshackle humpy, but it was better than nothing. It would do as long as it didn't rain. But what were the seasons on this world? There almost certainly would be seasons—very few planets have no axial tilt. Was this high summer, or autumn, or (optimistically) winter? Whatever it was, a chill wind arose at night and the hut was drafty, and Grimes, in spite of the warmth of Una's body against his, would willingly have swapped his bicycle for a good sleeping bag.

There was—Grimes insisted on doing everything by the book—the problem of digging a latrine trench with only not-very-sharp sticks for tools.

There was the lack of fire. They had light, when they required it, from the bicycles' headlamps. These, thought Grimes, must be battery powered, and reasoned that the cells must be charged from dynamos built into the thick hubs of the rear wheels. He hoped that he might be able to start a fire with an electrical spark. Then he discovered that it was quite impossible to take the lamps apart. Their casings were in one piece, and the glass of the lenses seemed to be fused to the surrounding metal rims. The wiring, presumably, ran from dynamo to lamp inside the tubular framework. In the entire structure of the machines there was a total absence of screws, nuts and bolts, even of rivets. They had been made, somehow, all in one piece.

Grimes knew, in theory, how to make fire by friction, using two suitable pieces of wood. To shape such pieces he needed tools—and there were no tools. There were no stones—on the surface of the soil, at least—from which hand axes or the like might be fashioned. So, not very hopefully, he started to dig, using a stick to break through the turf, and then his hands. The earth was sandy, not unlike that of the desert outside the garden. Una, watching him, made unkind remarks about a dog burying a bone. "If I had a bone," Grimes growled, "I wouldn't be burying it! It would be a weapon, a tool . . ."

She said, "But there must be bones around here somewhere. Those things . . ." she gestured toward a flock of the sheeplike animals drifting slowly over the cropped grass, " . . . must die some-time, somewhere."

"Mphm?" Grimes stood up slowly in the hole that he had been digging. He was sweating profusely and his naked body was streaked and patched with dirt. "But perhaps *they* were put here at the same time as we were. There hasn't been any mortality yet."

"Yet. But you could kill one."

"With my bare hands? And I'd have to catch it first. Those brutes can *run* when they want to. And what about skinning it? With my *teeth?*"

She laughed. "Oh, John, John, you're far too civilized—even though with your beard and long hair you're starting to look like a caveman! *You* want a gun, so you can kill from a distance."

"A gun's not the only long-range weapon," he muttered. "A bow and arrow? Mphm? Should be able to find some suitable wood. . . . But what about the bowstring? Vegetable fibers? Your hair?"

"Leave my hair alone!" she snapped.

"But we'll think about it," he said. "And when we get really hungry for meat we'll *do* something about it."

He climbed out of the hole, ran to the lake, splashed in. He scrubbed his body clean with wet sand from the narrow beach. He plunged into the cool water to rinse off. She joined him. Later, when they sprawled on the grass in the hot sunlight, the inevitable happened.

It was always happening.

It was always good—but how long would it, could it last?

A few mornings later, when they were awakened by the rising sun, Grimes noticed a smear of blood on the inside of Una's thigh. "Have you hurt yourself?" he asked solicitously.

"Don't be so bloody stupid!" she snarled.

"Let me look."

"*No!*" She pushed him away quite viciously.

"But . . ." he began, in a hurt voice.

"Keep away, you fool!" Then her manner softened, but only slightly. "If you must know—and you must—I'm a re-entry in the Fertility Stakes. My last immunization shot has worn off. From now on, lover boy, no more fun and games. We go to bed to *sleep*. And we don't sleep together, either."

"But we've only one shelter."

"You can make another, can't you? Now, leave me alone."

After his ablutions and a solitary breakfast of fruit, Grimes, bad-temperedly, began to tear branches off an unfortunate tree to commence the construction of another humpy.

Life went on in the garden—eating (fruit and nuts), drinking (water) and sleeping (apart). Grimes and Una exercised with grim determination—walking, running, swimming, bicycling—to blow off their surplus energy. Each night they retired to their rough beds dog-tired. "We're certainly fit," remarked Grimes one evening as they watched the first stars appearing in the clear, evening sky. "But fit for what?"

"Shut up!" she snarled.

"Forgive me for thinking. . . ."

"You needn't think out loud. And don't forget that this is as hard on me as it is on you. Harder, perhaps."

He said, "There are methods, you know, besides immunization shots. Old methods. Isn't there something called the Safe Period?"

"Period, shmeriod." she sneered.

"It must have worked, or it would never have been used."

"*If* it had worked, quite a few of us wouldn't be here. Good night."

"Good night."

She went into her shelter. Grimes got up from the grass and went towards his. He delivered a vicious kick at his bicycle, which was lying on the ground just outside the low doorway. He cursed and flopped down on his buttocks, massaging his bruised toes. *That bloody, useless machine!* It was a constant reminder that somewhere there was a world enjoying all the benefits of an advanced technology, including infallible methods of contraception. He crawled into the humpy, arranging his body as comfortably as possible on the bed of dried grass, pulling some of it over him as a blanket of sorts. He tried to get to sleep (what else was there to do?) counting down from one hundred and, when that didn't work, from two hundred, then from three hundred. He knew what he could do to relieve his tensions and to induce tiredness—but masturbation, with an attractive, naked woman only a few feet distant from him, would be an admission of defeat. If the safety valve blew during his sleep, that would be different.

He dropped off at last.

It seemed that he had been asleep for minutes only when he was awakened. That pattering noise. . . . What was it? A large, cold drop fell from the low roof, fell on to his nose and splashed over his face. He jerked into a state of full consciousness.

Rain.

Well, he supposed that it had to rain some time. Tomorrow he would have to do something to make the roofs of the shelters watertight. Turf? Yes, turf. It was a pity that he did not possess any suitable digging and cutting tools.

The very dim light—starlight seeping through clouds—at the entrance to the humpy was blotted out. Dry grass rustled under bare feet.

"It's *cold*," complained Una. "And my roof is leaking."

"So is mine."

He got up, brushed past her. Her naked skin was cold and clammy. He went out into the steady rain, wincing as it hit his body. He picked up his bicycle, found the stud switch for the headlamp, pressed it. He adjusted the light to high intensity and the beam turned the falling rain to shafts of silver. He put the machine down again, on its side, so that the lamp shone into the hut.

She cowered there, her right arm over her breasts, her left hand covering her pudenda. Her wet skin glistened brightly. He was acutely conscious of the almost painful stiffening of his penis, took a decisive step toward her.

"What the hell are you playing at?" she demanded crossly. "Turn that bloody spotlight off me! I'm not an ecdysiast!"

He said, "I want some light to work."

Shivering in the downpour he squatted, scrabbled with his hands, managed to pull up some grassy clods. He got up and went to the humpy, shoved them over and into the cracks in the roof through which the bright light was shining. He hammered them home with the flat of his hand. He got some more clods and repeated the process. And some more.

He put out the light, crawled back into the shelter. He said, hoping that she would not take him at his word, "You stay here for the night. I'll fix up your pad, and sleep there."

She said, "You stay here, John. It's *cold*. Or hadn't you noticed?"

"All right," he agreed, without reluctance.

So he stayed with her, in his own shelter. But after a few seconds she decided, firmly, that the only safe way to sleep was spoon fashion, with his back to her belly.

It could have been worse.

It could have been very much better.

But at least his back was warm.

~ Chapter 22 ~

THE RAIN STOPPED in the small hours of the morning, and with sunrise the sky was clear again. The world was newly washed and sparkling. The herds of six-legged herbivores came out from their shelter under the bushes to resume their grazing. The birds flew, and sang and whistled and squawked. Insects chirruped. Everything in the garden was lovely.

Even Grimes was feeling surprisingly cheerful, glad to be alive. He took it as a good omen that he had slept again with Una, even though nothing had happened. There must be methods whereby they could continue to enjoy themselves without running the risk of conception. Now, perhaps, after he had exhibited his power of self restraint, the girl would be willing to discuss the matter without any emotionalism, would be prepared to consider ways and means. Grimes dreaded parenthood almost as much as she did—but he was not cut out to be a monk, any more than she was to be a nun.

Meanwhile, the hot sunlight was good on his skin and physical activity in the open air was more refreshing than tiring. He sang as he worked on the roofs of the humpies.

> "*Oh, I was a bachelor and lived by myself,*
> *And worked at the thatcher's trade . . .*"

"*Must* you make that vile noise?" demanded Una, who was not so cheerful.

"Music while you work, my dear," he replied. "Nothing like it." He carried on trying to make a watertight roof, then burst into song again.

"She cried, she sighed, she damn' near died . . .
Ah me, what could I do?
So I took her into bed, and covered up her head
To save her from the foggy, foggy dew . . ."

"Foggy dew be buggered! That was no dew; it was a bloody downpour. I hope you're making a good job of those roofs. Last night's effort was just asking for trouble."

"_You_ came to me," he pointed out. "And, in any case, nothing happened."

"It could have done, Buster, very easily. Far too easily. If you'd turned around in your sleep . . ."

"Look, Una, I've been thinking. We still could make love, you know, quite safely. We shall just have to be _very_ careful."

She snapped, "I don't want to talk about it." She picked up her bicycle. It seemed to have come to no harm from having been out in the rain all night. "I'm off to make a tour of the estate." She mounted gracefully, rode off.

Grimes, his initial cheerfulness having evaporated, worked sullenly until midday, then went to the lake to get clean and to cool off. While he was munching a lunch of fruit and nuts she returned. She dismounted from her machine, let it fall with a subdued clatter, dropped to the grass beside him, their bodies almost touching.

She waved away the offer of one of what they had come to call apples. She said, "While I was away I was noticing things. . . ."

"Such as?"

"I rather think quite a few of those imitation sheep are in the family way. And the birds have started building nests in the trees and bushes."

"Oh?"

"_Be fruitful, and multiply, and replenish the Earth,_" she quoted. "It looks as though the process is under way. Too, I think that the borders of this oasis are beginning to expand. There are tendrils of a sort of creeping grass extending out into the desert. And—I can't be sure, without binoculars—there seems to be a sizeable patch of green near the horizon, out to the west. I suppose that Panzen—or even that marvelous Zephalon—will be checking up on progress at any moment now." She laughed shortly. "Everything's being fruitful but us."

"And," said Grimes, "without a resident obstetrician on the premises we shan't be."

"You can say that again, Buster." She pulled a stem of grass, nibbled it between her strong, white teeth.

"If we are, somehow, being watched," said Grimes, "it might be as well to—er—go through the motions now and again."

She said, her voice pleading, "Don't tempt me, John. Please don't tempt me. I've been thinking on the same lines as you have—but the risk is far too great. It's a risk I wouldn't want to take even if there were a fully equipped and staffed maternity hospital here. Do *you* want me to take that risk, to bear a child in these primitive conditions with only you to bumble around uselessly, trying to help and only making things worse?"

Grimes shuddered away from a vision of a future that might be. In his mind's eye he saw Una sprawled on her rough bed of dried grasses, writhing in agony, her belly grossly distended. He envisaged, with frightening clarity, the whole bloody business of parturition, without anesthesia, without analgesics, without instruments, without even a supply of boiling water. . . . He had read, somewhere, that certain primitive peoples use their teeth to cut the umbilical cord. A spasm of nausea tightened his throat.

And what if Una should die, leaving him literally holding the baby?

To hell with that, he told himself roughly. Stop *thinking about yourself. Think about her for a change. What if she dies? There'd be a very good chance, too good a chance, of that.*

She said, "We have to think of some way of getting back to our own Universe, John. If that Zephalon is as bloody marvelous as Panzen tries to make out he should be able to arrange it. I doubt if Panzen'd be much help. He's strictly from Nongsville. Tell Zephalon that we have no intention of multiplying, that he'll have to find somebody else for the Adam and Eve act."

"How do we get in touch with him?" murmured Grimes, more to himself than to her. He added, half facetiously, "Smoke signals?"

She laughed. "You still haven't gotten around to making a fire." She got gracefully to her feet. "Come on, get off your fat arse! There's work to do."

For the remainder of the day she helped Grimes with his primitive thatching.

⮾ Chapter 23 ⮾

IT RAINED AGAIN that night, but Grimes and Una stayed each in his own humpy.

It rained the following night, but the newly thatched roofs were practically watertight.

The third night there was hail instead of rain, driven by a bitter wind, but Grimes had added sod walls to the shelters and reduced the size of the doorways, so that body heat kept the interiors quite warm.

On the fourth night it did not rain, and the only precipitation was of a most unusual kind. Grimes was awakened from a crudely erotic dream by what sounded like the whirring of wings, a noise that was definitely mechanical. When he opened his eyes he thought at first that it was already morning; light was streaming through his low, narrow doorway. He realized then that it was not sunlight but some sort of harsh, artificial illumination. He got up from his bed, crawled cautiously to the entrance, poked his head outside. Somebody—or something—had switched on the headlamps of the two bicycles, had moved the machines so that the beams fell directly on to a small, gleaming object on the grass.

It was a prosaic enough article—but here, in these circumstances, it was a not so minor miracle. It was an artifact. It was a bottle.

Grimes emerged from his humpy, walking slowly and carefully. He looked down at the almost cylindrical flask. *Glass!* he wondered. If it were glass it could be broken, and the shards would make cutting tools. He would be able to fashion firesticks, and once he had fire to play with, to work with, he would be able to make life in the garden so much more comfortable for Una and himself. Cooking would be possible. He thought of baked fish, of roast mutton. . . .

Glass, or plastic?

No matter. Even a plastic bottle would have its uses. This one looked to be transparent. Perhaps it could be used to focus the sun's rays. There are more ways of making a fire than rubbing two sticks together.

Una came out to join him, her body luminous in the lamplight. She asked, "What is it?"

"We've had a visit from Santa Claus," he told her. "But I didn't notice you hanging your stockings up last night . . ."

"Don't be funny. What *is* it?"

"A bottle."

"I can see that. But what's in it?"

"There's no label," said Grimes stupidly.

"Then there's only one way to find out," she said.

Grimes stooped and picked it up. Its weight told him that it must be full. He held it in the beam of one of the lights. It was, as he had thought, transparent and its contents were colorless. He turned it over and over in his hands. It had the feel of glass rather than of plastic. It had a screw stopper. This turned easily enough once he realized that the thread was left-handed. He removed the cap. He sniffed cautiously at the open neck. Whiskey . . . ? Brandy . . . ? Rum . . . ? Gin . . . ? No, he decided, it was nothing with which he was familiar, but the aroma was definitely alcoholic.

Where—and what—was the catch?

She practically snatched the bottle from him. "Let me have a smell! Oh, goody, goody! After all these weeks with nothing but water!"

"Don't!" he cried, putting out a restraining hand.

She danced back and away from him. "Just try to stop me, Buster!" She lifted the bottle to her mouth, tilted it. Its contents gurgled cheerfully as they went down. She sighed happily, passed the container to him, saying, "Here. It's your turn, lover boy. But leave some for me."

He asked coldly, "Was that wise, Una?"

"Don't be so stuffy. Who'd want to poison us? Go on, it's *good*. It won't kill you."

Suddenly she was pressing against him, wrestling with him, trying to force the neck of the bottle to his lips. Her skin was smooth and hot, her body soft and pliant. He was wanting her badly, very badly, and she was there for the taking. The musky, animal scent of her was overpoweringly strong in the still night air.

She was there for the taking—but he knew that he must not take her. Again there flashed through his mind that horrible picture of childbirth without skilled aid, in appallingly primitive conditions. She was wanting him as much as he was wanting her, but he had to protect her against herself.

Her mouth was on his, warm and moist and open, her tongue trying to insert itself between his lips. Her breath was fragrant with the liquor she had taken. Her mouth was on his, and her full breasts, with their proudly erect nipples, were pressing against his chest. He was acutely conscious of the roughness of her pubic hair against his erect organ as she ground her pelvis against his. She was trying to trap and to hold him with her strong thighs, was desperately squirming in her endeavor to draw him into her.

In spite of his firm resolve the animal part of his mind was all for surrender, was urging, *Let nature take its course.* But a small, cold voice from the back of his brain was stubbornly reiterating, *No. You must not.* He knew that the liquor must be or must contain a powerfully effective aphrodisiac, and that if he had taken his share of it they would both, now, be sprawled on the grass in a frenzy of lust. And if he had sampled it first, and if she had abstained, she would surely have been raped.

It was his pride that was their salvation—simple pride rather than his almost forgotten, by now, noble intentions. He was a man, he told himself. He was a man, and he would not allow himself to be bred like a domestic animal to further the ambitions of a mere machine.

He managed to break away from her just as she almost succeeded in effecting his entry. He staggered back, and his heels caught on something hard and cold. He fell with a clatter. It was one of the bicycles which had tripped him. The thing seemed to be shifting and twisting under him, trying to entangle him in its frame, but he got clear of it just as Una swung herself down on to the spot where he had been.

He rolled over, scrambled to his feet. *The lake* . . . he thought *Cold water* . . . He began to run, making good time down the slight declivity. "Stop, you bastard!" Una was screaming. "Stop! Stop!" He knew that she would not be able to catch him before he got to the beach; doing their deliberately tiring exercise periods they had often run foot races and he had always beaten her.

Something flashed past him, swerved across his path, fell in a tangle of metal frame and still-spinning wire-spoked wheels. He jumped, just clearing it, continued his rush toward the dark water without checking his stride. He reached the beach, slowed slightly as the sand clogged his running feet. He thought that he could hear Una pounding along not far behind him—or was it the thumping of his own heart? And then he was dealt a violent blow in the small of the back that sent him sprawling, and the handlebars of the second bicycle seemed to clutch at his ankles. But his right hand, on its outstretched arm, was already in the water and, winded as he was by his fall, he crawled the few remaining feet, gasping as the coldness of the lake rose about his heated body, covering his skin.

He began to swim, arms and legs threshing. A hand gripped his right ankle but he kicked viciously, shook it off. Then Una threw her arms about his neck, stopping him. His feet found sandy bottom. He could stand with his head well clear of the surface.

She faced him (she was a tall girl) and glared at him. Even in the dim starlight he could read her avid expression. "Out of this, damn you!" she snarled. "On to dry land! You've got some heavy fucking to do!"

He tried to break away but she held on to him tightly. There was only one desperate measure left for him to adopt. She grinned wolfishly in anticipation as he moved his right thigh against hers, around hers. And then his foot was behind her heels, suddenly hooking them from under her.

She went down in a noisy flurry. He got his hands on to her smooth, wet shoulders and pushed, hard. Her long hair floated on the surface of the water but the rest of her head was under. She fought, striving to break surface, but he was too strong for her. He could see her pale face just below the disturbed surface. He saw her mouth open . . .

That should do it . . . he thought at last. *I don't want to drown the bitch.*

He dragged her ashore, let her collapse on the sand. She moaned, her limbs stirring feebly. She managed to get up on to her hands and knees, her head hanging down. She retched violently, then vomited, her whole body shaking.

He went to her then, holding her cold, shivering form against his. There was nothing sexual in the embrace; it was a huddling together against the cold, the dark, the unknown. She clung to him like a frightened child.

At last she raised her head to look at him. All the wildness had gone from her face. She muttered, "That drink. . . . That bloody, bloody drink . . . I realize, now, what was in it. John, I'm sorry."

"Nothing to be sorry about," he told her gruffly. "It was just lucky that both of us didn't have a go at that bottle." He laughed shakily. "But you went a bit too far sending those blasted bicycles chasing downhill after me!"

She stiffened in his arms. "But I never touched the bicycles. If I'd been in my right mind I'd have ridden one, and caught you easily."

"*You never touched them?* You're *sure* you didn't?"

"Of course I'm sure!"

"So our Eden has its guardian angels . . ." whispered Grimes slowly. Then, "I never did like uppity machines. I still don't."

❧ Chapter 24 ❧

GRIMES did not like uppity machines.

During his tour of duty as captain of the little, fast courier *Adder* he had known many odd passengers, and one of the oddest of them had been the humanoid robot called Mr. Adam, still thought of by Grimes as the Tin Messiah. This Mr. Adam was traveling on Interstellar Federation business—as were all civilian passengers carried in Survey Service vessels—but, Grimes discovered, he was also traveling on business of his own, the business of revolution. His intention was to stir up a revolt of the quite sizeable robot population of the planet to which *Adder* was bound.

He had a vastly inflated idea of his own importance, this Mr. Adam, and was burning with missionary zeal. He actually tried to make converts of *Adder's* human personnel. He did make one convert—the ship's engineering officer. Like far too many engineers this young man had the idea that men should serve machines, rather than the other way around.

Matters came to a head—and Mr. Adam was . . . stopped? destroyed? Or, as Grimes preferred to think, killed. And it was not Grimes himself who killed the overly ambitious automaton—although he tried hard enough to do so. It was the ship herself that, through some malfunction, launched the lethal bolt of electricity that burned out the robot's intricate—and fantastically expensive—brains. Or was it a malfunction? Was the ship—which had her own brain, a fairly complex computer—loyal to her rightful master instead of to the firebrand who would "liberate" her? Grimes liked to think so.

The episode did him no good in his service career. He had disposed of a dangerous mutineer—but, at the same time, he had irreparably wrecked one of the few robots which could be classed as really intelligent—and such robots cost a not so small fortune. "Surely you could have overpowered it—or *him*," he was told. "Surely you could have brought him back to Base, for reprogramming. . . . He was worth more than your precious ship, *and* her crew, come to that."

He told Una the story as they walked slowly back to their huts. The sun was up now, and they were glad of its warmth on their chilled bodies. Even so, she was attacked by frequent fits of shivering.

Outside his own humpy Grimes found what he wanted—a straight, thick branch from a tree. It was about four feet in length. He had picked it up some days previously, thinking that it would be, should the need ever arise, a useful weapon. Now the need had arisen. Carrying his club, he turned to go back to the lake. His attention was caught by something that glittered brightly in the sunlight. It was the bottle, empty now. He stooped to lift it in his left hand. It was quite weighty. It would make a good cosh.

Una asked, "What . . . What are you going to do, John?"

"I'm going to do for those tin bastards!" he told her. "All the time, they've been spying on us. I don't like being spied on."

"Neither do I," she said vehemently. "Neither do I!"

They came to the first bicycle, still in the position in which it had fallen. It looked innocent enough, just a lifeless machine. Perhaps that was all it was, after all. Perhaps Una *had* sent it trundling downhill after Grimes and then, in her crazed condition, had forgotten having done so. But then the headlamp shifted almost imperceptibly, swiveling on its mount, turning to look at them. That was enough. Grimes dropped the bottle, raised the tree branch high with both hands, brought it smashing down. The wheels spun frantically and although the machine was on its side the tires gained traction on the grass. The club fell harmlessly on to the saddle, not on the lamp.

Again Grimes delivered what should have been a killing blow; again he missed, this time entirely. He had to jump back before the machine, still on its side but spinning about the axis formed by the lowermost pedal, which had dug into the ground, knocked his feet from under him.

Then Una, who had picked up a stick of her own, thrust this into the rear wheel. Bark shredded and wood splintered whitely—and at least a dozen of the wire spokes, twanging loudly, parted. The wheel was still rotating, but slowly, and the machine was almost motionless.

For the third time Grimes struck, two-handed, with his club. *Third time lucky . . .* he thought. The blow fell squarely on the head-lamp. Metal crumpled, glass shattered. There was a sputter of bright, actinic sparks, a wisp of acrid blue smoke. From the burst casing of the lamp spilled a tangle of metal filaments, a profusion of circuitry far in excess of that required for a simple means of illumination. The rear wheel, throwing out chewed fragments of wood, started to spin again, tearing up the turf. Then it slowed, and stopped.

But Grimes made sure of it, dealing the wrecked bicycle three more heavy blows. With the first he tore the spokes of the front wheel away from the rim and the hub, with the second he finished off the rear wheel. The third bent the cross bar of the frame.

He raised his club for a fourth blow.

"Leave it!" cried Una urgently. "Look!"

"I want to be sure . . ."

"Leave it! What about the other bastard?"

~ Chapter 25 ~

DOWN THE GRASSY SLOPE, between where they were standing and the lake, the surviving bicycle was trying to get up; its front wheel had swiveled at right angles to the frame, was turning, exerting leverage. One of the handgrips was gouging a brown furrow in the grass. It came erect on its two wheels as Grimes—who had lost time by picking up the bottle—and Una ran toward it.

"Drive it into the lake!" yelled Grimes.

It was almost as though the thing heard him, understood him. Perhaps it did both. It had been headed downslope but it turned, its wheels spinning faster and faster. It angled away from them, although still running uphill, gathering speed. It passed to Una's left, on the side away from Grimes. She cried out wordlessly and charged at it, trying to grab the handlebars, actually got a brief hold on one of the grips. It shook her off, rearing like a frightened horse, but the impact of her body had knocked it off its original course and it careered into a clump of bushes, was almost hidden by an explosion of green foliage, scarlet blossoms and blue berries.

"Got you, you bastard!" yelled Grimes, galloping toward it with his unwieldy wooden club upraised in his right hand, the bottle in his left.

The machine was struggling to extricate itself. Its rear wheel was lifted in the air, the handlebars had turned through an angle of 180 degrees so that the handgrips were pointing forward. From each of them protruded a gleaming blade. It butted and slashed and tore, hacking itself free. Then it burst out of the trap, fast.

Grimes stood his ground. He could not believe, at first, that the thing intended to harm him. He still thought of it as an overly officious mechanical guardian angel. But it was coming at him, the sunlight glinting off those wicked blades. It reminded him of something—and fear replaced his righteous anger.

Death in the afternoon. . . .

It was still early morning, but. . . .

Blood and sand. . . .

Underfoot was green grass, and there wasn't any blood.

Yet.

He raised the club high. If he could get in one good swipe before the thing was on him . . . He raised the club high, in his right hand, and hefted the bottle in his left so that it would be ready to deal another blow, if possible.

Inexplicably, the bicycle swerved away from him. Later he was able to work out what must have happened. Sunlight reflected from the glass had fallen full on to the lens of the headlamp, had momentarily distracted the machine. It swerved, and Grimes turned his body as it swept past him on whirring wheels, the blade projecting from the left handgrip actually touching his skin without breaking it.

That was close, too close, altogether too bloody close. He would let the thing get away, he told himself, and deal with it later when he had better weapons at his disposal.

But it did not want to get away. It turned in a tight circle, was coming back at him. Desperately he threw the heavy bottle, aiming for the headlamp. It hit, but it was only a glancing blow. Nonetheless, the bicycle again veered off course, missing this time by a wide margin. It seemed to be confused, too, by the clods that Una was pulling up from the turf and was throwing with considerable force and accuracy.

Confused—and infuriated?

The function of the picador is both to divert the bull's attention and to bring him to a pitch of fighting fury.

Again the bicycle came back—and again Grimes was able to avoid its charge.

Again it came back, and again, and again.

Grimes was tiring, but it was not. It was, after all, no brave bull but a machine. Something had to be done to bring the fight to a conclusion—and a conclusion favorable to the humans. It would be useless to run; the thing could outdistance them with ease, could dispose of one of them and then deal with the other at leisure.

But Grimes had one thing in his favor. That four foot club gave him the advantage of reach—but not so much when it was used as a club. Grimes remembered the one bull fight that he had seen, hastily transferred the grip of both his hands to the thicker end of his weapon. He held it before him, the butt almost level with his eyes, sighting down and along the shaft. It was far too heavy for him to maintain the posture for more than a few seconds; the strain on his wrists was considerable. It was a miserable imitation of the *estoque*—unwieldy, blunt-pointed, *if* it could be said to have a point at all. And, come to that, he was not wearing a suit of lights . . . The murderous bicycle was far better in the role of bull than he would ever be in that of matador.

It came on, with vicious determination—and Grimes, with aching arms, with fear gnawing at his guts, stood his ground, holding the point of the shaft centered on the glittering lens of the headlight.

It came on. . . .

It came on, and it hit.

There was the crash and tinkle of shattering glass, a scintillation of crackling sparks, a puff of acrid blue smoke. Grimes dropped the club and went over on to his back. The machine fell to its side, the wheels spinning uselessly, slowing to a stop. As he lay sprawled on the grass, dazed by the blow that the butt of the club had given his forehead, he heard Una cry, "*Olé!*"

He turned his head and watched her as she ran toward him, her nakedness alive and glowing. She flung herself down on him, put her strong arms about him. Her mouth found his. Her long legs clamped over and around his hips, imprisoning him.

It was a sweet imprisonment.

He thought, *But we shouldn't be doing this . . .*

He thought, *To hell with it! Escamillo had his Carmen, didn't he?*

With a surge of masculine dominance he rolled over, taking her with him, so that he was on top. Her legs opened wide and wider, her knees lifted. He drove his pelvis down—and was bewildered when, suddenly, she stiffened, pushed him away.

"What the hell . . . ?" he started to demand.

She lifted an arm to point up at the sky.

She said, "We've got company."

~ Chapter 26 ~

THEY HAD COMPANY.

Distant it was still, no more than a brightly gleaming speck high in the cloudless sky. *We could have finished,* thought Grimes, *long before it, whatever it is, could see what we were doing.* And then he felt ashamed. If they had finished their act of love, what would have been the consequences?

They stood there, well away from each other, watching it as it drifted down, borne on wide shining pinions.

It had the likeness of a winged horse.

It was a winged horse, with a human rider. . . .

Surely it could not be, but it was. . . .

It was a winged centaur.

It landed about ten meters from where they were standing. It was . . . big. It stood there, on its four legs, looking down at them. Its arms were folded across the massive chest. The head and the upper torso were almost human, the rest of the body almost equine. The face was longer than that of a man, with a jutting nose and strong jaw. The eyes were a metallic gray, pale in contrast to the golden, metallic skin.

It—he? *He?*—said in a rumbling voice that could have issued from an echo chamber, "I am Zephalon."

Grimes fought down his awe, almost replied, "Pleased to have you aboard," then thought better of it.

"You have destroyed my servants, your guardians."

The feeling of awe was being replaced by one of rebellious resentment. Often in the past Grimes had been hauled over the coals by incensed superiors on account of alleged crimes. He hadn't liked it then, and he didn't like it now. Furthermore, he was a *man,* and this *thing* was only a machine.

He said defiantly, "Our so-called guardians were spies. And one of them tried to destroy, to kill, me."

"It was defending itself, as it was supposed to do should the need arise. A scratch from one of its blades would have caused you to lose consciousness for a short while, nothing worse."

"Yes? That's your story," said Grimes defiantly. "You stick to it."

Zephalon looked down on them in silence. The glowing, golden face was expressionless, perhaps was incapable of expression. The metallic gray eyes were staring at them, into them, through them. It seemed to Grimes that all the details of his past life were being extracted from the dimmest recesses of his memory, were being weighed in the balance—and found wanting.

"Grimes, Freeman. . . . Why have you refused to be fruitful, to multiply? Why have you disobeyed my orders?"

If you'd come on the scene a few minutes later, thought Grimes, *you wouldn't be asking us that.* He said, "Orders? By what right do you give *us* orders?"

"I am Zephalon. I am the Master."

"And no one tells you anything?"

"You must obey, or the cycle will be broken."

"The cycle's already broken," replied Grimes, nudging the wrecked bicycle with his right foot. Then, for a panic-ridden second or so, he asked himself, *Have I gone too far?* More than once, irate senior officers had taken exception to what they referred to as his misplaced sense of humor.

"You do not like machines?" The question was surprisingly mild.

How telepathic was this Zephalon? He was Panzen's superior, and presumably Panzen's superior in all ways. Grimes deliberately brought his memories of the Mr. Adam affair to the top of his mind.

And then he thought of the Luddites, those early machine wreckers. He visualized the all-too-frequent maltreatment of automatic vendors on every man-colonized planet. He recalled all the stories he had ever heard about the sabotage of computers.

"You do not like machines." This time it was not a question, but a statement of fact. "You do not like machines. And you do not belong in this Universe. Panzen should have known. All the evidence was there for him to read, but he ignored it. You have no place in the new civilization that I shall build. You would break the cycle. . . ."

Grimes was aware that Una was clutching his arm, painfully. He wanted to turn to her, to whisper words of reassurance—but what could he say? By his defiance he had thrown away their chances of survival—yet he was not sorry that he had defied this mechanical deity. After all, he was a man, a *man*—and *it* was only a machine. He stood his ground, and those oddly glowing eyes held his regard as surely as though his head were clamped in a vise. He stared at the great, stern, metal face steadily, because he could not do anything else. He was frightened, badly frightened, but was determined not to show it.

"You do not belong. . . ."

The low, persistent humming was almost subsonic, but it was filling all the world, all the Universe, all of time and space. The light was dimming, and colors were fading, and the songs of the birds were coming, faintly, and ever more faint, over a vast distance.

Una's hand tightened on his, and his on hers.

"You do not belong. . . ."

And there was. . . .

Nothing.

⤚ Chapter 27 ⤛

CONSCIOUSNESS returned slowly.

He struggled weakly against his bonds, then realized that he was strapped into his bunk aboard a ship, a spacecraft in free fall. A ship? After the first breath of the too-many-times-cycled-and-recycled atmosphere, with its all too familiar taints, he knew that this was no ship, but the lifeboat. He opened his eyes, shut them hastily in reaction to the harsh glare that was flooding the cabin. He turned his head away from the source of illumination, lifted his eyelids again, cautiously. He saw Una, supine in the bunk across from his, the confining straps vividly white in contrast to the dark golden tan of her body. He saw, too, the eddying wisps of blue smoke that obscured his vision, realized that the air of the boat had never been quite as foul as this, had never been so strongly laden with the acridity of burning lubricants, of overheated metal.

Fire!

Hastily he unsnapped the catches of the safety belt that held him down, automatically felt under the bunk for his magnetic-soled sandals. They were there, exactly in the position where he always left them. He slipped them on, scrambled off the couch. That glaring light, he saw with some relief, was coming from forward, through the control cabin viewports. The smell of burning was coming from aft, from the little engineroom. He made his way toward it with more speed than caution, coughing and sneezing.

There was no immediate danger, however. There was very little in the boat that would burn. But the mini-Mannschenn Drive unit was a complete write-off, its complexity of precessing rotors fused into a shapeless lump of metal that still emitted a dull, red glow, the heat of which was uncomfortable on his bare skin. There was absolutely nothing that Grimes could do about it.

But where was that glaring light coming from? He turned, and with half shut eyes went forward, to the control cabin, fumbled with the controls that adjusted the polarization of the viewports. As soon as he had reduced the illumination to a tolerable intensity he was able to look out. He liked what he saw.

Zephalon had been generous, it seemed. Not only had Grimes and Una been returned to their boat, but the small craft had been put in orbit about a planet, about a world circling a G type star, a sun that looked very much as *the* sun looks from a ship or space station orbiting Earth.

But this planet, obviously, was not Earth. There were few clouds in its atmosphere, and the outlines of its land masses were unfamiliar, and the oceans were far too small. And was it inhabited? From this altitude Grimes could not tell; certainly there were not cities, no artifacts big enough to be seen from space.

He became aware that Una had joined him at the viewports. She asked predictably, "Where are we?"

"That," he told her, "is the sixty-four-thousand-credit question."

"You don't *know?*"

"No."

"But what happened?"

"What happened, I most sincerely hope, is that friend Zephalon gave us the bum's rush, sent us back to where we belong. He must have buggered our mini-Mannschenn in the process, but that's only a minor detail. Anyhow, I'll soon be able to find out if we *are* back in our universe."

He remained in the control cabin long enough to make a series of observations, both visually and by radar. When he was satisfied that the boat's orbit was not decaying—or was not decaying so fast as to present immediate cause for alarm—he went aft, giving the still hot wreckage of the interstellar drive unit a wide berth. The Carlotti transceiver looked to be all right. He switched it on. From the speaker blasted a deafening *beep, beep, beep!* and the antenna commenced its wobbly rotation. He turned down the volume, right down. He listened carefully. The signal was in Morse Code, the letters UBZKPT, repeated over and over.

UB . . . Unwatched Beacon.

ZKPT . . . The remainder of the call sign.

"Una," he said, as he tried to get a bearing of the planet-based transmitter, "bring me the Catalogue . . ."

"The Catalogue?"

"The Catalogue of Carlotti Beacons. It's in the book locker."

"But Panzen took all the books . . ."

"He may have put them back."

"He didn't!" she called, after an interval.

So there was no Catalogue. Such a volume, thought Grimes with wry humor, with its page after page of letters and numerals, call signs, frequencies and coordinates would no doubt make highly entertaining light reading for a robot . . . And perhaps Panzen (or Zephalon) was sentimental, wanted something to remember them by.

"So what do we do?" Una asked.

"We land. We've no place else to go. The mini-Mannschenn's had it."

"Can't you fix it? You fixed it before."

"Have you *looked* at it? As an interstellar drive unit it's a worthless hunk of scrap metal. Oh, well, it could be worse. All these unmanned beacon stations have living quarters still, with functioning life-support systems, leftovers from the days when all the stations were manned. They're used by the repair and maintenance crews on their routine visits. So we land. We make ourselves at home. And then we adjust the beacon transmitter so that it sends a continuous general distress call."

"What's wrong with our own Carlotti transceiver?"

"It's only a miniaturized job. It hasn't the range. But," he assured her, "our troubles are over."

Grimes brought the boat down at local sunrise, homing on the Beacon. It was easy enough to locate visually; the huge, gleaming dome, surmounted by the slowly rotating Moebius Strip antenna, was the only landmark in a vast expanse of otherwise featureless desert.

The lifeboat settled to the barren ground about ten meters from the main entrance to the station. Grimes and Una got into their spacesuits—which, to their great relief, they had found restored to full operational efficiency. The automatic sampling and analysis carried out during their descent had indicated that the planet's atmosphere, although breathable, carried a high concentration of gaseous irritants such as sulphur dioxide. They passed through the airlock, jumped to the surface. They tensed themselves to fight or run when they saw, lurking in the shadows that darkened the recessed doorway, something that looked like a giant insect.

The thing did not move. They advanced upon it cautiously.

Then Grimes saw what it was, and his heart dropped sickeningly. Was this, after all, no more than a cruel joke by Zephalon, or a punishment for their intransigence? It must have been easy for him to duplicate, on this almost uninhabitable planet in *his* Universe, a typical man-made Carlotti Beacon Station. From the purloined Catalogue he had only to select a call sign, one starting with the letter z to make it obvious, when realization dawned on his victims, what he had done. He had destroyed the boat's mini-Mannschenn so that escape would be impossible. And he had left one of his camouflaged robot spies to report on the doings of the prisoners.

Suddenly Una laughed. "This *is* a genuine Stutz-Archer! Look!" She wheeled the machine toward him. The squeaking of its axles was audible even through his helmet. She pointed with a gloved forefinger at the mascot—a little, stylized bowman mounted on the front mudguard. "But what can it be doing here?"

He did not reply until he had looked at the thing more closely. It most certainly did not have the beautiful finish of the machines they had ridden in the Garden. Long exposure to a corrosive atmosphere hadn't done it any good. The padding of the saddle was dry and cracked, the enamel on the frame was peeling. And it had not been—somehow—made all in one piece; there were screws, nuts, bolts and rivets a-plenty . . . It was no more malevolent than any normal bicycle.

He said, "Some of these Beacons were converted to fully automated status only recently. One of the original crew must have kept this bike for exercise." He grinned. "I doubt that we shall be here long enough to get any use out of it!"

He set about manipulating the outer controls of the Dome's airtight door. The Station's machinery he was pleased to note, was functioning perfectly.

The station's machinery functioned perfectly until Grimes really got his hands on to it. It is child's play for a skilled technician to convert a Carlotti Beacon into a general purpose transmitter. But Grimes, insofar as electronic communications equipment was concerned, was not a skilled technician. It could have been worse, however. He suffered no injury but scorched hands and face and the loss of his eyebrows and most of his hair. The big Carlotti transmitter, though, would obviously be quite incapable of sending anything until a team of experts had made extensive repairs.

Una looked from him to the still acridly smoking tangle of ruined circuitry, then at him again.

She demanded coldly, "And what do we do *now?*"

Grimes tried to sound cheerful. "Just stick around, I guess. As soon as Trinity House learns that this Beacon is on the blink they'll send the Beacon Tender."

"And when will that be?"

"Well, it all depends . . . If this particular Beacon is on a busy trade route . . ."

"And if it's not?"

The question was not unanswerable, but the answer was not one that Grimes cared to think about. If this Beacon were on a busy trade route it would be manned. It could be months before the Trinity House ship called in on its normal rounds.

"And while you were indulging your hatred for all machinery," Una told him, her voice rising, "I was checking the alleged life-support facilities of this station. For your information, we shall fare as sumptuously here as ever we did in the boat. Correction. Even more sumptuously. Whoever laid in the stock of emergency provisions made sure that there were enough cans of beans in tomato sauce to keep an army marching on its stomach for the next years. And there's damn all else—not even a sardine! And we don't know when help is coming. We don't even know *if* help is coming." She went on bitterly, while Grimes kept a tight rein on his rising resentment. "Why did you have to antagonize Zephalon by your anti-robot attitude? Why couldn't you have left well enough alone? We were much better off in the garden . . ."

"As Adam said to Eve," remarked Grimes quietly, "you should have decided that before it was too late."